The HardBody Chronicles

Jake Smyth & Luca Barbieri

Acknowledgements

Jerry Chasen, Darrell Granger, Danny Lemos, Lanz Lowen,
Scott McLaughlin, Augusto Luis Newell, Peter McQuaid,
Kenny Phillips, Scott Russell, Jillian Rutenberg,
Andrew Werner, Ed Yezo

We would like to thank all our friends who helped make this
book possible.

And a special thanks to our husband for inspiring us to write
this book.

About the Photographer

Jeff Palmer, along with several other pioneering gay photographers from the '70s and '80s, planted the seeds for the reemergence of the male nude into the mainstream visual arts. "The male body is an amazing creation – a sensual machine of power, grace and beauty. I want to capture these powerful images in intimate moments. This is my art." His work has appeared in numerous publications. He has published three books: Sensual Men (1999), Temptation (2004), and Touch (2007).

Note from the Authors

We were there in the mid-1990s as both witnesses and instigators. It was a transformative moment in the evolution of the gay community, culminating with the celebration of Stonewall 25. The HardBody Chronicles is a roman à clef, a fictionalized retelling of actual events from those times. We hope you enjoy reading these stories as much as we enjoyed living them..

Jake & Luca

INTRODUCTION

Autumn 1994

November 1994 - *White Party Weekend*
South Beach
Saturday

By late November the humidity of summer finally gives way to cool ocean breezes. One autumn morning you wake up and the air seems to have lost all its weight. Instead of the heavy fragrance of night blooming jasmine, there's a hint of gardenia floating in the morning air. Season has begun and the Delano Hotel becomes the center of the universe.

The Delano doesn't hire staff, it auditions them. Casting calls are held to fill positions. Beauty trumps ability. Young men who look as if they'd just stepped out of a Calvin Klein ad work the front desk with great charm, but without a clue as to what their actual job might require of them. It's as if the Philippe Starck stage set in the lobby is intended to make up for the foibles, follies, and failures of the staff, and to a certain extent it does.

After you pass through the lobby with its dark wood floors and towering, ethereal white draperies, you exit onto the outside terrace of the Blue Door restaurant. It's as famous for its exorbitant prices and extravagant food as it is for its beautiful waiters. The terrace has a wide awning that allows guests to dine at the edge of the hotel's garden. When you descend the terrace stairs, you can't help but notice that the steps are so far apart that you're forced to slow your pace. It feels as if you're in a play, making your grand entrance. Of course, in this world, you are.

The landscape is high tropical drama. A grove of perfectly clipped orange trees offer up shade and scent the air. Arrayed along the north side of the pool area are private two-story bungalows, their balconies hidden behind two-story-long shear white draperies, which the staff draws in the evening for privacy. Appropriately, each bungalow comes with its own poolside cabana.

The bungalows are furnished like all of the other rooms in the hotel. White. And more white. White walls and white epoxy floors create a slightly institutional feel. An eclectic mix of overstuffed furniture is slip-covered in white canvas. Beds have white upholstered wraparound headboards. Potted white orchids sit on white bedside tables, and of course there are the ubiquitous shear white draperies. There is, however, one splash of color – a single, bright green Granny Smith apple sitting on its own small shelf by the entry.

Big Daddy & Bobby

Big Daddy decided to treat his boy-toy Bobby to some celebrity watching. Ever since their move to nearby Fort Lauderdale, they'd heard rumblings about the Delano. Was it true that Madonna had opened a restaurant there? According to their New York friends, Tomàs and Paolo – a duo from Rio de Janeiro whom everyone referred to as the Brazilians, the answer was yes. There was also a spa on the roof that was the creation of Madonna's "gal-pal." It was all too juicy and practically in their own backyard. It would be an adventure to travel from the suburban safety of their Fort Lauderdale home into the exotic demimonde of South Beach

But it wasn't quite that simple. In South Beach, where money can buy most anything, if you aren't beautiful, you're relegated to the sidelines. And Big Daddy was more than a few pounds overweight. Would his big bucks guarantee them a table with a view? Bobby was handsome enough to get them to the front of any line, but would beauty get past the velvet ropes while the beast was left behind? Big Daddy was not about to let that happen. Here at the Delano he felt he was in his own element, the world of money. Yes, this place was filled with perfect specimens in a perfect setting, but it all came down to being able to pay the tab. Big Daddy could play by those rules. So he'd treat Bobby to an afternoon glimpse of the rich and famous.

"Big Daddy, do you see how much they charge for a hamburger?" gasped Bobby, shocked that it was several times the cost of a Big Mac. "Oh, my God!" He scanned the menu to see if there was something more affordable.

"Sweetheart, in a place like this you're paying for the view." Big Daddy surveyed the moneyed crowd. "Just look around you."

Bobby took in the view. It looked liked a convention of *Men's Fitness* cover models. "Look at all the muscle guys. Do you think any of them are famous?"

"I'm sure they're all famous, but not the way you think, honey," replied Big Daddy. *I wonder who's picking up their tab?* he thought.

"I don't see any of the guys from New York."

The Brazilians, along with fellow New Yorkers Karl and Curt - fashionistas of the first order, were guests at the Delano. Big Daddy and Bobby would hang out with them by the pool after

4

lunch.

     "We'll find them." Big Daddy knew Bobby was eager to show off his new bathing suit. They'd hit a dozen swimwear shops in Fort Lauderdale to find just the right one. "Here comes our waiter. Let's order so we can join the boys. You'll knock 'em dead with your suit."

     "I hope they like it."

     "They'll love it," replied Big Daddy, "and you've got the body to show it off. I say 'Why hide your light under a bushel?' Show off what God gave you, honey." He then turned to the waiter, who was taking it all in. "I'll have the cheeseburger with fries. And I'd like a vanilla milkshake with that." Big Daddy announced.

     "I'm sure we can accommodate you, sir," the waiter responded coolly. There were no milkshakes on the menu.

     "And my Bobby will have the same."

     "Of course." The waiter collected their menus and thought to himself, *Why didn't they just go to McDonalds and save us all the trouble?*

***

After they'd paid their bill, Big Daddy, in his khaki shorts and pink Polo shirt, and Bobby, in his barely-there Daisy Duke shorts and spandex aqua tank-top, walked down the terrace stairs toward the pool. They gazed around at the wall-to-wall crowd of muscular men and found their four pale friends. All were wearing black designer bathing suits. After a round of hugs and air kisses, they settled down to chat.

Before sitting, Bobby began to strip off his clothes. The Brazilians and the Fashionistas watched with fascination. There wasn't much left to the imagination given what Bobby was already wearing. As his shorts were peeled away from his thighs, a leopard print thong was slowly revealed. The four boys were speechless. Granted, his ass was perfectly round and tanned, but his big dick looked ridiculous stuffed into the tiny pouch. He looked like a cheap stripper who had somehow tumbled into the world of Gucci and Versace.

     Tomàs finally broke the silence and managed to say, "Wow, that's really something . . . . Don't you love this place?" he asked Karl in an attempt to lead the conversation in a different direction.

     Karl laughed. "When I woke up this morning and looked around, my first thought was, 'Why am I in the deluxe wing of Bellevue Hospital?' It's all very white and minimalist."

"I adore it! It's a total fantasy-world here," exclaimed Curt, always one for the most *au courant* hotels and restaurants. Nothing fabulous escaped his attention. "Isn't that what you want when you go on vacation? I mean, who wants to stay in a place that reminds you of home? I want to feel like I'm in a movie . . . and I'm the star," he stated, rather grandly.

"Are you ready for your close-up?" asked Tomàs, offering Curt a bottle of suntan lotion.

"Speaking of movies," offered Paolo, "can you believe how gorgeous the crowd is? I mean, where are the . . . ugly people?" He stopped himself before he said "fat." Once again the conversation came to an awkward halt.

Big Daddy slurped on his creamy piña colada.

"They don't admit ugly into this hotel. Just look at the staff," Curt sniffed. "The hotel owner figures that if you have to look at them, they *should* be pretty."

"I think you should be able to have sex with them," Karl joked.

Curt shot him a dirty look. He suspected Karl played around behind his back, but it wasn't going to happen *this* weekend, and certainly not with the hotel staff.

"Look who's come down from their room," observed Karl as he spotted Rob and Erik. Everyone turned to catch a glimpse of the infamous couple. Both were wearing wife-beaters and matching black Addidas warm-up pants. They looked like Mr. America contestants.

"They're a handsome couple," Big Daddy said with a leer, enthralled with what he saw. "How do you know them?"

"From out on Fire Island," replied Karl. "They were our neighbors last season. They own Jocks, the hot bar in Chelsea. It's a huge hit with the boys. Packed every night."

"Did Rob have something new done? His face looks different," Curt questioned, knowing the answer was yes.

Karl went for the bait. "Well, he had a cleft put in his chin this past spring. So it's probably a neck lift this time. He *is* getting to that age," he said with a laugh.

"That age?" asked Bobby.

"Darling, we all need a little nip and tuck," replied Karl. "It's all about maintenance. You're just not supposed to do too much at one time. Little bits, so no one can tell. But not everyone believes in subtlety," he pronounced with a nod toward Rob.

"Oh, I see," replied Bobby, feeling well informed.

"Speaking of those two, I hear they're involved in this weekend's muscle-boy sex party, like the one they threw for

Gay Pride," Tomàs reported.

"You mean the one none of us were invited to?" quipped Curt.

"Yeah, that one. Well, rumor has it that there's a group, HardBodies or something, in South Beach. They're quite selective. Everyone's been talking about it since the Morning Party. They'd love you, Bobby," Tomàs said too quickly, regretting it before he was finished.

"There's no way my baby is going to an orgy without me," Big Daddy snarled.

"Well, I guess none of us will be going," Paolo jumped in, trying to smooth over Tomàs's faux pas.

As soon as they'd finished their poolside cocktails, the bill for which Big Daddy insisted on picking up, the Fort Lauderdale couple got ready to depart.

"So . . . we're picking you up tomorrow for the White Party at 6:00 pm sharp," announced Big Daddy. "If you're not ready, we're not waiting," and with that, he and Bobby got up and left.

When they were out of earshot, Karl asked, "Was he serious about leaving people behind?"

"Dead serious," replied Paolo with contempt in his voice. "We've gone on vacations with them, and His Largeness *demands* punctuality." *That, and sex with him and Bobby,* but he wasn't about to admit that to these friends.

Rob & Erik
Taking in every inch of tanned muscle on the way to where their Fire Island neighbors were sitting, Rob and Erik commanded the attention of everyone.

"Hey guys. What's shaking?" Rob said in greeting. Hugs and kisses all around.

"We were working on logistics this morning. Any of you know the best way to get to the White Party?" asked Erik.

Paolo spoke up, "We're taking a limo that our friends have arranged. In fact, that's them on the stairs."

"The one in the Daisy Dukes?" Rob asked, trying not to smirk.

"You noticed him?" Tomàs asked. *How could anyone have missed that perfect ass?*

"I'm sure everyone noticed him. Great little body," Rob replied.

"We'll talk to Big Daddy. He'd love to have the two of you climb out of his limo," Tomàs offered.

"Small problem. It's not just the two of us. We're here

with the Rocks," Rob replied.

"OK, that's ten in total. I'm sure the limo can hold us all. Big Daddy never does anything on a small scale. And Tomàs is right, he'd love to have plenty of attention-grabbing muscle piling out of his limo," replied Paolo.

"He's a Southern queen, and you know how they like making entrances," Tomàs added. "I'll talk to him and work it out. Don't worry, you and the Rocks won't have to arrive in a godforsaken taxi."

Ira & Beau

Ira and his trophy-boyfriend Beau had arrived from LA the previous afternoon, checked into one of the Delano's bungalows, and dined late at the Blue Door. As the light of the morning sun crept across the snow-white floor, they awakened to breakfast delivered with *The New York Times* and *Los Angeles Times*. They drew back the sheer draperies to their private balcony and inhaled the fresh ocean air. They ate their brioche French toast with grilled half-grapefruits, washed down with plenty of café con leche. After they'd showered and shaved, they helped each other apply a thorough coat of sunscreen. No premature aging for Beau (too late for Ira).

In a Versace bathing suit that showcased his body to perfection, Beau walked over to the cabanas on the other side of the pool. He noticed that several had small "Reserved" signs on them. Then Beau saw the sign "Reserved for Mr. Ira Gould and guest."

Guest? Beau felt the blood rise in his face. Excuse me!" he practically yelled across the pool at the Cuban towel boy.

The poor guy, who was already sweating through his white polo shirt, came at a clip. "Yes, sir?"

"There's been a mistake. I'm registered along with Mr. Gould. I know because I made the reservation myself. Make sure that for the rest of our stay, my name, Beau Fournier, is added to this reserved sign!" Beau said imperiously.

"Yes, sir. I apologize for the mistake. We'll make certain it doesn't happen again."

"Thank you," Beau said as he sat down on the chaise.

Ira had watched the entire scene from where he stood on their bungalow's patio. When the towel boy left, he walked over to Beau. "Beau, darling, next time, you might want to take him aside so no one else can overhear what you're saying. You can get what you want without letting everyone else in on your conversation," Ira explained.

"Sorry," Beau answered. Just then he spotted Rob and Erik. "I'll be right back. I want to say hello to my friends from New York." He sauntered over to their chaise lounges. "Fancy meeting you here," Beau said.

"Oh, my God!" exclaimed Erik. He jumped up to give Beau a hug and kiss. "What are you doing here?" he asked.

"I'm here with Ira," answered Beau. "We're staying over there in one of the bungalows."

"You mean celebrity row?" Rob joked. "I guess life in LA is treating you quite well."

"You can't even imagine. I'm auditioning for film roles and everything. But let's talk about this weekend's parties. What are your plans?" Beau asked. "I don't know which ones to go to. Where are all the hot guys going?"

"Well, tonight we're going to the HardBodies party," Erik answered. "And depending on how we feel afterward, we may go to the Underwear Party at the Arena. They're expecting thousands."

"Hold on. What's the HardBodies party?" Beau asked. "I got a card for it when I was on Fire Island."

"You met one of the guys who's throwing it," answered Rob. "Remember the tall dark blond guy you played with when you stayed at our place? Our friend Jake? He's the one who gave you the card. He and his boyfriend are throwing a sex party. It's invitation only. Can you imagine the crowd they're going to get with this much beefcake in town?"

"Where is it?" Beau pleaded.

"You're supposed to go to a certain address on South Beach at 10:00 to get directions. If you show up, you'll get in. I mean, the host thought you were hot enough to fuck. You're practically a twin for his boyfriend, Luca" Rob said.

"Is Luca a porn star?" Beau asked.

"Yeah," Erik replied.

"He's the guy who I was photographed with in LA. I had sex with him, too, really hot sex," said Beau with a smile.

"It's a small fucking world, when you're fucking the world," quipped Erik. "So come along with us and the Rocks. They're still getting pretty in their room."

"Trust me, this is one party you don't want to miss," Rob explained.

"I'm not sure what Ira has in mind," replied Beau. "I'll have to see. I don't exactly set our agenda," he said dejectedly. "Well, I better get back to him before his hair gets any grayer."

The Rocks

"Jesus, you can't believe the message on their answering machine," exclaimed Alcatraz, a short thick bodybuilder.

> *"Gentlemen, South Beach HardBodies has a strict door policy - muscle guys only. That means rock-solid pecs and six-pack abs. Expect to take off your shirt to prove it. If you don't measure up, you won't get in."*

"These guys are fucking serious. You gotta listen to this." Alcatraz handed the phone to Gibraltar, who was unpacking. The bed was already littered with white t-shirts, white tank tops, white 501 jeans, and he kept pulling more out of his duffle bag. Gibraltar hit the redial button. Over the past several months, the chatter about South Beach HardBodies had become deafening.

> *"Pick up directions to the party between 10:00 pm and 10:30 pm. Doors to the party open at 10:30 pm and close promptly at 11:00 pm. Don't be late."*

So those were the ground rules. The HardBodies guys obviously didn't operate on Cuban time. And they made it quite clear that they didn't suffer frail fools. Gibraltar was hoping his bowling-ball shoulders would let him sail through the whole intimidating process. *But what about Alcatraz's extra few pounds? What if only one of us gets in?* Gibraltar was ready to skip the party entirely rather than face the possibility of rejection.

PART 1

The Backstories

Erik Christiansen

November 1989 - *Five Years Earlier*
Phoenix - *Arizona State University*

FUCK! Get your balls out of my face, Erik screamed in his head. *Jeez, this guy's got huge nuts. And that smell . . . .* He'd gotten a whiff of lots of other guys over the years in locker rooms and at meets, but never this musky and masculine. It was all Erik could do to stay focused.

He pumped his hips to try and get the bastard off his chest. The Bulgarian heavyweight kept grinding those bull balls into his face. Erik drove his chin up and forward, into those big balls. His opponent let out an angry grunt and gave Erik the opening he was looking for. Erik rocked his hips hard and flipped out from under him. In this position, Erik knew he could beat the guy. *Now, get the right grip and bring him down.* Before he could, his opponent shoved his sweaty armpit right into Erik's face. Erik spit out the fur, but his face was soaked. He couldn't get this guy's smell out of his nostrils. Distracted, the guy mounted Erik from behind before he knew what was happening.

Erik was used to all kinds of dirty tricks, but this was different. Erik's face flushed. *Why is this guy getting to me like this?* The Bulgarian drove Erik into the mat with his crotch against Erik's ass. Erik pushed back with his butt, squeezing his big glutes, but the guy didn't budge. *Man, this guy weighs a ton. I can feel the heat pouring out of him. I can't lose. I won't lose.* Erik arched his back, lifting his opponent with his ass and got his foot loose for some leverage. That was enough to get Erik out from under. He flipped his opponent on his back and pinned him. Panting, the guy locked eyes with Erik and smiled. Erik didn't know what to think.

September 1990 - *Ten Months Later*

For the first time in his life, Erik had his own place. After three years in the university dorms, he had worked enough summers to be able to rent a small apartment not too far from campus. It was a studio with no real living room, just a maple desk, a chest of drawers, and an old easy chair across from the twin-size bed. But Erik finally had his own kitchen. It would be sweet being the king of his own castle with no roommates to complain if he made a protein shake at 2:00 am. *Which box has the blender?*

Erik wanted his apartment to feel like home, so he'd packed a half-dozen framed photos that his mother had stored away in a box in the basement. He'd wrapped his t-shirts around the frames to keep the glass from breaking. When Erik started to unwrap them, he came across a photo of himself with Hulk Hogan taken in the stadium where Erik had seen his first pro wrestling competition. *I must have been about 12.* He'd always liked the Hulk. Erik's grandfather Jack, whom everybody called Coach, had met the Hulk at a wrestling camp, and a couple of months later, tickets arrived for the whole family. Coach made friends with everyone. Erik had been dumbstruck by the Hulk's size. He towered over Erik. To this day, Hulk Hogan was the largest man Erik had ever encountered.

He unwrapped another photo. It was Erik and his twin brothers, all dressed in singlets, sitting on a dock on a lake. Erik smiled to himself when he noticed the name painted on the back of the tethered row boat below their feet. *Cheetah*, it read, in big black letters. It was all part of his grandfather's obsession. Erik rummaged through his things for his favorite photo of his grandfather. In a chipped burl frame was Coach's smiling face with Johnny Weissmuller's big arm thrown over his shoulder. *"To my pal, Jack"* was written across the bottom of the photo.

He remembered all the stories he'd heard Coach tell over the years. Erik knew the tales as if they were his own. As a young boy, every Saturday after wrestling practice at the YMCA, Coach would spend the afternoon at the movies watching Tarzan. It was the Tarzan legend on which he built his summer wrestling camp – Camp Tarzana. Erik could picture Coach cheering as Weissmuller saved the day by wrestling man-eating lions to the ground and taking down ever-hungry crocodiles. Tarzan always won. If the King of the Jungle had inspired Jack, he'd inspire his boys every summer with a simple philosophy at Camp Tarzana: wrestle to win. Erik hung the photo over his bed, like he'd done in the dorms. It was nice to think that Coach was still with him, watching over him.

January 1991 - *Four Months Later*
San Diego

Erik knew he couldn't avoid it any more. It was time for the

16

sacred pilgrimage to San Diego before the start of the spring semester, with the requisite side trip to Tijuana for steroids. The guys on the wrestling team talked about this tradition like it was Thanksgiving dinner. Erik used the juice from time to time but liked to keep his distance from the actual acquiring process. In all honesty, crossing the border with a bag full of illicit drugs scared the shit out of him. He was told, and believed, that guys his size were targeted for searches specifically looking for steroids.

This weekend, however, his three best buds on the team were San Diego-bound, and there was no excuse that Erik could think of that could get him out of the trip. He'd avoided it for the last three years and his time was up. Erik suggested that they take two cars so that he could at least have his own set of wheels.

***

After stopping by the motel office for directions, they headed to the nearest place for breakfast, the Serendipity Café. It seemed as if every bodybuilder in San Diego was there. A quick tour of the neighborhood proved why. Powerhouse Gym was right next door. The boys ate quickly and headed over to work out.

Erik looked around the gym. He saw some big guys over by the bench presses and decided he'd work out chest. He found an empty bench, loaded up several forty-five pound plates, and took his position.
"Need a spot?"
All Erik could see from his angle on the bench was the guy's huge legs, covered in thick black fur. From the smell of him, he'd been doing a lot of cardio. "Sure." Erik took a deep breath and got the bar off the rack with no problem. *Bigger. Stronger,* he repeated in his head. *I'll show him what I'm made of.* Somewhere around his tenth rep, Erik set the bar back effortlessly. He sat up on the bench to get a look at the guy.
"I'm Tzoni," he said offering his hand.
"I'm Erik." *And I thought my eyes were blue? This guy's got eyes like a husky.*
"Do you wrestle for the Sun Devils?" asked Tzoni.
"Yeah, I do." Erik smiled. His face felt hot. *Jesus, am I blushing?* He always got this way when fans came up to him after meets. He never knew what to say.
"We've met before. We wrestled last season. You beat

me. Not many guys do. No bullshit. That's how I remember you."

Erik watched the cleft in this guy's chin move as he spoke. *This is the guy who smelled so . . . .* Erik felt his face go beet red. He had gotten into the practice of not washing his jock to see how strong he could get it to smell. No matter how much he sweated, he could never conjure up that overpowering male scent. "What happened to you? I didn't see you this past season," Erik asked.

"I was out with an injury. I think things might have turned out differently in a rematch," Tzoni said, almost as a challenge.

"I guess we'll never know, but you can always dream," laughed Erik.

"So, what are you doing in town?" Tzoni asked, never breaking his gaze.

"Here for the weekend with some of my teammates, blowing off some steam. How about you?"

"I'm here for a family wedding."

"Listen, it's been great seeing you again, but I've got to finish up my workout. My buddies over there are getting ready to leave," Erik explained.

"Sure, no problem," Tzoni said. "I need to pump some more iron and get out of here, too."

Thinking fast, Erik suggested, "Hey, if you want to grab a beer later on, we're going to Hooter's around 7:00."

"Thanks," Tzoni answered. "I'd enjoy that. Don't hesitate to ask for a spot if you're going to be pushing all that weight. Remember, no injuries," he said, with a look in his eye that made Erik a bit nervous.

***

"Got room for one more?" It was Tzoni from the gym. He'd taken Erik up on his offer to meet him at Hooter's.

"Hey guys, this is Tzoni. He's on the UCLA team. We wrestled last year. I ran into him at the gym today."

Tzoni pushed his way into the crowded booth and sat next to Erik.

Their waitress brought another round and flirted shamelessly with Erik. "You're a big guy," she cooed. He was tongue-tied when she asked if she could feel his bicep. Just as Erik flexed his arm for her, his face flushed crimson. Under the table, right under his buddies' noses, he felt Tzoni's burly thigh press up against him. Erik didn't know where to look or what to do.

18

"So what's on tonight's roster?" Tzoni asked, utterly unfazed by Erik's trembling leg.

"We're headed down to Tijuana for some action," answered one of Erik's buddies.

"I think I've got all the action I'm looking for right here in town," Tzoni replied.

Erik froze. He'd been part of a circle jerk a few times at summer wrestling camp, but never before had a guy come onto him like this. Embarrassed by all the attention he was getting, Erik finally said, "I've got to take a piss." He practically leapt from the table.

"Sounds like a good idea," chimed in Tzoni, "I'll join you." Once inside the men's room, he turned to Erik and said, "I'm not interested in Tijuana. I'm interested in you."

Erik took a deep breath. He couldn't believe this was happening. "They've got their own car. They'll go without me," he stuttered.

"Great. Sounds like a plan. We can hang out here until they leave then head back to your motel for a few beers," Tzoni proposed.

"No, we can't. I'm sharing a room. I can't be sure when those guys will turn up with some girls," Erik did his best to concentrate on pissing but his legs were trembling. Adrenaline was pumping through his body.

"Well, we can't go back to my family's place. So, plan B," Tzoni said matter-of-factly.

"And that would be?" Erik hesitantly asked.

"We get a room at the bathhouse."

The whole idea made Erik shudder. *A bathhouse?* He'd heard of them but never dreamed he'd ever go to one. But he wanted to be with Tzoni. His maleness was overwhelming to Erik. He wanted to follow his feelings and see where they led him.

***

The drive to the bathhouse was quicker than Erik had expected. They pulled into a warehouse parking lot with a sign that read, *The Club*. Erik followed Tzoni, barely able to put one foot in front of the other. The small lobby had wood paneling and a shiny black speckled floor. The lighting was dim, but the place smelled clean.

"Just get a locker," Tzoni directed. "I'll get a room."

Erik's heart was pounding.

The cute young boy behind the glass window slid a towel and locker key through the slot below. The kid looked all of eighteen and was staring holes through Erik.

"Thanks," Erik managed to get out.

"Any time," the kid said with a huge smile.

"Hang your clothes in the locker and put your towel on," Tzoni instructed. "Meet me in my room." Looking at his key, he said, "It's number 215."

"Be right there," Erik replied.

Straight ahead was the locker room. It was nice except that the red lighting made it feel like a nightclub. The smell was familiar though, the smell of men mixed with the dampness from showers and steam room. Erik had been surrounded by those smells all his life. He stripped naked, aware of the stares from the other men around him. He gripped the locker door to steady himself. Erik felt lightheaded. He kept thinking about Tzoni's hairy body pressing down on him.

He got lost on his way out of the locker room. The club was a maze of hallways. *Don't panic. This is what you want.* Erik started counting the numbers on the doors and finally arrived at room 215. He knocked.

"Come in, it's unlocked," answered Tzoni. Erik turned the knob and entered the darkened room. The linoleum floor was cool under his bare feet. When his eyes adjusted, he saw Tzoni. He was naked and lying on his stomach on a twin-sized bed that was built into one corner of the small room. A wall sconce barely illuminated the tiny space. Over his shoulder, Tzoni said "I've been jacking off thinking about you ever since we wrestled. It's all yours, big boy."

Erik was speechless. He thought that big hairy Tzoni would be the aggressor, that Tzoni would be the one pinning him to the bed. "Uh, I'm confused. I thought we'd fool around a little first, I guess. I'm sorry . . . , I'm not very experienced at this," Erik stammered.

"Are you serious? You're not a top? The way you handled yourself on the mat, I figured you were an aggressive topman. I should've known. The bigger they are, the harder they bottom. I mean look at the two of us," Tzoni said with a chuckle.

"I'm a . . . , I don't know what I am." *God, I feel so stupid. How could I have been so wrong about all this?* "I thought you'd be, you know, the aggressive one," Erik said, his confusion clearly evident. He didn't know what more to say.

This wasn't what Tzoni had planned on either. He could tell just by looking at Erik that he was in over his head. Maybe a few pointers would help him out. "Well, at least we're in a bathhouse," Tzoni said. "We can both find what

20

we're looking for here. It's pretty clear who's a top and who's a bottom. Look for the guys who are showing off their hard-ons. They're gonna love your big blond butt. You won't have any problem finding someone. As for me, I'll leave my door open and see who comes along."

"I think I'll drive back to the motel," Erik said, crestfallen.

"You're already here. Have some fun. Here's a deal. If I find a good top, I'll tell him to look for you." Tzoni offered Erik a handshake to seal the deal.

"OK. Well, maybe I'll look around or take some steam. I'm already here, right?" Erik replied nervously.

"Right," Tzoni agreed.

With that, Erik headed out the door, leaving it open. He was utterly deflated.

***

His first thought was *military* when he saw him round the corner. The big man with the white crew cut stood out not only because of the authoritative set of his shoulders and the way he carried himself, but also because he was fully dressed. He was wearing a black t-shirt, black jeans, and black boots. Erik was transfixed. The guy was looking directly at him. Erik broke out into a sweat. He felt like he should move, break his gaze, but he couldn't. He felt his heart pounding in his chest.

The man strode right up to Erik and said, "Follow me."

For an instant Erik wasn't sure what to do, but something inside him said, *Go.*

The guy didn't even turn around to see if Erik was following. He marched down the hall to a room, unlocked the door, and walked in.

Erik stepped into the room.

"Close the door."

Erik followed his instructions.

"You're quite the specimen. But I know what you want, what you came here for."

How does he know what I came here for? Erik thought. *How can he tell?*

"I'm the General, boy. From this point on, you will address me as Sir. Is that clear?"

"Yes, Sir."

"Good. Now, drop the towel and kneel in front of me."

"Yes, Sir." Erik did as he was told. The man towering above him was still fully dressed. Erik had never felt so naked. He held his body in a position that showed it off.

Years of hard training had turned him into an imposing piece of manhood. Erik wanted to impress this man, to prove to him that he was worthy of what was to come.

"Unzip me," the General commanded.

Erik raised his hands and realized they were shaking. He was mortified. He didn't want the General to notice. Finally, he got his hands working on the General's fly. It was then that Erik noticed the size of the General's crotch. It took a bit of work, but out came the most enormous set of balls and fattest cock Erik had ever seen. It was uncut with a foreskin that hung down well below his cock head.

"Smell me, boy."

"Yes, Sir." Erik buried his face in the warm meat in front of him. He'd never openly smelled something so male. It was overwhelming. Erik got lost in the smell. He reveled in the freedom of enjoying it.

"Show me what you can do with your mouth, boy. Show me how hungry you are for my cock."

"Yes, Sir." Erik opened his mouth and took in the blunt head. The feeling surprised him - it was firm, spongy, and warm. Erik slid his tongue up underneath the foreskin. It was slick and slightly salty. He couldn't get enough. He tried to move his tongue the way he used his hand when he jacked off, swirling it around and around. He felt the cock start to grow. The big man above him groaned. He stuffed more cock into Erik's mouth. The foreskin slid back, fully exposing the shiny pink head to his tongue. He then felt the fat head pushing against the back of his throat. Erik tried to relax and swallow but kept gagging. Spit was running down his chin. He could feel the veins standing out along the General's thick shaft. He opened his jaws as wide as he could, but no matter how hard Erik tried, there were still inches of cock between his lips and the General's big hairy balls.

As if reading Erik's mind, the General said, "Get on all fours on the bed. Let me look at that ass of yours."

"Yes, Sir."

"Rest your shoulders and head against the bed and relax. Keep that ass nice and high in the air."

"Yes, Sir."

"I'm gonna eat that ass."

"Yes, Sir. It's yours, Sir." With that, it felt like a dam burst inside Erik. He was overwhelmed, as if speaking the truth for the first time in his life. He wanted to give this man complete and total control of his body, to make him proud.

Erik snapped back to reality as the General's big

hands, like the paws of an animal, gripped his big round ass cheeks and spread him apart. He was exposed as he never had been before. Next a scalding tongue lapped at the ridge that ran up from his balls to his ass. It felt right to give up any resistance, to open his body to another man, his superior. He thought, *Yes, Sir, anything you want. I'll make you proud. Use me for your pleasure. Teach me, I want to learn.* He lost the separation between his body and the General's tongue. He felt joined to this man. *It feels like electricity flooding my body.* Erik felt pressure against his hole and instinctively tensed.

"Relax, boy, and breathe deeply."

"Yes, Sir."

A thick finger, well lubricated with spit, slowly worked its way into his ass. Erik felt a slight burning sensation and took a deep breath, gritting his teeth. As he relaxed, the burning went away. It was replaced with a growing feeling of pleasure as his prostate was massaged. His dick was so hard it almost hurt. He could feel precum spilling out of him. Erik felt a bit more pressure and responded by taking another deep breath and bearing down. In went another finger.

"You're a natural."

"Thank you, Sir. It feels so . . . good." It was hard to speak. Erik felt like he was being massaged from the inside out. Several thick fingers slid in and out of him. Each time he wanted more, to be completely filled. This was a flood of pleasure he'd never felt before coming from a place deep inside. It was better than any dick-centered pleasure he'd ever experienced. Erik had discovered a secret new world.

"I'm gonna fuck your ass, boy," the General said. "You're never gonna forget this one."

"Yes, Sir. Please, Sir." Erik started breathing deeply. He felt what he thought was a hot fist, rubbing against his hole, then the whole arm. *Oh God, that's his dick! It'll never fit inside me.*

"Just relax and keep breathing. Follow my instructions and you'll be just fine. You're gonna surprise yourself, boy."

"Yes, Sir. I trust you, Sir."

"You're a big boy. You can handle me." The General used two hands to roll a condom all the way down to his balls.

Erik could see back through his legs as his Sir applied lube to his bull-sized dick. He felt those thick fingers massaging lube onto his hole, then a slick finger slid in and spread more lube inside him.

"Bring your ass back onto your heels, boy. It'll open you up more."

Erik followed orders. He felt the General's cock head massaging his exposed hole. He pushed back, he wanted it so badly. It felt as big as a billiard ball as it pushed into him. *It's gonna split me in two!* He kept concentrating on his breath. He forced the air in and out of his lungs. *I can't believe it's going deeper inside me!* The huge cock filled him to the hilt. The General's big hairy balls were pressed against his furry ass. Erik melted into the bed.

"You like that big cock up your ass, don't you, boy?

Erik had a hard time finding his voice. "Yes, Sir. Thank you, Sir." He had to stop speaking. Tears welled up in his eyes. He felt as if a light had gone on in his head that would never be dimmed.

"Relax and enjoy the ride, boy."

Erik felt the thick cock start to withdraw. Instinctively, he gripped it with his ass muscles. *No, don't take it out,* he yelled inside his head.

The General slowly withdrew his dick to the point where the big head almost popped out of Erik's hole. Then he plunged it back in.

Erik felt like he was being turned inside out.

"Good boy. Squeeze it with your muscles then relax and let me sink it in deeper."

"Yes, Sir." Erik could barely get the words out. His entire being was focused on his ass. His insides were being filled with the kind of pleasure that he usually experienced for a moment just before orgasm. His body shuddered as if he was coming, but the feeling didn't end, it went on.

The General knew that Erik was his completely, so he picked up the pace. The big man pounded away at the athletic butt in front of him, knowing that the harder he hammered, the more the boy enjoyed it. He grabbed Erik by his broad shoulders. *Damn, this fucker is big!* He wasn't afraid he was going to break him. The General drove his massive cock in deeper with each stroke.

Erik's head was spinning. He saw stars. He had to keep breathing deeply otherwise he felt like he'd lose himself and pass out. Finally, he let go, gave up all control. Erik could feel the General's cock growing harder, pushing out in all directions.

Then the General let out a series of loud grunts.

Erik knew the General was pumping out his load. He could feel the volume, the heat filling the condom. Then, without touching himself, in one big convulsion, Erik blew his load all over the sheets. He came like he'd never cum before.

24

Slowly, Erik felt the still-huge cock start to back out of him. He didn't want to give it up, but knew his Sir's will was to be obeyed. Anything he wanted, Erik would give. At last, the fat cock head popped through the last ring of muscle.

"You made your Sir proud tonight. You can stretch your legs."

Erik's entire body trembled as he got off the bed and stood up.

The General grabbed him under one arm to keep Erik from crumbling to the floor. "You'll be alright," he stated. "It's shower time. Come. Follow me."

Erik picked up his towel and wrapped it around his waist. He felt like he was on autopilot. His head was still swimming from what his body had just experienced. His brain was still catching up.

The General locked the door behind them.

Erik felt proud following him. He wondered if the men they passed could sense the connection.

They reached the wet area and hung their towels on adjacent hooks. It was then that Erik could fully appreciate the size of the General compared to the other guys present. Everyone turned and stared at the two giant men who'd taken over the shower room. Instead of feeling embarrassed by his nakedness, Erik felt more aware of his body than ever before. He flexed as he lathered up. Several times he bent over to soap his lower legs, fully realizing that he was showing off his just-fucked ass to all. He wished the General would fuck him right there in front of all these men.

Erik was shocked out of his daydream by the General's voice, "Soap up my back, boy."

"Yes, Sir." He started soaping away. Not only had he never felt another man's body like this, but now he was doing it in public. Erik's dick started to harden again. He made no attempt to hide it.

They rinsed off and headed for their towels. Erik had so much he wanted to say but wasn't sure where to begin.

"We'll meet again. I have a playroom in New York that I want to show you."

Playroom? "Thank you, Sir, I'd like that very much. May I give you my phone number, Sir?" Erik stumbled over his own words. "I have my own place," he continued. "I . . . I graduate in May."

"You're eager to please. I like that in a boy. Write down your number and drop it by my room before you head out."

"Yes, Sir."

Erik dressed quickly, still damp as he pulled on his clothes. He jotted down his name and number and headed for the General's room. The door was closed. He knocked.

"Slide it under the door, boy."

"Yes, Sir," Erik said. He slid the precious piece of paper under the door.

March 1991 - *Two Months Later*
Phoenix

It was just before spring break, and even in Arizona you could sense a freshness in the air. It had a sweetness to it, the smell of things coming to life. *Why not take advantage of this beautiful weather?* Erik changed into his running gear and headed out. The phone rang just as he was locking the door. *Let it go. The answering machine will get it.*

He'd worked up a sweat and an appetite by the time he got home. Tonight, he'd treat himself to some baby back ribs at Chili's, but first a hot shower. It wasn't until he was toweling off from his shower that he noticed the flashing light on his answering machine. It was the call he'd missed on his way out.

> *"Boy, this is the General. I want you to come to New York. It's time to take your training to the next level. Call me to arrange your flight."*

Erik sat down, his legs felt weak. His heart was pounding. He quickly dialed the number the General had left and drew a breath to steady himself as the phone rang.

"Hello," answered the deep voice.

"Hello, Sir. This is your boy Erik in San Diego. I'm sorry I missed your call."

"Not a problem. I understand you have a life at school. Aren't you graduating soon?" the General asked.

"Yes, Sir," Erik said, pleased that the General had remembered. "I finish in six weeks."

"Do you have any plans?"

"No, Sir. I'm all yours." Erik's dick was hard as a rock. He had to stand up to straighten it out before it snapped in two.

"Good. I'll have my travel agent book your flight. She'll call you to set it all up. You'll be here for a long

26

weekend, with only one stipulation: You'll obey my every command. Are you ready for that, boy?" the General asked.

Erik's heart was pounding and his mouth was dry. His voice was on the verge of cracking. "Yes, Sir. I'm ready. I'll serve you all weekend and make you proud, Sir. I know I need your training to be a better boy for you, Sir."

"Good boy," the General said. "Expect her call tomorrow morning. I'll see you soon."

"Yes, Sir. Thank you, Sir." The phone clicked off. Erik couldn't believe what was happening. His hunger was replaced by butterflies in his stomach. His cock was so hard it ached.

May 1991 - *Six Weeks Later*
New York

It was late evening and the industrial area along the West Side Highway had shut down for the night. All the mechanics and manufacturers had closed up shop. Only the new high-rise building that had sprung up in this fringe neighborhood was ablaze with light. It was here that the General lived. He'd left an envelope with Erik's name on it at the security desk. There was a key to the apartment and a note:

> *Make yourself at home in the guest room. Clean up in the master bath shower. Be waiting for me in the sling at midnight.*

Erik had never seen anything like the General's playroom. The walls and ceiling were mirrored. The floor was covered in black rubber. Restraints, dildoes, and assorted paraphernalia were displayed on chrome racks. Erik marveled at it all. He couldn't even guess at what some pieces were used for. He hoped he'd find out. Erik climbed into the sling. It was almost midnight.

The front door opened and Erik heard two men's voices. The General had brought another man with him. Erik's dick instantly got hard, but he knew better than to touch himself. His Sir had told him that a boy had to have permission to do that. Even then, he had to control his orgasm. That was under complete control of his Sir as well.

He heard their footsteps coming down the hallway. Erik's heart pounded in his chest. The first thing he noticed as they entered the room was the smell of warm leather. He couldn't get enough of the scent. Then he saw the source of the aroma.

"Boy, let me introduce you to Rob. I want you to follow his orders as you would follow mine."

"Yes, Sir," replied Erik.

The General and Rob were both in chaps and had on knee-high leather boots like the ones motorcycle cops wear. Rob was taller than the General. He was completely hairless, like a statue, a Greek god. He wore a leather harness that crisscrossed his beefy chest and focused all attention on his bulging pecs. Even his nipples were huge, like big eraser stubs.

Erik was mesmerized and couldn't stop staring at Rob. He had beautiful full lips. Erik wanted to kiss him. It was all so strange. He'd never thought about kissing another guy before. When their eyes locked, Erik's heart beat faster.

Rob smiled like a movie star. His green eyes never left Erik's.

Erik watched Rob's strong smooth muscles flex as he stroked his dick. It was long and straight with a perfectly shaped head. His free hand reached forward and touched Erik's hole.

Erik felt like a cattle prod had landed on that sensitive private part of his body. He moaned in ecstasy.

"Good boy," Rob said in a deep sexy voice.

"Thank you, Sir."

"Call me Daddy."

"Yes, Daddy."

Rob turned to the General, "You made quite a find with this big one."

"He's a natural," responded the General. "The harder you give, the more he'll take. He's hungry for it. I think he's been waiting all his life for this. I'm gonna sit back, have a beer, and watch."

Rob wasted no time. Without removing his finger from Erik's ass, he unrolled a condom down his dick. It had grown to enormous proportions. He squatted between Erik's upheld thighs and replaced his finger with his tongue.

Erik loved it. He wanted to open his hole completely so Rob could slide his tongue in as deep as possible. His breath was taken away when Rob removed his tongue, stood up, and pressed the perfect head of his cock against Erik's sphincter. He was so wet and ready from being eaten that it

28

entered him like a hot knife into butter. He felt Rob's balls pressing against him. Erik shuddered. His body gave into Rob's beautiful cock. It was skin against skin. All the time, those green eyes stared intensely at him.

"Are you alright, boy?" There was that million-dollar smile.

"Yes, Daddy. Thank you, Daddy." Erik's heart skipped a beat.

Without withdrawing his cock, Rob leaned his body forward and brought his lips to meet Erik's.

Erik opened his mouth and felt the hot silky tongue enter him. He could smell the male scent of his own hole all over Rob's face. This was too much, being totally connected at both ends to this god.

Their tongues melted together as Rob started to fuck Erik's ass. He started to swing the sling back and forth, driving his cock into Erik.

Every time Rob's dick slammed into his ass, Erik saw stars. He tightened his abs to draw his pelvis upward, and Rob sank in even deeper.

"You want it, boy, don't you? You want your Daddy to cum?"

"Yes, Daddy. I want it."

"Then take it, boy!" Rob became a blur. His balls began to make a wet slapping sound against Erik's hungry ass. He paused to suck in air and then with a roar drove his blast of jizz deep into Erik. With Rob's last spasm, Erik shot all over his own abs and pecs. Rob slowly stopped, still embedded in Erik. He was dripping in sweat. Every muscle was gleaming. Rob reached down to Erik's navel and dipped his fingers into the cum that had shot out of Erik. He brought his fingers up to his nose and inhaled deeply, then slid his finger into his mouth. "Mmm," Rob said. He lowered his lips to share the taste with Erik in a deep kiss, his mouth tasting of Erik's cum.

Later, after the General had pummeled Erik's ass, they headed to the shower. Even under the harsh unflattering light of the bathroom, Rob was the most handsome man Erik had ever seen. Rob's smile was just the beginning. He had a square jaw and a strong angular nose. All this was topped with short, brown, curly hair.

Rob chuckled when he realized that Erik was transfixed. "You're quite the handsome all-American boy."

"Thank you, Daddy. You're . . . you're . . . ." Erik was at a loss for words. Then they all stepped under the multiple shower heads and washed away the sweat and cum. Erik lathered up each of the men's backs. He spent extra time on Rob, whose back was so broad that it blocked Erik's view of the General. It reminded Erik of locker room showers with the team, except now he didn't have to just fantasize about touching the men around him. This time, he was there to tend to their needs. He was in heaven.

***

The three of them were sitting in the den drinking beers when the General made a proposal. "I'm going away on assignment for a month or so and need someone to take care of this apartment. I think you're capable of it. Consider the option, boy."

Without thinking twice, Erik said, "Yes, Sir. I'll square things with my family."

"Then it's a done deal. I leave next week. You can send for whatever you need."

"I've got everything I need with me," Erik replied, barely able to contain his excitement.

The General turned to Rob, "Do you have a job at your bar for this boy? He'll need some spending money and something to occupy his time here in the big city. I wouldn't want him to get into any trouble." The General knew exactly what he was setting up. He'd seen the connection between Rob and Erik. He certainly didn't have the time to take on Erik as a full-time boy, but perhaps Rob did. This boy was a diamond in the rough.

"Of course. He'll look great behind the bar. The customers will love him. He'll make a mountain in tips with that body and face." Rob turned to Erik, "It's not very complicated. It's mostly serving beer and a few simple mixed drinks. You'll pick it up in the first week, guaranteed."

Erik didn't know what to say. It was better than a dream come true - an apartment in New York and a job working for a god. "Thank you, Daddy! I won't let you down."

"You don't have to call me Daddy all the time, big boy, just when we're in the playroom. Otherwise, call me Rob." He glanced at Erik. "So, is anybody else hungry?"

Still intimidated by this god's looks and authoritative manner, Erik somehow found the nerve to reply, "I'm starved, Dad . . . I mean Rob."

"The Empire Diner is nearby. It's open 24/7 and has great burgers. How's that sound?"

"Terrific!" answered Erik.

"You guys enjoy yourselves," announced the General. "I've got a date with my pillow. Erik, use your key and lock up

30

after yourself. I'll see you in the morning. I like my boy to drain my hard-on when I wake up."

"Yes, Sir. I won't be late, Sir. I'll service you first thing in the morning, Sir."

Rob and Erik took the elevator down together. Erik was on cloud nine. They made small talk, mostly about Rob's bar, as they walked to the restaurant, but Erik only heard every other word. The City on a gorgeous spring night, walking down the street with Rob was more than Erik could absorb. All he could do was grin ear-to-ear and bask in this handsome man's attention.

Abruptly, Rob came to a stop, mid-block, and said, "You know, Erik, I've got a very good feeling about you." He couldn't hold back when it came to this beautiful boy. They'd made a connection that had taken Rob by surprise.

Looking into Rob's sparkling green eyes, Erik smiled and said, "So do I." Rob pulled Erik in close and wrapped his big arms around him, smothering him in the sweetest kiss of the evening.

Rob van Buuren

May 1988 - *Three Years Earlier*
Philadelphia

One of Rob's University of Pennsylvania classmates was presiding over the critique area in the drafting studio. "I met this guy on Fire Island last summer," he said, pointing to a photograph in the latest copy of *Town and Country*, the magazine he was flipping through. "Had really hot sex with him. He was working on a fabulous beach house." The classmate handed the magazine to Rob and continued chattering, going on about the architect and how he was married to a wealthy heiress who had inherited her fortune from baby food. Her smiling baby face was on every jar. Appropriately enough, her nickname was Baby.

Rob thumbed through to the article about the architect in question, Ellis Conrad-Wright. *He's hot for an older guy,* Rob thought. The architect was in great shape, like an ex-gymnast. Rob couldn't tell his height from the photo, but he was taller than his wife, who was also very attractive albeit as wide as she was tall. There were photos of the couple's Upper East Side townhouse filled with art and European antiques. Reading on, Rob learned that the architect was a partner in a well-known Manhattan firm. They did projects that got plenty of press. Rob's mind started to calculate. *I'd love to land a job at a firm like that.* Then he came up with a brilliant, if unorthodox, idea. Along with sending his resume with a letter of recommendation from a professor who'd gone to school with Conrad-Wright, Rob enclosed a photo that had run in Penn's *Daily Pennsylvanian* of him after a rowing meet. Rob was captain of the team. It was a great face shot, and his sweat-soaked tank top and shorts showed off his impressive physique.

New York

Conrad-Wright was indeed impressed and scheduled an interview within days of receiving Rob's application. Rob dressed in his best old money uniform: blue blazer, button down shirt, striped tie, and khakis. He wanted the architect to feel that he was already a member of the same club.

The firm was in a loft in Chelsea. Stainless steel and sand-blasted glass balanced exposed brick and wooden rafters. The furniture in Conrad-Wright's office was designed by le Corbusier and Mies van der Rohe. It was masculine in character and suited its occupant. The architect was shorter than Rob had expected but in a sexy "toss him around in bed" way. The image that came to mind was of a bantamweight boxer, a scrappy little ball of energy. He was in his early forties with a full head of close-cropped gray hair.

The interview went well. Conrad-Wright, "please call me Ellis," liked the fact that Rob had gone through a demanding program at an Ivy League university. He smiled when Rob mentioned where he'd attended prep school and spent summers. It seemed they had a lot in common. If Ellis was impressed with Rob's resume, he was visibly awestruck by Rob's size and chiseled good looks. He didn't even try to hide it.

If this was a bar, thought Rob, *I could get him into the sack without any further discussion.*

***

Rob found an apartment in Chelsea on 23rd Street, within walking distance of the firm. It was in a simple, pale brick, postwar building with a beautifully maintained inner courtyard. He couldn't believe this little bit of paradise existed in the middle of such a grungy neighborhood. A walk around the area's small shops and restaurants validated Rob's choice. He'd landed in the new, up-and-coming gay hotspot.

After a week without a single sighting of Ellis, Rob was surprised when he received a visit late in the day on Friday. "I thought I'd deliver your first paycheck in person. After all, I'm the one who'll be held responsible for your performance here. I have to keep an eye on you," Ellis said in a slightly flirtatious manner.

"Don't worry about my performance. I always try to exceed expectations. You'd be amazed at what I can do," Rob replied with confidence.

"I bet I would be," Ellis said with a smile. "I have big expectations for you." He took Rob's hand but didn't shake it. He just squeezed it. Rob's large hand dwarfed Ellis's, and he squeezed back.

***

Rob began working out at Chelsea Gym. Swimming and rowing had helped Rob develop an outstanding upper body but kept him lean. He wanted to be as big as the bodybuilders working out around him. One evening after his workout, Rob showered next to one of them, a sleek black guy who looked like he was carved from onyx. Rob couldn't believe his build, so big and so defined.

The bodybuilder smiled at Rob.

Once in the locker room, he turned and offered his hand to Rob. "Hi, my name's Charles. Are you new here?"

"Yes, I just moved from Philadelphia. My name is Rob. It's a pleasure to meet you. Cool accent. Where are you from?" Rob thought, *You sound whiter than I do.*

"I'm from the Bahamas. Is this your usual workout time?"

"Yes, I come straight from work."

"Me too, I head uptown from Wall Street." After a few more pleasantries, Charles made Rob a proposal. "I recently lost my workout partner. He's found religion and thinks he can turn straight. Anyway, I lift heavy, and it helps to have a partner spot me. Would you like to work out together tomorrow?"

"I'd love that."

"Great! I'll see you here, same time. It's a leg day, so be prepared." Charles said with an evil grin.

Charles's workouts were intense. Rob was so sore that he had to take a hot shower just to loosen up before Charles put him through his paces on the gym floor.

"You're trying to kill me," Rob said in frustration after a particularly brutal bicep workout.

"No, I'm trying to get you bigger and stronger," answered Charles.

"Well, it isn't working!"

"What do you mean? Have you looked in a mirror lately?"

"Yeah, but I'm not as big as you. How long is that gonna take?"

"That's easy enough to solve. A little juice and you'll put on ten pounds of muscle in ten weeks."

"Juice?" asked Rob. "You mean steroids?"

"Of course I do. You think I got to this size by jumping rope? You want?"

"Yeah, I'm game," answered Rob. "Give me the who, where, when."

***

Around quitting time one Friday, Ellis brought Rob his paycheck as usual. It had become their weekly ritual. They flirted shamelessly but never said anything directly. Rob found it more and more arousing. He could feel the sexual tension building.

"Have you been working out?" Ellis asked as he clapped Rob on the shoulder.

"Oh sure, got to stay in shape, so I go to Chelsea Gym. It's right around the corner.

"Yes, I know the one. It's on the corner above the video store. I've never been, but I hear it's a lot of fun."

"I wouldn't know. My workout partner is a tough taskmaster. It's what I want though, so I can put on some size."

"Size? Aren't you big enough? My God, if you get any bigger, we'll have to get you a bigger office."

"Do you promise?" Rob asked.

June 1989 - *One Month Later*
Fire Island

Charles invited Rob to be his weekend guest on Fire Island in a small house he rented with his buddies, the Rocks - two short white bodybuilders. The traffic to Sayville was surprisingly light. Rob made it with time enough to grab a beer at the ferry dock and cruise the after-work crowd. It was one fine-looking group of men. Most were tan, in shape, and looked like they had money. *This is a crowd I'd like to get to know,* he thought.

Any tension he felt from the day's activities and long drive melted away as the ferry made its short way across the dark waters of the bay. There was no question that the Pines - one of the most upscale communities on the barrier island - was the place to be. It was where the Velvet Mafia, the richest of the rich, held fabulous parties at their fabulous beachfront homes filled with fabulous men.

As the lights of the Pines' marina came into focus, Rob's excitement started to build. Disembarking from the ferry, he was met by an unusual sight. Everyone was waiting for their friends and lovers with little red wagons, the only way of transporting goods and luggage along the wooden walkways that snake through the pine trees. There were no cars allowed.

He made his way down Pines Boulevard - so named because it's twice as wide as all the other walkways and it runs the entire length of the community. There was no light along the way except that which spilled from the homes built into the woods. Rob felt like he was away at summer camp.

It was a bit of a hike to Charles's house. Rob was the first to arrive. The house was empty and unlocked - very strange to one coming from the City - but it was the tradition on this isolated island. The crime rate was nil, just a few drunk-and-disorderlies. And it was quiet. No wonder those who could afford it fled the City's noise and traffic for this little paradise. Rob dropped his bag in the living room and headed back to town.

"Town" consisted of a few commercial buildings – a bar, a disco, the ubiquitous liquor store, and an overpriced gourmet market – all joined together and covered in the same gray, weathered cedar. He marveled at the "quaintness" of it all. It wasn't much, but out here, it was all you needed. That and a wad of cash. Rob headed straight to the bar to wait for Charles.

***

The next morning, Rob was awakened by the buzz of barber's clippers coming from out by the pool. He opened the sliding doors from his bedroom to the pool. The Rocks - Gibraltar and Alcatraz, so named because of their huge but rather squat physiques - were helping each other clipper spots that had become difficult to reach. Hair removal was part of every weekend's activities.

"Good morning," said Gibraltar.

"Did we wake you up with the clippers?" Alcatraz quickly asked.

"Sorry. I told him to wait until everybody's had their first cup of coffee," Gibraltar offered up as an apology.

"Not a problem," answered Rob. "I'm going to the beach for a swim."

The beach was deserted. Rob had the Atlantic all to himself. He loved the ocean and didn't mind that is was cold and dingy green. He liked the challenge of ocean swimming with its waves and currents. The constant struggle tired Rob out in half the time he would have spent in a pool.

As he got out of the water, he saw a man dressed in gym clothes waving to him from down the beach. When the man got closer, Rob realized that it was Ellis. There were no secrets now.

"Hello, stranger!" Ellis shouted out with a big smile. "What a surprise seeing you here! His eyes roved up and down Rob's torso.

"Are you headed to the gym?" Rob asked, startled to meet his boss outside of work, let alone in an all-gay enclave. He thought Ellis looked better than he'd ever seen him. He was tan and smiling.

"No, I just finished. You can probably smell me from where you're standing," Ellis said.

"As a matter of fact, I can," Rob answered with a laugh.

"I got out here on the first ferry. A friend of mine is hosting a party here tonight." He pointed up the hill to the enormous cedar-clad home perched high on the dunes. "Come back to the house for a cup of coffee," Ellis offered, "I want you to see the work I've done on it." Rob grabbed his towel and followed Ellis.

After chatting about various projects and sharing office gossip, Ellis invited Rob to stay for breakfast. They were joined by Ellis's host, Mr. Underwear, and his latest boyfriend, an Olympic swimmer. Rob was impressed by the company that Ellis kept. He tried to be nonchalant about the host's home. Ellis had turned a beach shack into a home that had been featured in *Architectural Digest*. It was minimal and masculine. The rooms were a series of attached boxes with glass walls facing both the ocean and pool. The views were staggering. Tonight's party, to which Rob had just been invited to attend, was the official "reveal" of the house. Everyone who was *anyone* would be there.

***

Rob spent the rest of the day working on his tan and grooming. He didn't have much body hair, just a patch between his pecs. The rest of his body was perfectly smooth. So he decided to take the plunge. He borrowed the Rocks' clippers and used them on his chest.

Then he thought, *What the hell, why not?* Off came his pubes.

Seeing Rob through the open sliding glass doors, Charles was shocked and impressed. "Damn, boy. What got into you? You look like a statue, absolutely perfect."

Rob cringed. *I'm far from perfect*, he thought. As a gay man in a straight world, Rob felt inherently flawed, particularly when it came to his looks. Every time Rob looked into the mirror he failed to see the handsome face that he'd been blessed with. To Rob, his chin wasn't strong enough, his cheeks weren't prominent enough, his lips weren't full enough. Lost in thought, he finally answered Charles. "Thanks. You really think so? I want to look my best. My boss invited me to tonight's party at Mr. Underwear's house."

"Are you serious? Who do I have to fuck to get in?" asked Charles.

"I'm not sure. I ran into my boss on the beach this morning and he showed me the place. He remodeled it over the winter. And are you ready for this? It has a 50-foot lap pool."

"I've heard. The one for the Olympian? That's old news out here."

"Anyway, the house is amazing. And I got to meet Mr. Underwear. Right now, though, I need to lay out in the sun and get some color. I want to make a good impression."

"Every guy at that party will be trying to make an impression on somebody. Watch out that one of them doesn't steal your boyfriend."

"He's my *boss*, not my boyfriend," Rob shot back.

***

Rob felt like a celebrity as he was ushered in past security. The house looked even more beautiful than it had at breakfast. The lighting was perfect. It was decorated with white candles, white orchids, and fresh Casablanca lilies that filled the air with their erotic sweet smell.

Rob saw the Olympian and asked if he'd seen Ellis. At first, the Olympian acted as if he hadn't met Rob. *I had breakfast with you this morning,* Rob thought, *what is this little game you're playing?*

"Oh, right. You're that muscle boy. I think I saw him out on the deck with some cute guy."

"Thanks." *What a bitch*, Rob thought as he walked away. He got himself a glass of champagne and headed to the ocean-side deck, hoping to find Ellis.

Ellis spotted him first and rose from his seat to get Rob's attention. "Come on over, I've saved you a choice spot."

"Thanks," Rob answered. He sat down on the fluffy white canvas cushions next to Ellis. "I ran into the Olympian on my way in. He acted like he was clueless as to who I was when I asked him about you."

"I'm not surprised," replied Ellis. "After you left, Mr. Underwear kept going on and on about your physique. The

41

Olympian's been in a huff all day. I think it's a hoot."

***

The house darkened as candles burnt out, and guests began to leave.

"Let me show you the suite I'm staying in," Ellis said to Rob. "It's my favorite room in the house."

"I suppose we could take a peek," Rob replied. They quietly mounted the stairs. Rob's mind was racing. It was one thing to meet on the beach and strip each other naked with their eyes, but this was leading up to something entirely different. When they reached the end of the hallway, Ellis pulled out a key and unlocked the door in front of them.

"This is our host's little sanctuary, where he does his more private entertaining," explained Ellis, ushering Rob in and locking the door behind him. Only moonlight illuminated the all-black room. It was hard to see anything. Rob's eyes slowly adjusted to the darkness. He could make out a black platform bed in the middle of the room. It was upholstered in black leather and sat on a black slate floor. Before Rob could notice anything else, Ellis pulled him into an embrace, and the passion that had been building burst forth. They devoured each other like it was the last meal either would ever have. They tumbled onto the bed.

"You have no idea how long I've waited for a man like you," Ellis confessed when he finally came up for air. "You push all my buttons."

"Careful," Rob replied. "I might push buttons you don't even know you have."

"Promise?"

"I'm a man of my word,"

"Spoken like a true Daddy," Ellis noted.

"A Daddy? That's a first."

***

Ellis managed to meet Rob on the Island every third or fourth weekend at Mr. Underwear's beach house. Over the course of the summer he gave himself entirely to Rob. For the first time in years Ellis felt free to explore some of the darker realms of his sexuality. He appeared one weekend with a duffle bag of toys.

"Take me anywhere you want to," he'd whispered to Rob as he handed him a set of handcuffs and a blindfold.

Eager to please, Rob took control.

"A true Daddy wears leather," Ellis told Rob when he presented him with the gift of a harness from The Leatherman. Within days, Ellis had arranged for a complete fitting at the West Village store and had Rob outfitted in a pair of custom-made chaps.

As the end of September approached and the prospect of weekends on Fire Island came to a close, Ellis suggested a plan for getting together in the City. "Baby's social calendar determines most of my schedule," he dourly explained, "but I make a point of keeping a few evenings a month free for myself. We could meet at the Eagle on those nights, if that works for you?"

"I'd enjoy that enormously," Rob replied. He'd come to care for Ellis in a way he'd never anticipated. But a voice inside his head cautioned him: *Don't get too involved. Protect yourself.*

April 1990 - *Ten Months Later*
New York

Ellis's business partner suggested lunch at the Empire Diner. They never ate at that noisy diner unless there was a compelling reason. Obviously, his business partner didn't want anyone to overhear their conversation. *What the hell does he want to talk about?* Ellis wondered.

"You know, Ellis, we've been through a lot together over the years. I hope you know that I only want what's best for you and the firm."

"What is it?" Ellis asked.

"Far be it from me to judge what you do in your personal life, but when it comes to business, our business, I have to lay it on the line."

"OK, shoot," Ellis replied. He began to get a knot in his stomach.

"It concerns some rumors that are going around the office about you and Rob van Buuren. It's become a bit too obvious that you're doing more than mentoring the boy."

Ellis could feel his face flush with embarrassment. "I'll do what I need to do."

On the walk back from the diner, Ellis and his partner passed the sports bar project that they'd been working on for a Saudi prince. His partner asked, "Have you heard anything from our client lately?"

"No. Why?" Ellis responded.

"Rumor has it that the prince's father had a religious rebirth and has called all of his children home to Riyadh. Our billing department has been getting the runaround from his accountant. Not only are our fees stacking up, but several of the contractors have been calling about getting paid. They're threatening to walk off the job, and some of the subs won't start any new work without some up-front money."

"But his family has more money than God. Don't they own oil fields?" Ellis asked.

"That may be, but it doesn't change our situation. Got any ideas on how to move forward?"

***

"I have a problem that I need your help with, Rob," Ellis said gravely.

"Sure. Just name it," Rob replied, puzzled by the look on Ellis's face. Something was clearly troubling him.

"You know that we're having some problems with the sports bar project, right?"

"Well, I've heard the client is being difficult in paying his bills."

"It seems his father, who holds the purse strings, has shut the purse. We're stuck with angry contractors. We could sue, but it would take years. The only way to get our money out of this is to take over the bar. It's just about finished, and it wouldn't take that much more to get it up and running."

"Makes sense, I guess, but how can I help?"

"I want you to run it," Ellis said.

At first Rob thought he was joking, but he saw the seriousness in Ellis's eyes. "I don't have any experience running a bar. I'm an architect," he explained, not understanding where this request was coming from.

Ellis took a deep breath and continued, his voice quavering. "My partner told me that people around the office are discussing our relationship. He thinks it's a bad idea all around." It broke Ellis's heart to have to speak those words.

Rob looked like he'd been sucker punched. "You want me to leave the firm, to give up architecture?"

"It wouldn't have to be forever. Once the bar makes a profit, we could sell it. It wouldn't take long, a year, maybe two."

"What about me? What about my dreams, my life? While you're protecting yourself, where do I fit?" Rob's calculating, fight-to-survive instincts kicked in.

"You'll have no money worries, I'll see to that. You'd make much more than you're currently making. This may be the opportunity of a lifetime."

"Where does all this leave me?" Rob asked. "Running a bar for the rest of my life?"

"I'll give you half ownership upfront and full ownership once the debts are paid. Help me out of this hole and you'll have a business all your own. I really need your help on this. I'd be eternally grateful," Ellis said almost begging.

***

Charles slapped Rob on the ass, "You gonna lift or what?" he asked.

"Sorry, I'm having trouble focusing."

"What's up, stud? Can't figure who you're gonna fuck tonight?"

"Ha ha. Very funny," Rob said. He took his position on the flat bench.

"Then what gives? Come on now, push, if you want to get big and strong."

Once he'd finished his set, Rob confessed, "Well, I already know you're going to say 'I told you so'." They traded positions on the bench.

Charles stopped and looked up at Rob, "The words, 'I told you so,' will not be crossing my lips. OK?"

Rob took a deep breath, "Apparently, the whole firm knows about my relationship with Ellis. His partner told him that he had to fire me."

"You're not serious!'

"Oh, yes I am," Rob replied.

"Well, what did Ellis tell him?"

"Basically, that he'd take care of it."

"Meaning?" Charles asked incredulously.

"That it would be best that I leave the firm," Rob said.

"I was afraid of this. He has everything and you get left with nothing!"

"It's not all bad. I have an opportunity. I'm just not sure how to work it out," Rob responded

"You of all people should know how to take advantage of a opportunity."

"It's complicated, but the deal is that the firm has found itself with a nearly completed sports bar on its hands."

"What does that have to do with you?" Charles asked.

"Ellis will be the silent partner, and I'll run the bar."

"Are you serious? What the fuck are you thinking?
You don't know anything about running a sports bar. Have
you lost your mind?"
"You're right. I can't see myself running a straight
sports bar. That's just the point. But what about a gay
sports bar? Are there any in the City that you know of?" Rob
asked.
"Only the Dugout on Christopher Street, but I don't
really think that counts. It's a dive.
"The Village and Christopher Street are so tired. I'm
talking an upscale sports bar. I think the right bar in this
neighborhood with the right vibe could work."
"I hate to bring up this little detail, but . . . , I mean
great, Ellis is the owner. What about you?"
"He'll give me fifty percent ownership up front for
giving up my job."
"Well, this is sounding better."
"After the bar pays off its debts, Ellis said he'd give me
the other fifty percent."
"Sounds pretty good. Just get it in writing."
"First things first. I have to present the idea to Ellis. I
feel like I need a hook. I'm not sure the sports angle is
enough. I've got to make it sexy."

***

When Rob met Ellis for lunch the next day, Rob was
beaming. After they placed their orders, he said, "I've given
the bar a lot of thought since our discussion, and I know how
to make it work."
"I knew you'd come up with something."
"I spend a lot of time in this neighborhood. I work
here. My gym is here. Lots of my buddies live here. Chelsea
is the new gay heart of the City, the perfect spot for a gay
sports bar."
Shocked, Ellis asked, "Are you serious? We never said
it would be a gay bar."
"I know, but if you want me to make this a success, it
has to be *my* bar. It has to have *my* personality. I know I can
make a gay sports bar work. I know a lot of guys like me and
what they're looking for. I can promote it through my network
of friends. I want to call it Jocks, and I have a hook."
Unrolling his rough drawings, Rob showed Ellis his idea.
"You know the raised area where the booths are going in? We
replace those with a small stage. The stage can be a locker
room with a glassed-in shower. We hire guys with great
bodies to dress in sport uniforms and have them strip down

46

and take showers. It's every gay man's fantasy."

September 1990 - *Five Months Later*

It was Ellis's idea that Rob use his own photo - the one from the university newspaper that he'd sent to Ellis with his resume - as the cover of the invitation for the grand opening of Jocks. At first, Rob was hesitant, "Don't you think it's a bit much? Using my own photo?"

"No one will know it's you if you don't identify yourself," Ellis said.

"I don't know," Rob laughed, "it seems a little egotistical, even to me."

"Don't be ridiculous. You want this bar to be a success. You know it needs your personal touch. I can't think of a better image, and unless you can, I suggest you use it."

The invitations went out just before Labor Day for a series of opening nights. The first night was for the press and the usual crowd of celebrities who would show up for the opening of an envelope. The second night's party was for the staff's family and friends. Rob figured it was a sure way to get the word out through people who had a stake in the bar's success. Finally, they would have the big official opening for "gym members only." Rob had gone to every gay gym in the City and left a stack of invitations. This little tactic sealed the deal. Everyone was abuzz as they drifted back into the City from all points around the globe. The first question, "How was your summer?" The second question, "Are you going to the opening of Jocks?"

***

Within twenty minutes of the doors opening, the bar had reached its legal capacity. All of Rob's bartenders were muscled studs in their prime. They were dressed as soccer referees in black and white striped shirts and tight black shorts. Multiple TV screens around the bar were tuned to cable sports channels with no audio, only captions providing the play-by-play. At about 9:30 pm, the lights came up on the locker room stage and the volume of the music subtly increased. The crowd's attention shifted, all heads turning as a handsome young man swaggered onstage wearing full boxing gear.

Without acknowledging the crowd, the boxer slowly started to undress. He unwrapped the bandages protecting his hands and sat down on the bench to remove his boots. As he stood, off came his hoodie and down came his shorts. He was in front of his locker in his jock strap. The crowd was mesmerized.

Rob beamed from his position behind the main bar. *Yes, they get it!* The boxer onstage peeled down his jock strap and wrapped a towel loosely around his waist. His cock slapped against the thin white terry cloth when he sauntered over to the glass-walled shower. He reached in and turned on the water. Hanging his towel on a hook, he stepped in. After making quite a show of sensuously soaping himself up and rinsing off his muscular body, he slowly dried himself. When the boxer finished, the crowd went wild. Everyone was hooting and hollering. They'd never seen anything like it.

The next day, everyone was talking about the "locker room studs in Chelsea." Jocks, and the excitement it generated, seemed to be the final acknowledgement that Chelsea was the epicenter of gay Manhattan. Every night of the week there was a waiting line outside, even as winter's chill fell on the City.

May 1991 - *Eight Months Later*
New York

"Jocks, this is Rob speaking. How may I help you?"
"Hey Rob, it's Ellis. I know it's short notice but is there any chance of you meeting me at the Eagle tonight at 10:00? I'd like to introduce you to an old friend of mine. He's leaving town for a few weeks and asked if I'd join him for a beer."
"I'm a little short on staff this evening, but I think I can make it," Rob answered.
"Come in full leather, if you can."

The cab dropped Rob off at 21st Street and the West Side Highway, a rundown neighborhood of derelict warehouses and auto repair shops. On the corner was The Eagle, an old longshoreman's pub that had become a leather bar in the early '70s. Reeking of stale beer and cigar smoke, the interior was all black with an old Harley Davidson hanging from the ceiling. It was a world away from Jocks.

Rob entered and saw Ellis at the bar speaking to a big

leather-clad man with a white crew cut. He made his way through the packed crowd. "Sorry I'm late. I was short one bartender this evening and had to man the bar myself. Can I buy a round of beers?"

"That'd be great," answered Ellis. He polished off the last of his mug. Rob signaled to the bartender for three drafts. "Rob, I'd like to introduce you to the General. We've known one another for twenty-some years. When I was in my 20's, he was my leather mentor," Ellis said proudly.

Rob was startled by the information.

The General nodded. "Ellis was one of my best boys," he said with a smile. He and Ellis had had a scorching relationship long before Ellis met Baby. When Ellis's career took off and he began to move in different social circles, he and the General parted ways but always kept in touch with one another.

The General sized up Rob. With his chaps and harness displaying his bulging muscles, Rob looked like he was ready for a COLT photo shoot. Ellis couldn't have been prouder of his Daddy. "You're quite impressive, Rob" complimented the General. "Leather suits you well."

"Thank you, sir," answered Rob, flattered at the compliment. "Ellis tells me you're leaving town for awhile. Where are you off to?"

"I'll be on assignment for a month or so in San Diego. I spend quite a bit of time there," the General responded. "I work with the Marines and the Navy."

Rob was fascinated. He'd never met a career Marine, let alone a top-ranking one.

The conversation continued. The General filled Rob in on his past. He'd been a prisoner of war in Vietnam. "I learned all about bondage during my extended stay in Hanoi."

"Were you tortured?" asked Rob, uncertain if he was crossing a line by asking such a question.

"Torture is a matter of perspective," answered the General. "Is it torture if both men get some sort of pleasure from it?"

Rob didn't know what to say. When he'd handcuffed Ellis to the bed and blindfolded him, Ellis had begged for more. "Rape me, Daddy," he'd pleaded to Rob.

"Another round, gentlemen?" asked Ellis.

"I'd love to stay longer, but I've got a boy waiting for me in my playroom, an all-American college wrestler from Phoenix," announced the General as he placed his empty mug on the bar.

"Really?" remarked Ellis. "If it would be alright with you Sir, perhaps you might consider having Rob join you?" suggested Ellis, much to Rob's surprise. "I'm certain he could learn a lot from you."

A curious smile crossed the General's lips. "It'd be my pleasure, Ellis. I'd be more than happy to see your young Daddy in action. Are you free to join me?"

Beau Fournier

May 1993 - *Two Years Later*
New York

I'm here! he thought. *I'm in New York!* For the last several weeks Beau had carried a small notepad in the back pocket of his uniform. He'd asked every flight attendant he knew where he should go, which places were fun, where the hottest guys were. The list he'd compiled was burning a hole in his pocket. Every few minutes he'd check to make certain it was still there. Beau had three days to soak up Manhattan.

Traffic crawled and then roared forward. Without warning, the cab swerved to avoid a truck, and Beau slid to the opposite side of the back seat. Times Square opened up before him.

"Oh my God . . . ," whispered Beau to himself as his eyes traveled upward. Towering in front of him was a massive billboard of a hunk wearing nothing but underwear. It dominated everything around it. No matter which way he turned, his eyes kept coming back to the massive photo. *So fuckin' cool!*

After a quick shower and a slow drawn-out shave (*please, no nicks!*) he put on his tightest 501 jeans. They fit him like a second skin. Then he reached for his little bag of essentials. Beau pulled out his favorite leather cock ring and snapped it around his dick and balls. He stuffed his meat into his 501's, leaving the lowest button undone for maximum basket. "Nice package," he said to himself when he checked his profile in the bathroom mirror.

He remembered the time his mother had done Tom Jones's makeup at the Toronto television station where she worked. Beau had been transfixed by how Jones stuffed his mammoth cock into double-knit pants. You couldn't mistake that bulge for anything other than a huge dick. No wonder the women screamed and threw their panties at Jones. Beau had no compunctions about showing off his biggest asset. He checked out the rest of himself in the mirror. His thick black hair was cropped close. His full lips and pale blue eyes, with their enviably long lashes, made heads turn. He was handsome enough to be mistaken for a model. He was ready for his first night out on the town. He headed to Jocks.

***

He couldn't believe his eyes. He'd never seen this many

gorgeous guys in one place. It was man candy from wall to wall. Beau headed toward the bar. The bartender was bent over opening a box. His tight black referee shorts showed off his ass and golden fur-covered legs. When the guy stood up, Beau tried to keep his jaw shut. The bartender was huge and blond. His black-and-white striped shirt was stretched over massive pecs, and the sleeves were hiked up over enormous biceps. He was a god.

"Can I get you something?" the god asked.

"How about another view of your butt?" Beau had no idea where he got the balls to say that but he was glad he did when he saw a smile spread across the god's face.

"You mean this big ol' thing?" he said as he turned halfway around. "Glad you like it. Flattery will get you *everywhere.* My name's Erik."

"I'm Beau. Pleasure to meet you."

"Welcome to Jocks, Beau. What can I get you to drink?"

"I'll take a light beer on tap." *It's got to be the cheapest thing in here,* Beau thought.

Erik grabbed a mug and pulled the tap. "Here you go. Wasn't sure if you liked a lot of head or not."

"I'll take as much as I can get." Beau actually blushed. He couldn't believe he was even talking to this guy, let alone flirting back.

"You look like you've got some hot body under that shirt, Beau. Do you like to show it off?"

"Not a shy bone in my body."

"Want to prove it?"

"Sure"

"Here," Erik said, sliding a sheet of paper across the bar.

Wow, Beau thought. *That was easy.* When he looked down, he realized it wasn't Erik's phone number but a form to fill out for that night's Mr. Southern Sizzle contest. The winner would represent Jocks at the Atlanta competition in August. "What do I have to do?" asked Beau.

"It's easy. Get up on that stage over there, get undressed, and take a shower. Then it's up to the judges."

"Who are the judges?"

Erik smiled, "I'm one of them. And I think you should enter."

"What the hell? Sounds like fun. I'm in."

"Great, go see the big guy with the clipboard over there."

Beau found the guy Erik had pointed out. He was even bigger

and more handsome. Beau was in awe when he shook his hand.

"I'm Rob. Thanks for signing up. We're just about ready to start. There are four guys on ahead of you. When I call out your name, I'll hand you a towel. You climb these stairs and go up on stage. Put your clothes in one of the lockers. When you're naked, go over to the shower and turn the water on. The temperature's set, so you have nothing to worry about. Once you're in the shower, you can do anything you want. Just don't jack off." Rob clapped Beau on the back. "Enjoy yourself!"

***

"And now a special treat, let's give a warm welcome to a guy who's come all the way from Toronto. Let's give it up for Beau!" Beau slowly climbed the steps onto the small stage. He looked out into the crowd. Every eye in the house was on him. They were all smiling and clapping. They loved him, and in that instant Beau loved them.

A huge smile lit up his handsome face, and the crowd went wild. *This is great!* Beau felt a surge of adrenaline. The Pet Shop Boys' "It's A Sin" filled the air and he took center stage.

After kicking off his shoes and socks, Beau turned his back to the audience and slowly started to peel off his t-shirt. Once it was free of his head, he flexed the muscles in his back, making his lats spread like wings. He spun around, held the t-shirt behind his head, and posed to show off his abs. Beau looked into the crowd and made eye contact with a cute redhead who mouthed the words, "Marry me." Beau laughed and his abs rippled. He was enjoying himself as much as the crowd was. He turned his back to the crowd again and quickly undid his jeans. Grinning over one shoulder, he bent over and pushed his 501's to his ankles, revealing his muscular ass. The wave of energy that swelled from the audience was overwhelming. It was a sexual rush. Beau wanted more.

He grabbed his towel. Instead of wrapping it around himself, he hung it over his rock hard erection. He turned in profile and walked to the shower. The cheering and applause nearly drowned out the music. The towel seemed to bob up and down to the music's beat. It was actually Beau's own heartbeat that was making his dick throb. He loved the attention his big equipment was getting him. He hung the towel up on its rightful hook and stepped into the shower. Slowly he started to lather himself up. He looked out over the crowd to try and catch Erik's eye, but all he could see were smiling faces, all looking at him adoringly. *You're a star!* shouted a voice in his head. Despite the hot water, he got goose bumps. He'd dreamed of being famous since he was a kid. He'd seen how stars like Tom Jones were treated, and he never forgot it.

Beau stopped lathering and pushed his body up against the glass. Then he started humping it. The crowd began to clap along to his thrusts. Beau turned around and pushed his butt up against the glass.

Then Beau heard Rob over the speaker system, "We better turn on the cold water before members of our audience have heatstroke."

Beau took that as a signal to wind things down. He slowly, sensually rinsed himself off. He didn't want to rush his exit like the other contestants. He'd take his own sweet time. He turned off the water and grabbed his towel. There were several boos from the crowd. *Don't worry, boys, it ain't over yet,* he thought. Instead of drying off, Beau threw his towel on the stage floor and stepped out of the shower onto it. He then very slowly squeegeed the water off of his body with his hands.

The crowd lost it.

"Gentlemen," Rob announced, "we have our new Mr. Southern Sizzle contestant! Let's hear it for a man of many talents, Beau from Toronto!"

Toronto - *Two Weeks Later*

Rob had a lot riding on Beau and was doing everything in his power to groom him as a winner. Shortly after he'd won the contest at Jocks and returned to Toronto, Beau received a package from Rob containing travel-size shampoo bottles filled with testosterone and deca-durabolin. In a separate letter were a check to cover grooming expenses and instructions on how to administer his weekly injections. Beau called Rob immediately. "I just opened the box you sent me. I don't do drugs. I thought you said my body was perfect. Why do I need steroids?"

"Relax, you don't have to do them forever, but everyone else you're competing against will be using them. I want to level the playing field. It'll help you get bigger. You wouldn't want to look puny compared to all the other big boys, would you?" Rob asked.

"No, I wouldn't . . . but just this once." Beau conceded. "I'll do it so I can win the contest."

Beau trained hard at the gym. Almost immediately, he felt the effects of the steroids. His strength increased and he lifted heavier weights. He started to put on muscle. In addition, his sex drive went through the roof. He was constantly yanking on his dick. First thing in the morning in the shower (but he did that every day anyway), in the shower at the gym, in bed at least once before nodding off. He even woke up at 3:00 am during the first week with such a throbbing hard-on that he had to jack off before going back to sleep.

The week before the competition, Beau went to Bumble & Bumble, Toronto's premier salon and day spa, where he got his first everything - manicure, pedicure, facial, and full-body waxing. He was the only male client in the salon that day. The entire staff hovered around him. Since Beau already looked like a star, the staff simply assumed he was. He was waited on hand and foot, and offered glass after glass of champagne. Beau let himself revel in it. He couldn't quite get the image of the Cowardly Lion being groomed in the Oz salon out of his head.

"Ready for your body waxing?" asked a gorgeous girl with a Swedish accent.

Beau didn't think he had that much body hair until the girl started tearing it out strip by hot sticky strip. "Fuuuuuuuck!" he shouted at the top of his lungs when she yanked the strips on his inner thighs. *How the hell do women live through bikini waxes?!? Straight men have no clue what their women do for them.* But the pain of removal had its dividends. The first time he showered, he couldn't get over how sleek and muscular his body looked and felt. Water rolled right off of him, catching only on his dark black pubes.

August 1993 - *Six Weeks Later*
Atlanta

It was a gathering of the tribe. On this sultry evening, a steady stream of young men was filling the downtown Apparel Mart. The thumping bass of the music, pounding away somewhere deep inside, reached the sidewalk entrance as a visceral beat. You could feel it in your chest.

The dance floor was the ground level of a multi-story atrium.

It was filled to capacity with a sea of shirtless guys. Fog machines were pumping out clouds of smoke that transformed the space into a cauldron of lust. Strobe lights flashed, making it look like the entire scene was happening in slow motion. Computerized banks of lighting swirled above, painting the crowd in brilliant colors. Laser beams bounced off a huge mirrored ball suspended overhead.

In front of the atrium's glassed-in elevators was a raised stage upon which the *crème de la crème* of male perfection were about to strut their stuff in the Mr. Southern Sizzle competition. Onstage was a group of men flagging to the rhythm of the music. The fluid movements of their white scarves created ever-changing shapes in the colored light.

Beau was tanned and buff. Backstage, with the pounding music barely muffled, Rob helped him slip into a brand new Versace bathing suit. Beau couldn't believe the extravagance of the gift. He'd never worn anything so expensive. He was beaming with pride.

"I've checked out the competition, and believe me, you have nothing to worry about. Try not to pay attention to anyone else. Tonight is all about you."

"Thanks, Rob. I could have never done this without your support. I won't let you down."

"That's my boy," Rob said proudly. "You're number nine out of ten. Make sure the judges don't even notice the last guy. See you in the winner's circle."

"OK!" Beau replied. All he had to do now was oil up. Rob had told him a little secret – use Neutrogena's light sesame oil instead of baby oil. It absorbed better and wouldn't leave him looking greasy.

"Hey, could you give me a hand? I'll do your back if you do mine."

"Sure," Beau said without looking up. When he did, he took a gulp. An enormous, overly-tanned, blond beast, who looked like he was about to burst, was standing in front of him. He resembled a barracuda with too many bright white teeth stuffed in his mouth. His eyes were a disturbing shade of blue that reminded Beau of those scary children in *Village of the Damned*. Beau thought, *You might look great up on a stage, but close up you don't look real.*

"I'm Mr. LA. You're on just before me, right? You're from New York."

"Nice to meet you. I'm Beau. I'm actually from Toronto, but Jocks in New York is my sponsor."

"So you're a Canadian boy? How sweet," Mr. LA said with an attitude. "A word to the wise - the judges will disqualify you for stuffing your bathing suit like that."

Looking down at the rather small bulge in Mr. LA's trunks, Beau smiled and said, "This? It's all real." With that he pulled down his Versace suit, and out fell his slab of meat.

With a look of shock on his face, Mr. LA only said, "Oh."

Beau stuffed himself back in, his dick a bit aroused from being shown off. It nearly reached his hip.

"Will you put this on my back?" Mr. LA asked, handing Beau a bottle of baby oil.

"Sure, bend over and let me oil you up." Beau applied it heavily so that Mr. LA's already broken-out back would shine like a greasy pizza. "Done. Now you do me," Beau said. He handed his bottle of sesame oil to Mr. LA.

Applying it to Beau's back, he said, "This is interesting. I've never used it. It feels lighter than baby oil. Maybe I should towel off and use some of yours."

"Too late," announced Beau. "They're starting the contest." He tossed the bottle into his duffle bag and moved forward into the lineup. *Take that!*

Rob was right, Beau thought. *This guy has good looks and a nice body, but I can beat him.* In his heart, Beau didn't think the judges would respond to all that overkill – the bloated muscles, the dyed hair, the bleached teeth, the artificial tan, and those fake blue eyes. The only word that came to mind was "vulgar."

The photographer who would be taking Beau's onstage photos was David Fujimoto. According to Rob, he was the hottest guy in the industry. Fuji, as he was known professionally, had tapped into a whole new genre of homoerotic books, cards, and calendars. The winner of tonight's competition would be flown to LA for a photo shoot with Fuji.

"He's the man who'll make you a star," Rob stated.

From your lips to God's ears, Beau thought. He'd heard that last year's winner was currently being squired about the world by an English pop star.

"Contestant number nine, Beau Fournier, from Jocks in New York." Beau took a deep breath and stepped out into the bright light. At first, the large space was overwhelming. Beau felt dwarfed by it, as if it would suck him up into an enormous void and he'd disappear. He tried to look out into the crowd, but with the flashing lights and fog, he couldn't see anything. In a way it was easier. It was almost as if all those guys weren't there. He slowly walked out to the beat of the music onto the center of the stage.

He heard someone to his left say, "You look fabulous! Show them what you've got." Beau turned toward the voice and saw Fuji, camera in hand. He then turned to the crowd and gave them a big wave hello.

"I love you!" Beau heard someone yell.

Beau's smile beamed. "I love you, Atlanta!" Beau yelled back. *Where did that come from?* he wondered. A cheer went up from the crowd and rushed like a tidal wave toward Beau. *Jesus,* he thought, *this is it!* He walked toward the edge of the stage. Hundreds of hands shot up, reaching for him. Making sure to keep just out of reach, Beau slowly turned and began to slide his hands over his slick body. Then he began doing his stretching routine as if warming up for a track meet. It felt natural to him. He could never have posed like a bodybuilder. His instincts were right.

"Fantastic!" Fuji said.

FLASH

"Hold that for a second longer."

FLASH

"Great! That's even better."

FLASH

Before he knew it, Beau heard, "That's contestant number nine from Jocks in New York." Beau took a deep bow to the audience and slowly walked back to the opening in the curtains. Before stepping through, he turned and waved back at the crowd.

"Alright, Mary, get out of the way. It's my turn in the spotlight." Mr. LA pushed past Beau, leaving him covered in baby oil. Beau barely noticed. Nothing was going to burst his bubble. He was riding the high he'd gotten from the crowd's adoration. Thousands of men had focused all their attention on him and him alone. He could feel their raw lust. He wanted to run back out there and get more. Through the closing curtain, he managed to see Mr. LA slip on his own greasy bare feet and barely catch himself from falling face first onstage.

Rob surprised Beau from behind, wrapping his big arms around him, and lifting him off the ground. "I can't get over that performance. You were born to the stage! Now, change into your jeans. I left Erik with my best friend Charles. It's time to go dance with them. Besides, they won't announce the winner until the end of the party. They want to keep the crowd in suspense until the end of the night."

60

Beau quickly changed into his jeans and sneakers but left his shirt off. He followed Rob through the crowd. All along the route, the sexiest men were reaching out and clapping Beau on the back.

"I love you!"

"You're gorgeous!"

"How's that for ego stroking, champ?" Rob said. "They all want to see what you have hiding in your bathing suit. I'd hazard a guess that you could take home just about any guy in this crowd tonight."

What a feeling of power, Beau thought.

Finally, they found Erik and Charles. "Here, take this," Rob said. He opened up at Tic Tac container and handed them each a small pill. Beau watched as Rob, Erik, and Charles took theirs. "It's E. You know, Ecstasy. Cheers!" Rob handed the bottle of water to Beau.

What the hell? Everyone else is doing it. It's my night! I'm gonna celebrate in style. "Bottoms up!" Beau said as he swallowed the bitter tasting pill with a big swig of water. "When will I feel it?" he asked.

"You should feel it in a few minutes or so," Erik answered.

"How will I know it's working?"

"Oh, you'll know. Don't worry."

Beau tucked his water bottle into his back pocket and started shaking his hips to the music. Sweaty, shirtless bodies pressed in on him from all sides. *This is paradise,* Beau thought. He closed his eyes and focused on the rhythm engulfing him. Then he felt someone come up from behind him. The mystery man put his arms around Beau and start rubbing his chest. Beau looked down and saw the dark, thick muscular arms of Charles. His solid chest felt warm against Beau's back. He started kissing and nibbling the back of Beau's neck. *God, that feels so good.* It gave Beau goose bumps.

Charles's hand slowly worked its way down Beau's stomach to his crotch. His hand started to squeeze Beau's hard-on to the beat of the music.

Beau could feel bubbles of sensation rising from his feet up to the top of his head. He became part of the stranger behind him. He felt Charles's hot tongue enter his ear. Beau felt like his body was building up to an orgasm. He'd never felt anything like this. *This is better than sex, it's Ecstasy!* Beau began to laugh and couldn't stop repeating, "I feel it. I feel it!"

Rob whispered into one ear, "I thought you'd like it. We're just catching up to the crowd around us. Don't you feel like fucking every guy in sight?"

"Yes, and being fucked at the same time," Beau surprised himself by saying. This stuff is incredible."

Erik whispered in the other ear, "Stop talking and focus on Charles. He's really into you."

Just as Beau was beginning to feel weak in the knees, Charles turned him around. Beau closed his eyes and slid his tongue between the softest lips he'd ever kissed. He couldn't tell where he ended and Charles began. It was all hot sweaty muscle grinding and humping against more hot sweaty muscle. His erect cock was sticking straight up above his belt, rubbing against Charles's six-pack abs. Beau wished he was naked.

The music slowly faded. Beau heard a voice announce, "And the winner of the Mr. Southern Sizzle contest is . . . ." There was a pause that seemed to stretch on endlessly. ". . . our contestant from New York, Beau Fournier!!!"

Good for him, Beau thought. *Lucky guy!*

Rob's voice shook Beau from his bliss. "I told you!" he shouted, hugging Beau.

Beau couldn't stop laughing.

September 1993 - *One Month Later*
West Hollywood
Friday

Beau awoke and looked around his rather small but clean room. It was all beige-on-beige. When he climbed out of bed, he still couldn't believe it. His boyhood dream was coming true. He was in Hollywood! Well, the San Vincente Inn was in West Hollywood, but close enough. He'd arrived late last night from Toronto after a grueling month. He'd worked his usual hours and picked up extra flights so he could afford to take a week off. He'd arrived at LAX exhausted and wanted to get a good night's rest before his big day. Everything was riding on this photo shoot. He was in the best shape of his life. He'd spent every extra waking moment at the gym. The Southern Sizzle contest was one thing, but this was different. The camera didn't lie. He'd be frozen in time. Every minor flaw would be brought into sharp focus by the camera's critical eye.

Beau showered, shaved, and headed out in search of breakfast.

"Are you looking for a scene or for cheap and easy?" the front desk clerk asked.

"Cheap and easy," Beau replied, thinking, *I like the sound of that.*

"I would have pegged you for more of a 'scene' kinda guy. Anyway, walk down to Santa Monica Boulevard, the double wide street just down the hill one block. Make a left and keep going until you see IHOP's big blue roof. You can't miss it."

"Great, thanks. Oh, one other thing. Where's the nearest gay gym?" Beau asked.

"Honey, they're everywhere. Just try to find one that isn't gay!"

Beau smiled and thought, *We're not in Kansas any more, Toto.*

After an egg white omelet, Beau headed to the gym he'd passed. It was so gay that it didn't even have a women's locker room. Guys worked out without shirts. To top it all off, there was a nude sun deck on the roof. After a sweaty workout, Beau headed back to his hotel for a swim. He swam a couple of lengths and climbed out of the pool to dry off. When he picked up his towel, he caught the eye of a beautiful guy who had sat down in the chaise next to his.

"Hi, my name's Luca. We haven't met yet."

"My name's Beau." He was mesmerized by Luca - his smile, his pale blue eyes. Luca was model material. Beau smiled back while he tried to think of something to say. "I'm here to shoot with David Fujimoto," he said.

"You're not here for the porn shoot?" Luca asked. "Sorry. I didn't know there were any outsiders staying here. I figured from the way you're built that you worked for Priapus Studios as well."

"Thanks, but no," Beau stammered. "Are you a porn star? I mean, you seem to have everything that I'd look for in one." Beau wasn't using a line. This guy was built every bit as well as Beau – tiny waist, muscular shoulders, and pecs like half melons.

Luca just laughed. "How long are you in town for?" he asked.

"Just a few days," Beau answered. "How about you?"

"I'm working at a fundraiser on Sunday afternoon. I head to Laguna on Monday morning to shoot a video."

Saturday

Beau woke at dawn and dressed exactly as instructed - loose
fitting clothes and no underwear. Fuji had been quite
specific. He didn't want Beau to have an elastic waistband
mark on his body. It was something that made perfect sense,
but Beau would never have thought of it on his own. He
waited at the entrance of the San Vincente until Fuji pulled
up in a Ford SUV.

"Nice car," Beau said as he buckled his seat belt. It
smelled like it had just been driven it off the dealer's lot.

"Thanks, but it's not the car I should be driving," Fuji
replied.

"Oh? What kind of car should you be driving?" Beau
asked, confused.

"A Range Rover," Fuji said as they drove off.

"Really?" Beau decided to take the bait and ask the
next obvious question. "Why is that?"

"Out here, it's all about image. If you look successful,
then you are successful. And that's all that really matters in
LA," Fuji said matter-of-factly before changing topics.
"There's an old mausoleum in Pasadena. I'd like to shoot
there this morning," he said.

Beau was stunned. "You mean one of those places
where they bury dead people? You want me to get naked in a
cemetery?"

"Exactly," answered Fuji. "This place was built in the
'20s and has huge stained glass windows. I want to shoot you
against them. The colored light they cast is just amazing."
Beau didn't know what to say.

Pasadena

Fuji turned down one side street after another. "We're
going to go into the cemetery through the back," he
announced to Beau. They pulled up to what looked like a
service entrance to a city park. Fuji parked under an oak tree
that arched over the road. "OK, let's get going. We've only got
so much time before the sun's too high."

The mausoleum was a long low structure built into the side of
a hill. Huge balustraded staircases framed either end. It was
a grand palace for the dead. From where they stood, Beau
could see the stained glass windows sparkling in the early
morning sunlight.

"The guard opens up the place at 10:00 and then goes

64

on his rounds. We have little more than an hour to get in, shoot, and get out."

"OK," replied Beau, not sure of what was expected of him in such circumstances.

They watched the guard unlock the massive doors. After he got back into his golf cart, Fuji and Beau made their way up the hill. They left footprints in the dew-covered grass. Roses surrounded the mausoleum. Their scent was everywhere. Beau inhaled deeply. The smell of the morning air reminded him of Toronto's all-too-brief summers. They ascended the staircase and entered. Suddenly they found themselves in darkness. The silence was unnerving. They lowered their voices to a whisper. Even then, their words echoed in the empty marble hall. Every twenty feet or so, a cascade of colored light poured in through the stained glass windows.

"Alright, I want you to strip and climb up on the window sill," directed Fuji. Beau hesitated. It seemed somehow sacrilegious to be stark naked in a place dedicated to the memory of the dead. "Are you sure about this?" he asked.

"We have about fifty minutes before the guard circles back. He'll wander in here, so I need you to get up on the sill now," Fuji said authoritatively.

Beau complied. He shivered when his bare feet touched the white marble floor. *This is so wrong*, he thought. *It's not right to be naked in here. What if someone comes in?*

"I know what you're thinking," said Fuji. "Don't worry. These people have been dead for so long that no one ever comes to visit them."

It didn't reassure Beau. The mausoleum was cold and unwelcoming, despite the light pouring in through the windows. Due to fear and the cold, his dick and balls had shriveled to nothing.

Fuji had to give Beau a boost up onto the narrow sill. He struggled for a moment to get his footing. It would be a hard fall if he lost his balance.

Fuji then fiddled with his camera. "Here, hold this light meter at arm's length from yourself and push the button on top of it when I say so," ordered Fuji. Once again, Beau did as he was told.

"OK, I've got my reading. Let's start."

Beau flinched. This was it. This was his dream coming true. Not quite in the location he'd envisioned, but here he was being photographed by one of the best known gay photographers in the country. He fluffed his dick to try and awaken it from its chilled slumber.

"Flex those abs for me. I want see your perfect body framed against the light," instructed Fuji.

Beau exhaled and held his breath. He tightened his abs.

"Perfect," said Fuji. "Give me that angelic face."
FLASH

"Turn your head slightly toward me. Now lower your chin. Give me a slight smile."
FLASH

Beau could feel the goose bumps on his back begin to fade as the light warmed him, but his bare feet were like blocks of ice.

"Reach to the left as if you were getting ready to hold a baby. Think Michelangelo and the Sistine Chapel. I want muscles and tenderness. Can you do that for me?" asked Fuji.

Beau did his best. Arms outstretched. Head held aloft. Muscles tensed to show off every ripple and line.
FLASH

Within an hour they were done. The lighting had indeed changed. The intense colors of the morning had warmed to pastels. Their window of opportunity had literally come and gone.

Beau was relieved to be able to hop down from the sill and put his pants back on. "Damn, that was fast," he commented to Fuji.

While Beau was getting dressed, Fuji made a call to his old pal, Ira. "You free for an early lunch at the Abbey around 11:30?"

"Sure," Ira responded.

"Great! We're just leaving Pasadena," Fuji said.

"We?"

"Yes. I want you to meet my new model, Beau. He's just your type, hung and handsome. He's this year's winner from that contest I judged in Atlanta – an innocent Canadian boy. I just finished the most amazing shoot with him," Fuji explained.

"Sounds interesting. I'll see you at the Abbey."

"Hungry?" Fuji asked.

"Starving!" was Beau's answer. "I haven't eaten since last night."

"Let's head back to West Hollywood. I know a great place that all the boys love. It's one of my favorites. And it's not too far from where you're staying. I hope you don't mind, but I took the liberty of inviting a friend of mine. He's in the business and well connected."

Beau was intrigued. He'd yet to meet someone who worked in the film industry, let alone someone who was "connected."

Fuji continued, "Ira's a genius. He's someone you should get to know."

West Hollywood

Fuji parked in front of an antique shop that was filled with huge garden urns. They walked a short distance to a walled-in brick courtyard. At the center table sat a handsome older man who was very tan. He stood out like an exotic bird. He was wearing a Panama hat and a brightly colored Hawaiian shirt.

"Always on time," Fuji commented. He reached out to shake his friend's hand.

"Always with a beauty!" Ira responded. He clapped Fuji on the back and gave him a bear hug. "You must be Beau. Fuji's told me all about you. I'm Ira Gould."

"It's a pleasure to meet you, Mr. Gould." Beau made sure to remember this bigwig's name.

"Please call me Ira. Mr. Gould was my father."

Beau smiled, "OK, Ira."

"So, Beau, I must say that Fuji wasn't exaggerating when he described you. You've got to be the most handsome man here, and there are a lot of contenders."

Beau blushed at the shameless flattery that was being tossed his way.

"Trust me, I've got an eye for this kind of thing. You've got something special. You're more than just a pretty face," Ira said.

Beau began to feel a bit uncomfortable. *What exactly had Fuji told Ira? Was this how everyone "in the business" warmed up their next catch?* "Well, thanks, Ira. I don't know what to say."

"You're doing just fine, Beau. Just fine. Are you hungry? They have a great Caesar salad with grilled chicken. It's what I always get. Let's go inside and place our orders. Fuji, why don't you stay here and save our table?" Ira said, not waiting for Fuji to answer.

Suddenly, Beau stopped in his tracks. He turned to Ira. "Is that who I think it is?" he whispered. There, surrounded by her gaggle of gays, with a fluffy little dog on her lap, sat the Living Legend. Her violet eyes were piercing, more stunning than they ever appeared on the silver screen.

"Who else could it be? " Ira nonchalantly replied. "It's her favorite place for lunch. She's here at least once a week. She calls it 'her pub'."

***

Ira and Beau were chatting when they came back with their drinks. "So, Beau, I'm throwing a little charity event tomorrow afternoon at my home in Beverly Hills. A lot of industry people will be there, and I'd like to introduce you. I know it's short notice, but I hope you're free."

Beau hesitated. Of course he was free, and even if he weren't, he'd cancel any and all plans to attend a Beverly Hills party. "I don't have anything on my schedule," he answered. "When and where?"

"It's at 3:00. It's a pool party. Did you bring a bathing suit?"

"Yes, I did. A Versace," Beau said proudly.

"That's perfect. Fuji's going to be shooting some photos in the pool. You wouldn't mind posing for some more photos, would you?" Ira asked.

"By Fuji? No, of course not. His work is great. I've seen some of his photos that were shot in a swimming pool. Was that yours?" Beau asked.

"That would be the one. He's making my pool famous with his photos. Soon people will be referring to me as the guy with the Fuji pool," Ira laughed. "I guess there are worse ways to be known."

"What are you two conspiring about?" Fuji asked,

"I've invited Beau to my benefit tomorrow," Ira said. "Would you be a dear and pick him up on your way over? I told him to be prepared for another photo shoot. I think he'd look smashing in my pool, don't you?"

"Brilliant idea. That crowd will eat him up."

"And speaking of eating, here's our food. Just in time, too. I was about to take a bite out of Beau!" Ira laughed.

Beau cringed. There was something off kilter about the entire lunch. He wasn't sure if Ira was harmless, but if Ira could get Beau into the office of a casting director, then Beau would put up with his ever-so-polite lecherous comments.

Beverly Hills
Sunday

Beau stepped out of the SUV and looked up at Ira's house - no, make that estate - as Fuji handed his car keys to the valet. Its style reminded Beau of photos he'd seen of old movie star's homes. It had corkscrew-shaped columns and dozens of pointed archways.

"Wait 'til you see the inside," said Fuji, knowing full well that Beau would be knocked out. Everyone had that response the first time they came to Ira's home.

As they walked through the house, Beau couldn't get over its grandeur. Every room, and there seemed to be dozens, was furnished to the n'th degree with Art Deco furniture. Fuji greeted and shook hands with at least half the crowd.

He seems to know everyone. Beau smiled and shook hands as he was introduced, knowing he'd never remember anyone's name. There were just too many introductions.

Finally, Ira appeared and swept toward Fuji and Beau with open arms.

Beau realized that he was dressed in the same style as yesterday – Panama hat and Hawaiian shirt. *You gotta have a gimmick*, Beau thought.

"It's the man of the hour," Ira gushed. "Beau, it's wonderful to see you again. Now the party can begin. Let me get you some champagne." Ira grabbed a shirtless hunk with a tray and handed Beau and Fuji glasses of champagne.

Beau knew he'd seen the waiter before. *Isn't he the porn star I met by the pool?* But in a flash, the waiter was gone.

"Welcome to my home," Ira said with a grand gesture.

"It's beautiful. I've never seen anything like it," Beau said, feeling way out of his league.

"I'm so glad you like it. I'm very proud of it. It's one of the few examples of 1920's Moorish architecture in LA. I went in the opposite direction when I had the pool designed. I wanted something sculptural. I think I succeeded. At least Fuji seems to like it. Don't you Fuji?"

"Absolutely," he replied.

"Speaking of which, Fuji, why don't you get set up while I show Beau around?"

"OK, sure," Fuji replied.

Ira put his arm around Beau's shoulder and ushered him forward.

From what he could gather, Beau surmised that this was a fundraiser for Project Angel Food to which Ira had invited the A-list gays of Hollywood. It was a mix of well-dressed older men and their beautiful boyfriends. *Not a bad gig,* Beau thought.

Suddenly, a tall rotund black man with a little redheaded bodybuilder by his side pushed his way in front of Beau and thrust out his hand. Before either Ira or Beau could react, the stranger said in a way-too-loud voice, "I'm Otis Mercer, but everybody calls me Big Daddy. And this is my Bobby. We love your videos. When is the next one coming out?"

Beau was speechless. He shook the huge man's paw.

Ira took charge of the moment. "I'm so sorry for the confusion," he interjected. "Beau's my special guest, and I'm your host. You've must have him confused with one of the staff. They're all porn stars from Priapus Studios. Perhaps you'll find your favorite among them."

"I'm sorry, Big Daddy. I really thought he was Gianni d'Angelo," the little redhead said apologetically to the over-sized black man. The big man shot the redhead a look and the two stepped back into the crowd.

"One can't always handpick the guests who attend a fundraiser," explained Ira. "In any event, it's time to get into your swimsuit and try out the pool. Fuji should be ready to photograph you. Let's head over to the cabana so that you can change."

Once inside, Beau stripped out of his shirt and jeans. He'd worn his Versace bathing suit underneath.

Ira's eyes opened wide as Beau bared his body. "I knew you were handsome, Beau, but I had no idea that your body was so beautiful. You're perfection!" When they emerged from the cabana, all eyes were on the flawless specimen of manhood at Ira's side.

Fuji was already photographing several young men who had apparently lost their bathing suits. When he saw Beau, Fuji said something to the boys, who swam off, perhaps in search of their missing apparel.

Ira took Beau's champagne when he entered the water.

The pool was heated. *This is perfect,* Beau thought.

Fuji posed Beau on the steps of the pool but then stopped and said, "You've got to lose that suit. It's beautiful, but too distracting. This isn't a Versace ad."

Beau discreetly slipped his trunks off. When he went to put them by the pool's edge, Ira was there with a hand.

"I'll hold onto this for you. Now go on. Be gorgeous."

Beau returned to the steps and draped himself over them.

"Stunning!" Fuji said. And so it went, Fuji suggesting positions while Beau improvised. Beau was surprised by how naturally it came to him. Fuji called to Ira, who was watching every move Beau made, "With your permission, I'd like to borrow one of your waiters."

"Oh, you like them? I thought it would be fun to have porn stars staff the party. They're shooting a video at my Laguna house tomorrow. So by all means, my staff is at your command."

"There's one who's a mirror image of Beau. They're exactly the same size and proportion. I'd like to photograph them together. I'll go find him."

Beau took the opportunity to stretch and swim a few laps.

In less than a minute, Fuji was back with the porn star.

"Hi! It's nice to see you again. Small world, huh?" smiled Luca.

"So, you already know each other. You certainly don't waste any time," Fuji said.

"We're staying at the same place. He's in the room next to me." Beau replied.

"How cozy," Ira added, none too pleased. "Well, for Christ's sake, Fuji – do your thing."

"OK. Luca, would you take off your jeans and get in the water, please?" Fuji asked.

"Sure," Luca replied. He slipped off his Levis unashamedly and stepped into the pool.

Fuji was thrilled with the shoot. *These two are naturals. The way they move, the way their bodies fit together.* Realizing he was just about out of film, he said, "Hey, let's have some fun. I'd like a shot of you both coming up out of the water. Have fun with it. We're just about done. Beau, how about you get on Luca's shoulders? Let's see how that works," Fuji suggested.

He saw it as soon as it appeared in his viewfinder - the look of pure joy on their faces. It was different than all those perfectly posed shots. This looked totally candid, two beautiful boys having the time of their lives.
FLASH

What a perfect moment caught on film, Fuji thought to himself.

Ira had an enormous Hermès towel waiting for Beau when he climbed out of the water. Beau followed Ira and Fuji to the cabana to change back into his clothes. Ira didn't miss a thing as Beau stuffed his dick into his jeans.

Once Beau had tucked in his shirt, Ira said, "Would you like to have dinner with President Clinton?"

Beau paused. "I'm sorry. Dinner with President Clinton?"

Fuji turned around to listen to the exchange. He always enjoyed watching Ira at his best.

"Yes. Would you like to be my guest? It's two weeks from this Saturday. Friends of mine in Holmby Hills are hosting it."

What the fuck? thought Beau.

Fuji had to stop himself from chuckling at the expression on Beau's face.

"I'd love to . . . but . . . I, um, I, you know, live in Toronto," sputtered Beau.

"I'll take care of that," assured Ira. He handed Beau his business card. "Call me tomorrow, and we'll work out the details."

West Hollywood

It was a short drive back to the San Vincente Inn. "You boys have fun," shouted out Fuji when he let Beau and Luca out and drove off into the night.

Luca reached for Beau's hand. "I want to get naked with you," he whispered as he unlatched the front gate to the compound.

Beau couldn't believe his ears. He'd only fantasized about porn stars before now, and here he was face-to-face with the man of his dreams. "I'd love that," Beau managed to stammer. It was as if everything that had happened – New York, Atlanta, LA – had all led up to this perfect moment.

"Follow me," Luca quietly said. He led Beau to his room. Before he put the key in the lock, he pushed Beau up against the door and dove in with a kiss that took Beau completely by surprise.

Beau felt his legs tremble as adrenaline raced through his body. He gave in to Luca's kiss and returned it with a passionate fervor. "You're the most beautiful man I've ever met," Beau managed to say once their lips parted. Luca smiled. What Beau failed to realized was that he was just as handsome, just as perfect. For Luca, it was as if his own image had stepped out the mirror. They looked into one another's pale blue eyes. There was no need to rush. They had all night to explore each other.

Monday

Beau was exhausted from a night of spectacular sex with his next-door neighbor. Luca was everything, and more, that Beau imagined he would be. Beau had finally gone to bed around 5:00 am, his dreams filled with erotic images. He woke at 9:00 am when Luca knocked on his door to say good-bye. Beau convinced himself to wait another hour before calling Ira's office. He didn't want to appear overeager and blow his big chance with the guy in the Panama hat. *Who the hell wears Panama hats?* Beau stifled the urge to laugh. He was bowled over that Ira was interested in him. The clock finally hit 10:00 am, and Beau called the number on Ira's business card.

"Broad Spectrum Films," answered the receptionist.

"Ira Gould, please. Beau Fournier calling."

"Oh, Mr. Fournier, I have instructions to route you directly to Mr. Gould's private secretary. One moment, please."

In five minutes, Ira's secretary had Beau booked on a round-trip flight from Toronto to LA for the Clinton dinner. "Can you be ready in an hour?" the secretary asked. "There's some shopping we need to do," she explained.

It was short drive to the nondescript shopping strip in Little Odessa. The secretary walked Beau into a small shop filled with bolts of fabric. The air smelled dry and dusty. Sound was muffled.

A little man stepped out from behind some drapery near the cash register. "Always a pleasure to see you," smiled the gentleman.

"The pleasure is all mine," the secretary replied. "Our young man here is in need of a suit."

It dawned on Beau that he was meeting Ira's tailor. *I'm getting a fitting,* he realized. Beau was taken aback. He hadn't even thought about what he'd wear to meet Clinton. Ira obviously had.

The secretary and the tailor picked out four fabrics for Beau to choose from. *This feels like buttery silk,* marveled Beau at the first bolt. He ran his fingers over the fabric again and again trying to soak in its richness. He settled on a dark navy blue gabardine that looked like something Cary Grant would wear.

The tailor took Beau into the dressing room. "Does the gentlemen dress to the right or to the left?" the tailor queried as he measured Beau's inseam.

Beau had no idea what the old Russian man meant.

The tailor reached up and gently patted Beau's crotch.

"Oh," exclaimed Beau. He shifted his dick and balls to where it all felt comfortable.

"We make that pant leg a little wider," explained the tailor.

Holmby Hills – *Two Weeks Later*

All of the men wore dark well-fitted suits. They looked like Wall Street brokers. But it was obvious that they were packing serious hardware under their arms. There was a bulge next to their rib cage.

What kind of guns do these guys carry? All Beau could think of was Dirty Harry's .44 Magnum, but these guys looked a lot more sophisticated. Beau smiled at one the agents. He expected a blank face and no response, instead, the agent walked up to him.

"May I help you?"

Beau was startled. "Uh, no, that's OK. I'm with him," he stuttered. Beau pointed to Ira, who was a few feet away. It was then that Beau noticed sharp shooters in black fatigues stationed on the roof.

At the front gate, the Secret Service had installed metal detectors for all guests to pass through after exiting their limos. Everyone was expected to walk the long drive up to the Frank Gehry-designed house. *This is what Dorothy must have felt like when she approached the Emerald City,* thought Beau. Here in the middle of LA, these people lived in a house that was the size of an airport hangar looking out on nothing but woods and gardens. Beau had no idea that people lived in the style of the art collectors who were hosting the evening. Everything was over-the-top. He knew enough to recognize the Warhol paintings and Henry Moore sculptures, but there was art throughout the house. One room contained nothing except a bunch of gray rocks arranged in a circle. Beau assumed it was important and expensive if it got a room all to itself. When he saw Barbra Streisand walk in, he had the overwhelming feeling that it was all a dream. This party erased any doubts he might have had about Ira's connections.

74

Before dinner began, a handful of people - Ira and Beau included - were ushered into the gargantuan living room by the Secret Service. Twenty couples who had donated major bucks were to have their photo taken with the President, but Clinton was running late. Everyone made small talk while cooling their heels.

From across the room, Beau caught the eye of the Scientologist, a major film star. Once their eyes locked, he walked directly across the room toward Beau. For an instant, Beau thought the Scientologist must be heading toward Ira. But no, he was making a beeline for Beau.

"Good to see you again," the Scientologist greeted Ira while staring a hole through Beau and undressing him with his eyes. Beau was embarrassed by the attention. Star-struck and tongue-tied, he struggled for something to say. The Scientologist, still handsome but showing a bit of a paunch, shook Beau's hand and introduced himself. "Haven't we met before?" he asked Beau.

Before Beau could answer, the doors swung open and the entourage surrounding Clinton strode into the room. Beau was dazzled. Clinton filled the room with his presence. Even the massive painting on the wall seemed to recede. All eyes were on the President. Before he knew what was happening, he and Ira were standing next to Clinton. His heart was pounding so hard in his chest that Beau couldn't hear a word that was spoken. Then he broke out into a cold sweat. *This is all wrong. I can't have my photo taken with the President. Stop the camera!* Beau wanted to shout out. But it was too late. The photographer was focusing the lens. *Jesus fuck! I'm Mr. Southern Sizzle. I don't belong in this world. The National Enquirer will kill for this photo!*
FLASH

Ira Gould

October 1993 - *One Month Later*
Beverly Hills

Beau sat at Ira's huge desk and looked at the framed photos that covered most of it. There were more atop the credenza behind the desk. Many of them were familiar faces. Then he saw it. There in the middle of the credenza was *the* photograph, proof positive that Beau had met Clinton. The Presidential seal was even engraved into the sliver frame. Beau kept wishing that the photo could be color corrected so that his ridiculously bright red cheeks didn't stand out so much, but the sparkle in his eye at being in such company came shining through loud and clear. *I had dinner with the President of the United States at a billionaire's mansion filled with Hollywood movie stars. How's Ira ever going top that?* thought, Beau.

He studied some of the other photos. It looked as if Ira had been photographed with every Hollywood somebody. Photos of Ira with the Blockbuster Director were scattered across the desk. Beau had seen all of his films.

"It was his first big hit that put me on the map," Ira had told Beau. When it came time to produce the trailer, the Blockbuster Director went to Ira. They knew each other through mutual friends. It was a match made in heaven. With a keen instinct for audience titillation, Ira created a trailer that was more famous than the film itself. He'd come up with the tag line that catapulted the film into the realm of summer blockbusters. Those few simple words brought Ira millions in trailer production work and had built Broad Spectrum Films into the biggest producer of "previews" in the world. Ira became a legend in Hollywood. Every director came knocking on his door.

Beau picked up a faded black-and-white photo of Ira in full Navy whites graduating from the U.S. Naval Academy. *Every man looks great in a uniform,* he thought. It was taken when Ira was about the same age as Beau. He was quite a looker then, hair slicked back, and that big smile that always made people turn in his direction. While Ira could have used his good looks to his advantage, he didn't. It was too risky in the service. Instead, it was his ability to talk most anyone into seeing his point of view that got him recognized and placed in the media relations office of the Pentagon.

Being low man on the totem pole, Ira got the left-over work that no one else wanted to deal with. His assignment was handling special requests. Among his varied responsibilities was supplying B-movie directors with ships for their war films. Most were small productions requesting small crafts. Then, out of the blue, came a request from a hugely successful British director. He'd been hired by Paramount to direct a war epic, the first of its kind in more than a decade, and the studio was going all out. Dozens of ships, from frigates to aircraft carriers, would be needed. Suddenly, Ira was shuttling between San Diego, where much of the Pacific fleet was anchored, and Bangkok, where filming was to begin. He got three aircraft carriers and a host of other ships half-way around the world in less than three weeks. Everyone sat up and took notice. By the time Ira's tour of duty was complete, he was headed for Hollywood.

Toward the back of Ira's desk were a series of color photos that were beginning to turn magenta from too much sunlight. It was the photo of Ira with Barbra that made Beau pause. *She gave Ira a hug and kiss at the Clinton dinner. How well does he know her?* Beau wondered. Scattered among all the shots of Ira with Hollywood legends were several of him with Broadway's Betty Boop. Always a favorite of Beau's, he'd seen her in several productions that had played in Toronto. She and Ira had met when she'd come to Broad Spectrum Films to overdub some lines for the trailer of her first movie. He'd offered to take her to lunch and a life-long friendship was born.

"She's so sweet," Ira had mentioned. "I'd love for you to meet her sometime."

***

It was a well-known secret in the film industry that Ira rented out his Laguna beach house to gay porn studios. He'd make a point of visiting the house whenever there was a shoot taking place and assess the eye candy. He had a voracious appetite for young men with big dicks. Over the years, he'd squired several well-hung porn stars to some of Hollywood's most exclusive affairs.

When the idea of filming gay porn to be viewed on the Internet was presented to him by one of his film editors, Ira leapt. The beach house could be rented out for months at a time. There'd be an endless flow of male perfection to choose from. If it made money, than all the better. The film editor set up a lunch with a director from Priapus Studios to set it all in motion.

80

West Hollywood

The Abbey was packed. Ira looked around, hoping that the film editor had gotten there early enough to snag a table. Ira hated to wait for anything. He spotted his old pal sitting at a table in the corner with a pale, obese guy in a baseball cap. Ira walked up to the table.

"Ira, I'd like you to meet the director," the film editor said, gesturing to the hulk in the cap.

"Pleased to meet you," said the director, who looked like a teamster. The only difference? Teamsters have eyebrows. This guy was hairless.

"Have you gentlemen ordered? I'm starving," Ira asked.

"You're asking about food? Please! I dream about food. Big surprise! Look at the size of me," the director replied in an overly loud voice.

Ira let the comment slip.

"I'll order," the film editor announced. He got up from the table. "You guys stay put. Your usual Caesar salad with grilled chicken?"

"So talk to me," Ira stated in his business voice.

"It's simple," began the director. "All we need is to install video cameras in your beach house. After the initial setup, there's virtually no expense. There's a pile of cash to make in this." After seeing a smile cross Ira's face the director continued. "I've got the connections to get any gay porn star we want. Give them a free ticket to Laguna to spend a few days with a bunch of other porn stars, feed and house them, and they're a happy bunch who'll fuck all day long. Can you imagine how many guys will pay to watch? They'll blow a ton of money on this kind of setup." The director knew what he was talking about. A few "voyeur" porn sites had already appeared on the Internet, and they were raking it in. The director wanted to get in on it before the market became saturated. "We charge an initial access fee and an additional fee for viewing each individual room. It's all done with credit cards, and no one questions the charges."

Ira could see the big picture. *Thousands of visitors paying multiple fees would generate incredible cash flow.* His bank in the Cayman Islands could process everything. He was barely listening anymore as the gears in his head spun furiously.

"If it takes a few months to cancel a membership," added the director, "so be it. Fees might add up. Would you call MasterCard and tell them you didn't want to pay for jacking off?"

Beverly Hills

Fuji swept through the front door into Ira's mansion.

"Do you have the proofs from the photo shoot?" Ira asked as he greeted his friend.

"Do I ever! That boy Beau is going to be a star. Wait until you see the sexual energy he radiates. He's a natural."

"I can't remember the last time I saw you this excited," Ira declared. They sat down at the kitchen table where Fuji could spread things out. He handed Ira the first of several proofs. Ira's jaw dropped.

"Was I right?"

"A star is born," Ira proclaimed. "He's hotter than any of the boys in Mr. Underwear's ads." Finally, they got to the proof of the last role of film that Fuji had shot that day. It was the photos of Beau and Luca. "I can't get over how similar to Beau this other model is," Ira said. "They're practically twins."

"He's remarkably handsome with that strong Roman nose," Fuji responded.

"You've got his contact information, don't you?" Ira asked.

"Yes. Why?"

"Well, you know, it never hurts to have a spare warming up in the bullpen."

Luca Barbieri

Jesus, these goddamn lights are gonna fry my nuts, thought Luca as the cameraman slid on his back to get between his legs. The camera was less than a foot from Luca's freshly shaved cojones. The light attached to it was intense. Luca could feel sweat pouring down his legs. It felt like his balls were hanging halfway to his knees from all the heat. *I am so over this,* groaned Luca to himself. *I should be getting combat pay.*

"Gianni, try not to drip sweat onto the lens," asked the cameraman, who always addressed Luca by his professional name, "I'm almost in position."

Luca stood still behind his co-star, a hot young new face.

"Those lights are hot," complained New Face.

"Get used to it," the cameraman barked.

Luca decided to tease New Face. "I'm gonna fuck the hell out of you," he whispered.

A look of panic crossed his co-star's face. He'd seen Gianni d'Angelo's videos and knew what he was in for. "Don't hurt me," New Face pleaded with his innocent face.

"I'll play nice," answered Luca with a smile.

New Face shifted his ass.

"Don't move!" yelled the cameraman. Luca pulled his co-star back toward his roasting balls. He positioned him so that the camera would have a perfect view. The cameraman got his shot.

***

"Where the hell is our third guy?" the director bellowed. "Isn't this supposed to be a three-way?" The mystery of Luca's additional co-star was shortly solved. Luca had worked with him on his first film and it'd been a miserable experience. Since then he'd referred to him as Southern Discomfort. Dis was a prima donna, an arrogant fucker who played by his own pointless rules. Handsome as could be, Dis was from Alabama and spoke with a sexy drawl. Like every other porn star, he was built but he'd gone overboard at the tanning salon. His skin was orange while his hair was dyed jet-black. He looked like the spawn of Elvis.

"I want to see passion," proclaimed the director, a pale, obese, hairless, creature who looked like Jabba the Hut, "intense hard-core passion. Kiss like it's the last time you'll ever see one another."

It sounded pretty clear to Luca. It was the reason he'd been cast in the video. If nothing else, Luca, or at least the character he played, was known for his balls-to-the-wall performances. It was what sold. Priapus Studios was in love with Gianni d'Angelo.

"Quiet on the set!" yelled Jabba's assistant.

BOOM! On went the lights.

Southern Discomfort assumed his usual demeanor. Head back, mouth slightly open, eyes nearly shut. Except in this case, he might actually have been enjoying New Face's oral talents. It was so hard to tell with Discomfort. To Luca's eye, Dis had the same look on his face in every scene, a smug "worship me, I'm a god" expression. He was too old school for Luca.

With New Face's smooth, white hairless ass in front of him, Luca knew exactly what to do. He pulled New Face's ass cheeks apart. There wasn't a hair in sight, assuming New Face even had hair below the neck, other than his pubes. He spit on New Face's pink rosebud. Then he dove in tongue first.

New Face jumped a bit. His teeth scraped Discomfort's shaft.

"Bite my goddamn dick and you're dead meat," cursed Dis under his breath.

"Unnnhha," garbled New Face, his mouth stuffed with dick. New Face went back to what he seemed to be quite good at. From his vantage point, Luca was certain he had the ability to disengage his jaw. The boy definitely had a future.

Luca probed the boy's hole with his tongue, then pulled back. "Let's get that pretty fuckhole nice and ready. What do you say, boy?" Luca said in a dominant snarl.

The sound guy lowered the boom close to New Face to catch his response. New Face grunted his approval.

"Good boy," answered Luca. He reached for a bottle of WET Lube, making sure to keep the label in the camera's frame of view.

"Gianni, make certain we get a couple of shots of you pouring that stuff on his hole and on the condom before you bury your bone," Jabba reminded him. WET paid a lot for exclusive product placement.

"I don't like WET," was Dis's response.

Yeah, whatever, who even asked you? thought Luca. He drew circles around New Face's hole, moving in closer and closer with each rotation. Finally his finger was right on New Face's twitching rosebud. Luca slid it in.

"Unnnhha," mumbled New Face, his head still

bouncing on Dis's slab of beef.

"You want me to fuck you, boy?" barked Luca.

"Unnnhha," came the response.

"Well, let's open you up." Luca slid another finger into New Face's ass. He grunted and groaned as Luca massaged his prostate. Luca reached over to a box of ultra-thin Japanese condoms. The entire industry swore by them. He tore open a packet with his teeth and tossed the wrapper to the side of the bed. New Face pushed his ass back in anticipation.

Luca rolled the condom down and grabbed the bottle of WET. He held it up high for dramatic effect and let it drizzle down onto his dick. He'd seen bartenders mix drinks that way and had been impressed by the theatricality of it all. "Borrow from everyone and make it your own," he'd been advised by his roommate, a veteran porn star. Luca raised the bottle of lube higher. The cameraman focused in on the WET splashing on Luca's cock. "OK, boy, open wide for Chunky," ordered Luca.

But it wasn't to be. The cameraman burst out laughing.

New Face froze.

"Chunky?" yelled Jabba. "Where the fuck did you come up with that? This isn't a candy commercial!"

Luca couldn't keep a straight face. He stood up on the bed. "Well . . . it's a big fat chunky dick," he replied as his big fat chunky dick waved in the breeze.

"This is goddamn porn, not a fucking comedy," hollered Jabba, pissed that the scene had come to a halt.

Lights were adjusted. The microphone boom was positioned over their heads. Jabba lumbered over from where the monitor was stationed. "OK, gentlemen, let's try this again," he announced.

Luca rolled his eyes. Jabba had come back from the brief break with white powder surrounding each nostril. *Wipe your fucking nose*, thought Luca. *I don't need to know how much of a coke whore you are.*

"No more antics," Jabba growled as he stared at Luca. "I want something intense, something I can actually use. Got it?"

"Gonna fuck it up again?" murmured Dis.

That was all Luca needed to hear. If Jabba wanted intense, he was going to deliver intense.

"You, New Face," called out Jabba, "you're gonna suck Southern Boy's dick. I don't care how you position yourself, just get his dick in your mouth. As for you, Mister Chunky, I want you sitting on the top of the headboard getting blown by Southern Boy. Think the three of you can handle that?" All three nodded. "And show me some goddamn passion."

"You got it, boss," answered Luca.

"Yo, Southern Boy. Suck on Gianni's dick," screamed Jabba. Clearly the coke was having its effect. Irritability. "This isn't all about you!"

"Action!" the director's assistant hollered.

Dis leaned forward to swallow Luca's meat. "Fuck you," were the words his mouth formed. He knew enough not to let the microphone pick up his voice.

Luca smiled back. "Take it to the balls, big boy," he yelled. "Make me shoot."

The cameraman gave Luca a thumbs-up. They were on the same page.

Dis swirled the head of Luca's dick around in his mouth but didn't slobber all the way down on it. Every time Luca tried to push his dick deeper, Dis pulled back. It was as if he didn't want to or didn't know how to give decent head.

Then Luca flinched. Dis's teeth were scraping against the shaft of his dick. "Watch it, Southern Boy," whispered Luca. He wasn't sure if it was deliberate or not, but then a set of molars bit down on the head of his dick. That was it. "Come on, fucker. Suck my goddamn cock!" Luca grabbed Dis's head and rammed it as far down his dick as he could.

Discomfort sputtered and tried to come up for air.

Luca fucked Dis's throat even harder. He could hear him gasping for air. "All the way down!" he yelled.

"Keep going," motioned the cameraman.

Luca didn't need any encouragement. He disliked Dis. That whole, "I'm better than y'all" attitude rubbed him the wrong way. "Take my goddamn meat, you fucker!" demanded Luca to the complete satisfaction of Jabba. Luca continued to bounce Dis's head up and down like a basketball.

Finally, he let up. Dis's face was beet red. "You fucking asshole!" he half-screamed, half-gasped.

Luca wouldn't let go of his head.

Dis aimed a punch at Luca, but he couldn't see and didn't land it.

Luca shoved Discomfort as far as he could toward the end of the bed.

Dis lunged toward Luca.

"Cat fight!" shouted the sound guy.

Luca leapt off the bed toward the protective shield of the cameraman and his precious camera.

"He almost killed me," screamed Discomfort. "And he

fucked with my hair! Look at it!"

The cameraman stifled a laugh. Dis's hair looked like a fallen soufflé.

"You think it's funny, fuckface!" shouted Discomfort to the cameraman.

"Yeah, I do, asshole. Take one more step toward me and it's lawsuit city." Out of the corner of one eye Luca could see Jabba stomping toward them.

"WHAT THE FUCK!?!" screamed the director, the blood vessels on the side of his head bulging. It looked like he was ten seconds short of a stroke. "Gianni finally gives me what I want, and you wanna bitch about your goddamn hair."

"He nearly choked me to death!" screamed Southern Discomfort hurling himself at Luca. All bulk and no grace. Luca simply stepped out of the way. Dis tripped over the sound guy's cables and fell flat on his face.

"BOTH OF YOU! GET THE FUCK OFF MY SET!" roared Jabba, "NOW!" Dis stormed off to the makeup room.

New Face sat on the bed with a bewildered look.

The cameraman motioned to Luca. "I'll settle this," he said quietly. Jabba had thundered off to another room. The cameraman followed.

"I DON'T GIVE A FUCK WHAT YOU'VE GOT ON THAT TAPE," roared Jabba from somewhere in the dark.

The cameraman stood his ground. "Yes you do," he countered. "Gianni gave you exactly what you wanted. And if you won't finish this film, I will, you goddamn coked-up queen."

The director grew silent. He had been warned about doing drugs on the set. It wasn't just grounds for being fired. It meant being barred from any further work with Priapus.

The cameraman had the upper hand. He could work with whatever lighting challenge he faced, from blazing desert sun to dim candlelight. He knew how to get the most erotic, damn-I'm-gonna-shoot-my-load-jacking-off-to-this-scene shots, even if it meant hanging upside-down from scaffolding. Because of his technical ability, the cameraman was paid more than Jabba was able to command. "Do I have to show you the footage?" he demanded.

Jabba backed down. "Where's Gianni?" he asked. "We're gonna shoot this scene without Southern Boy."

June 1993 - *Three Months Earlier*
South Beach

Luca had been a piss-poor graduate student. He'd gotten a scholarship to the London School of Economics advertising program, but it'd been a miserable experience. Shortly before graduation, a classmate had arranged an interview for Luca with an ad agency in Miami. It was a favor for having helped the friend write his thesis. The opportunity to at least visit a warm place was more than enough incentive to get Luca to purchase a plane ticket to Florida. He'd deal with the credit card bill later.

He was sold on the swaying palm trees, blue ocean surf, and warm tropical nights. *I don't care if I ever see snow again. This is where I belong.* One of the first things Luca did when putting down roots in South Beach was to find the local gay gym. He knew that it could be a resource for all things gay. Almost immediately he found a possible place to live by searching the bulletin board for "roommates wanted." After a phone call to set up a meeting, Luca ventured down a quiet street to a small Mediterranean house built in the '20s. A hunky guy with salt-and-pepper hair and a big mustache opened the door.
"Welcome. You must be Luca," the swarthy hunk said as he ushered him in. "I'm Raul. Welcome to my home." He thrust out his hand to shake Luca's. "So, new to Miami?"
"Yes, just moved here from London." Luca studied Raul's face. He knew he'd seen him before. "You look familiar. Could we have met there?" Luca asked.
Raul laughed. "No, you probably recognize me from porn," he said proudly. "I put myself through law school working for COLT Studios. Went by the name Armando"
Luca's face turned crimson. *I've been jacking off to you for years.* He didn't know which way to turn.

***

For months Luca struggled to build a successful freelance copywriting career but the advertising market was changing rapidly. The local Miami agencies that Luca had initially worked for were being bought up by large national agencies. The pool of work was becoming smaller and smaller. Luca's checking account was getting lower and lower. It was reaching the point where Luca had no more notches in his belt to tighten. He found himself struggling to cover the basics. Something had to change.

90

One evening over a beer at Bazooka, a dive of a bar on South Beach renowned for its well-endowed "dick dancers," Luca found himself bemoaning his loss of income to Raul when Raul's pager went off.

"Sorry, but I've got to return this phone call. It's my agency."

"Agency?" asked Luca.

"Yeah, I escort," was Raul's casual response.

Luca gave him a quizzical look. Then a smile crossed Luca's face. "Tell me more," he asked, trying to sound nonchalant.

"It's a pretty cool gig. My immigration practice pays the bills, but I make my fun money working a couple nights a week. Of course, it doesn't hurt that I've done porn," he said in a matter-of-fact way. "Clients want the stars from the videos they jack off to. As Raul, I'd probably make $150 an hour, but as Armando I command $300. It's a sweet deal. I clear at least $1,200 cash a week, tax-free."

Luca was stunned. It wasn't a question of *if*, it was a matter of *when*. Any extra cash would help keep his head above water. "Who do you work for?" he asked.

"A guy right here on the Beach.

"Does he need anyone else?" asked Luca.

***

Nothing had prepared Luca for the world of escorting. It wasn't just about sex, though that of course was the starting point. Most clients were lonely guys who wanted someone to talk to, and that was where Luca's talents lay. He intuitively understood the roles he was being called upon to play – stud and therapist. If the sex was over and done in 20 minutes, it was the 40 minutes of conversation that was the most important part of the hour. If the clients felt you were listening to them, they would ask for you again and again.

Luca quickly realized that he needed to approach escorting as if it were as much of a business as his freelance copywriting. *Be available. Be on time. Be professional.* Within a month, he was clearing more in one week of escorting than he did with four week's worth of ad work.

One night, Luca had a call at the Kenmore Hotel. It was popular with gay tourists because of its proximity to the gay beach and cheap prices.

He knocked on the door and heard, "Come on in. It's unlocked."

In the dim light, Luca did his best to hide his shock at the humongous naked man propped up on the bed. The term "beached whale" didn't do justice to the man's size. "Relax, I just want to watch you strip naked and jack off," the mountain of flesh said.

"OK, sure. No problem," Luca replied, relieved. He slowly got undressed making several turns to allow his client a full view of his gymnast-trained body.

"You're beautiful. I can see every muscle on you. When you're about to cum, could you stand on the side of the bed and shoot on me?"

"Sure," Luca replied. Naked, he started to stroke himself to erection. Erotic images, far from what was happening in the room, filled his mind. He knew it wouldn't take long. He made his way over to the bed in time to explode all over the man's enormous white belly. Up close, he realized why the man looked so strange. It wasn't just his pale, obese body, but the fact that he was completely hairless. Even his eyebrows were missing.

"Thank you," he said.

"My pleasure," Luca responded. The man reached over to the bedside table to grab a pile of cash. He counted out $200 in twenty dollar bills and handed them to Luca, along with a business card.

"I'm always looking for new talent. Give me a call if you're interested."

"Thank you," Luca answered, uncertain of what the comment meant. Stuffing the money into the pocket of his jeans, Luca quickly dressed and left. Outside, he read the business card. He'd just been asked to work for Priapus Studios, the biggest and best known gay porn company in the country. Luca had to stifle a laugh at what fate had just thrown his way.

May 1994 - *Eleven Months Later*
South Beach

Even for the outrageous nightlife of South Beach, Amnesia was over-the-top. Modeled after a world-renowned disco on Ibiza, it was an open air amphitheater with mountains of pillows that rose up from the dance floor. It was gay on Sunday evenings. Every guy on South Beach went there for the fierce music, cheap beer, and manic drag shows hosted by Kitty Meow. Because of its multiple levels, it was perfect for cruising. You could see the entire crowd from the upper reaches of the club. Guys wore shorts and little else.

Luca had been to Amnesia a few times. He enjoyed dancing with Raul and his friends, and flirting, but he seldom went home with anyone. He'd dated a few guys. If it became clear by date two or three that they weren't husband material, then they weren't worth dating again. He wanted commitment. It might have been a ruthless approach, but Luca longed for some sort of permanence. Anyone could find someone to fuck, but a husband was a true find.

From the balcony that looked out over the dance floor, Luca recognized Nutcase Neil. In a moment of weakness, Luca had played with the stunningly built go-go boy. He had biceps for days, sculpted pecs, and an ass that couldn't get enough dick. But his face was another matter all together. It looked like it had been beaten with a bag of nails. He'd look best with a paper bag over his head.

The nickname was well deserved. Nutcase Neil always had another grand scheme up his sleeve, but nothing ever came to fruition. Any time Luca ran into him, Nutcase was "this close" to his next big break. He operated from a vantage point of blind stupidity. If it hadn't been for his killer body and ability to gyrate on a box, he'd be living under a bridge somewhere.

Nutcase was dancing with two handsome guys. One was tall with dark blond hair and broad shoulders. Luca's curiosity was stoked. He'd always been attracted to that all-American look. Since he knew Nutcase Neil, what difference would it make if he casually joined in? Perhaps the tall, dark blond would take notice of him. Without hesitation Luca made his way through the crowd.

Jake Smyth

January 1992 - *Twenty-Eight Months Earlier*
Philadelphia

What the hell am I doing here? Jake sighed to himself as he sat in the living room of the modest townhouse in the questionable Fairmount area. *I can't believe an escort agency operates out of here.*

"I'm sorry, Robert isn't available this evening. Can I recommend Evan? He's a wrestler with impressive biceps. I know you like men with brawn." Jake listened intently. The thick-necked guy, built like a bulldog, who'd answered the door when Jake arrived, was now talking on the phone with a prospective client and trying to close the deal. He was reviewing schedules and noting appointments on a chart that was laid out on the coffee table in front of him.

Jake tried to imagine how Bulldog would sell him. *Tall, dark blond, and hung?*

"Frankie's expecting you. He should be here any moment," remarked Bulldog, looking in Jake's direction. The front door groaned open. Jake could hear grocery bags being placed on the kitchen counter. "Your six o'clock interview is here, Frankie," shouted Bulldog before the phone rang again.

Frankie walked into the living room. Jake was taken aback. He looked like someone's rumpled Italian uncle dressed in a baggy burgundy track suit. Frankie stuck out his hand to shake Jake's. "Well, you're more handsome than I expected," he gushed. Frankie's smile was as genuine as could be.

Jake blushed.

Alright . . . looks can be deceiving, thought Jake. If Frankie didn't look like a businessman, maybe that was the nature of this particular business. Maybe low-key was preferable to high profile. Suddenly it all clicked for Jake. *Why draw attention to yourself if your line of work isn't exactly above board? No one would question guys coming and going on this street. Maybe,* Jake thought, *Frankie has an ideal locale to meld into.* Jake's appreciation of Frankie suddenly increased.

"So, tell me about yourself. I see you're wearing a tie and you definitely look younger than your age. That's good," Frankie said.

"I work for an interior design firm a few blocks away. Because of the economy, my hours have been cut. I need to bring in some extra money to make ends meet," Jake confessed. He'd overheard a guy at the gym talking about the cash he was pulling in working for Prestige Escorts.

"We have all types of clients," explained Frankie. "Some are a little more challenging than others. Our goal is to offer them the best service possible with the best escorts available. I expect the men who work for me to be professional at all times."

Professional? Jake wondered. *What exactly is professional about getting paid to get laid?* "How does the agency work?" he asked.

"Well, the first hour is billed at $150 cash, with a third of that going to the agency," he stated. "Every additional hour after that is billed at $100, all of which you keep for yourself. We don't keep track of your hours with a client. Overnights start at $800 and go up to a thousand bucks or more, depending on the client and location. Two hundred of that goes to the agency. Does that work for you, Jake?" Frankie asked.

"Absolutely," he responded.

"So, tell me what you're comfortable with," prodded Frankie.

"You mean sexually?"

"That's a good place to start."

"I like to fuck," Jake said without hesitation. The blunt statement hung in the air like a smoke ring.

Frankie was struck by Jake's directness. He'd been in the business long enough to know that confidence, more than anything else, made a great escort. "How big's your dick?" Frankie asked without missing a beat.

"I've never measured," Jake answered, "but everyone who sees it seems to be impressed with its size."

"Shall we go upstairs for a moment?"

It's show time, thought Jake. He stood up and followed Frankie.

"Let's see what you got," and with that Frankie sat on the end of the bed to watch Jake undress. Jake slowly undid his tie and unbuttoned his shirt. "You have a very nice chest. I'd describe you as having a muscular, swimmer's build."

"Thanks. I go to the gym six days a week," answered Jake as he untied his shoes and stood up to unbuckle his belt. He slipped his pants off. Jake had come prepared for the interview with a metal cock ring already choking his dick and balls. He showed a bulging basket in his underwear. Turning to face Frankie directly, he paused for a moment and then casually stepped out of his Calvin Kleins.

"How big does it get?" Frankie asked.

"Well," responded Jake, "they use to call me Tripod in high school gym class."

"Nice nickname," laughed Frankie. The excitement of the moment caused Jake's dick to engorge of its own accord. "That's very impressive," stated Frankie with a smile. "We're going to make a lot of money together."

June 1992 – *Five Months Later*

Jake quickly proved to be one of Prestige's most popular escorts. Over the next several months he found himself raking in at least a thousand dollars a week. Frankie began to book him with some of the agency's elite clients, many of whom performed in the casinos of Atlantic City.

His first call to the Jersey resort was to see the Magician. Frankie's only word of advice was to be gentle. Jake was OK with that. It was in his nature to be sweet and kind. It wasn't until they were in the bedroom that Jake discovered the Magician's secret. He was shaved head-to-toe, not a hair on his body.

"Please call me Daddy's little girl," he asked in a quiet voice.

Caught off guard, Jake tried his best not to laugh.

***

The Comedian answered the door to his hotel room wearing an oversized Eagle's football jersey and track pants. "All I really need is a good back rub. Are good a giving massages?" he asked Jake.

"Well, I've got big strong hands for it," Jake sheepishly replied. He'd never given a massage before.

The Comedian stripped off his jersey and pants. Underneath he was wearing a pair of red fishnet stockings with garters and a matching g-string.

Jake acted as if he saw this kind of thing every day.

***

And then there was the Singer.

"Wear a coat and tie," Frankie said to Jake. "He's certain to take you to dinner."

When Jake arrived at the Presidential suite at Caesar's, the Singer welcomed him like an old friend. "It's so good to see you," he said with a hug. "I've made reservations for us at Nero's Grill.

"That sounds great," Jake responded.

"We can get to know each other better," the Singer smiled.

After dessert, they headed back to the suite. "I'd enjoy it if you'd undress me. Are you OK with that?" asked the Singer.

"Sure," Jake answered. "It'd be my pleasure." He proceeded to undo the Singer's tie and unbutton his shirt. Off came the shoes and socks. Jake then undid his belt buckle and unzipped his fly. At first, he thought the Singer was wearing an athletic cup. To Jake's surprise, it was made of polished metal. He'd never seen anything like it. Then it dawned on him. The Singer was wearing a chastity device that locked over his cock and balls.

Jake looked to the Singer for an explanation but none was forthcoming, all he said was, "Lie back and enjoy. I'll do all the work."

It was over and done in less than twenty minutes.

"I'll get our shower started," said the Singer. He padded off toward the bathroom. When Jake joined him, he noticed that the contraption still in place as the Singer soaped himself up.

***

"You passed your audition in Atlantic City," Frankie exclaimed.

"Huh?" Jake asked. "What are you talking about?"

"The Singer. He called and said he wants to take you to London for ten days. You really impressed him. You're my first escort to travel across the Atlantic. I'm so excited for you. You can go, can't you?" Frankie practically pleaded. "Listen, even if you don't have vacation time coming at work, he'll pay you enough that it won't matter. I quoted him $1,000 per night, and he didn't bat an eye! Now I wished I'd asked for more. After my commission, you'll make $8,000 and all your expenses will be paid. Pretty good, huh?"

Jake was speechless.

"Are you there?" Frankie asked.

"Yeah, yes, I'm here. I don't know what to say. Ten days in London?"

July 1992 - *One Month Later*
London

After checking into the posh Grosvenor House in Mayfair,

100

Jake and the Singer took in the sights, went shopping, and, just as in Atlantic City, dined in gourmet restaurants. Although Jake enjoyed each concert, after a few days he could practically perform the show, including the banter. Following the concert, it was back to the hotel for what the Singer thought was fantastic sex. Afterwards, Jake would head back to his own room to preserve the appearance that he was part of the Singer's entourage.

On Sunday evening the Singer's road manager got a call from one of the London tabloids asking who the tall young man was who seemed to be with the Singer night and day. The Singer panicked. He was a major celebrity in the UK and a family man. He feared what the tabloids would print.

Jake woke on Monday morning to find that an envelope had been slipped under his hotel room door. He read it and stopped dead in his tracks. Jake needed to talk to Frankie. He had the hotel operator place a call to Philadelphia. "I've been dumped!" Jake practically shouted into the phone.
"What are you talking about?" Frankie asked.
"The Singer. He's left me high and dry!"
"Wait, slow down. This isn't making sense."
"His road manager left me a note that said my services were no longer required. The Singer packed his bags and left the hotel. He's paid me in full, but I don't know what to do."
"I'll contact him. You stay put. Don't do anything until you hear back from me," Frankie said as he tried to calm down Jake. *Great! My first escort to travel to Europe and he gets the boot?*
"Trust me, I'm not going anywhere. Call me as soon as you know something and tell me what I'm supposed to do," Jake pleaded.

The call finally came. "He was very apologetic, but I made him feel really guilty. You can stay put for the rest of the week on his tab. He'll cover all your hotel expenses. Relax and enjoy London. I'm sure you can find some trouble to get into. You're a resourceful guy."

***

Jake climbed the steps up to the second floor to Earl's Court Gym, London's most popular gay gym. It was a no-nonsense kind of place with a slightly musty smell.
The guy behind the front desk looked to be in his early

forties, a hot daddy with a dusting of gray in his hair. He had huge arms, huge shoulders, and a crew cut. "So where in the States are you visiting from?" he asked Jake.

"Is it that obvious?"

"Your baseball cap is a dead give-away. Only a Yank would wear one," Hot Daddy replied.

"I'm from Philadelphia," Jake answered.

"And how long are you visiting London?"

Jake was beginning to feel like he was being interviewed. "I leave on Sunday and I don't know where to go or what to see," he said, honestly disappointed.

"You've at least been to Heaven, haven't you?"

"Excuse me? Heaven?"

"The dance club. Everybody goes there on Saturday nights," Hot Daddy explained.

"Oh, the disco. No, I haven't been. I've only gone to a few of the pubs in this neighborhood," Jake said, relieved that the conversation now made sense.

"Well, you've still got your chance before you leave. You really should go," Hot Daddy said with a smile as he handed Jake a locker key. "Have a good workout."

"Thanks," Jake replied, not sure if Hot Daddy had actually winked at him.

After his workout, Jake headed to the showers. He soaped up and checked out the naked bodies around him. He was amazed at how white and tattooed all these lean English boys were. Just then a pint-sized Adonis stepped up to the shower head next to his and turned on the spray. The guy was quite a bit smaller than Jake, but gorgeous. He had blond hair, brown eyes, and was deeply tanned. The only hair on his body was the thick sprout above his dick. As the water ran over his muscles, he flashed a dazzling white smile at Jake.

Jake toweled his hair dry in front of his locker.

"Excuse me."

Jake instinctively moved out of the way.

"My locker is right below yours." It was the Adonis from the showers. He was squatting to get into the locker that was indeed directly below Jake's. "You're visiting from the States, aren't you?" he asked.

"Yes," Jake said. "How did you know?"

"My friend at the front desk told me there was a tall Yank in the gym and that I should keep an eye out for you," he explained. "He knows my type," the Adonis said with a laugh.

Jake smiled at the comment. "My name's Jake," he

said offering his hand.

Standing up, the Adonis took Jake's handshake. "My name's Sean. Sorry I can't chat, but I'm late for a date with the tanning machine. I'm here this time everyday. I hope to see you around." And off he went, towel wrapped around his waist, his Walkman headphones in his ears. He turned and smiled again at Jake when he left the locker room.

When Jake returned his locker key to the front desk, Hot Daddy handed him a piece of paper. "I'm having some mates over on Saturday night before we all go to Heaven. Sean will be there. If you're free, you should stop by for a beer and go with us," Hot Daddy smiled.

***

Jake arrived late. It had taken much longer by taxi than he'd anticipated getting to Hot Daddy's flat. London was more like LA than New York. The city spread out into endless suburbs. He grabbed a beer and, with the host nowhere in sight, stationed himself by the front door. It would make a quick exit easier if he began to feel awkward in the room full of strangers. Then Jake spotted a familiar face across the crowded living room. It was Sean. He was dressed in a barely-zipped-up Air Force jumpsuit and seemed to know everyone around him, giving kisses to all.

Jake casually made his way toward him. "Can I get you a drink?" he asked as he slid up behind Sean.

"I recognize that American accent," Sean answered. He spun around to greet Jake. "How are you?" Sean flashed his brilliant smile. "Let me guess. You met our host at the gym and voila'!" he laughed.

"You got it," Jake said. How'd you know?"

"I've known him for quite a while. He's a sly one."

After an hour or so, the party began to wind down. Guys started grabbing their jackets and heading toward the door.

It's now or never, thought Jake. He took a deep breath and turned to Sean, "Are you going to Heaven tonight?"

"I am if you are," replied Sean.

"Would it be OK if I tagged along with you? I've no idea where it is, and I'm afraid I'd get lost on the Tube by myself," Jake said, knowing full well that his host had promised they'd go as a group.

"Of course you can. I'd like that. I'm parked just around the corner."

Sean drove a tiny MG that Jake had to fold himself into. Fortunately, it was a convertible and Sean put the top down. Jake felt odd seated on the left with no steering wheel in front of him. Sean gave Jake a quick sightseeing tour as they drove along the half-empty streets of London. He pointed out landmarks: Buckingham Palace, Big Ben, and the Houses of Parliament. Sean popped in a cassette tape of the Pet Shop Boys. The song was appropriately titled, at least for Jake, "Where the Streets Have No Name." Jake had no clue as to where they were driving. They made small talk along the way. Sean thought it was funny that a butch guy like Jake was an interior designer. He told Jake he'd been a personal chef for the past fourteen years. Jake had been raised around the restaurant business. They talked about the current trend of Nouvelle Cuisine with its huge plates and tiny vegetables.

Finally, Sean squeezed the car into a tiny spot and said, "We're here. But first, I have a little treat for us. Do you like to do Acid?"

"Acid, like LSD? I've never tried it," Jake said, feeling a bit apprehensive.

"Have you ever tried Ecstasy?" Sean asked.

"Sure, but I didn't bring any with me because of Customs."

"Well, I think Acid is better. We can split a hit of it. Trust me, you'll like it."

"OK, I'll trust you," Jake replied warily.

"Open your mouth and hold this under your tongue," Sean said. "It's a tiny piece of paper. Keep it there for as long as you can and let your body absorb it. Then chew and swallow it." Jake opened his mouth as if accepting communion. He then unfolded himself and climbed out of the car. Much to Jake's surprise, Sean took his hand. They headed down the street under a series of marble-covered arches where their voices echoed and bounced. This was the way to Heaven.

A doorman, with an angelic face and a body that looked like a stack of bowling balls, gave Sean a big kiss and waived the cover charge. Sean quickly found the group of guys from the party. Hot Daddy tried to make introductions, but it was impossible to hear one another over the music. Then Madonna's voice pierced through the wall of sound. A cheer went up on the dance floor. The whole group made their way into the mass of swaying bodies, shedding shirts as they went.

Jake and Sean were dancing crotch to crotch. In spite of the heat, Jake felt chills run up his spine. It was an endorphin rush from the Acid kicking in, stronger than any E he'd ever taken.

He looked into Sean's eyes and brought his lips to his. It was as if everything in the world came into a bright new perspective. *This is the man I'm meant to be with,* thought Jake.

***

As they drove back to Sean's place, he told Jake that he worked for a rock star. Jake recognized the name. He knew the guy and his group had had a few major hits but didn't think of him as being all that famous. Of course he kept that opinion to himself. *Who knew? Maybe over here, he's a big deal like the Singer.*

After what seemed like a lot of twists and turns through the exclusive neighborhood of Belgravia, they arrived at their destination. The two of them walked along a stretch of brick wall for what seemed like an eternity before reaching a gate with an intercom and security camera. Sean punched in a code and the gate clicked open. He turned to Jake, "Everyone will be asleep so we should keep quiet."

Behind the gate was a petite mansion set in a spectacular garden. Everything was green and seemed to be in flower.

Jake couldn't believe he was still in dreary London. *Am I hallucinating?* He felt like Alice in Wonderland as they crossed the perfectly groomed grounds. Beautiful weeping willows swayed in the late night air. Sean used another keypad to open the ornately carved front door and led Jake inside.

Sean's suite was down the hall from the kitchen. It was done in a simple Japanese style. All the furniture was shiny black lacquer. Jake followed Sean into the bathroom. It was covered in black marble. Floor. Walls. Ceiling. The tub looked to be carved from a single block of black marble. Sean opened the door to a glass-walled shower. It was bigger than Jake's entire bathroom at home. Sean turned on the water and sprays came out from every angle. They stripped off their clothes and stepped in. Jake felt like he was somehow outside of his body watching the whole scene, then Sean started to lather him up.

It snapped Jake right back into his body. *God, that feels so good.* The hot water washed away the smoke and sweat. Sean's hands slid up and down. He paused for a moment and started soaping up Jake's cock. Jake nearly fainted as all the blood in his body flooded his manhood. He focused enough to take the soap from Sean and start soaping his body in return. Sean was so smooth and hairless. Jake's hands slipped over Sean's well defined muscles down to his cock. They kissed while their hands caressed each other's lathered bodies.

Sean broke the kiss and said, "Let's rinse off and get horizontal."

Once in bed, Sean's legs instinctively wrapped around Jake's waist as they kissed, pulling his cock toward its target. Without breaking their kiss, Sean reached into a drawer that was full of condoms and lube. "Put this on before my ass sucks you in," he said.

Jake paused and lubed his aching cock. His sense of touch was heightened. Once on Fire Island, he'd taken a shower on Ecstasy and shampooed his hair for what seemed like an hour. This Acid was like, that but better. He'd never felt his cock this hard before. He couldn't wait to bury it deep inside Sean. Finally, the head of Jake's cock found the sweet spot.

Sean tilted his pelvis, taking Jake's cock into him in one motion. "Oh, fuck!" Sean moaned.

"Shh! You'll wake up the house," Jake whispered with a laugh.

Three hours later, minds buzzing, bodies covered in each other's sweat and cum, Jake and Sean relaxed back onto the pillows.

Then it dawned on Jake. "Shit, what time is it?" he asked, nervous that he'd miss his morning flight.

Leaning over, Sean checked his watch, "It's 5:00. Why? What time is your flight?"

"At 10:00. I have to get back to the hotel and pack," Jake replied with a bit of panic in his voice.

"Relax. We'll take a shower, and I'll drive you to your hotel. You'll have plenty of time to pack and get to the airport," Sean calmly said.

"OK. I wish I didn't have to go. I want to get to know you."

"There's this really cool invention called the telephone. There's nothing to stop us from using it."

"I'm afraid if I leave I'll never see you again," Jake said. "I don't want that to happen."

"So we won't let that happen. Trust me. Something

tells me this is just the beginning for us," Sean said with a smile.

Philadelphia

Jake called Sean the minute he arrived home. His heart skipped a beat when Sean answered.

"I knew it was you even before I picked it up," said Sean. "It's so good to hear your voice."

"It still feels a bit unreal to me," Jake said. "Was it as special as I thought it was? It wasn't just the Acid was it?"

"Trust me. It wasn't the drugs," Sean confidently replied.

"I can't figure out where we go from here," Jake stated. "I mean, an ocean separates us."

"Listen," Sean continued. "Things are kind of crazy here. They have been for a while. There're rumors about the Rock Star. The press follows me to the gym asking all kinds of questions. I turn up the volume on my Walkman and ignore them. Anyway, the Rock Star is going to make a statement to the press next week. I wanted to warn you so you wouldn't be shocked. It'll be big news. Sorry to be so vague, but it's something I can't talk about yet."

"Sure, Sean," Jake replied, feeling a bit out of the loop.

"Good, I wouldn't want you to think I was avoiding you. It's just that we met at a hectic, difficult time. Right now, it's all about the Rock Star. I'll be able to talk more after the press release."

***

As per their Friday after-work ritual, Jake met his best friend Karl – one half of the Fashionistas - for happy hour at Woody's, Philadelphia's barely upscale gay bar. Karl was a high-end hair stylist whom Jake had known since childhood. His boyfriend Curt was an even higher-end stylist on Madison Avenue in Manhattan.

"I wish Sean were here," Jake bemoaned.

"That boy really got to you, didn't he?" Karl asked.

"We've talked every day since I got back. My phone bill's gonna be through the roof. But I don't care. He's worth it. This is the first time I've ever felt this way. I think I'm falling in love."

"You're crazy. He lives in London."

"I know but there's something different about him."

"Yeah, the gorgeous mansion he lives in."

"No," Jake corrected him. "He's just the live-in chef."

"Listen, I brought *The New York Times* with me because I know you don't read it. I thought you'd want to know as soon as it hit the news," Karl said.

"What is it?" Jake asked, reaching for the folded newspaper. Scanning the front page, nothing jumped out. Then in the lower left hand corner he saw it. Jake's jaw dropped.

***

Finally, Jake got the call he'd been waiting for. "Hello, stranger." It was Sean.

"Are you alright?" Jake asked with great concern.

"No, I'm a mess. I wish you were here."

"I wish I was there, too. I read about his death in yesterday's paper."

"The press went crazy. They mobbed the house. We were trapped inside. His doctors had to have police escorts. It was horrible. He was terribly sick, suffering so much." Sean started to cry. "Now, I've been told by his lawyers that I have a week to vacate. I've lost my home, my best friend, and my job all at once. It's so overwhelming. I mean, what do I do now?" Sean asked, sounding utterly lost.

"Well, until you figure things out, you can come and stay with me. Get away from London. Take your time here to decide what you want to do," Jake offered.

"Thanks, I might do that. I've been thinking of heading back to the States," Sean said. ""How much do you know about South Beach? I've read a lot about it lately. How'd you like to meet there for a vacation? I want to spend time with you. I think about you all the time."

"I'd really like that," Jake replied, surprised and excited that he might be seeing Sean soon.

Switching gears, Sean took a deep breath. Sounding desperately sad, he said, "Listen, before we go any further, there's something you need to know." After a long pause Sean broke the silence, "I'm . . . I'm positive."

"I'm so sorry," Jake said in a barely audible whisper. His heart broke for Sean. If he could, he'd have hugged Sean as hard as possible.

"So I'll understand if you want to end this now," Sean said tearfully. "I don't want to put you through what I've gone through with the Rock Star. He lost so many battles and was in such pain. He was unrecognizable in the end." Sean broke down in tears.

His voice trembling, Jake said, "It's different for each

person. Just because he got sick doesn't mean that you will."

***

"So, I heard your boyfriend's a millionaire," exclaimed Karl on the phone.

"What?" Jake asked.

"I was watching MTV this afternoon in the salon and they did a story on the Rock Star's will."

"Are you serious? They discussed the details of his will on MTV?"

"Yes. Apparently a few close friends, your Sean included, each got a million pounds. You have a very rich boyfriend," Karl replied.

Jake was speechless.

August 1992 - *One Month Later*
South Beach

The water on both sides of the causeway was bright blue, just a shade darker than the clear blue sky. The taxi's windows were rolled down. Jake could smell the ocean. Instead of staying on South Beach's fashionable Ocean Drive with its newly renovated Art Deco hotels, Sean had found them a charming gay bed-and-breakfast within walking distance of the gay beach. He told Jake that he preferred the privacy of a garden outside their cottage door rather than a bunch of tourists. Jake agreed.

A friendly young Australian with curly blond hair and a gift for gab greeted them. "Hi, welcome to SoBe Cabana," he said. He led them through the main house and into the backyard. Sean was right. The place was charming. All of the paving had been done in a kaleidoscope of broken ceramic tile. The garden was filled with fragrant tropical plants. Jake and Sean were staying in the cottage at the rear of the garden. It was bright and cheery, decorated with white furniture. Lots of windows let in cross breezes of fresh air. It was their own little paradise.

***

One afternoon while soaking in the guesthouse hot tub, Sean said to Jake, "I have an idea I just can't get out of my head. Could you live in South Beach?"

"Are you serious?" Jake answered.

"Absolutely," Sean replied. "I have enough money for

us to live anywhere. Why not start our new life in a place that's on the upswing, filled with positive energy and sunshine? Not to mention beautiful people."

"I'd love that!" Jake replied, happily surprised by Sean's decision. "I've loved South Beach ever since I started coming here as a kid with my family. Spending time here with you has been heaven. I'm sure I could find design work. There's so much renovation going on," Jake responded, the enthusiasm building in his voice.

"Better yet. We could invest in a house and renovate it. You could design the interior. How does that sound?" Sean asked. "And maybe I'll finally get to write my book, *Entertaining the Rock Star*. I actually have an outline. It's part gossip, part cookbook. I'm going to write about the food I prepared for some of his outrageous parties. There are so many fans around the world that I know it would be a big hit," Sean cheerfully stated.

"That would be incredible. You could do the book and I could do the house. Maybe we could do one house a year. Each time we could buy a better home and keep trading up," Jake offered up, already seeing a game plan for their future.

"Well, let's do our research," Sean said. "We'll ask the Aussie to recommend a realtor."

***

The agent showed them a variety of listings, but one property in particular stood out. The house belonged to the owner of the gay bar, Bazooka. The small house was on "Millionaire's Row", the most exclusive street on South Beach. Houses on Biscayne Bay went for millions. Pop icons, movie stars, and best-selling authors lived here. Mr. Bazooka's house was on the dry side. No one had expressed any interest in the property because the place was decorated like Pee Wee Herman's playhouse. Living room walls were painted red, yellow, and turquoise with Dalmatian-spotted crown moldings. A vintage bowling ball collection was scattered throughout the entire house.

Although Sean was horrified by the décor, Jake could see beyond it. Almost every room had French doors that led to the outside, but it was the pool that sealed the deal. It was square and had an infinity edge that made it appear as if the water flowed over into the jungle-like garden surrounding it. Nothing the boys had seen compared to this. It was the perfect setting in which to start their new life together.

110

December 1992 - *Four Months Later*

By then end of the year, Sean had outfitted the kitchen with everything a professional chef could want - a six-burner Wolf gas range, a Sub-Zero refrigerator, and a full set of Le Creuset pots and pans. It was New Year's Eve and their new house smelled like the holidays. There was a roasted turkey waiting to be carved and a chocolate cheesecake cooling on a rack. They sat down at their new dining room table and began the first course.

"You're the best chef in the world. This lobster bisque is amazing!" exclaimed Jake. "I haven't had it in years. My father's restaurant only made it for the holidays."

"That's why I love you," Sean proclaimed. "We speak the same language – food. And you're in good company," he continued. "This soup is the reason I was hired by the Rock Star."

"I wondered how you got that job."

"It was surprisingly easy," Sean explained. "It happened when I was working as an assistant chef at one of the top restaurants in Boston. I'd created a recipe using an old Cordon Bleu technique of pulverizing the lobster shells with a mortar and pestle to extract their flavor. It really takes the bisque over the top."

"Does it ever!" Jake agreed. "But let's get back to the Rock Star. He loved your lobster bisque so much that he hired you?"

"Yeah. He was on tour and playing a concert at Fenway Park," said Sean. "His entourage came into the restaurant the next night and the Rock Star ordered my bisque. He raved about it and insisted that he had to meet the chef who'd created it. We took an immediately liking to each other. I was stunned when he asked if I would like to be his personal chef."

"Wow, that was some offer!"

"It was an easy decision. Stay in Boston? Or move to London and cook for rock royalty? So I packed my knives and off I went," explained Sean. "He entertained every celebrity you can name – Elton, Bowie, even Princess Anne."

"I can't even imagine."

"It was a dream come true," Sean sighed with a bit of sadness in his voice.

"Hence, your cookbook," Jake jumped in, wanting to lighten Sean's mood.

"Exactly," Sean brightened. "I can't wait to tell all the stories."

"Well, I'd like to propose a toast," Jake said. He raised

his glass of champagne. "To the success of your book!"

"That's very sweet of you, honey. And I'd like to toast to your fabulous renovation of our home," Sean added.

"Here's to us," they said as they clinked their glasses. "Happy New Year."

May 1993 - *Five Months Later*
Fire Island

The cool of winter gave way to springtime weather, but by the end of April the heat and humidity of summer had hit full force. Jake and Sean decided to escape and take a May-to-September share in a house on Fire Island with Jake's housemates from the previous year, the Brazilians and the Fashionistas.

Sunday morning of Memorial Day weekend, Sean was up early and cooked breakfast for the entire house before he and Jake went to the gym. Not feeling his best, Sean went back to bed after their workout. He told Jake that he thought he might have a sinus infection. He slept on and off throughout the day. Jake stayed in that evening with Sean.

On Monday morning Sean woke with a fever. Just to be safe, Jake put in a call to the Fashionistas' Park Avenue doctor. Since it was a holiday, they'd have to wait until Tuesday when the doctor had hours. They skipped the day's big parties and kept a low profile at home. Later that night, Jake woke up when he heard Sean rushing to the bathroom to vomit. Jake had to change the sheets. They were soaked with Sean's sweat. As the night wore on, Sean's fever got higher. Sean felt weaker and weaker. He tried, but couldn't keep water down. His lips and tongue were cracking from dehydration. Jake had to get him into the City to see the doctor.

At 6:00 am on Tuesday, Jake helped Sean get dressed. He was too weak to do it himself. Jake called his friend, the EMT, at the fire station in the Pines, who sent a golf cart from the grocery store to pick them up. Jake arranged for a car to meet them in Sayville and drive directly to the hospital in Manhattan.

New York

"Are you a relative?" the emergency room nurse asked.

"I'm his partner," Jake answered.

"OK, you're allowed to wait with him," she replied.

Sean was visibly nervous. "Here, put this on," he said to Jake. He slid off his Cartier ring.

Jake put it on the third finger of his left hand.

The team evaluating Sean feared that his sinus infection had spread. He had a high fever and trouble staying focused. They wanted to perform a spinal tap. Jake gave the OK. He knew Sean's immune system was not strong. His T-cells were below 200. There were no other options.

An older woman who was waiting nearby called Jake over. She'd been watching the scene unfold while she waited for her turn to be treated. "Are you his brother?" she asked.

"No, he's my boyfriend," Jake responded as if in a dream. *Was this all really happening?*

"He'll be alright. He's lucky to have someone like you looking out for him," she said. She reached out to hold Jake's hand.

"I'm scared. I don't know what's wrong," Jake replied. Tears rolled down his cheeks.

"He'll be fine," she reassured him. But Jake could barely hear her.

"Jake?" a voice from behind him asked. "You're with Sean, right?"

Jake turned and saw a doctor. "Yes, that's right. Is he OK?"

"We've done the spinal tap. His sinus infection crossed the blood-brain barrier. He has sepsis," the doctor explained. "We're pumping antibiotics and fluids into him, but his blood pressure is extremely low. I'm having him moved upstairs to ICU. Would you like to go with him?"

"Yes," Jake replied. He tried to soak in all that the doctor had said. The nurses wheeled Sean's gurney toward the elevators. Sean's eyes were closed. When they exited the elevator, Sean had a seizure. His body convulsed like he was being electrocuted and the sound of his breathing changed to a hard rasp.

"What's happening?" Jake begged for an answer. The sound of Sean fighting to breathe was unbearable. *Someone do something!* Jake screamed inside his head. Nurses came running with bags of ice. They were packing it around Sean. "What are you doing?" Jake pleaded.

"We have to bring his temperature down. He has a fever of 105. That's why he seized," one of the nurses said.

She brushed Jake aside to get more ice.

"Why is he breathing like that?" Jake asked. "Can't you do anything to help him?"

"Does he have a living will?" the nurse interrupted. "Are you his medical proxy?" she asked.

"Yes!" Jake practically screamed. They had signed documents at their lawyer's office when they'd bought the house.

"Please calm down, sir. Once we lower his fever, his blood pressure should stabilize, and we can put him on a respirator."

The day stretched on and became night. Jake sat next to Sean, holding his hand. Ever since the seizure, Sean had stopped responding. His eyes were closed as if he were sleeping. The only sound he made was a terrible labored rasp.

Jake kept talking to Sean. "Stay with me. Focus on my voice and come back to me," Jake heard himself saying over and over. Through shear strength of will he was not going to let Sean give up. They were just starting their life together. This was only a setback. Everything would be fine.

Somewhere around 4:00 am, Sean's breathing changed to a desperate croak. Jake rushed to the nurses' station. "You *told* me you were going to put Sean on a respirator hours ago. His breathing is worse. You've got to do something. Please!" Jake begged.

"He wasn't stable enough. I'll get the doctor. We'll try and get the respirator started on him now," the nurse explained. "You'll have to wait out in the hall." A medical team rushed into Sean's room. Jake could hear the concern in their voices. Then all sounds ceased. The room became silent. The doctor exited the room.

"How is he?" Jake asked in desperation. "Did you get him on the respirator?"

"We lost him," the doctor replied.

"What do you mean?" Jake's mind was racing, trying desperately to understand what the doctor was saying.

"We couldn't get him on the machine. He passed away."

Time froze. Logic failed. Jake stood under bright fluorescent light as his world collapsed.

The body was lying motionless in the white hospital bed. Jake put his arms around Sean's beautiful body as his heart broke. Sean was dead. He was gone. The man Jake loved so dearly wasn't in this room. What was left was recognizable, but Jake knew it wasn't Sean. He kissed the tanned forehead of his beautiful love and started to weep.

Fire Island

Jake arrived back in the Pines to an empty house. His housemates had left a bouquet of flowers on the kitchen table. The attached note read:

> Words can't describe our sorrow. We're your friends now and forever.

He went downstairs to the bedroom that he and Sean had shared. The Brazilians had stripped the room of all signs of Sean being sick. The bed linens were freshly laundered. The bathroom was sparkling and fresh. The Fashionistas had left him some audio tapes about death and dying by Maryanne Williamson. Over the weeks that followed, Jake learned to view Sean's death as the beginning of a journey, not an end. It was as if Sean had come into Jake's life, changed its direction, set everything up in its place, and then moved on. He was thankful for the time he and Sean had had together.

One afternoon, after grocery shopping at the Pines Pantry, the owner of the Sip and Twirl walked Jake home. "I hope you don't think I'm crazy. I was on the ferry the morning you took Sean to the hospital. I could tell something was terribly wrong. I watched the two of you for the entire trip. I'd never seen one man take such care of another. It was such an open display of love. It affected me deeply," he said.

"I had no idea," Jake replied, surprised and touched by the revelation.

"I got to witness the love it takes to care for someone."

Tears welled up in Jake's eyes. That happened a lot lately. He unashamedly let them fall.

"I just wanted to let you know, that it didn't go unnoticed," the owner said. He gave Jake a hug and turned to make his way home.

For Jake, Fire Island was the ideal place to mourn his loss and to heal, surrounded by friends. He spent time walking on the beach and sitting in the harbor watching the ferries come and go. He did a lot of talking to Sean, asking for guidance. He felt Sean's presence and it was comforting. By the end of the summer, Jake knew it was time to begin his new life on South Beach.

May 1994 - *One Year Later*
South Beach

Just before Memorial Day, Jake received a registered letter from Tallahassee informing him that he'd passed his Florida massage boards with flying colors. He was in a mood to celebrate. He dressed and was heading out the door.

"Wait, I'm coming with you!" Jake's roommate, the Aussie from the guesthouse, hollered out of his bedroom. It had been his idea to go to massage school but he'd dropped out after the first few weeks. For Jake, it clicked. He knew it was his future profession.

"I thought you had a hot date with that deaf guy?" Jake asked.

"I'm not seeing him anymore."

"What? He was gorgeous!"

"I know, but the communication thing was just too hard," the Aussie replied.

"But you can sign. I saw you do it. And he can read lips. So you're covered," Jake said, wondering what he was missing.

"It wasn't that. It was the phone calls."

"Oh," Jake replied, feeling stupid. "How did you guys handle that?"

"That's what I'm trying to tell you. It got too weird. He had to use a service."

"A service?" Jake asked, clueless.

"He would type into a machine on his end and a translator, usually the same black lady, would tell me what he was typing. Then I'd talk to this stranger, and she'd type my response back to him."

"Well, that seems simple enough."

"Yes, except that he liked to talk dirty on the phone and this poor black lady had to say whatever he typed," the Aussie said.

"For instance?" Jake wasn't getting it.

"Like, 'I can't wait to suck your dick then have you fuck me all night.'"

"Are you serious?"

"Do I look serious?" the Aussie responded. "It kills me to stop seeing him. He was so sweet and sexy, but I couldn't talk to a stranger about fucking his ass. I mean, I can only imagine how this poor woman felt. So I told him that I

116

couldn't do it anymore and ended it."

"I'm sorry."

"It just wasn't meant to be. That's why I'm heading to Amnesia with you," the Aussie said as he grabbed his wallet and keys. "Maybe we'll both get lucky!"

Jake and the Aussie were on the dance floor when they were joined by Nutcase Neil, a transplanted New Yorker. They both had history with him. Jake had picked him up at Bazooka where he was a "dick dancer." The Aussie had done him in the bushes of South Beach's Flamingo Park.

They were dancing under the stars with Nutcase Neil as their third wheel when out of the corner of his eye Jake noticed a handsome guy with a ripped muscular body making his way straight for them. *Who's this?* Jake thought, hoping neither the Aussie nor Nutcase would lay claim to him first. The guy had thick black hair and pale blue eyes. Jake was taken by his strong Roman nose. He was shorter than all three of them and walked right up to the dancing trio.

"Hi, Neil. Mind if I join you guys?" he asked.

"Sure!" Nutcase responded.

"I'm Luca," he said as he shook Jake's and the Aussie's hands. All four continued dancing, unable to make any conversation above the music. Finally, drenched in sweat, the boys took a beer break.

The Aussie announced that he needed to hit the men's room.

Nutcase Neil said he'd go along, too.

The Aussie shot Jake a look as he and Luca walked away. *Don't leave me alone with him!* was the expression on the Aussie's face.

Jake just smiled back. Grabbing a beer together would give him a chance to talk to Luca.

"So, how do you know Neil?" he asked.

"Well . . . we've crossed paths." Luca responded, trying to be truthful without saying too much. "He's quite the character."

"A nutcase?" asked Jake.

"Absolutely!" answered Luca with a laugh.

Thank God, Jake thought, *he passed the test.*

Otis "Big Daddy" Mercer

October 1974 - *Twenty Years Earlier*
Atlanta

This is gonna be one fun night, thought Otis as he drove his fraternity brothers out to the Mount Zion Baptist Cemetery on the edge of town. All the senior frat guys were gathering a half an hour earlier than the pledges. Each had been given a blindfold and a ping-pong paddle.

The captain of the football team instructed them as to the proper ritual. "First we blindfold 'em. Then we line 'em up against these tombstones and have 'em drop trou. You tell 'em to turn around and bend over the tombstone. Ask if they deserve to be in this fraternity. If they say yes, then you tell 'em they gotta learn to take it like a man. Whip out the paddles and let 'em have it. Then we hightail it out of here. Anybody got any questions?"

As ordered, the pledges lined up in front of a row of tombstones. Otis was pumped up. He could feel his heart pounding. He'd worked up a sweat even in the cool autumn air.

He took his blindfold out and tied it around the smallest guy in the group, a redhead. "OK, pussy. You do everything I tell you to do," Otis said in his most authoritative voice.

"Yes, sir," Redhead answered in a barely audible whisper, clearly intimidated by the 6'2" black linebacker in front of him.

"Drop your pants."

The kid fumbled with his belt and his zipper.

He's really scared of me. Otis liked this feeling of power. Other than using his size and brute force on the field, he couldn't remember having control over another person like this. "Drop everything, underwear, too," he barked.

"Yes, sir," Redhead replied. He hooked his thumbs into his briefs and slid them down to his ankles.

Lord! This kid's hung like a mule. Huge for a white boy, Otis thought when he saw the boy's pink dick flop out.

"Turn around and bend over that stone," he ordered. Otis got a strange feeling watching this boy's dick swing free.

"Yes, sir."

"Spread your legs," Otis commanded. When the kid spread his legs, Otis could see his pale dick pressed against the face of the dark tombstone. It had to be about a foot long. For some reason, Otis was glad nobody else had the same view. "Do you deserve to be in this fraternity?" he hollered.

"Yes, sir."

Otis took the paddle from his back pocket. "Let's see how tough you are. How old are you?"

"Eighteen, sir."

"Then eighteen whacks it is." Otis liked the way Redhead's white ass bounced every time he hit it. He almost lost count, he was enjoying himself so much. When he stepped back to admire his handiwork, the boy's butt was glowing red in the bright moonlight. That's when Otis noticed the dark stain on the light colored tombstone. *Did the kid piss himself?* Then it dawned on Otis exactly what had happened. He whispered into Redhead's ear, "I know what you just did and it makes me sick, you faggot. From here on out I'll have my eye on you. You better not pull any queer shit on me." Then Otis smacked the boy across the ass with his bare hand as hard as he could.

Otis's cock had been half hard all night from the excitement. Back in his bed he kept playing the scene over and over in his head. He couldn't get over the size of the kid's cock. *Fucking faggot! Shooting his goddamn jizz like that,* Otis thought as he stroked his dick. *Fucking tombstone was covered with his load.* He could feel the spunk churning in his balls. Otis began to tug on them, his left hand getting closer and closer to his ass. *Fucking faggot,* he kept repeating in his head as he slid a finger up his own hole. "Unnnhha," he grunted as he shoved another finger in. He started to jack his dick faster.

October 1993 - *Nineteen Years Later*

Otis had gone to work with a slight fever and a cough. By mid-week his cold had gotten worse. He chalked up his shortness of breath to being overweight. At 260 pounds, he was a large man. Then, late one afternoon after walking the warehouse to check on inventory, he collapsed. His office manager called 911. The EMT didn't like the way he was breathing. An ambulance took him to the emergency room.

"I'm sorry to tell you, Mr. Mercer, but we're going to have to keep you overnight and run some tests," the young intern at the hospital informed Otis.

"I can't stay in a hospital. I've got a business to run. People are counting on me," he replied in a sharp tone.

"Well, I think you have pneumonia, Mr. Mercer. And while we still have to run some blood work, I'm afraid this is very serious."

The gravity of the situation failed to hit Otis. "OK, but just overnight. I'm healthy as a horse. I've never missed a day of work in my life," he proudly attested.

The next afternoon Otis was resting comfortably, talking to his wife, when the doctor entered the room. "Mr. Mercer?"

"That would be me," Otis said.

"I'm here with your test results. I think we should discuss this in private," he said.

His wife turned to Otis.

"Anything you have to tell me," Otis replied, "you can say in front of my wife, doc."

"Alright, I've got the results of your blood work. You have pneumonia, Mr. Mercer. It's a type called Pneumocystis pneumonia or PCP. I have some bad news," the doctor continued, lowering his voice.

Otis turned ashen. "Go ahead. What is it?" he asked.

"Yes, please tell us," his wife said, grabbing Otis's hand.

"Your initial blood work shows that you've tested positive for HIV."

"What?" Otis yelled. "That's impossible. The test must be wrong."

The doctor spoke up, "We're going to run the test again. It's possible to get a false positive. But your blood work confirms PCP. It's an unusual form of pneumonia that we only see in people who have AIDS."

The room fell silent.

"How dare you say that my husband has AIDS!" she finally shouted, unable and unwilling to hear any more about it. "He's a very religious family man." Then his wife pulled her hand away as if Otis's hand was on fire.

***

Just like he'd done before he was married, Otis picked up his old habit of visiting adult bookstores when his wife was pregnant with the twins. As her stomach expanded, their sex life withered away.

A man has to find an outlet to blow off some steam, doesn't he? Otis reasoned. After his discovery that more went on in the video booths than just viewing, he was hooked. The sexual thrill of seeing another man's erection was like a drug to Otis. How could he not suck it?

One day a voice whispered through the glory hole telling Otis to turn around. He did and felt a man's hot tongue in a place he'd never dared to dream of. It wasn't long before Otis found himself backing up onto the rock hard dick that followed. After all that tongue action, the cock slid in easily. Jacking off while his prostate was getting pummeled gave Otis the best orgasm in his life. He'd never felt anything like it. He couldn't help but keep going back for more. It was then that he began to hunt for the biggest dicks he could find to fuck his ass, and find them he did. Several times a week, he'd stop on his way home from work and "blow off some steam."

***

Otis's wife didn't come to pick him up when he was discharged from the hospital. He came home to an empty house. All that she left was a note:

> *You should be ashamed of yourself. You're a filthy pervert.*

"Well, I guess that pretty much sums it up!" Otis yelled to the empty house. "Good luck with your lawyer. You think you'll screw me? Well big surprise! You have no idea where I put all my money." In a fury of frustration, Otis screamed at no one and everyone.

November 1993 - *One Month Later*
Key West

"Welcome, can I help you with your bags?" asked a voice.

Otis turned around. *Wow,* he thought, *who's this handsome little redhead?* "Sure, I'm here to check in. I have a reservation under the last name Mercer," he said.

"Great! I'm Bobby, the assistant manager. I just finished making up your room, Mr. Mercer," the little hottie replied.

"Please, call me Big Daddy. Everyone does."

"Ooh, Big Daddy. I like that," Bobby flirted shamelessly with the big hulk of a man. He liked big guys, and big guys liked Bobby. From his strawberry blond ringlets to his muscle-bound physique, Bobby was some package, and he knew how to work it. Wearing only a bright blue Speedo and flip-flops, he picked up Big Daddy's bags and carried them up the front steps of the porch.

Big Daddy watched Bobby's butt as he walked ahead.

124

I could eat up that little boy like candy, he thought. He felt a stirring in his loins. As Bobby led him to his room, Big Daddy made small talk. "So where in the South are you from?"

"I'm from the Florida Panhandle but everyone refers to it as lower Alabama."

After Big Daddy had settled into his room in one of the cottages that formed this clothing-optional resort for men, he undressed and headed for the pool. Half of the lounges were taken, by men of all shapes and sizes. Big Daddy checked each one out from behind his sunglasses and scored them as potential playmates. Most checked him out as well. Big Daddy had the body of a solid football player well past his prime, but then there was his pride and joy. He had a dick like a beer can. With all the attention he was getting, it started to expand. It was impressive, massive in its girth. He spied a hot tub over in a private corner of the resort and decided that's where he'd settle down.

Bobby appeared out of nowhere as Big Daddy was lowering himself into the steaming bubbles. "Can I get you a cool beverage, Big Daddy?"

"That would be great."

"It's my job to see to it that you enjoy yourself while you're staying here. Would a Diet Coke be OK?" Bobby offered.

"Perfect."

"Be right back."

Bobby returned in a flash with two Diet Cokes. "Mind if I join you? It's my break and I'd like to get a little sun. I hate tanlines, don't you?" he asked, unaware that it might be an odd question to pose to a black man. He slid his Speedo down his tanned thighs. Out popped a dick that was twice the size Big Daddy had expected on a little guy like Bobby. He was 5'6" if he was lucky. Bobby walked naked toward Big Daddy, his long pink dick swinging from side to side. He put the drinks down on the edge of the hot tub and slipped in next to Big Daddy. They made small talk and sipped their Diet Cokes. Big Daddy's hand boldly crawled up Bobby's thigh until it reached his dick. Bobby followed suit. Big Daddy had been rock hard from the minute Bobby had exposed his python.

"Now I know why they call you Big Daddy," Bobby said.

By now, Big Daddy was stroking Bobby's ever-growing manhood. "You should talk. That's some big equipment for a sweet little boy," Big Daddy said under his breath.

"Oh, that ain't nothin'. You should see some of the things I can do with it," Bobby replied. His green eyes sparkled. Big Daddy had never had such a beautiful boy come on to him so blatantly.

"Well, maybe after you have dinner with me tonight, you could give me a demonstration," Big Daddy smiled.

"I can meet you at your room around eight o'clock," Bobby said without hesitation. "It's when I get off work."

"Eight it is. I'll let you pick the restaurant since you're the local," Big Daddy suggested, thrilled with the direction the conversation was taking.

"I haven't lived here long enough to be considered a local, but I do know a few great restaurants in town. I'll call Louie's Backyard and make a reservation. We can eat outside on their ocean-front deck. It's what Key West is all about." Bobby was confident that Big Daddy would like his choice.

"Well, that's what I'm here for, to find out what Key West is all about. It's a date, then."

"Sure thing! I hate to leave you, but my break is over. It's back to the front desk," Bobby said as he climbed out of the hot tub. Instead of slipping on his Speedo, as Big Daddy expected, he simply picked it up with his empty can and walked away with his erection standing out from his groin like a fishing pole.

After the most relaxing day he could remember in a long time, Big Daddy took a nap and a shower. He was dressed and ready when Bobby showed up at his door with a bunch of flowers. He looked so cute dressed in chinos and a light blue polo shirt.

"I thought these would look cheery in your room. You can take those tired old silk flowers out and fill the vase with some water for these." Then he caught himself. "What am I saying? You're the guest. Let me do it for you. Won't take but two shakes of a lamb's tail." A minute later he returned. "Okie dokie. All done."

"Don't you look handsome all dressed up?" Bobby said, cheerily.

"Thank you. I was just thinking the same about you," he replied. Big Daddy was smitten with Bobby's red curls, tan, and dimpled smile.

Bobby took Big Daddy's left hand.

Shit! I should have taken off my ring. Now he's gonna ask about my wife, Big Daddy realized in a flash.

"Your watch is *so* pretty. I've never seen one like it," Bobby gushed as he took in every detail.

Relieved, Big Daddy said, "I love that watch. It's a

Rolex. I bought it to celebrate the opening of my second paper products distribution center in Atlanta."

"A real Rolex? It really looks great on your wrist. It's so big, just the right size for a Big Daddy," Bobby giggled at his own joke.

Not sure what to say, Big Daddy asked, "Where to for dinner, baby?"

"I got us a table at Louie's."

"Great. How do we get there? Do we walk?"

"No, it's a little too far. We could drive your beautiful car" Bobby proposed.

Big Daddy nodded. They walked through a side gate out to the street to where the silver Jag stood.

Bobby looked at it admiringly. "I've only seen these in TV commercials. Boy, this is sweet!"

Big Daddy loved the way Bobby's face lit up looking at his car. It had been a long time since he'd been that impressed with anything. *How could a boy this gorgeous be so unspoiled,* Big Daddy wondered?

The young hostess at Louie's showed them to their table. They could see the ocean from where they were seated.

"Isn't this just nifty?" cooed Bobby.

"It really is beautiful. Do you come here often?" Big Daddy asked, trying to make conversation.

"On my paycheck? No, I've only been here once, for a drink with a friend." It was the first time Big Daddy had seen Bobby deflate a little. "But the past is past, isn't it? Onward and upward, otherwise it's down and out," Bobby said, brightening.

"I couldn't agree with you more. The future is already looking brighter. Where's our waiter? I want to order us a bottle of champagne."

"May I help you, sir?" the young Latin waiter asked.

"I'd like a bottle of Domaine Chandon," Big Daddy commanded. It was his favorite brand and not particularly expensive.

"Yes, sir. Coming right away."

"Gosh, I feel like Cinderella at the ball. What are we celebrating, Big Daddy?" Bobby asked, his cheerfulness fully restored.

"We're celebrating a new beginning in a new place between new friends," Big Daddy said. Bobby smiled and his beautiful face lit up.

Bobby Billbray

October 1993 - *One Month Earlier*
Pensacola

Gaylord was six feet tall and extremely thin. He had yellow hair and no eyebrows. He'd been plucking them since he was a teenager and eventually they'd stopped growing back, so he penciled them in daily. As if he weren't exotic enough, he often wore a woman's scarf tied around his neck. He liked the attention it got him. The women who came to Curl Up & Dye, the hair salon where he worked, loved his choice of colors and constantly asked him for fashion and makeup tips.

He'd been part of the Florida drag pageant circuit – Pensacola, Tampa, Fort Lauderdale, Key West. He'd competed in all of them, and Crysta Shanda Lear (he loved his drag name) won more often than not. She had seven crowns to her credit and had retired to Pensacola. Or more accurately, had been forced to move back home when her credit cards were maxed out.

One afternoon when there weren't any clients in the salon, Gaylord was going through his mail. He'd received a postcard from an old friend. It read:

> *Crysta,*
>
> *Remember the old days, girl? Doing each other's makeup and competing for the crown? Well, Miss Thing's still at it. I'm running the Miss Diva Florida Pageant now! The next one's in Pensacola. You should come. Too bad you're too old to compete. Ha, Ha!*
>
> *Blanche*

Gaylord walked over to Bobby, the salon's clean-up boy, a little muscle muffin with strawberry blond curls down to his shoulders and a bit of a swish. "How'd ya like to make some extra money, sweetie?"

"Sure, you know I'm saving up to buy a used car," Bobby said. He saved his money by freezing folded-up twenty dollar bills in an ice cube tray. That way he had to think twice before defrosting one to spend.

"Well, an old friend of mine is running a drag contest, and I thought you'd be perfect." Bobby had done drag for Halloween at the salon. Gaylord had convinced him to go as Dorothy from *The Wizard of Oz*, even though he looked more like Rebecca of Sunnybrook Farm in his gingham skirt.

Whatever. He was just dumb and beguiling enough to charm anyone. "It'll be fun. I'll help you with your talent," Gaylord said.

"Talent? I don't have any talent," Bobby replied, looking confused.

"Who needs talent when you have a face like that! Besides, it's easy. You can lip-synch to 'Somewhere Over the Rainbow' in one of my gowns."

"What's lip-synching?" Bobby asked.

"Don't be ridiculous, Bobby. It's when you pretend to sing. Even Madonna does it."

"Really? Madonna lip-synchs?" Bobby asked, amazed by this information.

"Of course she does, honey. How else do you think she can roll around on the stage while she's singing? Now you want to win that money, don't you?" Gaylord practically demanded. He reached out and grabbed Bobby's chest. "These pecs are going to look fantastic in a plunging neckline. You won't even need falsies!" When Gaylord teased and combed Bobby's long red curls into a feminine style, a goddess was born.

***

"Welcome to the Miss Diva Pensacola Contest!" Gaylord's old friend announced. "I'm your hostess for the evening, Blanche Dubois. And what an evening it's going to be."

That was all Bobby heard. His attention was focused on Gaylord.

"Now, honey, you lucked out and got the last spot to perform. That's perfect. You'll leave a lasting impression on the judges. You just go out there and do the song. You'll be fine. And remember, the audience is on your side. Make them love you," Gaylord implored.

"Don't worry. I'm going win, and first thing tomorrow morning, I'm going to buy a car," Bobby said without an ounce of fear in his voice.

It was Bobby's turn on stage. "Ladies and gentlemen, I'd like to introduce a newcomer to the pageant scene, Cherry Delite." Gaylord gave Bobby a pat on the butt and then dashed into the audience to watch. The musical introduction started and a spotlight hit Cherry. Compared to all the queens who'd gone on before her, she looked positively virginal in a simple white chiffon gown. Gaylord had altered it so that the neckline dipped just low enough to show off her natural, smooth cleavage. Like that little girl in the movie, she was about to step out of her run-down black-and-white life into a new Technicolor future.

Bluebirds seemed to fly across the stage as Cherry nailed the song. By the time she was done, everyone had to touch up their mascara.

Gaylord was so proud he started sobbing. His creation had stolen the show. "I knew you could do it," he cheered. "I just knew it! Now it's time for Cherry to hit the road and win another crown," he chirped. "How'd you like to go to Key West? There's a pageant there next month and I know you can win it. The prize money would pay for the whole trip," Gaylord cajoled. *Anything to get away from this hick town,* he thought. *If only for a few days.*

"I don't know. Key West is a long drive," Bobby answered, uncertain about Gaylord's idea.

"Don't worry, honey," Gaylord said confidently. "I can spot a winner."

November 1993 - *One Month Later*
Key West

The Copa, the biggest nightclub on Duval Street, was packed. It seemed as if everyone in town was there for the Miss Diva Key West Contest. It was the biggest and most popular contest on the pageant circuit. Careers were made and destroyed on that stage. Unlike Pensacola, Key West was all about excess. Lip-synching to Judy Garland would prove to be too old school for this crowd. In the blinding glare of the spotlight, Cherry waited for applause, but only a few uncomfortable laughs were heard.

The emcee broke the awkward silence, "Let's hear it for Cherry Delite." A light smattering of applause helped her off the stage.

What went wrong? Bobby wondered. His pale freckled cheeks flushed red.

Watching from backstage, he was mesmerized by the next contestant, a drag queen from South Beach named Kitty Meow. Bobby was confused. Kitty was a black man with a shaved head and a tall thin body. He didn't try to look like a girl, but he didn't look like a boy either. He was dressed as neither - in fact, he was practically naked. His wildly made-up face looked like a cross between a clown and a space alien. Bobby had a hard time telling where Kitty's black g-string ended and his body began. Kitty was crawling and gyrating to Madonna's "Express Yourself" and the crowd was going crazy. Bobby had never seen anything like it. Even Madonna seemed tame by comparison. Kitty looked like some wild thing about to pounce on the audience at any second and devour them.

Bobby didn't wait around for the winner to be announced. He had no illusions that it might be him. The crowd had made that abundantly clear. Backstage, he got undressed and combed the hairspray out of his hair. Then he removed his makeup, washed his face, and got dressed. Bobby packed up Gaylord's gown and high heels and made his demoralized way back to the guesthouse.

When he got back to his room, he found an envelope resting against the pillow. He opened it and read the note inside.

> *Bobby,*
>
> *Seeing the other contestants tonight made me realize that I want more than what Pensacola has to offer. I'm going to South Beach. I need to be in a place that understands my kind of talent. I feel that if I return home, I'll just die.*
>
> *Gaylord*

At first Bobby didn't understand what he was reading. Then it hit him. *How could Gaylord do this to me?* Bobby had no money to pay for the room, no money for gas. "Oh sweet baby Jesus," he cried out, as if someone had punched him in the gut. He fell to his knees and prayed out loud. "Sweet baby Jesus, I know I got myself into this awful mess. I'm pleading for your help. I know you love me. Please show me a way out." Bobby climbed into bed, tears streaming down his face.

First thing in the morning, Bobby rushed into the guesthouse office.
"How can I help you?" the tall handsome man behind the counter asked in a voice deepened by cigarettes and booze.
"My name's Bobby and I'm staying in room 201. You're the owner, right? I need your help."
"Yes, I am. Room 201, you said? Your friend paid half the bill last night. Kinda late to be checking out, but I've

134

stopped questioning what other people do and try to maintain my own life. How do you need my help?" the owner asked.

"Well . . . he stranded me here. I was supposed to win last night's contest, but I didn't, so I have no money."

"Can't you phone home for some help?"

"I don't have any family," Bobby answered, trying to hide the fact that he was trembling.

"You said you were in a contest?" the owner asked, curious about where the conversation might lead.

"A drag pageant," Bobby answered.

"Are you serious? I mean you don't look anything like a drag queen."

"I did it once before in Pensacola, and I won enough money to buy a used car."

The owner knew this beautiful boy was telling him a true, if slightly bizarre, story. "I think we can work out a deal to pay off your bill," he said. "Why don't we get ourselves something cold to drink and head to the hot tub?"

***

Bobby met Big Daddy for dinner every night. They sat at the same table at Louie's Backyard and every night Big Daddy ordered a bottle of Domaine Chandon. During the day they barely saw one another. Big Daddy spent more time on the phone with his lawyer than he did in the hot tub.

"How could she leave me on my death bed?" Big Daddy demanded. "Whatever happened to 'til death do us part'?"

"First things first, buddy boy," his lawyer said. "I've had the locks changed on your house. If she needs something, she's going have to go through me. I've also restricted her access to all your bank accounts. She can't get a dime out of you. I've canceled all her credit cards. We'll see how long she lives off the kindness of strangers."

"I owe you big time," Big Daddy replied.

"I'm just doing my job," the lawyer answered as he tallied up the fees in his head. He could already envision the new Mercedes that Big Daddy's divorce would pay for.

"Speaking of houses, I'm interested in finding something down here in Florida," Big Daddy said. "I've heard that Fort Lauderdale is a very nice place." Actually, he'd heard that Fort Lauderdale was a very gay place.

Fort Lauderdale

It was a four-hour drive north from Key West. Big Daddy met

the real-estate broker at his office on Las Olas Boulevard.

"I've got about a dozen homes to show you, all in the million-dollar range," said the broker. "Why don't we start at the low end and work our way up? I think it'll give you a good perspective on the market." By the end of the day, Big Daddy had seen a number of possibilities. They had one more house to visit. It was on one of the islands that make Fort Lauderdale so famous. Big Daddy loved the neighborhood. All the homes were on the water. They parked on the driveway's pink concrete pavers and walked across a small bridge to the front door.

Now, this is how rich people are supposed to live. The McMansion was bright and cheery, all white with yellow trim. The roof was powder-blue barrel tile. The colors reminded Big Daddy of Key West. Without even seeing the interior, Big Daddy was taken by the house. The broker rang the door bell. A uniformed maid opened the front door, and Big Daddy knew he'd found his new home.

Key West

It took a week to finalize the deal. Big Daddy let his lawyer do the haggling while he hung out by the guesthouse pool. When the lawyer called and let him know that a price had been agreed upon, Big Daddy immediately found Bobby.

"Sweetie, I have some good news," he began. "I've decided to move to Fort Lauderdale. I've bought a beautiful home on the water."

"Oh, my! That's wonderful news. How exciting!" Bobby chirped, not exactly sure where Fort Lauderdale was.

"You know how much I've grown to care for you. I'd like you to drive up with me next week to see it. And I was thinking that maybe you'd like to move in with me. It's an awfully big place. I sure could use your help. You can't stay here in Key West forever, can you?" Big Daddy asked in his sweetest Southern drawl.

"Are you serious? That would be a dream come true," Bobby said with stars in his eyes. "You're my knight in shining armor, Big Daddy. I love you." He jumped up and gave Big Daddy a big hug and a kiss.

December 1993 - *One Month Later*
Fort Lauderdale

Big Daddy and Bobby were happily ensconced in their pastel

136

palace by the end of the summer. They'd bought the place furnished. It was almost mandatory. Everything, from the sculpted carpets to upholstery fabrics, had been custom-made to match each other. All the happy couple had to do was move their clothing into the walk-in closets. They didn't have much to unpack so they spent most of their time shopping for new wardrobes. Big Daddy got a kick out of spending money on himself and his boy-toy knowing that every dollar spent would not be going to his wife. Bobby was beside himself. He thought he must be in heaven.

In order to make sure that Big Daddy's breakfast was ready at 9:00 am sharp, Bobby's day started at the crack of dawn. He was at the gym by 6:00 am. He loved working out at Better Bodies in the neighboring town of Wilton Manors. The owners had spent a fortune remodeling and filling it with all the latest equipment. Bobby loved that it smelled like new carpet and fresh paint. Within weeks, he had a workout partner, a big guy whom he saw at the gym every morning. The big guy owned an insurance company with his boyfriend and looked like Popeye's arch nemesis, Bluto. He was about six feet tall and six feet wide with black hair and a heavy black beard.

Bobby idolized him and was stunned when he suggested that they train together. "You're the only one I know who works out at this hour," explained Bluto. Bobby would have worked out at midnight with Bluto if that had been the only option.

Chatting in between sets, they realized that they were both big fans of gay porn. They talked about all the latest releases that they'd rented. One day they recognized a Priapus Studios porn star, a chatty Southerner with jet-black hair, who'd spent too many hours in the tanning salon. Bobby and Bluto worked up their nerve and introduced themselves. The porn star was surprisingly eager to talk about himself and his travel plans for the near future. He outlined his "dancing" appearances across the nation, which would end with a stint filming a new video for Priapus in Laguna. But the gig that he was really looking forward to was being a celebrity bartender at an LA fundraiser. He figured he might meet someone famous who was looking for a new boyfriend. Bobby and Bluto marveled at his exciting life.

***

Big Daddy had been reading about gay resorts in Palm Springs. They sounded more upscale than Key West, and several were clothing-optional. Just thinking of the young studs he could lure into his suite with little beefcake Bobby as bait gave Big Daddy a hard-on. It was then that Bobby mentioned the LA fundraiser with porn-star bartenders.

"Will any of our favorites will be there?" Big Daddy asked.

"Yes," squealed Bobby. "Bluto and I talked to that porn star, the one with the Southern accent and hair like Elvis, at the gym today. He told us that all of the Priapus porn stars will be there," he exclaimed, barely containing his excitement. "He was so sweet to us. Just went on and on about his traveling and such. That's when he mentioned this benefit that he'll be bartending at. It's for some charity called Angel Food Cake or something like that," Bobby said, trying hard to remember the details. Truth be told, he was star-struck at the time and only half listening. He'd ask Bluto. Maybe he'd recall.

"Well, why don't you do your homework and get us some tickets. We can easily make a stop in LA on our way to Palm Springs. I don't mind spending some money on a charity if we get to meet some of our favorite porn stars. That sounds like my kind of party!" Big Daddy declared.

May 1994 - *Five Months Later*

The telephone rang. *Where's Bobby to answer that?* Big Daddy fumed. He put his Diet Coke and bourbon down, hauled his considerable bulk out of the poolside lounge chair and waddled into the house.

"Hi, Big Daddy." Tomàs cringed every time he had to say that name. It made him feel like a character in a Tennessee Williams play.

"Who is this?" Big Daddy barked into the phone, unhappy that his siesta had been interrupted.

"It's Tomàs, from New York," he explained, "Paulo's partner."

"Oh," replied Big Daddy in a more civil tone. His mind flashed back to Palm Springs and the hot sex he and Bobby had had with the two Brazilians. "Are you boys coming down to spend a naked weekend with us?"

Tomàs shuddered. "Actually I'm calling on behalf of a friend. He's a newly licensed massage therapist looking for clients. And I know how much you like getting massages."

"Especially with happy endings!" Big Daddy laughed.

Tomàs chose to ignore the comment and continued, "His name is Jake and he was our housemate last summer on

138

Fire Island. He's a real nice guy and lives in South Beach. That's not too far from you, is it?"

"How big is his dick?" Big Daddy blurted out.

"I don't think that's part of his service," Tomàs answered, uncomfortable with the question.

"Everyone has a price," Big Daddy replied.

PART 2

The Chain of Events

Spring 1994

May 1994
South Beach

Jake & Luca

Finding time to spend together was a challenge. They were both self-supporting boys working long hours, seven days a week. Finally, they agreed to take a Sunday off and meet at The Palace for happy hour. The Palace was one of the oldest cafés on Ocean Drive. Because of its location at 12th Street, directly across from the gay beach, it was *the* place to hang out. The parade of beautiful boys was constant. Everyone went to The Palace. The Extravagant Italian Designer with the annoyingly high-pitched voice had breakfast there almost every morning. The Ultra-Modern French Designer, a mass of muscles on a compact body, would have cocktails by the bar with one of his ever-changing "personal trainers." And the Up-Start Parisian Designer, with his shocking white hair and staggeringly bad teeth, often held court at the table on the south corner.

The wait to be seated could take more than an hour, but both Jake and Luca knew the owner. He snagged them one of the more private tables on the upper patio.

How do I handle this? thought Luca. He wasn't quite sure how to reveal secrets about himself, secrets that would inevitably become obvious. It was a matter of finding the right moment to lay everything out on the table.

Jake too, was concerned about the secrets that he was keeping locked away. *How do you tell someone that there's more to you than you've already told them? At what point do you turn the half-truths into the truth?*

Both were confident that the other would understand. Do you risk losing a new love because you choose to tell the truth?

Sipping his beer, Luca decided the time had come. Jake couldn't, or at least wouldn't, get up and walk away from the table amidst so many acquaintances and friends. Besides, they had placed their order for turkey burgers and sweet potato fries. It would be a good half hour before anything came out of the kitchen.

"I have something I want to talk about," started Luca. He held his breath before he launched into it.

In that moment, Jake's expression slid from a smile to a painful grimace. "What is it? Are you OK?" The concern in his voice was palpable. Jake couldn't bear the thought of falling in love with another man who was positive. He knew he couldn't face that kind of loss a second time.

From across the table, Luca could see that Jake thought the worse. There was no turning back now. He had to tell him the full story. "I'm fine, big guy. I need to tell you a few things before you hear them from someone else," he cautioned.

Jake's face went blank. "Alright. I'm seated. Hit me with it."

Luca took a long swig of his Corona. "Awhile back, I was at the Kenmore Hotel," he began. *How do I put this in the best light possible?* "And this guy complimented me on my body. He gave me his business card." Luca looked at Jake, whose expression had changed to one of curiosity. Luca dove into the deep end. "Turns out he's a director for Priapus Studios, the big porn company in LA."

Jake's jaw dropped just enough for Luca to notice. "So tell me where this all leads," he encouraged Luca.

"Well . . . ," Luca chose his words carefully. "I showed the card to my landlord, Raul. He worked for COLT Studios a few years ago under the name Armando. You must have seen his videos."

Jake loved the look of COLT men. Thick muscles covered in fur. COLT men were legends. Jake couldn't believe that Luca knew one of them.

"Long story short, Raul had heard of the director and told me that he was legit. So . . . after several weeks of debating with myself, I gave him a call."

He's a porn star, thought Jake. *I'm dating a porn star! Wait until Karl hears about this.*

Luca wasn't certain how to read the smile on Jake's face. He took another big swig of his Corona and finished it off. "I've flown out to LA a few times now and made some films for them. The first one just came out. Guys in South Beach will see it and start talking. Can you handle that?" Luca absent-mindedly picked up his beer, hoping there was another gulp left, anything to fill the awkward moment before Jake replied.

"I . . . I think that's great!" Jake was thrilled that his worst nightmare had turned into a remake of the Lana Turner story. "I can't imagine what it's like to be in one of those videos. Did you enjoy it? Did you meet anyone interesting? Are you going to do more?" Jake had a thousand questions. "Let me find our waiter and get us two more beers. I want to hear all about this." Jake gave Luca a big kiss and got up from the table.

Luca shuddered before smiling. The worst was over. He took the wet napkin from under his empty beer bottle and wiped his forehead. Without even knowing, he had been sweating bullets throughout the entire conversation. He closed his eyes and could feel the sweat covering his upper lip. He quickly grabbed some napkins from the table next to theirs so he'd look his best, or at least passable, once Jake returned.

Alright, now's the time to come clean, Jake thought, returning to the table. "Since we're being upfront about our part-time jobs, I need to tell you that I sometimes do more than massage my clients," declared Jake. "I used to work for an escort agency in Philly. It was an easy way to make a lot of cash. Anyway, a lot of my massage clients want a little extra, so I give it to them for a fee."

"Really?" Luca asked. He wasn't surprised given Jake's looks and considerable endowment. He took a deep breath and spilled the rest of the beans, "We're on the same page. I do some escorting on the side, too. My copywriting just isn't making ends meet."

"That's the same situation I was in before I moved to South Beach. I know exactly where you're coming from. Escorting is nothing more than a well-paying job," Jake replied. "It can't compare to sex with the person you're in love with."

Luca laughed. "Does this mean you're falling in love with me?"

"Damn right," answered Jake.

"Well, it's mutual," Luca replied. He leaned in to give Jake a kiss.

"So when will we be able to see each other if we're both working all the time?" Jake asked.

"Can you afford to take Sundays off?"

"Yeah," Jake answered, "that's not a problem." He wasn't sure if he really could but he'd do it for Luca.

"Then let's make Sundays our day to spend together."

"It's a deal."

They clinked their Coronas. "Here's to us!"

May 1994
Beverly Hills

Ira & Fuji
It was rare that anyone called Ira after 8:00 pm. Like everyone else in Hollywood, he was early to bed. Instead of letting the answering machine take the call, he decided to pick up the phone.

It was Fuji calling from New York. "Have I got news for you! I just came from a dinner party with the gallery owner who's exhibiting my work next month for Gay Pride. It's a twenty-five year retrospective of gay art."

"Well, I'm happy for you, but what's the big deal with Gay Pride?" Ira asked. "It's all Beau's been talking about."

"Ira, it's the 25th anniversary of the Stonewall riots and it's the Gay Games. You should know these things. They're expecting over half a million to attend. Trust me, all the A-list gays in LA will be there."

"Really?"

"Absolutely! I wish you'd been at the dinner. The group that's producing the parade is having trouble finding someone to put up the bond to secure Central Park for the afternoon rally," Fuji explained. "It's all politics. Conflict of interest and that sort of thing. So they're looking for an outsider to post a million-dollar bond. That's when I thought of you. For $100,000, you can be *the* top private sponsor of the entire Gay Pride weekend, right up there with American Express and American Airlines. Your name will be plastered everywhere."

Ira was listening intently. He let Fuji continue.

"Here's the deal. In exchange for your posting the bond, Empire Pride will corral their East Coast celebs into attending a Saturday night benefit which you, of course, would host. And if *you* work the West Coast crowd, you'll have a "Page 6" party on your hands. It doesn't get much better than that! Best of all, when it's over, you get your 100K back. Doesn't cost you a dime. It's a deal you can't refuse."

Ira was elated. This was the prize opportunity he'd been waiting for. He began working out the details in his head. *Perhaps my old friend the Movie Star will lend me his Park Avenue penthouse.* Who'd turn down an invitation if the advance PR sold it as *the* benefit of the weekend? He knew the A-list gays on both coasts would sit up and take notice. It was virtually guaranteed that they'd all attend. He'd own Saturday night. It'd be the perfect occasion to show off his latest trophy – Beau!

***

"Beau? How'd you like to help me throw a fundraiser in New York, the last weekend in June?" Ira asked.

"Gay Pride weekend? Oh, my God, are you serious?" Beau replied, practically jumping up and down.

"That's when you wanted to go, isn't it?"

Summer 1994

June 1994 - *One Month Later / Gay Pride Weekend*
New York
Friday

Big Daddy & Bobby

"This is a goddamn freak show," muttered Big Daddy under his breath. He and Bobby were standing in the middle of the lobby of the Paramount Hotel trying to figure the place out. Dozens of red roses stuck out of the marble walls. An enormous oddly-angled staircase ran up one side of the lobby with a dangerous-looking glass handrail. Groupings of bizarre furniture filled the two-story space. "What the hell were the Brazilians thinking?" complained Big Daddy, disgusted with the hotel they'd recommended.

A beautiful boy who could have been a model stepped up to them. "Welcome to the Paramount. My name is Xander. May I be of assistance?"

"Yeah, we're looking for the front desk and haven't been able to find it," grumbled Big Daddy. "We need to check in."

"Please follow me," Xander said with a gleaming white smile.

Big Daddy had to nudge Bobby to get him moving. He was still staring at all the odd furnishings. There were ornate gilded chairs next to what looked like a carved-out log. Big oversized upholstered pieces sat next to rickety looking modern metal chairs. Neither of them had ever seen anything like it. Neither knew what to say to the other.

Once they'd checked in, the bellboy, another stunner named Weston - *Does anyone have a normal name here?* Big Daddy wondered - led them to their suite. Big Daddy and Bobby walked around the space as if they'd landed on another planet.

"What kind of a hotel is this?" Bobby asked.

"I have no idea," barked Big Daddy. "It's an asylum for crazies."

Bobby stared blankly at the bed. "There's no headboard, Big Daddy. Just a giant painting." He frowned and shook his head in what seemed to be disappointment. "It isn't cheery like the guesthouse in Key West. Everything's the same color brown."

Big Daddy was doing a slow burn. Pissed about being in a prissy hotel, he reluctantly began to unpack his bags. If he was going to get any more action out of the two sexy Brazilians, he'd have to make nice with them, but this would be the first and last time that he'd ask them for a hotel recommendation. He opened his garment bag and hung up his tux. "What the fuck . . . ," he cursed to himself as he stuffed his socks and underwear into the top drawer of an incredibly small dresser. *Who the hell stays here,* he thought, *Ken and Barbie?* Then he went to put away his toiletries. From across the suite he called out, "Wait until you get a load of this. You're not gonna believe this bathroom!"

Jake & Luca

There was something exciting about being away from home. It felt like they were on an adventure. After they'd settled into their hotel room, Jake and Luca headed off to Jocks to meet the Fashionistas.

Manning the door of the bar were Gibraltar and Alcatraz, friends of Jake's from Fire Island. Rob had met them through Charles and had hired them away from The Roxy, the City's hottest nightclub, to work as bouncers at Jocks. Jake and Luca were ushered in like VIPs. They went up to the bar to order some beers.

The bartender was a handsome all-American guy. He looked like a football player. "Hi, guys. Welcome to Jocks. What can I get you?"

"Two Coronas with lime," answered Jake. The bartender looked familiar. Jake studied the back of his head, hoping he'd recognize him when he turned around. The bartender came back with two brews. When Jake reached into his wallet to pay for them, the bartender turned to him.

"Don't I know you from out on the Island?" he asked. "Weren't we neighbors last summer?"

Suddenly it clicked for Jake. This was one of the guys who owned the bar. "Yeah, I remember," said Jake. "Rob's your boyfriend, right?"

"Bingo, big guy! I'm Erik. I manage this place." A smile as bright as the sun crossed his face. Jake and Luca couldn't help but smile back. Erik had that something about him that made you want to make him your new best friend.

"I've got something for you," Erik said. He handed them each a card.

"What is it?" Luca asked.

"An invitation to a private sex party tomorrow night."

That was not the answer Luca was prepared to hear. Compared to Jake, he'd led a relatively sheltered gay life. This was the first time Luca had gone away for a weekend like this.

152

He knew there would be dance parties, but he hadn't counted on sex parties, let alone being invited to one. Maybe Jake was used to this, but it was all new to Luca.

"These will get you in," Erik continued. "We have a strict door policy. Muscle guys only. So keep it to yourselves or you'll have some very disappointed buddies to deal with."

Well, I guess we know what we're doing tomorrow night, thought Luca. This would be a first.

Out of the darkness came a voice: "Well look who's here!"

Jake froze for a second. "It's my best friend Karl. Don't mention anything about a sex party to him. He'd be hurt if he knew what he was missing."

Luca slipped the cards into his pocket.

"OK, break it up, you two," Karl joked as he came up behind Jake. His hair was cropped short and colored burgundy. He reached out his hand to Luca. "I'm Karl. You must be Luca. Damn, you're handsome! Now, I can understand why Jake's so crazy about you."

"Thanks, nice to meet you, too," Luca said, blushing.

"You guys ready to start this weekend off with a toast?" Karl asked. "Curt and I are over there. We're waiting for the Brazilians."

Jake filled Luca in on the back story. "They were my housemates on Fire Island. You'll like them. Tomàs is a painter - he does all those racy covers for trashy romance novels - and Paolo is a graphic designer. They're very sweet."

Saturday Night

Ira & Beau
The Movie Star's penthouse overlooking Central Park was sleek and modern, beyond spectacular, with shiny white granite floors and 12' ceilings. The white walls were covered with modern art. Ira pointed out works by artists whose names Beau recognized - Andy Warhol's celebrity portraits, Jasper Johns's flags, and Roy Lichtenstein's giant comics. The sweet smell of dozens and dozens of Casablanca lilies pushed the already impressive space completely over the top. The flattering candle light would make everyone look beautiful. Beau had on a Versace silk shirt printed with scenes of South Beach. Its pale blue color matched his eyes.

Ira and the Movie Star went way back. They knew each other from the '60s, when the Movie Star worked for Roger Corman. The Movie Star was a sweetheart and had a soft spot for the underdog. He didn't hesitate when Ira presented the idea of holding a benefit in his penthouse.

Beau had steadied his nerves with one of Ira's Xanax, but it did nothing to alleviate his disappointment. He was dying to attend Rob and Erik's private sex party. They had made a point of inviting him. Beau hated to decline his friends' invitation, but he had a role to play at Ira's side.

Beau was introduced to an unending stream of men whose names he'd read in magazines. He was astonished that Ira knew the Movie Mogul. He'd produced several blockbuster films and knew every major star on a first name basis. His fortune was legendary. He held onto Beau's hand after he'd shaken it. After talking to Ira, he turned to Beau and suggested he get in touch when he returned to LA.

Ira didn't miss it. "Look out for that one. He goes through boyfriends like Kleenex. If he had any idea what you were hiding in your pants, he'd steal you away."

"You have nothing to worry about," Beau responded. "You know that don't you?"

"Of course I do," answered Ira. "But I know how these men work. They see something they like and they'll do anything to get it." Still, Beau couldn't help but be intrigued by the attention that the Movie Mogul had shown him. *What kind of world does one of the richest men in Hollywood live in?*

Sunday Morning

Ira & Beau
Ira awoke to the smell of fresh coffee wafting into the bedroom. For him, the aroma of Blue Mountain java was the perfect alarm clock. Soft and subtle. That was the way mornings were supposed to be. He could hear the cook at work in the kitchen. Ira knew the director of New York's Culinary Institute and had arranged to have a chef-in-training sent over each day to prepare breakfast.

So as not to wake Beau, he showered in one of the guest bathrooms. As the hot water hit his sunburned shoulders (he was perpetually tan in spite of his dermatologist's pleas), Ira thought about last night's success. Everyone who was anyone was in town, and all had been seen rubbing elbows at his spectacular party. Ira had made a point of inviting *the* Condé Nast Editor, who walked in with *the* Gossip Columnist. That practically assured a mention on Page 6 of *the* New York tabloid and possibly in *the* Editor's glossy magazine. And there would be plenty of photos to supply to the press. He'd commissioned Warhol's Protégé to document the entire *soiree*. Instead of running from the camera, his guests practically pushed one another out of the way to get in front of the Protégé's lens. Ira smiled to himself. It had been a perfect party.

As he walked toward the kitchen to grab a cup of coffee, the smell of warm citrus drifted down the hallway. Ira paused and closed his eyes. The scent engulfed him. Someone had obviously mentioned to the chef that broiled grapefruit sprinkled with chopped mint leaves was one of Ira's favorites. The morning was off to a great start. Ira couldn't wait to surprise Beau with breakfast in bed.

Although he didn't do it often, Beau loved sleeping in late, and today his body was cradled in the softest duvet of Egyptian cotton, bleached the purest white. He'd been dreaming about last night's party and the A-list crowd that had attended. Beau couldn't believe how many famous Hollywood people were gay. Much to his astonishment, Ira knew them all on a first name basis.

"Honey, it's time to wake up," Ira said. He set down the breakfast tray and opened the blackout curtains. Sunlight flooded the room.

With his face buried in a down pillow, Beau felt the sun's warmth before he opened his eyes. Squinting, he asked Ira, "What time is it?"

"It's after 10:00. Did you have a good night's sleep?"

"The minute my head hit the pillow, I was out like a light. Was last night *all* a dream?"

"I can assure you it happened. I've been listening to my phone messages this morning. There was the first group, who called to say, 'Last night's party was fabulous! Thanks for inviting me.' Then there was the second group who want to stay in my good graces and said, 'I heard your party last night was fabulous. So sorry I couldn't be there.' Then there were a few who actually called to say, 'Why wasn't I invited to your fabulous party last night?'"

***

The view from the balcony was dizzying. Beau doubted if birds flew this high. The people down on the ground looked like a swarm of insects. "Look at that rainbow flag! It goes on for blocks. That's amazing!" Beau exclaimed.

155

"I want to know who had the time to sew the damn thing," Ira said with a laugh. He took a sip of his Mimosa. He never drank anything harder until the sun went down.

"I bet it's exciting to be down there. All that positive energy," Beau said, trying not to sound disappointed. He wished that he was on the street with all the shirtless men.

As if reading his mind, Ira said, "Trust me, you wouldn't like it. That crowd is seen better at a distance. They're all sweaty in this heat. It's much better from this vantage point. Have another Mimosa. I have a massage therapist coming by to work on both us before tonight's big surprise," Ira said as he adjusted the brim on his hat to block the sun from his eyes.

"Tonight? I forgot to talk to you about tonight," Beau said sheepishly.

Rob & Erik

By the light of day, it looked like the aftermath of some demented children's party. Hundreds of multi-colored condoms, and their torn-open wrappers, were scattered everywhere. Half-empty beer cans and bottles of water covered every possible surface.

"Where's the mop and bucket?" Alcatraz asked Gibraltar. They rummaged around in the kitchen closet for anything and everything that could be used to clean lube and cum off of floors, walls, and furniture. It would be a long day.

"Wow!" exclaimed a buck naked Erik when he staggered into the living room. "This place looks like hell. What happened in here?"

Alcatraz handed Erik a cup of black coffee. He knew Erik couldn't function without a serious jolt of java in the morning.

Rob looked at Erik and laughed, "Hey, slumber bunny." He came over and gave his big boy a hug. "You missed something," he announced when Erik turned around. With a flourish, Rob plucked a condom wrapper off of Erik's hairy blond ass.

"I'll take condom duty," Gibraltar said. He snapped on the housekeeper's rubber gloves and grabbed an empty trash bag. *"He loves me, he loves me not,"* he sang to himself as he started picking condoms off the kitchen counter.

"I can't believe they were fucking in the kitchen," Rob said. "Men are such pigs!"

"And your point is?" asked Gibraltar. "I had about a dozen prove that to me last night. One right here against the sink."

Rob gave him a stern look as if to say, *Don't tell me you contributed to this mess.* "I'm opening the windows to let some fresh air in here. This place reeks of poppers and jizz," he declared as he marched toward the sliding glass doors.

I kinda like how it smells, thought Gibraltar, hoping that Rob would keep the windows closed just a bit longer.

"We're going to have to burn the bed," Erik called out from the bedroom, "but the good news is, we'll never need another towel for as long as we live." Nearly everyone had brought hotel towels with them. He began to separate the Paramount and Royalton towels from the Marriott ones. Then he glanced at the bed. *Where the hell are the sheets?* There was nothing on the bed except a mattress pad. *I slept on that?* He found the bottom sheet scrunched up under the headboard. The top sheet was tossed over a chair in the corner. By the looks of it, the mattress pad had taken some serious punishment. Cum and lube stains covered it. Erik smiled to himself. He'd fallen asleep on a bed reeking of semen. If Rob hadn't been cleaning up the next room, Erik would have crawled back onto the rank bed and taken a nap.

***

If the bed could talk, it wouldn't shut up for days. Dozens of men had been fucked on it last night. At the start of the party, everyone was walking around with towels on. A few brave men had dropped theirs and were getting blow jobs against the bedroom wall, but no one was getting fucked. Erik decided to change that and kick the party up a notch. He stood in the doorway, looking into the candle-lit bedroom. He couldn't see anything but large shapes. All he could hear were slurping noises and groans. As his eyes adjusted to the dark, he surveyed the room again. Off to one side was a handsome guy with a big dick getting serviced by a short Asian fireplug. Erik watched as Fireplug practically disengaged his jaw to swallow Handsome's cock. In the flickering light, Erik could see spit dripping off Handsome's fat tool. It was what Erik liked best. A long dick always made him feel like his guts were being massaged from within, and that felt damn good, but it was girth that pushed Erik over the edge. The fatter the dick, the more it pressed against his prostate. With each thrust of a fat dick into his hairy blond ass, Erik's eyes would roll back as waves of electric sparks fired off in his head. That alone could get Erik high as a kite. Add some quality weed, or Ecstasy, or Special K - or better yet, all three - and Erik would be so zoned that he'd let his hole be hammered for hours. Erik's favorite was Special K. He loved to do a few bumps. It sent him on an out-of-body experience like no other drug.

Fireplug paused to take a breath.

Erik saw his chance and seized it. Flaring out his lats so that he looked as huge as possible, he walked over to Handsome. "I want you to fuck me," he whispered in Handsome's ear. Erik grabbed an XL condom from the bowl on the dresser and pushed it into Handsome's hand. In his other hand was a packet of lube. He tore it open and poured some onto the head of Handsome's beer-can dick and stroked it until it was hard as steel. Then he squeezed the rest of the packet into his left hand and lubed up his ass. Erik pushed his way through the crowd to the bed.

Handsome followed.

A few guys turned to watch.

Erik sat on the edge of the bed and slowly reclined until his ass was in front of Handsome's crotch, then he grabbed his ankles and pulled them back. "Come on and pound my ass," he said, loud enough for everyone to hear.

More heads turned to watch.

Handsome played with Erik's ass then rolled the sheer condom down his throbbing member.

Someone handed Erik a bottle of poppers. He inhaled the vapors and everything melted. Erik was zooming.

Handsome banged the head of his dick against Erik's lubed hole. Slowly he worked his meat into Erik.

Fireworks shot off in Erik's head when Handsome's cock slid up to meet his prostate. "Fuck, yeah!" he bellowed.

Handsome rammed it deeper.

"Pile-drive my ass, you fucker," demanded Erik.

The room fell silent. Everyone's eyes were on the huge blond and Handsome.

Erik began to rock back and forth on Handsome's thick pole.

Another guy got onto the bed on all fours, doggie style. A tall red-haired guy began to fuck the daylights out of Doggie. In short order the entire bed was covered with men getting plowed.

Erik was rock hard from all the fucking going on around him. When the hit of Ecstasy he'd taken began to wash over him, Erik grabbed Handsome's thighs. With every thrust, Erik pulled Handsome's entire body toward him with such force that the headboard began to slam against the wall. *Bam, Bam, Bam!* It sounded as if a wrecking crew was demolishing the bedroom wall.

158

Big Daddy & Bobby

The Brazilians were waiting at Big Cup in the heart of Chelsea for Big Daddy and Bobby, whom they had come to refer to as the Beverly Hillbillies. "Good morning!" they sang out when they saw Big Daddy come through the front door and push his way through the crowd. He cut a wide path.

Scampering behind him was Bobby in a shimmering blaze. He looked like a peacock on steroids. "Howdy!" exclaimed the perennially perky redhead.

Tomàs and Paolo froze when they saw what he was wearing.

Oblivious to their shocked expressions, Bobby asked, "Don't you *love* these colors?"

Neither knew what to say. There wasn't a color that was missing from his iridescent spandex tank top and shorts.

"I've always loved rainbows since I was a little boy. They make me think of Noah and the Ark," Bobby added.

"Oh?" Tomàs said, waiting for Bobby to continue down this strange path.

"Well, after the flood was over, God put a rainbow in the sky. It was a sign of his unconditional love. We learned that in Bible class. Isn't that what the gay rainbow stands for? Unconditional love?"

Stunned silence.

"I think Bobby looks fantastic. I'm so proud of my baby," boasted Big Daddy, never one to hold back praise when it came to Bobby's tight muscled body. "He's been working so hard at the gym to look perfect for this weekend. And I think that outfit really shows off his assets."

"Well, you certainly can't hide *that* asset," Paolo said, pointing to Bobby's dick. It wrapped over to his right hip. *I can tell your religion from twenty paces.*

"He tried to tuck it down under his balls, but I thought it stuck out too much. This way looks more natural," Big Daddy proudly stated.

"Yeah, natural," was all Tomàs could say.

"We need to place our orders so we can get down to the Village for the start of the parade," Paolo said.

Big Daddy surveyed the crowd. The clientele was pure Chelsea - buffed boys shorn of every hair from the neck down. The uniform was either jeans or cargo shorts, every pocket filled with an absolute necessity - Tic Tac container of Ecstasy, a bumper of Special K, and last but not least, condoms (just in case).

"I've gotta tinkle," announced Bobby and he twirled out of his seat. The entire coffee shop watched his rainbow-butt bounce toward the little boys' room. Once he was out of sight, a quiet chatter began. "He's one of the Flying Wallendas," was the best of the comments that Tomàs overheard. The waiter brought café con leches for the Brazilians and mocha raspberry coffees with scoops of vanilla ice cream for the Beverly Hillbillies.

"Don't you just love flavored coffees?" asked Big Daddy.

Paolo kept his nose in his coffee cup for fear of laughing. *I guess it's never too early in the day for dessert*, he thought.

Tomàs kicked him in the shins.

Paolo took the hint and changed the subject. "We're meeting our friends Karl and Curt - the Fashionistas - on Christopher Street. They're from our house on Fire Island. I think they'll have our South Beach buddies with them, Jake and Luca."

"You mean the massage guy with the big dick?" asked Big Daddy. "We know him very well. We haven't met his boyfriend, but we've seen enough of his videos to know that we'd like to."

OK, I'm uncomfortable, thought Paolo. *Let's find another topic.* Bobby returned to the table just in time to hear Paolo say, "This year, the parade begins down in the Village at the Stonewall Inn with an army of drag queens. If it wasn't for a bunch of pissed-off drag queens twenty-five years ago, we wouldn't be celebrating today."

"Drag queens? That's how I got to Key West and met Big Daddy. I just love drag queens!" Bobby practically shouted.

"And I bet they love you too," responded Tomàs.

***

The four of them arrived just in time to grab a spot on Christopher Street. Big Daddy and Bobby couldn't believe the size of the crowd.

All these people are here because they're gay and they're proud of it, Bobby marveled. Hundreds of participants in the parade marched by. Gay firemen. Gay police officers. Proud parents with their gay sons and daughters. Then the din of the parade suddenly stopped. Bobby strained to see over the crowd. A huge group was marching by. Their total silence spread to those on the sidewalk behind the barricades. Each marcher held aloft a placard with a person's

160

photograph. A name, a birth date, and a date of death were written beneath each photo. These were people who had died from AIDS. Their friends and partners were marching in their memory. It was, tragically, the largest group marching in the parade. The effect was like a sledge hammer to Bobby's heart. Tears ran down his cheeks. *Their suffering is over and they're with sweet baby Jesus, now.* He turned and put his arms around Big Daddy and buried his head in his chest.

Jake & Luca

They met the Fashionistas at their apartment on Beekman Place. It was very luxe. Karl and Curt were quite proud of their building's heritage. Greta Garbo had lived there for 40 years after her film career ended. Jake had warned Luca to expect a gorgeous apartment of the sort that only two flamboyant gay men could create and live in. Luca wasn't quite prepared for the extravaganza that flooded his vision as the door opened.

"Good morning, good morning! And how are the love birds today?" teased Karl. Always outgoing, he gave Luca a big hug and kiss. Since Friday night, he'd dyed his hair black and cut short bangs *a la* Julius Caesar.

Totally blocking Curt from reaching the door, Karl hadn't realized his faux pas. "Move," commanded the tiny elf behind him. He seemed smaller than when Luca had first met him at Jocks. "Yes, I'm the forgotten husband," Curt said, exhibiting his singularly bitchy sense of humor. His haircut matched Karl's but was bleached platinum blond. He gave Luca a hug and said, "God! You're even more gorgeous than I remember from Friday night. Then again, I had so many cocktails that I could barely remember what my own husband looked like!"

Karl and Jake caught up with each other while Curt gave Luca a quick tour of the small apartment. First, there was the postage stamp-sized black and white marble foyer with leopard wall paper and a Baroque cut-crystal chandelier that looked like it had belonged to some Bavarian prince. The tiny dining room was the next stop. About the size of a walk-in closet, the room held a round Empire table accented in gilt. It looked like Napoleon would have breakfast on it. Two matching chairs upholstered in zebra print were squeezed into the cramped space. The living room had a fireplace with a marble mantle stolen from the same Bavarian prince. Two enormous windows flooded the room with light that bounced off the East River. The canary yellow walls were done in alternating stripes of matte and semi-gloss paint. Vibrant yellow taffeta curtains puddled on the parquet floor. The room had a golden glow.

"It's based on one of the queen's morning rooms in Drottningholm Palace in Stockholm," explained Curt.

Of course it is, thought Luca. While it wasn't to his taste, the overall effect was a knockout. "Your place is amazing," Luca said. "Jake tried to describe it but didn't do it justice."

"Thanks, we like it. I think it expresses who we are," Curt responded.

Oh, does it ever! Luca thought.

"Are you guys hungry?" Karl asked. "There's a cute place just around the corner. Garbo used to eat there every day."

***

The tiny eatery was packed with gay men being waited on by generously proportioned black ladies in pink uniforms. They served enormous portions of steaming pork chops and grits. After a short wait, the four of them were seated at a small table by the front window.

"Hot coffee, please," Luca asked the waitress when she handed them their menus.

"Uh-huh. I hear ya, sugar," she replied.

"So, Jake tells me you guys went to a sex party last night," Karl blurted out after they'd placed their breakfast order.

"Karl!" Jake nearly shouted.

"Well, that's what you said, wasn't it?" Karl stated with a devilish gleam in his eye.

"Well, if you must know, it was amazing, happening in every room," Jake explained. "At least a hundred guys all built like go-go boys and strippers."

"It was hot watching Jake fuck another guy because when the party was over, I knew he was coming home with me," Luca said.

"I don't know how you can do that. I mean, you've just started dating. Karl and I are completely monogamous. We couldn't handle knowing that each of us was having sex outside of our relationship," Curt replied.

"It's not like we're cheating behind each other's backs," Jake said. Karl gave Jake a hard look. Jake knew that Karl was not exactly monogamous.

"I believe that men can be emotionally monogamous

162

but not physically. We're hard-wired to spread our seed far and wide. That's simply a given," spouted Luca, much to the Fashionistas' surprise. "Besides, I think the more you try to deny someone something, the more they want it. It's the forbidden fruit," Luca continued.

Curt squirmed. "What happens if they like someone else better?" he asked.

"Then maybe that's who they should be with," Luca answered. "If someone else can steal your boyfriend away with a better fuck, then maybe he's not the right partner for you."

"Do you really think you can hold onto someone by saying 'No, you can't do that'?" Jake asked. "I think that leads most guys to wonder if maybe the grass isn't greener elsewhere."

"Jake has a point," Karl added.

"You're opening up a can of worms," Curt scowled. There was no smile on his face.

"Speaking of a can of worms, here's breakfast. Everybody dig in," Karl said, relieved to stop talking about monogamy or the lack thereof.

*

Jake and Luca decided not to join the Fashionistas on their trip downtown to meet up with the Brazilians and the Beverly Hillbillies. They wanted to spend some solo time together. This trip to New York was turning out to be a sort of honeymoon for the two of them. Besides, the Village would be a madhouse. Jake and Luca liked the idea of heading over to Central Park to attend the big rally on the Great Lawn.

On the walk to Central Park, Luca convinced Jake to pop into an art gallery that had a show entitled *Gay Art: A Twenty-Five Year Retrospective*. The first piece to catch their eyes was a large black-and-white photograph of an innocent-looking prepubescent boy. The photo was surrounded by text written by David Wojnarowicz, the artist. It told the story of how one day the boy would discover emotions that would make religious men want him dead and how the government would write laws to make his life unlivable. There would be those who would brutalize him. This boy would wish for his own death because living his life was so painful. All this because of his love for another boy. With eyes filled with tears, they read that the artist had died of AIDS two years earlier. He was their age.

Memories came flooding back to Jake. Soon after coming out, he'd gone to see the AIDS Memorial Quilt in Philadelphia. It had affected him so deeply that he volunteered to work on the quilt display when it covered the entire National Mall in Washington, DC, the following year. Up to that point in his life, he'd not known anyone who'd died from AIDS. The memory that was forever burned into his heart was of meeting the mother of a young man who had died. His quilt was part of the section that Jake was overseeing. When it came time to fold up the quilt for the evening, the young man's mother asked if she could help. She lovingly folded the large section containing her son's quilt and helped put it in its storage box. Before the box was placed back in the truck for overnight storage, she asked Jake if she could say goodnight. Jake held the heavy box. The mother wrapped her arms around it and wept, saying goodnight to what was left of her son.

***

The Park was already teaming with people when Jake and Luca arrived. They had never seen anything like it. There were gay men and women as far as the eye could see. Jake and Luca had both had grown up feeling as if they were absolutely alone in the world. Now this. Half-a-million strong were willing to stand out in public to proclaim that they were gay and not ashamed of it. The closet of the past had been kicked open by the Stonewall riots. Now the door was off its hinges. Nothing would ever be the same.

At 3:00 pm, everything stopped. Voices fell to a whisper. The Great Lawn drew quiet. For one entire minute, there was complete silence. Heads bowed. Tears flowed. In the quiet of that moment, everyone reflected on the devastation that had befallen them, the horrific loss of so many lives.

Jake's thoughts were of Sean. *I hope you can see this. Thank you for being in my life and changing me for the better.*

Luca's mind was flooded with the memories of dozens of men he'd known who were no longer alive. He thought of how much he hated crossing friends' names out of his address book. It was a record of loss.

The silence was broken by the emcee's simple, "Thank you." The crowd's unified voice, from Central Park all the way down Fifth Avenue, yelled in a spontaneous moment of joy and rage. Life carried on.

Although Jake felt the rage inside him begging to be let out, to join the voices around him, he stayed silent. He was afraid that once he started yelling, he wouldn't be able to stop.

Sunday Afternoon

Big Daddy & Bobby

"It feels so good to get out of these sweaty clothes," announced Big Daddy, "and away from that crowd! I thought this was Gay Pride. What are they so proud of? A bunch of weirdoes prancing down the street half naked, I've never been more disgusted." The irony of Bobby's outfit was lost on him.

"I thought the drag queens were pretty, but what about those scary guys in leather? Some of them had whips!" Bobby said incredulously.

"I'll just never understand some people's kinky habits. Well, tonight's crowd will be far better. We'll be with VIPs. The Brazilians got us great tickets for tonight's concert."

"I can't believe they cost so much money," Bobby exclaimed.

"Hardly anything, baby," smiled Big Daddy as he settled back onto the bed. "It's a cheap price to pay to play in the big leagues. Get used to it, kiddo."

Curling up under Big Daddy's arm, Bobby asked, "Will we see any movie stars tonight?"

Sunday Night

Ira & Beau

Ira had used his network of friends wisely. When he'd gotten wind of the Barbra Streisand concert, he went into planning mode. Of course, he and Beau *had* to go. Every A-list gay, would be there. Ira wanted to bump it up a notch. Beau would turn plenty of heads, but Ira also wanted the perfect woman on his arm. Then it came to him. *Broadway's Betty Boop! She's perfect. Gorgeous. Always pulled together. So much fun.* Ira knew Betty Boop would offer to use her connections to get them the best seats in the house. *Talk about killing two birds with one stone*, Ira thought.

***

Beau looked out at the people who were peering into their limo. Their faces were practically stuck to the window. For a moment, he felt like an animal in a zoo. Then he looked over at the beautiful woman who was sitting next to Ira. Betty Boop had always been one of his favorites. She looked like a girl from another time with her pale skin, bee-stung lips, and golden ringlets. Beau half expected her to say, "Boop-oop-a-doop," when they first met. He should have been thrilled that he was spending the night with her, but what he really wanted was to be with the hottest boys in the world, dancing on an aircraft carrier just blocks away. Tonight was the big circuit party on the *USS Intrepid.*

Big Daddy & Bobby

Dressed in matching tuxedos with rainbow-striped bow ties and cummerbunds, the Beverly Hillbillies stepped out of their taxi onto the red carpet. They both felt like a million bucks. They had *arrived.* Well, they had indeed arrived, but it was at the back of the VIP ticket line. They were so far back in the crowd that they couldn't even see the entrance.

Big Daddy said to Bobby, "You stay here. I'm going to the front of the line to get us in." He strode up the red carpet, bumping into men who never waited in line . . . but this was Streisand. Once he'd barreled his way to the doorman, he tucked a hundred dollar bill under his two tickets. "Excuse me. Am I in the right place? Isn't there a special entrance for us?"

"Yes, sir, this is it," answered the bright-eyed young man.

"Should I get my partner?" Big Daddy asked.

"I'm afraid you'll have to wait in line with all of these folks, sir," the young man said as he continued to tear tickets.

Big Daddy waved his tickets and hundred dollar bill in the young man's face, again. "Shouldn't this be enough to get us in?" he demanded.

"Yes, sir, those are the correct tickets. You'll have to wait like everyone else," the young man replied, still maintaining a smile.

"But we're VIPs," Big Daddy said, a little too loudly.

"Sir, everyone in this line is a VIP. I think you've got your money mixed up with your tickets. You don't want to lose a hundred dollar bill."

Big Daddy turned on his heels and strode back to Bobby. "I'll never understand these people," he snarled. "They're the rudest bunch I've ever come across."

***

By the time the Beverly Hillbillies reached their seats, the Brazilians and the Fashionistas were already there chattering away. Big Daddy and Bobby sat down with their souvenir programs in hand.

Karl pointed toward a group of people in front of them. "Look, its Betty Boop with the Velvet Mafia."

"Velvet Mafia?" Big Daddy queried.

"They're the gay power brokers who run Hollywood," Karl was incredulous that he had no clue.

"There's the Movie Mogul and the Media Mogul. I don't know the guy in the Panama hat or the hottie next to him, but they must be important if they're sitting with *that* crowd," Tomàs said.

"Hey, we know the guy in the hat from Beverly Hills," Big Daddy bragged. "Remember the fundraiser in LA that we told you about? That's the guy who threw it! And I think that's his boyfriend. He was being photographed naked in the pool. Now who's Betty Boop?" Big Daddy asked.

The Brazilians stared at one another.

Karl knew what his boyfriend was thinking and shot him a look.

Curt rolled his eyes.

"Betty Boop has done movies and Broadway," explained Karl. "She's a big star."

"There's your movie star, baby!" Big Daddy said to Bobby. He pointed toward her, his hand nearly knocking into the head of the gentleman seated in front of him.

"Oh, my God! I love her!" Bobby squealed. "She was in my two favorite movies! We should say hello." Bobby had a grin as big as a kid's on Christmas morning.

"Let's go down there now," Big Daddy suggested. They pushed their way back down the narrow row of seats toward the aisle with Big Daddy's ass hitting everyone in the face as he squeezed by.

Bobby practically sprinted to the front of the theater.

"How nice to see you again," Big Daddy said, extending his hand to Ira.

Ira shook it and said, "Yes, it's very nice."

Big Daddy could tell he wasn't being recognized. "We were at your lovely home in Beverly Hills for your benefit. We're from Fort Lauderdale. I'm Otis Mercer, but everyone calls me Big Daddy, and this is my Bobby."

"It's so nice to see you both," Bobby said. He leaned over the front row of people to shake Ira and Beau's hands. Then he turned his focus on Betty Boop. "It's a real pleasure to meet you. I've been a fan ever since *Blazing Saddles* and *Young Frankenstein.* You're so funny," he said.

Who are these bumpkins? Ira wondered.

"Well, thank you," replied Betty Boop, utterly unperturbed by Bobby's gaffe.

"Please sign my program," continued Bobby. "I love you."

Big Daddy stood there beaming. He could see the joy on his boy's face.

With a swirl of his arm, Bobby shoved his program in Betty Boop's face.

Ira suppressed a scowl when the program bounced off of his arm. He graciously handed it over to Betty Boop.

She pulled her lipstick out of her purse. She'd been through this before. *Give them what they want and they'll go away.* She nudged Ira ever so slightly, and he turned to watch her scribble her John Hancock in Lancôme Coral Blush on the cover of the program. *"Always, Madeline Kahn."* Luckily, the house lights flickered.

"Well, we better get back to our seats. We're just a few rows behind you. Let's meet for a drink at intermission," Big Daddy suggested.

Ira, Beau, and Betty Boop just stared.

"OK, then. See you later," said Big Daddy. He and Bobby made their way back to their seats.

Unable to control himself, Ira let out a laugh that was far too loud. "You're so sweet, Madeline," he chortled.

"I didn't want to disappoint one of her fans," she said as she put away her lipstick.

Jake & Luca

They took a taxi to the West Side where the *USS Intrepid* was docked. When they opened the cab's door, they could hear the thump-thump-thump of dance music. Off to one side of the entrance to the party was a group of twenty or so Navy veterans who held signs protesting the "desecration" of a great battleship.

NO FAGS ON OUR SHIP, read one sign.

"You're all going to hell," yelled one of the vets to the mass of men emptying out of cabs and limos.

From one cab stepped a couple dressed in formal Navy whites.

"Take off those uniforms," roared another vet.

The partygoers paid them no attention.

This was a first. Never before had the *Intrepid* hosted a gay event, let alone one so massive. Thousands of tickets had sold out the day they went on sale. Jake and Luca could sense the excitement in the crowd. They entered on a lower level into a vast open area and marveled at the sheer size of the space in the belly of the ship. They then climbed metal

168

stairs up several stories through an interior that was painted battleship gray. It radiated masculine energy. Finally, Jake and Luca emerged onto the main deck where the aircraft landed and took off. They were high above the streets of the City. If the view was unbelievable, the scene before them was surreal. Thousands of men, most of them buff and shirtless, filled the deck of the ship where sailors once hurried about their duties. Hugely muscled bodybuilders, many still wearing the medals they'd been awarded earlier in the day in Yankee Stadium at the closing ceremonies of the Gay Games, were dancing on raised platforms. How incongruous it seemed to have a US Naval ship filled with openly gay men at a time when sailors were dishonorably discharged for being gay. Change was in the air.

Jake and Luca bought drink tickets and headed over to one of the bars to grab two beers.

To Jake's surprise, the first bartender they came to was one of his buddies from Fire Island, the volunteer EMT. "Hey, Jake! How's it hanging, big boy?" the EMT asked.

"Great! Meet my boyfriend, Luca," Jake said proudly. The boys shook hands across the bar.

"You've got a real keeper there," the EMT said to Luca.

"Thanks, I think so too," he answered.

"Can I get you something to drink?"

"Sure. We'll have two Coronas with lime," Luca said, handing him their drink tickets. Jake put a five-dollar bill into the tip jar.

"Thanks, guys. It was great seeing you again. Hope to see you at the Morning Party in August," the EMT said as they walked away.

They strolled toward the starboard side of the ship to a slightly more private spot. Luca took out a Tic Tac container and retrieved two small pills. He gave one to Jake, they clinked their beer bottles, and swallowed their Ecstasy. Jake took Luca's hand and led him into the heart of the dance floor. It felt like they knew almost everyone they saw. The men surrounding them were bursting with energy. You could feel it in the air, almost lifting you off the ground. It felt like gay men finally had a reason to celebrate. They had borne witness to a decade of death and had survived. Jake and Luca were bouncing up and down with the crowd when a new song's lyrics rang out: *Things can only get better!*

A cheer went up from the crowd.

The energy around them intensified and kicked their Ecstasy into high gear. They were rolling. Luca grabbed Jake and kissed him passionately.

"I love you, big boy," Luca said, his eyes wide and sparkling.

"I love you, too."

They kissed again. Things could only get better.

July 1994 - *One Week Later*
Coconut Grove

Jake

After returning from his trip to New York, Jake couldn't wait to tell his friend Hunt, that he'd fallen in love. Huntington "Hunt" Carter had been one of Jake's first massage clients. They'd met while Jake was still in massage school and took to each other from the start. Hunt was a born story-teller. At times it seemed as though the seventy-year-old was more interested in having someone listen to him than actually getting a massage. Jake had never met a gay man with such a rich history. In Jake, Hunt found the perfect audience.

Hunt's estate was buried deep in Coconut Grove, hidden behind a fifteen-foot tall ficus hedge.

Jake pulled up to the intercom outside the wrought iron gate and pushed the button.

"I'm so glad you're here," Hunt answered happily.

A moment later the gate rolled aside and Jake pulled into the paved courtyard. The house had been built in the roaring '20s as a winter home for a Chicago financier. Little expense had been spared. With eight bedrooms and a dining room that could hold thirty, it was very old money Miami.

Jake had picked up bits and pieces from Hunt's stories as to where his fortune had come from. Before there was Calvin Klein or Ralph Lauren, Hunt had been one of the premier designers in the country. He'd started his own line of women's fashion in the 1950s and was enormously successful. He dressed the stars and socialites of his day. His stores were in Palm Beach, Palm Springs, and New York. Oscar de la Renta and Bill Blass were his close friends.

Jake carried his massage table up the travertine steps.

Hunt gave Jake a big kiss and a hug to welcome him. "I've missed you so much!" he said as he ushered Jake into the marble entry hall.

It seemed an odd comment to Jake. He'd only been gone for a long weekend. There was an awkward moment of silence.

Finally they reached the master bedroom.

Jake unpacked and got set up. "Why don't you get undressed while I wash my hands," he said.

Once on Jake's table, Hunt cheerfully bounced from one topic to the next. Today Hunt was recounting tales of Miami in the 1950s. "I use to dress Ava Gardner when she was Frank Sinatra's wife," he started off. "She'd always get me a table right up front when he performed at the Fontainebleau. Did you know Sinatra won an Oscar? I designed the dress Ava wore to the Academy Awards when Frank accepted the award."

Jake was duly impressed, but wasn't about to interrupt the tale.

Hunt continued. "She was a stunning woman, but explosive, cursed a blue streak at the drop of a hat. You know her famous line, don't you? 'When I lose my temper, honey, you can't find it anywhere.' She was a handful at fittings. 'Make my tits look luscious,' she used to tell me." And so it went for the next hour, inside gossip about the rich and famous.

"Are you hungry?" Hunt asked when Jake finished the massage. "I thought we'd go to Abbracci in Coral Gables tonight." Hunt always insisted on taking Jake to dinner after his massage. Jake readily agreed. He was not about to turn down invitations to dine at the best restaurants in town. Hunt had celebrated their first meal with a bottle of Cristal champagne. "Here's to us!" he toasted.

"I love our dinners together. I wish I'd met you thirty years ago," Hunt said before he climbed into the shower.

Over the sound of the water, Jake started telling Hunt about what a wonderful time he'd had in New York. He told Hunt that the guy he'd met a few weeks ago had been there too and that they'd spent most of their time together. "I really like him a lot," Jake said. He was still riding the high of the weekend.

Hunt came out of the bathroom and began to dress. "Don't be silly. You're my sweetheart. I don't want to hear another word about other men."

In that instant, Jake realized that Hunt had grossly misinterpreted his interest in him.

"Here, I have something for you to read," Hunt said. He gave Jake a handwritten note on his personal stationery. Jake unfolded it and read:

In the winter of my old age, you are spring.
In the desert of my heart, you are water.
My life was at a dead end, you showed me the way.
My withered heart is once again
Overflowing with love.

Jake was taken aback. He felt his face flush. No one had ever written him a love poem. He saw a spark in Hunt's eyes that hadn't been there before. Jake couldn't bear to break the sweet old man's heart. "It's beautiful. I can't believe you wrote this for me. I don't know what to say," Jake stumbled over the words. "Thank you."

July 1994
South Beach

Jake & Luca
Finally their coffee arrived. Jake and Luca were having breakfast with Raul at the Front Porch Café on Ocean Drive. Every Friday morning they'd meet at the eatery to catch up on the week's gossip.

"I can't believe *you*, of all people, missed the hottest party of the weekend. Why weren't you at Rob and Erik's on Saturday night?" asked Jake.

"Unfortunately, I was busy making money. An old client of mine from Palm Springs hired me for the evening," Raul explained. "We were 'partying' and played 'til dawn. I could've kicked myself. It's the one party that *everyone* has been talking about."

"As well they should. It was incredible," Jake said. "I wish someone would throw one here on South Beach."

"Hello! Why don't you guys do it yourself?"

"What?" Luca responded. "You want *us* to throw a sex party?"

"Sure. It can't be that difficult to organize. White Party weekend is coming up in November. Tons of guys will be in town from all over. Host one then," Raul encouraged.

"Where?" asked Jake.

"At your house. It's the perfect setting. You have that incredible pool. And you've got total privacy with the jungle that surrounds it."

***

"I've been thinking about your party. Let me give you a few

words of advice from a legal viewpoint. You need to have the guys attending your party sign a waiver," Raul informed Jake and Luca.

"A waiver? What kind of waiver?" Jake asked, thinking, *He's going overboard.*

"You have to make everyone responsible for their own behavior. Make them sign something that says they'll play safe and use condoms," he pointed out. "That way no one can blame you for getting an STD, or worse, at your party. I know a guy at county health department. I can get you all the condoms you need. And I know I'm the last person you'd expect to hear this from, but I think you should make it clear that your party is drug-free."

"I like the idea of a waiver. And I bet I can get free lube from WET through my connections at Priapus," said Luca.

"Point two. How are you going to screen guys?" Raul asked.

"We're only going to invite hot muscle guys," Jake answered, as if it weren't obvious.

"But what if someone brings their ugly cousin or some fat guy hears about it and shows up? Trust me, the last thing you want is to turn away some pissy queen at the door and have him start trouble. Here's a thought, you guys could use my place to do the screening. It's easy for anyone staying on South Beach to walk to," Raul offered. "Besides, that way I get to preview who I want to play with. There are some privileges to playing host," he said with a Cheshire Cat grin.

***

"How do we let guys know about the party?" Luca asked.

"Have some cards made up and hand them out to every hot guy you see," Raul suggested.

"And what do we call ourselves?" Jake asked Luca.

"What do you mean?" Raul asked.

"We need to have a name for ourselves so that guys can refer to it by something other than Jake and Luca's sex party."

"It should sound like a private club for muscle-boys only," Luca answered, calling on his copywriting talent. "How about South Beach HardBodies?" he said, knowing he'd struck the perfect name.

Ira & Beau

"Ira, honey," Beau began in his sweetest voice.

"Yes, Beau, what do you want?" Ira asked with a smile.

"Why do you think I want something?" Beau responded, hurt.

"The only time you call me 'Ira, honey,' is when you want something. No big deal," he replied.

"You know my New York friends, Rob and Erik? They asked me to be their guest for the Morning Party out on Fire Island in August. It's a benefit for a big AIDS organization. I know it's not your style, but I'd like to go if you wouldn't mind," Beau said, bending the truth slightly. It was he who had called Rob and Erik and asked if he could stay with them over the party weekend. It was the premier weekend to be out on the Island. The A-list gays mixed with all the hot young hunks. Beau wanted, no needed, to feel he was a part of that. Staying with Rob and Erik would be a real coup.

"Sure. Go and have fun with your buddies. I can always catch up on stuff here. Maybe I'll go down to the Laguna house," Ira said over his cup of coffee.

"Great. I'll book my flight. It's the last weekend in August," Beau replied, relieved that it had all gone so easily.

"Any auditions coming up?" Ira asked.

"I have one lead. I have to call the casting director. It's for a Greg Araki project. He's an independent filmmaker who does some pretty cool gay films. I'll let you know what comes of it. Keep your fingers crossed," Beau answered.

"I'll make a few calls to some of the casting people I know and see if I can stir the pot for you. Have a good workout today," Ira said. He got up from the breakfast table. "I've got to get to work."

Safely locked behind his office door, Ira made a phone call to his friend. "Fuji, it's Ira. I'll only be a minute. Remember the porn star who posed with Beau in the pool? Looked like his twin?" Ira inquired.

"Yes, why?"

"I'd like him to be my guest in Laguna the last weekend of August. Do you think you can arrange that?"

"There's an escort agency here in LA that books all the porn stars. Consider it done."

174

July 1994 - *Two Weeks Later*
South Beach

Jake & Luca

"I can't believe you won't be able to go to the Morning Party!" bemoaned Jake when Luca told him the news. "Is there any way you can change the dates? Everyone is expecting both of us."

"I wish I could, but I can't turn down $4,500 for three nights," Luca explained. It was his first call from the escort agency that all the gay porn stars worked for. The client list was a who's who of Hollywood. This was Luca's opportunity to get his foot in the door with an exceptional agency that catered to an exceptional clientele.

August 1994 - *One Month Later / Morning Party Weekend*
Fire Island
Friday

Jake & Karl

Karl, his wavy brown hair now straightened and highlighted blond, was there to greet Jake with open arms when the ferry pulled into the harbor. Hugs and kisses all around. Jake wished he could tell his best friend about his and Luca's plans to throw a sex party over White Party weekend. He had a pack of cards announcing the HardBodies party that he intended to hand out to every hot guy who crossed his path, but he couldn't tell Karl. Neither he nor his boyfriend, Curt, were HardBodies material.

"How was your flight?" Karl asked.

"Packed with hot boys. I swear South Beach must be a ghost town this weekend. Everyone we know is here."

"Except your boyfriend."

"Yeah, doesn't that suck? But show business calls." Although Karl knew all the details of Jake's escorting in Philly, Jake decided not to spill the beans about Luca's side job. Besides, he was kind of telling the truth. He'd gotten the job because of his porn career.

"Here, put your bag in my wagon. I'll show you the house we rented this summer. We're on the dry side of Ocean Walk."

"Ooh, movin' on up?" Jake remarked.

"We have 'partial views of the ocean' from the pool deck, which means, if you stand on your tip toes and look between the expensive houses, you can see a bit of water."

175

Los Angeles
Friday

Ira & Luca

At LAX, Luca was greeted by Ira's houseman holding up a card bearing his last name. "Hello, Mr. Barbieri. Did you check any bags?" he asked Luca as he took his carry-on.

"No, just this one," he replied.

"Excellent. We'll pick up Mr. Ira and then continue to the beach house."

"Great," Luca responded. He followed the houseman, climbed into the back of the black town car, and dozed to the soft music that was playing as they drove to Beverly Hills.

"We're here, Mr. Barbieri," the houseman said.

Luca opened his eyes. They were pulling up to the house where the Project Angel Food fundraiser had been held and where Luca had been photographed with Beau. Standing on the front steps with a Vuitton duffle bag by his side was the owner. He was wearing a Hawaiian shirt and a Panama hat. *Practically the same outfit he was wearing at the party,* Luca thought. *I guess this must be his "look."*

"Hello, Luca. It's so nice to see you. You're looking well. How was your flight?" Ira asked as he climbed into the back seat.

"It was pleasantly uneventful. I watched *Forrest Gump.* I've wanted to see it since it came out."

"I worked on that one. Fascinating what you can do with digital technology."

Luca nodded in agreement.

Ira then placed his hand on Luca's knee. "I've been looking forward to this weekend with you," he said.

Luca just smiled. He knew better than to ask about Beau.

***

As they approached the seaside resort, Ira told Luca the history of the house. It had been built as a wedding gift from Orson Welles to Rita Hayworth. The home's interior had been redone in a minimalist style, in contrast to its hacienda architecture. It was as if someone had hollowed out a Spanish Mediterranean mansion and refurbished it in the latest modern style. Granite countertops. Stone floors. Pale wood. Stainless steel. A small fortune had been spent. An enormous bower of bougainvillea covered the outdoor dining and living areas, a beautiful and perfect way to keep the

176

bright California sun from roasting midday guests.

After dinner, Ira led Luca out onto the deck overlooking the Pacific. The cool evening air gave Luca a slight chill. It was a refreshing change from the humidity of Miami. Ira lit up a joint and offered it to Luca. Luca took a deep toke. The weed was fragrant. Luca guessed it must be good and strong. He passed the joint back to Ira, who inhaled as if it were his last breath. Ira finished and stubbed it out in an ashtray.

"Let's go upstairs, shall we?" Ira asked with a wide grin. "Dinner was delicious, but dessert's going to be even better."

What Luca didn't know was how simple it was to satisfy Ira. He was a pig for sucking the big dicks of young men. Sometimes on business trips, he'd arrange for a half dozen studs to be sent over by the local escort agency. Once he'd finish sucking one dry, another would show up eager to be drained. Ira preferred to prescreen his partners, whether through a friend like Fuji or through an escort agency. He didn't like gambling when it came to cock size. For him, bigger was always better.

Ira would never reach orgasm while playing with his partners. He liked it best when he could jack off the next day in the shower, thinking of the big cocks he'd serviced the night before. He couldn't wait to unzip Luca's prize piece. If his memory served him, it was every bit as big as Beau's. He was eager to impress this young porn star with his oral expertise. In the morning he'd replay the whole scene while soaping up under the hot water of the shower.

Laguna
Saturday Night

Ira and Luca arrived at Mark's Bistro shortly after 8:00 pm. The place was mobbed with men.

"Right this way, Mr. Gould. Your guests are waiting," the maitre d' said as he escorted them to their table.

Your guests are waiting? Luca thought. *We're not dining alone?* Suddenly before them was a round table with three older gentlemen and three young men. There were two empty seats. Everyone rose for a round of hugs and kisses.

The only guest Luca recognized was the photographer David Fujimoto. With him was a young stud who looked all of twenty-one with wavy brown hair down to his shoulders. Luca was introduced to a film producer in his 50s with short salt-and-pepper hair and steel blue eyes. His younger "friend," had shoulders like bowling balls. Rounding out the table was a film director with a mane of gray hair and a striking young black man.

At first, Luca was a bit uncomfortable. Usually when a gentleman hired him it all took place discreetly behind closed doors. This felt like show-and-tell. Luca sat between Ira and Fuji. He noticed that none of the arm-candy were seated next to each other. Each had an older man on either side of him.
　　Talk about jock block, Luca thought.

Almost immediately the conversation turned to Hollywood gossip and the soon-to-be released film that everyone was talking about.
　　"How did you get that closet case to play gay?" asked Ira. He'd just received a rough print in order to create the trailer. "Isn't that just going to fan the rumors?"
　　"Are you kidding? Every actor, gay or straight, wanted that role. The book was a pop culture phenomenon," explained the director. "With his back-end deal, no pun intended, he'll walk away with a $15 million paycheck. That's enough to sue anyone on the planet who suggests he prefers boys over girls."
　　"He's just not credible in that role, too much of a lightweight in my opinion,' quipped the producer. "I'd have gone with Malkovitch or Irons, even Sting for that matter.
　　"Well . . . ," said the director, "once the Movie Mogul decided to produce the film there was no question as to who would play the lead."
　　"Was it all decided over pillow talk?" asked Fuji.
　　"I assume our leading man still has a key to the Movie Mogul's Malibu hideaway," answered the director.

The evening went on for several courses and many cocktails. With each round of drinks the conversation became more animated and the stories more salacious. Luca could hardly believe what he heard. These men knew *everyone's* secrets.

Fire Island
Saturday Night

Jake & Beau
After dinner, Jake, the Fashionistas, and the Brazilians went

178

to the Sip & Twirl for cocktails. Since the key to surviving and enjoying any circuit weekend was pacing, the boys planned on a quick drink, a spin on the dance floor, and home for a solid night's sleep.

On the dance floor, Jake bumped into Rob and Erik. With them was a friend of theirs from LA. Jake thought he was gorgeous, almost a carbon copy of Luca.

"This is our friend, Beau," said Rob.

Beau was dazzled by Jake's good looks. It didn't take long for him to invite Jake back to Rob and Erik's house for a moonlight swim and a midnight romp.

Afterwards while in the pool, Beau asked Jake, "Are you out here alone this weekend?"

"As a matter of fact, I am. I'm a porn widow," Jake said jokingly.

"A what?" Beau asked.

"A porn widow. My boyfriend is filming a video in California."

"Your boyfriend's a porn star? That's hot. We have a house in Laguna that we rent out to porn studios," Beau said, as if he owned the place.

"What about you? Is your boyfriend out here?" Jake asked.

"No, it's not his scene."

Oh, really, Jake thought. *He has boyfriend like you and he doesn't like circuit party weekends? I get the picture.*

They got out of the pool and dried off.

"How do you know Rob and Erik?" Beau asked.

"We were neighbors last summer," Jake answered. "And you?"

"We met at the bar. I represented Jocks in the Southern Sizzle contest. When I won I got to shoot with David Fujimoto in LA. Now I'm out there full-time pursuing a career in films," Beau said, sounding quite self-impressed.

Jake thought about telling him that Luca had been photographed by Fujimoto as well, but it would have sounded like he was trying to compete. Instead he changed subjects. "Were you in New York for Stonewall 25?" Jake asked as he put on his jeans.

"Yeah, wasn't it great?"

"How did I miss you at Rob and Erik's party?" Jake rewound the images of that night in his head.

"I wasn't there. I was hosting a benefit."

"Oh, so I guess you've heard all about it," Jake said.

"Oh, yeah. They've done a great job of rubbing it in. Apparently every hot guy in the world was there. And please don't ask me if I danced on the deck of the *Intrepid*. No, I got to sit front row to hear Babs sing," Beau said ruefully.

Jake felt sorry for the guy. He obviously knew he'd missed the high points of the weekend. No reason to make him feel worse. We all have to make sacrifices. "Well, I have some good news for you. If you're coming to South Beach for White Party, there's going to be a muscle-only sex party," Jake said.

"Now that sounds like a distinct possibility," Beau responded. Jake reached into his pocket and handed him a HardBodies card.

Autumn 1994

September 1994 - *One Month Later*
South Beach

Jake & Luca

No matter where he went, Jake carried the HardBodies cards with him. He handed them out at the gym, at the beach, at the Palace. Even at the supermarket when he got cruised. If you were built, Jake handed you a card. It was just a matter of days before he'd handed out all of the cards he and Luca had had printed. They ordered another hundred.

"I can't believe how easy this is," exclaimed Luca when he looked up from the computer. They were now living together with the Aussie from the guest house as their roommate. Luca had converted Jake's spare bedroom into an office. He'd just upgraded from a black-and-white monitor to a full-color screen and was thrilled with his new toy. "Every gay guy in the country must be on AOL." Every city had at least one chat room, often two or more, that was M4M. With a quick perusal of profiles, you could find exactly what you were looking for. And Luca did. There were countless buff men who were interested in attending the HardBodies party.

As Luca collected e-mail addresses, his list of possible attendees grew exponentially. Tell ten guys about South Beach HardBodies and they'd each tell ten more guys. Before you knew it, one hundred guys were talking about SBHB in a heartbeat. "It's only been three weeks and I've already got a list as long as my arm of muscle guys who are coming to South Beach for White Party," Luca told Jake. Their combined efforts were paying off. SBHB was rapidly becoming an underground phenomenon before the first party had even been thrown.

Rob & Erik

They checked into the Kenmore Hotel at the corner of 11th and Washington, the gayest hotel on South Beach. They loved the location but weren't all that impressed with the accommodations. It looked like somebody had simply slapped a few coats of paint on the walls and laid down new carpet to spruce the place up. The bathroom fixtures and tile, for better or worse, were all original from the '30s, but at least it was clean, everything worked, and the nightly rate was less than half that of anything in New York.

It was easy to spot the gay section of the beach at 12th Street.

Rainbow flags flew on top of the volleyball nets. Rob and Erik stared at the bodies of the boys who were hooting and hollering as they pummeled the ball over the net. Sweat gleamed on their rippling abs. It was like a Herb Ritts video. They continued their walk toward the shoreline. The aqua blue of the Atlantic Ocean came into view when they crossed over the dunes. They stopped and took in the vista.

"I can't believe the size of this beach," Rob remarked. It stretched as far as he could see and was as wide as a football field from the dunes to the water's edge.

"And look at the color of the water!" Erik exclaimed. "God, it's beautiful!"

"This is like a photo out of one of those travel brochures that you swear they've retouched," Rob replied.

"Even the sky looks a brighter blue," Erik said. They set their beach towels where the sand sloped down toward the water. They'd taken off their tank tops as soon as they'd left the hotel. Every other guy on the street seemed to be shirtless, so why shouldn't they? They both hit the water and dove under. A gentle wave washed over them. "This is heaven," Erik sighed. He dove back under the crystal clear saltwater.

Once the sun started to set, they followed the crowd to the Palace. All the beautiful boys who had covered the beach were there.

"Can you believe this place?" Erik asked under his breath. He didn't want to sound like a tourist. "I hear so many different languages that I don't feel like we're in the States. And look at the bodies!"

"I know. Everywhere I look, I see the most perfect men," Rob said.

"Hey!" Erik protested with a chuckle.

"You know you're the love of my life, but honey, I'm a man. And this is almost too much. All the hype didn't prepare me for all this," Rob admitted. After they'd had a round of Coronas and their fill of eye candy, they called Jake and Luca. It was decided they'd meet at Warsaw at midnight.

***

Rob and Erik were easy to spot. Jake and Luca simply walked up to the two biggest boys waiting in line. There were hugs and kisses all around.

"It's so great to see you guys on our turf," Jake said, noting that something looked different about Rob. *Are his lips bigger? His cheekbones?*

184

"Enjoying your visit so far?" Luca asked.

"Everything's been great," Rob replied. "The hotel is like a bathhouse filled with *GQ* models. Hardly anyone bothers to close their door. And we've fallen in love with the Palace!"

Looking at the line that stretched for half a block, Erik added, "Well, this certainly looks like the place to be tonight."

"Oh, believe me, it is. Warsaw is one of the best clubs on the beach. But don't let the line worry you. There are some privileges that come with being a local," Jake said. He led their little group to the front of the line.

Luca embraced the short Cuban doorman.

"How many in your group?" the doorman asked.

"There are four of us. These are our friends from New York. They own Jocks," Luca responded.

"VIPs! Come on in, gentlemen. I've heard great things about your bar. Here are some drink tickets. I hope you enjoy tonight's party," the doorman said as he ushered them in.

The place was packed. They paused to get their bearings. It looked like a set for a Fellini film. Tonight, Susanne Bartsch, a wild looking German woman, was throwing one of her infamous bashes. The theme was Caligula. On a raised dais just inside the entrance was an enormously overweight woman lounging on a gilt chaise. She was dressed in a Roman toga, her face powdered lily white. She calmly ate grapes from a golden bowl balanced on her lap. Then, someone or something bumped into Erik's ass. He turned around to see a muscular midget in a gold lamé toga pushing his way through the crowd with a giant phallus, twice his height.

"Did I just see what I thought I saw?" asked Erik.

While they waited to catch the eye of the blond toga-clad surfer boy who was bartending, they watched a stripper mount the bar. A red spotlight fell on him. He was a porn star from the '80s known for his ridiculously large cock. He was wearing gladiator sandals and a g-string. The first thing he did was to haul out his massive member and let it flop over the top of his g-string. The boys looked at each other in amazement when he started stroking it to the music. It kept growing and growing.

"That is so fucking hot," Rob said.

"And it's only the start of the evening," commented Luca.

The music slowly faded when Bartsch, the Mistress of the Evening, took to the stage. "Having fun, boys and girls?" she asked in a strong Teutonic accent. "It's time for my favorite part of the night, the strip contest." With that, ten young men marched out behind her, all clad in gold lamé g-strings. They were supposed to be amateurs, but given their perfectly chiseled bodies, it was obvious they weren't. They took turns in the spotlight, each shaking his moneymaker and trying to outdo the competition. The winner was a beautiful sinewy black boy who, for his finale, whipped out his extraordinarily long cock, bent over, and sucked it. The crowd went wild.

***

By Saturday, after a few days in the sun, Rob and Erik felt like part of the tanned, buff local crowd. They could pick out the new arrivals by their pallid skin. That evening they approached the corner of 12th and Washington and saw a mob. It appeared to be the waiting line for admittance to Paragon, a massive gay dance emporium, but there was clearly something else going on. The crowd was clapping along to music coming out of Meet Me in Miami, the clothing store on the corner. A drag queen was performing in the shop window. Her energy was contagious. She was lip-synching to "Proud Mary" and seemed to be channeling Tina Turner on speed. The crowd grew to where it flowed out into the street, stopping traffic. Drivers climbed out of their cars to see what was happening.

At one point, one of Tina's platform stilettos flew off, nearly shattering the shop window, but nothing could stop her. The crowd went wild as she hobbled and hopped through the finale. Soaked with sweat, the drag queen took her bows to a cheering audience. Rob and Erik were amazed. They'd never seen anything in New York remotely like what had just happened in front of them.

Erik spotted Jake and Luca at the entrance to Paragon talking to the door person, Kitty Meow. His face was made up like Divine's in *Pink Flamingos*, but his unadorned head was as bald and black as an eight ball on a billiard table. He was wearing thigh-high silver platform boots and micro shorts made of gold mesh. An enormous codpiece displayed his manhood front and center. Across his sculpted chest he sported a rhinestone harness that held a back-piece of black ostrich feathers splayed out like a peacock's tail.

186

Jake and Luca introduced Rob and Erik to Kitty, and the four of them were immediately admitted through the massive doors of the club into the enormous lobby of what once was an Art Deco movie theater. Along one wall, a grand staircase rose to a balcony. Guys in various states of undress and inebriation paraded up and down the stairs doing their best Norma Desmond impressions. Jake and Luca led the boys to the lobby bar for their first beer of the evening.

"Oh, my God! I can't believe I found you in this crowd!" a voice hollered out from the multitudes. It was Raul. He was practically jumping up and down. "I had to come out tonight. I missed you guys. Let me buy you a drink!" he shouted over the music.
"Raul, these are our friends from New York, Rob and Erik," Jake said in an attempt to calm down the little dynamo.
Shaking their hands vigorously, he said, "Pleased to meet you. What would you like to drink?" As always, the beverage of choice was Coronas with lime.
"Where have you been?" Jake asked. "We haven't seen you in weeks."
"Ibiza! I go every August. You have to go. It makes South Beach look like a farm! All the hottest gay boys in Europe are there. The clubs are twice the size of this one. And there's sex all day in the dunes behind the beach. It's paradise!" Rob and Erik were both fascinated and a little horrified by this seemingly crazed character. "I've decided that you're coming with me next year. You won't regret it." He handed out the Coronas along with sloppy kisses and then dashed off into the crowd.

"Now, who was that again?" Rob asked, his head still spinning. "He looked vaguely familiar."
"That was our friend Raul. He used to be a COLT model. He went by the name Armando. He's a bit like a Cuban Chihuahua on steroids," Jake said.
"I think he's on more than steroids, tonight," Luca threw in.

At midnight, the doors to the main club finally opened. A wide ramp flowed down to a circular dance floor large enough to hold several thousand partiers. It was filled in a matter of minutes. Jake and Luca led Rob and Erik to the far side of the dance floor, closest to the raised stage. Moments later, the curtains opened, and an enormous roar filled the entire club. Kitty Meow, in all his opulent glory, came skidding onto the stage riding an iridescent purple Harley-Davidson motorcycle.

"It belongs to Prince," whispered Luca into Erik's ear. "He's supposedly here tonight in the projectionist's booth, the ultra-VIP lounge above the balcony."

Kitty roared off into the wings, and the lights came up on stage to reveal a huge swimming pool with massive angled mirrors hanging overhead allowing for all to see. The pool was ringed by a dozen muscle boys in matching purple Speedos and a dozen drag chorines in purple one-piece swimsuits and matching bathing caps. With what sounded like a clap of thunder, the show began. It was a synchronized swimming routine set to Prince's song "1999." The muscle boys dove on cue and the chorines drenched the crowd with their high kicks in the water. They partied on stage as if it were the turn of the century. As the song built to its clattering climax, mountains of purple Mylar confetti rained down on the dance floor. It was impossible not to smile. The crowd cheered for more.

"Well, that tops it for me," Rob confessed.

"Just another Saturday night on South Beach," Jake and Luca said in unison.

Monday

Jake & Raul

"Where do I start with Ibiza? The men get more gorgeous every year," Raul began. The waiter who'd taken their order promptly returned with two iced teas. It was a slow afternoon at The Palace. "I tell you, it's tough keeping up, but somehow I managed. Speaking of gorgeous men, everyone I talked to in Ibiza seemed to be coming to the White Party. So of course, I mentioned that I was best friends with the two guys who will be throwing the most spectacular sex party of the weekend. I made sure to write down all of their e-mail addresses. I assure you that each and everyone one of these guys is amazing. I got fucked by most of them," Raul boasted as he handed the e-mail list to Jake. "The nightlife in Ibiza starts as late as ever. Every night you meet friends at the early bars around 2:00 in the morning. I've gotten to know the owner of Dome, one of the most popular gay bars in Ibiza."

Jake interjected, "And I bet he has a huge, uncut dick."

"How'd ya guess? OK, back to me. It's at the early

bars that you get your free passes to that night's event. You have to be gorgeous or know somebody who is somebody. Anyway, every night a different club has a gay party. Of course, you can't show up before 4:00 or it'll be just you and the bartenders, but by 5:00 the clubs are packed, and we're talking thousands. Of course it's never totally gay. It's a mix. Some of the hottest straight boys take their girlfriends home and come back out to pick up guys. It's so wild," Raul said, pausing to catch his breath.

"How do you stay up so late? Cocaine?" Jake asked.

"Cocaine is so '80s. No, the drug of choice is Tina."

Jake looked confused.

"It's crystal meth, speed. Tina sounds so much better, like a friend's name. It turns you into an insatiable sex pig," Raul explained. "Around sunrise everyone goes to Space, an afterhours club. It's right at the end of the airport runway, so as you're dancing, there are planes taking off over your head. The vibration is incredible when you're on Ecstasy. They play light, happy music outside on the terrace. Everyone is beautiful and flirty. It's my favorite place to go before the beach."

Finally, their turkey burgers arrived. While Raul paused to take a bite, Jake took advantage of the moment, "OK, I need your help with something," he said.

"Sure, anything."

"Every time I bring this subject up with other big guys, I get total denial. It's very frustrating. I think you're the only one I can talk to about this," Jake confessed.

Looking serious, Raul said, "You can always talk to me about anything. You know that."

Lowering his voice, Jake said, "I want to talk to you about steroids."

"Is that all? Oh, honey. You had me scared for a second. Sure, ask away."

"The deal is, I'm stuck below 200 pounds and I can't get any bigger. I mean, I'm 6'4"! I see guys my height who are so much bigger than me."

"Jake, you've got a beautiful body. You can hold your own in any crowd. Plus, you've got a big dick. Still, I know what you mean. There's always that competition between men," Raul admitted.

"Exactly. Plus, I'm married to Mr. Body. Luca's been a gymnast since he was eight years old. I don't just want to be known as the tall guy with the big dick. Besides, I'm getting nervous about our HardBodies party. How am I going to be the guardian of the gate if *my* body doesn't measure up?"

"OK, I can get you steroids. No problem. Me and everyone I know who is positive is over-prescribed. I'll sell you my extras. But you have to work out harder and eat more. You don't just sit there and grow muscles. It's like a part-time job. Nobody ever said looking this good is easy," Raul laughed.

Fort Lauderdale – *One Week Later*

Big Daddy & Bobby
"It's pronounced *Ee-beetha,* but it's spelled I-B-I-Z-A," Jake explained. "It's an island off of Spain that's built around nightlife. My friend Raul hasn't stopped talking about it since he returned. Apparently all the hot Euro-boys go there in August."

"Sounds interesting," replied Big Daddy, always on the hunt for the hottest gay destination. The massage table creaked and groaned under his weight. "Have you and Luca been?"

"No, but if it's half of what Raul says it is, than Ibiza must be a gay paradise," Jake answered.

"I'll have to ask the Brazilians. I'm sure they'll know all about it. Perhaps there are some nude guesthouses. I'll have Bobby look into it. He's good at finding things on the Internet."

Beverly Hills - *One Week Later*

Ira & Beau
Ira was mapping out his strategy. His benefit in New York had been a huge success. The Gossip Columnist had written a glowing account in *the* New York tabloid and the Protégé's photos had been featured in *the* Condé Nast glossy magazine. It was more than Ira could have hoped for. He intended to build on that buzz with another fabulous evening.

"Honey? When are you done shooting your movie?" Ira asked, thinking to himself, *So that's what qualifies as a movie these days.* In fairness, it was a film short. Beau had auditioned and gotten the role of "Unattainable Stud." His one scene was to take place in a steam room, and he had one line:

> *Moving his towel aside, Beau's character says, "So you like this?" as he exposes his dick (off camera).*

190

While Ira wasn't impressed, at least Beau was pursuing an acting career of sorts.

"It'll be finished by Halloween. Why?" Beau responded.

"I was thinking we might go to South Beach for the White Party at the end of November. Would you like to go?" Ira asked, already knowing the answer.

"I'd love to," Beau replied, thrilled at the prospect.

"Would you be a dear and call my travel agent? Have her book us a bungalow at the Delano," Ira said.

November 1994 - *Two Months Later / White Party Weekend*
South Beach
Saturday Night

Ira & Beau
By the time the sun had set, the Velvet Mafia had arrived for champagne at Ira and Beau's bungalow at the Delano. Only Mr. Underwear had declined the invitation, as he was dining with the Italian Designer. The timing never seemed to be right with Mr. Underwear. He always had a more fabulous party to attend.

Ira had been very selective in whom he invited. He gazed around room and gauged his success. Over in the corner, the Media Mogul was chatting to the director of a just-released movie. Ira's trailer had gotten better reviews than the film. The Movie Mogul was sitting on the high-backed white sofa talking to Ira's long-time Laguna neighbor and frequent dinner guest, the producer of last summer's blockbuster. Of course, Ira had done the trailer for that one, too. In the only chair in the room, a tall white wingback, the Lesbian Designer was holding court.

David Fujimoto arrived last, with a surprising guest. Instead of his usual trophy-boy, he'd brought an unattractive guy who was dripping with sweat despite the cool evening. Fuji introduced him as one of the leading party promoters in the country. "We both grew up in Palm Springs."

The Party Promoter wouldn't be able to join them for dinner because he was hosting one of his famous underwear parties at the South Beach Arena that evening. He gave everyone VIP passes to the event.

Ira suggested that Beau attend the party.

Beau was thrilled.

"I have something for all of you," announced Fuji. "A little gift." He pulled a copy of his new 1995 calendar out of a small bag he'd brought with him. On the cover was the photo of Beau on Luca's shoulders in Ira's pool. He held it up for all to see.

"Is that really me?" Beau asked in awe.

"Yes, it is," answered Fuji as he handed out copies to everyone in the room.

"Oh my God, you're as good as Herb Ritts!" exclaimed the Lesbian Designer.

"Ritts takes beautiful photographs," declared the Media Mogul, "but you've captured a moment of real joy with these two boys."

Ira was beaming with pride.

"I knew the moment I saw the image in my viewfinder that it was perfect," Fuji said, unaware that he was singing his own praises.

"You're a master," the Party Promoter said. "I'd love to use that cover shot to promote my Underwear Party in Palm Springs. We can market your calendar at the same time."

"Synergy! I love it," Fuji replied.

The Movie Mogul turned to Beau. "You look flawless. Fuji, couldn't have found a better model."

Beau was tongue-tied. He had no idea how to respond to the compliment from such a Hollywood heavyweight.

The assembled group finished their champagne and started their short walk to the hotel's Blue Door restaurant.

Before leaving the bungalow, the Party Promoter pulled Beau aside. He'd taken a shine to the boy. "Follow me into the bathroom. I'll give you a little pick-me-up," he said under his breath. He closed the bathroom door behind them.

When he pulled a little bag of white powder from his pocket, Beau asked, "Cocaine?"

"No, it's much better. It's Tina. It'll give you energy and make you horny."

"Like Ecstasy?" Beau asked, his curiosity piqued.

"Yes, but this is better. It lasts much longer. You'll see," the Party Promoter said. He tapped out a tiny mound on the back of Beau's hand. "Just snort it."

Jake & Luca
The big night had finally arrived. The first guest rang Raul's doorbell and Jake answered it. When the first guy in line stepped into the small foyer, Jake felt a knot in his stomach.

192

His worst fear had come to pass. First In Line seemed like a nice enough guy, but evidently had never been to a gym in his life. He was short and dumpy. Jake knew that he hadn't been given a card. Obviously he'd called the HardBodies number and gotten Raul's address from the outgoing message. And he had clearly chosen to ignore the rest of the message regarding the physical requirements to attend.

Quickly, Jake went over the drill that he and Luca had prepared in the event something like this might occur. "This is a really difficult position you've put me in," Jake said to First In Line.

"What do you mean?" he asked, all wide-eyed innocence.

"Well, it's not going to work out for tonight's party," Jake said firmly.

"I don't understand," First In Line replied.

Jake suspected he understood completely but thought he could bully his way in. Backed into a corner, Jake pushed right back. "You're not in good enough shape to attend tonight's party. We made it very clear in our phone message," Jake stated in no uncertain terms.

"But I'm really into muscle guys, and I have a big dick," he replied, hoping this extra information would gain him entrance.

"I'm sorry, but you need to be a muscle guy yourself. It doesn't matter how big your dick is."

"I've got some great E. You can have as much as you want," First In Line offered under his breath.

"Thanks, but our parties are drug-free. I'm sorry," Jake said, gently putting his hand on First In Line's back and guiding him out.

***

Rob, Erik, and the Rocks walked from the Delano over to Raul's and discovered a whole new world. Gone was the neon-lit glamour of Ocean Drive. This was a sweet little neighborhood of two-story Art Deco apartment buildings and Mediterranean-style houses. When they arrived at the Euclid Avenue address, they were met by a dozen muscle boys, some of whom they knew from New York, all waiting on the front steps.

"This must be the place," Rob said as he scoped out the crowd.

The Rocks wasted no time introducing themselves to two strangers who spoke with German accents. They were both tall and built, with blond hair, blue eyes, and sunburns.

The door opened inward and let out a group of eight men.
Some spoke Italian, while others spoke Portuguese. Clearly,
word of the party had spread far and wide.

Rob spotted Jake over the heads of the growing crowd
and waved hello. "I'll be right with you," Jake said. "We've
got quite a full house here so it'll take a few minutes."

One hot stud took his time exiting so that the mere
mortals waiting in line could get a good look at him. Heads
turned and Jake overheard, "That's Mr. B, king of the B-list
porn stars. He's in *every* video they put out these days."

Rob
By the time he'd gotten his change back from the cabbie, Erik
and the Rocks were already inside the house. Rob walked
through a tropical garden to the front gate. Pink bromeliads
dotted the ground. Purple orchids clung to tree trunks.
Uplighting transformed the palm trees into towering columns
bursting with golden-lit fronds.

Rob climbed white terrazzo steps up to a black metal gate.
It swung inward to a courtyard and he handed his invitation
to a blond muscle boy with an Australian accent.

"Thanks, mate. Here's a bag for your clothes. Write
your name on it with this marker and stash it in a place you'll
remember," the Aussie directed.

In contrast to the wild jungle Rob had just walked through,
this Zen-like courtyard was perfectly manicured. He was
overwhelmed by the scent of gardenias that covered one of the
inner walls. Against that wall of green leaves and white
flowers were a dozen beautifully-built young men getting
undressed. Rob disrobed, wrapped a white towel he'd brought
from the hotel around his waist, and entered the house.

Clusters of candles flickered on black tables. Muscled bodies
moved in and out of the darkness. In the center of the room
were two huge black leather sofas covered with writhing
naked bodies. In their midst, Rob spotted the Rocks, with
their glow-in-the-dark tanlines, kneeling in front of the
muscle-bound Germans they'd spoken to earlier. Their heads
were bobbing up and down. Around them, several muscle
butts were being greedily eaten. It was only a matter of time
before hard cocks sank into those wet asses.

Just as the front of the living room opened to the courtyard,
the back opened to the lanai. Candlelit lanterns illuminated

an enormous white canvas canopy. The rhythm of drums came from speakers hidden in the foliage. Naked bodies of every color and size were engaged in all manner of carnal pleasure on the sleek outdoor furniture. To Rob's right was a thick bodybuilder burying his bone with incredible ferocity into a smooth gymnast's ass. A ring of guys surrounded them, urging them on.

Rob stepped out from under the lanai into the light of the full moon. Several couples were floating in the black-tiled pool. One impressive specimen was stretched out on his back on the pool's edge. The profile of his body against the huge palm leaves behind him was perfection. The water cascading around him over the infinity edge created the sound of a waterfall.

A swarm of guys, most with their towels around their necks, were crowded into a lattice arbor. Designed to serve as an outdoor shower, tonight a sling hung from its four posts. At the center of it all was Erik, his legs held high in the sling's stirrups. All eyes were riveted on the giant stud standing in front of Erik. His monstrous cock, slick with lube, curved upward and caught the moonlight. Rob watched long enough to see him sink his sheathed meat deep into Erik's hungry hole.

Rob walked around the pool to get something to drink. He grabbed a bottle of water from an icy barrel and spotted a sexy Latin hunk. Rob could have sworn he'd seen him in a Kristen Bjorn video. Rumor had it that the director lived on South Beach, so maybe it was true.

Latin Hunk smiled at Rob and said in a heavily accented voice, "Fuck me, Papi." Latin Hunk then turned around to offer Rob one of the most incredible butts he'd ever seen.

Am I dreaming? Rob took his towel off, hung it over his shoulder, and began to stroke his already-hard dick.

Beau
Beau did his best to walk calmly back to their bungalow with the group despite, his urge to run. He'd barely been able to sit through dinner, tapping his foot under the table. He hardly touched his food and was sweating through his silk Versace shirt. Beau couldn't believe that tiny bit of white powder had such an effect on him. The conversation didn't help either, as all they did was talk about how difficult it was

traveling around the world from one hot spot to another. The only place mentioned that caught Beau's attention was Ibiza. The Movie Mogul and the Lesbian Designer couldn't say enough about it. "Bianca and Mick's daughter, Jade, has made it her second home. It's young and hip. It's all about parties. You really must go in August. We'll all be there." Beau tucked that one away for later discussion with Ira.

Entering the bungalow, Beau went straight to the second floor bedroom and changed into jeans and a tank top. VIP pass in hand, he kissed Ira and said, "Don't wait up for me. It'll probably be a late night. See you at breakfast." And off he went. He looked at his watch. *Damn, doors to the sex party closed over an hour ago. Make the best of it. Head to the Underwear Party. I'll run into Rob and Erik there.*

***

Beau flashed his VIP pass and was ushered into the lobby. Towering silver curtains framed the entrance. He followed the crowd through the doors into the Arena itself and was overwhelmed by the scale of the party. The place was packed with thousands of revelers in various states of undress. At the near end of the dance floor, Beau spotted a sign that said VIP and headed in that direction.

A bouncer with a shaved head and biceps the size of canned hams checked Beau's wristband and admitted him through the velvet ropes without so much as a nod or a smile.

Beau went directly to the bar and asked for a bottle of water. To his surprise, it was free. *Not bad*, he thought, *this is the way to do a circuit party*. Beau assumed he'd easily spot Rob and Erik since they both tended to stand out on a dance floor, but there were simply too many men. It was one huge seething mass of bodies. Beau headed out into the crowd. He needed to move among them and feel the heat of all those men.

Suddenly Beau felt a surge of energy. It was electrifying, but not in a good way. A certain paranoia began to build in him. He felt like the guys around him, who usually stared at him in admiration, had a different look in their eyes tonight. He felt like they were measuring him up. *Who are they to judge me? Do they have any idea who I just had dinner with?* He was a *somebody*, and they were all nobodies.

Where the hell are Rob and Erik? he wondered as he

pushed his way through the crowd of dancers. *We should have picked out a spot to meet. This is insane.* A feeling of desperation rose in Beau. The adrenaline surge continued. Beau's heart was pounding in his chest. So what if he couldn't find his buddies - he'd make some new ones. With his looks and body, he could always meet a few hotties on the dance floor. A shiver ran down Beau's back. The music changed from the electronically-altered vocals of Madonna to the driving rhythm of a tribal beat. It wasn't going to be sing-along music tonight. No waving your hands in the air. This was going to be dark and pounding.

This wasn't at all like Atlanta. Tina had an edge that Ecstasy didn't. Beau was grinding his teeth like a madman. Bodies were closing in from all directions, swallowing him up. He had to get out. Using the tall silver curtains as a landmark, he steered his way through the crowd. But no matter how many near-naked men he brushed past, they were replaced by an endless stream of more men.

Finally, the crowd began to thin. Then he stopped in his tracks. Between Beau and the beckoning silver fabric was a sight that at first he couldn't quite grasp. *What are those EMTs doing to that guy? Oh Jesus, they're cutting open his shirt. They're putting paddles to his chest.* Beau was frozen, riveted to the scene playing out in front of him. All the while, the partiers kept dancing, the music kept playing. *I'm watching somebody die,* Beau thought. He finally turned and barreled his way toward the lobby, trying to stay focused on the silver curtains.

He shivered when he felt cool fresh air wash over him. At last, Beau could see the glass exit doors, and his panic began to subside. His brain kicked back into gear. *Where the hell are Rob and Erik?* Then the answer came to him, and with it a rush to his groin. *They're still at the sex party!* He dug around in the pocket of his jeans. *Yes!* The address for the sex party was there. Maybe there'd be a chance to salvage the night. He hailed a cab.

***

When Beau arrived, the lights inside were on and he could hear dance music thumping away. *Good sign.* He wiped the sweat from his brow with his tank top, pumped out his chest, and he rang the doorbell. He was hoping that his tanned muscles would gain him entry even though he was several hours late.

The door opened and a handsome Latin face peered out.

"I know I'm late," Beau said, "but I'm a friend of Jake and Luca's."

"You missed them. They left hours ago. I'm Raul," the Latin said, checking out Beau's physique. "But you're welcome to come in. I'm having a little private party of my own." Raul stepped into full view, revealing that he was stark naked.

Beau felt an overwhelming rush. *Damn, the Party Promoter was right! This powder is better than Ecstasy.* He climbed the front steps and joined Raul inside. Beau saw that there were several other naked guys hanging out in the living room, all well built.

"Wanna bump of Tina?" Raul asked. Beau was already flying, but how long would it last?

"Sure," he replied. He had no plans for the next morning. As long as he got home before Ira woke up, he'd be golden.

Raul pulled out a bumper, a small bullet-shaped device, and loaded it for Beau. "Snort this," said Raul.

Beau did as he was told. His body was tingling from head to toe and he couldn't wait for the sensation to increase. He felt like he could fuck an entire football team. Beau began to strip. As each piece of clothing came off his passion intensified. When Raul returned with a bottle of water, Beau took him in his arms and started to kiss him. He experienced such a surge of lust that he felt as if he could eat Raul alive. "I have to fuck you!" Beau demanded.

Raul turned around and bent over the arm of the sofa. "I'm all yours. It's all ready for you, big boy. Give it to me raw."

Overwhelmed by the Tina racing through his system, Beau spit on his dick and slid it into Raul's hot wet ass. The rush made Beau feel like he was levitating. *Damn, this is gonna be one fun night after all.*

Sunday Morning

Ira & Beau

Beau felt incredibly horny when he returned to the Delano. It was as if fucking until dawn had only increased his libido instead of satiating it. After he showered, he lay down on the bed next to Ira and tried to fall asleep. His body was exhausted, but his mind kept racing. One image after another popped into his head, all replays from that night's non-stop sexual smorgasbord. Hungry mouths sucking his cock. Hands tugging on his balls and nipples. Tongues buried deep in his ass.

He must have dozed off briefly before he was awoken by Ira turning on the shower. Beau arose with a throbbing erection and joined him. He told Ira to turn around, soaped up his cock, and fucked Ira brutally until he exploded.

"What's gotten into you, young man?" Ira asked.

"I must have had a sexy dream. I woke up with a hard-on that needed to be taken care of."

Beau spent the rest of the day poolside with an obscene hard-on in his bathing suit while Ira snoozed. He thought about dragging one of the many men who cruised him back into the bungalow for a quick fuck but didn't want to risk a surprise visit from Ira.

Sunday Night

Rob & Erik

They felt like movie stars when they walked past the long billowing white curtains of the Delano's glamorous lobby and out onto the front terrace. Rob, Erik, and the Rocks were surrounded by beautiful men all dressed in white. The four of them had selected white 501's and an array of white t-shirts and tank tops.

"I think this is what heaven looks like," Gibraltar said as he scanned the crowd waiting for their cabs and limos.

". . . if God is a gay movie director," Alcatraz shot back.

"Speaking of heaven, last night's party was un-fucking-real!" Erik interrupted.

"I have to hand it to Jake and Luca," Rob agreed.

"I couldn't have handpicked a hotter crowd myself," Erik said. "It wasn't just the quality of the men. It was the setting, too."

"Having sex with all those beautiful men, outside in that tropical jungle was incredible," Rob concurred.

"Last night's was a total fantasy trip," Erik admitted. "I mean, it's what South Beach is all about. I can't imagine a single guy having been disappointed."

"Except the ones who got turned away," Alcatraz said.

"Or the ones who didn't get invited at all," Gibraltar added.

A model-gorgeous doorman opened the Delano's front doors and out stepped the Fashionistas, in their white crinkled Issey Miyake shirts and white Dolce&Gabbana jeans with glittering gold D&G logos over the rear pockets. They were followed by the Brazilians, who were a sight to behold in their skin-tight sailor pants and white leather chest harnesses. The piece-de-resistance was their matching white crystal-organza capes.

Karl and Curt looked at Rob, Erik, and the Rocks as if to say, *Don't start laughing or we'll all lose it.*

Exactly as promised, a white stretch limo pulled into the hotel's driveway at 6:00 pm sharp. An ever cheerful Bobby, in a see-through white tank top, popped out of the sunroof and hollered, "Hey y'all! Come on in and let's party!" Every person within earshot turned and stared as the eight New Yorkers piled into their chariot.

Big Daddy popped open a bottle of Domaine Chandon.

Bobby, in diaphanous harem pants and a white thong, said what everyone was thinking but afraid to say to the Brazilians, "You guys are so cute. You look like a gay Batman and Robin!"

Miami - *Vizcaya Estate & Gardens*

Ira & Beau
Ira had made a sizeable donation to the AIDS charity sponsoring the White Party to ensure that he'd be docked front and center at the base of the coral rock staircase leading up to Vizcaya, the Italianate mansion built by the heir to the International Harvester fortune at the turn of the century and the setting for tonight's benefit. The dock master informed Ira that he'd be in very good company as his dockside neighbor would be the Italian Designer, who was rumored to be hosting the Diva. Ira couldn't have been happier.

The upper deck salon was a sea of white. In a mix of comfortable and chic, the Movie Mogul had on white Levi jeans and a white silk Armani sweater, his face half-hidden under a white baseball cap. The Lesbian Designer was resplendent in a hand-beaded white wrap dress, while the Media Mogul had on a vintage white dinner jacket. Everyone looked their best.

Ira uncorked the first of many bottles of Dom Perignon and started handing out champagne flutes to his guests.

When they pulled into the dock, Ira noticed that the boat

beside them was indeed an expensive yacht - modern, pure white, and overflowing with gorgeous European model-types.

The Lesbian Designer confirmed the pedigree. "Oh my God!" she screamed. "It's them! Ciao bello!" she yelled like a drunken fishwife from their boat. "I see Mr. Underwear, and the Diva's with them, too!" She acted as if she couldn't wait to get off of Ira's small tugboat to schmooze with her designer pals.

After a toast to a great White Party, Ira announced that the boat would be departing at 10:00 pm to return everyone to the marina in South Beach. The Lesbian Designer made a beeline for the Italian Designer's yacht.

Beau gave Ira a peck on the cheek and said he wanted to go round up his friends from New York to bring on board for a drink. Ira thought it was a great idea. Little did he know that Beau had a slightly different agenda.

Ira settled back on the white cushions of the upper deck and joined the conversation.

"My sources say they have a tough door policy," the Media Mogul said. "They supposedly turned away several celebrities and porn stars."

"I heard a couple of guys talking yesterday around the pool at the Delano," the Movie Mogul chimed in. "You must have seen them, both huge, but short bodybuilders. Even they were afraid they wouldn't make it past the doorman."

"Today at breakfast there were two gorgeous German guys talking about the party," the Media Mogul said. "I couldn't help but overhear them. They said it was in a neighborhood with mansions."

"I'll ask Beau, Ira offered. "He's in the know about all that stuff. He's friends with that entire crowd."

The gossip session was interrupted by the Lesbian Designer, returning from the Italian Designer's yacht. "He'd like to invite you all over for a glass of Cristal. The Diva's over there with her new girlfriend, and she looks like a beautiful Cuban choirboy!" she exclaimed.

"We'll be right over. We're dishing the dirt about last night's secret muscle-boy sex party," the Movie Mogul said.

"Oh, you mean the HardBodies party?" she laughed.

"How do you know about it?" the Movie Mogul asked.

"Darling, *everyone* on their yacht is talking about it. Three of his models attended and are giving all the juicy details. It almost makes me wish I had a dick," she said.

"You don't?" the Movie Mogul asked.

"Bitch!" she shot back.

Beau took a path that led him into the woods surrounding Vizcaya. Once there he did a bump of Tina. *This will spice up the night,* he thought. His erection was almost painful as it strained against the fabric of his white Versace jeans. He reached down into his pants and straightened up his cock. *That feels better. It's going to feel even better when I get a hot mouth on it.* He felt like a wild beast hunting his prey. Moonlight filtered down through the thicket of tree branches. He saw someone light a cigarette up ahead and decided to go in that direction.

Jake & Luca
They parked their car on the road outside the grounds of Vizcaya, near Sly Stallone's estate, just a few blocks from where Madonna had recently bought a home. Jake and Luca were wearing nothing more than skin-tight, white shorts covered in row after row of crystal-beaded fringe. Luca shook a bottle of baby oil into which he'd added a small amount of iridescent glitter and rubbed the oil over their bodies. It made their muscles glisten. Jake was proud of his improved physique. He'd put on almost ten pounds of muscle since starting his steroid cycle. He finally thought his body was almost a match for Luca's. And the extra boost it had given his sex drive wasn't a bad side effect, either.

The boys exchanged their tickets for wristbands and walked down a long, sloping pathway bisected by an elegant stone water trough that cascaded down the grade. On either side were tall hedges covered with twinkling white lights. The effect was magical. Jake and Luca spotted guys they knew from the beach, the gym, and the clubs. Everyone seemed to want to give them a hug and a kiss. Some had attended the party and privately thanked them, not wanting the guys around them to know what they'd been up to the previous night. If Jake and Luca were flattered and a little bit embarrassed by all the attention, they were unaware of the wild speculation that was circulating about them.

Some in the crowd were pointing them out to their friends, "Those are the guys who threw the HardBodies party last night."

"Aren't they porn stars?"

"Escorts?

"Trust fund babies?" The little bits of misinformation whispered down the lane were creating quite a stir.

At the end of the pathway, a circular drive surrounded an

enormous fountain. Jake and Luca had arrived at the front entrance. They filed through intricate glass-and-wrought iron doors with the rest of the crowd and walked around the atrium that rose the full height of the three-story mansion. Upper walkways with arched openings looked down upon the inner courtyard. The crowd flowed into a reception room with ornate mirrored panels covering the walls. Then Jake and Luca stepped out of the house onto the massive terrace that looked out over the formal gardens. The party unfolded before them.

Walking up to the nearest bar, they ran into Rob and Erik. "Hey, guys. Congratulations on such a successful party!" Rob said.

"Your party was everything I fantasized it would be," Erik added. "Everyone had an unbelievable time."

"We're headed back to the dance floor with waters for the Brazilians. They were very sweet and got us a ride in a limo. The whole gang is out there. Join us," Rob said.

"We just arrived. We're going to wander around the gardens first and check out the crowd. We'll meet you on the dance floor later."

Jake and Luca explored the manicured grounds. They felt as if they'd been transported back in time to some French aristocrat's extravagant masked ball. All around them, people in outrageous costumes strolled through the gardens. Some wore towering headpieces that looked straight out of Las Vegas. Others wore animal masks encrusted with glittering beads. Each outdid the last.

They circled the gardens, passing entrances into the woods that bordered the estate. There were bodies moving in the shadows. They both knew that where there were woods and gay men, there was sex. But after last night's party, sex was the last thing on their minds. They'd had as much sex as they possibly could with the cream of the crop. Tonight was about meeting, greeting, and dancing with their friends.

On the dance floor, they easily spotted Rob and Erik. They were with the Rocks, the Fashionistas, and the Brazilians. Their group was like a magnet drawing a circle of hot muscle boys to them. Everyone was rolling on Ecstasy. They felt connected and happy to be celebrating with their friends. After all the death and disease that had followed them like a shadow, they were here to celebrate life. They remembered friends who were no longer with them. They could feel them in spirit, surrounding them with love and happiness. Those who had passed whispered, *"Dance for me. Enjoy life to the fullest. It's over so fast."*

Suddenly, Raul emerged from the crowd that encircled the boys. "Oh, my God! You guys are famous!" he exclaimed to Jake and Luca, yelling over the pounding music. "Everyone's talking about your HardBodies party."

Jake and Luca froze, hoping that not everyone in their group had heard him.

"*You guys* threw that sex party?" Curt burst out. He looked at Karl, who was as surprised as he.

"I should have guessed that you two were behind it," Karl said. "I want every detail!"

Jake and Luca wanted to kill Raul for spilling the beans. Stalling to come up with a response, they were saved by Beau who popped up out of nowhere.

"I knew I'd find you guys at the heart of the dance floor. I've been looking for you all night to invite you onto the boat for some champagne," he said.

Everyone stared at him.

Beau was soaked with sweat. His silk Versace shirt was hanging from his waist and his white jeans had dirt all over them. He was the perfect distraction from an uncomfortable moment.

Luca seized the opportunity. "We'd love some champagne. Where's your boat?" he asked.

Beau pointed to the base of the stairs leading down from the dance floor to the water.

"You mean the big boat that's starting to pull away?" Jake asked.

Beau got a panicked look on his face, turned around, and made a mad dash, pushing his way through the crowd. Everyone stopped and stared as he ran screaming and shoving. Beau reached the edge of the dock and took a flying leap toward the yacht. He made it by inches, grabbing hold of the railing. One of the crew helped him onto the deck.

"Now that's what I call a dramatic exit," Curt commented.

November 1994
South Beach

In the Press –
THE HOUSE OF GUCCI VS. THE HOUSE OF HARDBODIES

Just when this man-about-town thought nothing could shock him, events of last weekend on this billion-dollar sandbar surprised even myself. "Millionaire's Row" saw quite a lot of action between two very different groups of the body elite.

On the bay side, in a Greek revival mansion recently abandoned by a Saudi sheik, the House of Gucci held a fundraiser. All of South Beach's glitterati were there. Across the street an elite group of a very different kind, whose membership is based purely on muscle, was having a very different type of *soiree*.

No less than this author's personal trainer proved an excellent source for an insider's view of the steamy goings-on. Every bit as organized as the Gucci event, the South Beach HardBodies ran a tight ship. Only gay muscle boys needed to show up at the appointed time at a secret location on South Beach. There, muscled guards checked out your body from head to toe to see if you measured up. The approved candidates were given invitations that allowed them entry to the private home where the party was held.

While the glitterati were dropping off their furs across the street, the HardBodies were dropping their pants. Yes, clothing check was mandatory at the door. While the Gucci guests were sipping champagne, the naked muscle boys were drinking beer and getting busy. My eye witness said that at one point, there was so much moaning going on around the pool that it sounded like a cattle yard.

The scene must have been priceless as celebutantes waited for valets to bring around their Rolls and Bentleys while muscle boys across the street waited for yellow taxi cabs to return them to their hotel rooms on South Beach. It was just another week on this crazy billion-dollar sandbar.

November 1994
New York

In the Press – THE BEST PARTY YOU NEVER HEARD OF

Last weekend, yours truly had the audacity to knock
on heaven's doors. And yes, dear Readers, they
opened. It seems a gorgeous boy from the Island
moved to South Beach and fell in love with a porn star.
I know what you're thinking. It happens every day!
But these boys put their muscles to work and created
the hottest underground party of White Party weekend.

I was given a HardBodies card by the former Fire
Island boy at Body Tech Gym, with a cryptic message,
"We throw parties that you might enjoy." So, curious
cat that I am, I decided to call the number for South
Beach HardBodies. Lordy! The standards seemed a
bit high even for this musclehead, but I thought I'd
take a chance. Am I glad I did.

After a nerve-wracking once-over, where my abs and
pecs were inspected, I was approved. Invitation in
hand, I cabbed it north to a ritzy neighborhood.
Something tells me our Pines boy hit the lottery.

I arrived at a tropical paradise with a mandatory
clothing check. After a few walk-arounds, cold beer in
hand, and my hotel towel wrapped around my waist, I
had scoped things out. There was sex in the living
room, there was sex in the bedrooms, there was even
more sex around the pool.

I must say it was the most astonishing display of
muscle in motion that this jaded gym queen has ever
seen. Even the super-buff hosts of NYC's most talked
about, muscle-only, sex party of the year were
indulging in the all-you-can-eat man buffet. I threw
my towel to the breeze and got to know a little Euro-
hottie under South Beach's full moon.

Back in Manhattan, I feel like Cinderella after the ball.
Did it really happen? Did I really dance with the
prince? I'm keeping my fingers crossed that my little
Euro-hottie will knock on my door, hotel towel in hand
and say, "Did you leave this behind?"

Spring 1995

March 1995 - *Four Months Later / Black Party Weekend*
New York
Saturday Night

Rob & Erik

Rob couldn't stop looking at his new eyes in the bathroom mirror. The swelling had gone down thanks to nightly ice packs. The bruising was easily disguised with a little concealer. *Do I look younger?* Rob wanted people to see him and say, "Wow! You look great. What's different?" He couldn't understand why anyone would want to go through all the trouble, not to mention expense, and not have people notice. Cleverly, he switched his contact lenses from clear to a bright emerald to accentuate his green eyes. That way, he could claim, "Oh, it's my new contacts." Tonight's gathering at the Fashionistas' place before the Black Party would be the litmus test.

Putting aside thoughts of his new eyes for a moment, Rob turned his attention to the outfit he'd laid out for the party. Motorcycle boots, a codpiece, and leather chaps. What better way to show off his sculpted ass? He wore a studded leather harness across his pecs and a leather armband on his left bicep to indicate he was a top. A leather wrist cuff to hold his money finished off the look. He'd wear a motorcycle cap with a stiff shiny brim that he'd carry to the pre-party. He didn't want his eyes hiding in the shadows.

Erik also decided to wear a leather harness, chaps, and codpiece. He wore an armband on his right bicep to show he was a bottom. He wanted to be sure he sent out the right signals. While Erik dressed, he thought about the night ahead. Before meeting Rob and getting into the bar business, he'd never been much for nightlife. If he had his druthers, he'd rather have a few beers at home. Now, everyone in their social circle seemed obsessed with circuit parties. Rob thought it was important that they be seen at these events as PR for the bar. If guys were out having fun somewhere, he wanted to be there in the midst of it so they'd know that Jocks was part of the mix.

Big Daddy & Bobby

I'm so glad we decided against staying in another crazy designer hotel. This place is much more our speed, Big Daddy thought as he looked around their suite at the Plaza Hotel. He sat on the rose chintz bedcover listening to the sounds of

Bobby taking a shower. The blue striped upholstery matched the rose patterned fabrics, and the needlepoint carpet picked up the yellow in the fringe of the swagged curtains. From the moment they checked in, the Beverly Hillbillies felt like they were in a royal palace. Everywhere they looked they saw marble and shiny gold trim. *Now this is classy!*

Once he heard Bobby turn off the shower, Big Daddy got up and started pulling his own ensemble out of the closet. When Bobby entered the room, Big Daddy said, "You should go just like that, sweetie. You look perfect!"

"If you think I look good now, wait until you see me in my outfit. I'm so excited. I've never gone to a Black Party before. I must have tried on a dozen outfits at the leather store. I'm so glad you helped me pick this one out," Bobby said. "I hope I can remember how to get into it."

"I'll help you get dressed as soon as I'm done. I'm excited, too. It's like going to a costume party."

Big Daddy looked like the villain in a Mel Brooks movie. He was dressed in black cowboy gear from his boots to his hat. His black leather vest featured ornate black stitching all over it. On a smaller man, it might have looked sexy. On Big Daddy, it looked ludicrous. He was a huge overwhelming mountain of black.

"Well, don't you look snazzy!" Bobby complimented.

"Thanks, honey. It makes me feel dangerous. Now come over here and let me see if I can remember what gets buckled where."

The Fashionistas

While Curt was putting the finishing touches on his outfit for the evening's event, Karl answered the door.

"You look fabulous!" he declared when he let the Brazilians into the foyer. "Let me take your jackets." They all traded air kisses. "So what do you think?" asked Karl. "I'm going as rough trade."

The Brazilians looked at him and laughed. "In head-to-toe Dolce&Gabbana?" they both quipped.

Karl was sporting a black D&G t-shirt and matching D&G jeans. "I thought it was very understated and butch," he replied defensively, "especially with these motorcycle boots."

"But they're D&G too," Paolo stated before they moved into the living room. He and Tomàs had gone to The Leatherman in the Village and bought matching ensembles. They were wearing shiny, black leather boots to the knee with

210

black leather jodhpurs, motorcycle cop shirts made of black leather, and regulation motorcycle helmets.

"I love the helmets, but aren't they going to be kind of hot on the dance floor?" Karl chuckled.

"They're just for our entrance. We'll check them once we've done a walk through the crowd," Paolo replied.

Curt made his grand entrance into the living room. "Champagne, anyone?" he asked, making a dramatic turn.

"Please don't tell me that's all Gucci!" Tomàs practically shrieked.

"Well, it's a little Gucci here and there," he said as he pointed out the crossed G's on his silver belt buckle. "Feel this perforated leather. It's like butter," Curt directed. Willing hands went to the supple black skin of his shirt.

"Are those black suede Gucci loafers? You're killing me," Tomàs exclaimed, stopping just short of crouching to touch them.

"You're too much," Paolo cried out, failing to see the irony of his statement given what he was wearing.

"Well, I threw something together that I'd feel comfortable in. I'm not the type for uniforms," Curt said, not really caring if he caused offense.

"Shall we get the party started? Care for a bump of Special K?" Tomàs asked. He filled the small plastic bumper by tapping it on the back of his hand.

"No, thanks," Curt said. "And be careful mixing that with champagne. I once had a not-so-pretty experience."

The doorbell rang. "Excuse me," Curt said. He left Karl to attend to their guests. "Come on in and have some champagne," he greeted the Beverly Hillbillies. Curt was glad to take their jackets into the bedroom so that he could compose himself while the rest of the guests got a gander of the Lone Ranger and Tonto. *What possessed them?* he wondered.

Stepping into the living room, Bobby couldn't wait to pull down his black spandex shorts to show what he was wearing. "I think they call it a sling shot," he said. Bobby turned, modeling it for all to see. Conversation stopped as the boys looked at what appeared to be a g-string attached to suspenders. It was made of black leather straps with silver buckles to adjust it. It was the kind of thing that no one would dare wear out in public, not even Cher, but Bobby was clearly breaking new ground. His entire ass was exposed and his dick was barely stuffed into the front pouch.

Karl brought Curt a glass of Veuve Cliquot. "I thought you could use this."

"If I have to look at those outfits with a straight face all night, I'm going to need a few of these," Curt said under his breath.

"Take these *after* you get there," Tomàs instructed Big Daddy and Bobby. He tapped out two pills from his Tic Tac container. "There's nothing worse than waiting in line when your Ecstasy starts to kick in."

The Beverly Hillbillies had become curious about Ecstasy since they'd started hanging out with the Brazilians. Tonight, they were taking it for the first time.

"I won't do anything crazy, will I?" asked Bobby.

"No, you'll be fine. Hang out with us all night. We'll keep an eye on you," Paolo promised. "Just remember to drink a lot of water to stay hydrated."

The door bell rang again. It was Rob and Erik.

"Check out the eyes," Karl whispered when he passed Curt with their jackets.

"Hey guys! Great to see you. You're looking particularly fabulous, Rob. I don't know how you do it, running that bar and going out all night," Curt said as he studied Rob's eye job. *He's starting to look like he's wearing a mask. Is he wearing makeup, too?*

"Thanks," Rob replied, relieved that he'd made the desired impression. "You look fabulous, too. I love your Gucci belt."

Tomàs stumbled his way over to Rob, Erik and Curt on wobbly feet. His bump of K had kicked in. "And look at his Gucci loafers, they're beautiful," Tomàs slurred. As Rob and Erik looked down at Curt's feet, Tomàs bent over and puked all over the beautiful black suede shoes.

After gingerly placing his soiled loafers in a trash bag, to be dealt with later, Curt changed into his black lizard cowboy boots. He wanted to kill Tomàs. Hadn't he warned him about mixing booze with Special K? By the time Curt emerged from the bedroom, Paolo had cleaned up the mess and Karl had lit a few more scented candles to cover the smell. Tomàs's little accident had pretty much put everyone off their Veuve Cliquot.

"Where are Jake and Luca?" Curt asked. "I talked to them when they got into town. They said they'd be stopping by."

"They just called. The newlyweds were having sex and

lost track of time," Karl explained. "They'll meet us at the party."

Curt had arranged for a limo to take all of them to the warehouse where the Black Party was being held. They wanted to get there on the early side, around midnight, so they'd be able to see the show. Well, maybe "show" wasn't the best word to describe the entertainment that the Black Party provided on its stage. "Demonstrations" might be more apt. Tonight, as in previous years, lots of unusual sex acts would be performed for the enjoyment of the crowd. There would be something for everyone. At least one guy would do something disturbing with a giant python. It wasn't every day that you got to watch total strangers having sex under theatrical lighting.

***

The gang checked their jackets, and Bobby checked his shorts. Curt led them through the crowd toward the section of the dance floor closest to the stage.

"Now that we all know our *rendezvous* point, who's going to go get us waters?" Karl asked.

"We will," Big Daddy volunteered. "I want to show off my boy in his new outfit." He led Bobby through the crowd by the hand. Big Daddy loved all the stares they were getting. *Eat your hearts out, boys. He's all mine.*

Bobby was beaming from ear to ear from all the attention. He felt his dick begin to harden and push out of the inadequate pouch. If it were up to him, he'd walk around stark naked.

They ordered eight bottled waters from a stud that was nude except for riding boots. Big Daddy gawked at the enormous cock that swung as he walked. "Now I've seen everything," he said to Bobby while he waited for change from his fifty dollar bill. He was shocked when all he got back was two dollars, which he begrudgingly handed back to the bartender.

The Rocks appeared out of nowhere and stopped the Beverly Hillbillies in their tracks. "Boy, are we glad to see you," Gibraltar exclaimed.

"You're looking particularly special this evening," Alcatraz said to Bobby, warming him up for the request that was to follow. "We spotted you from way over there. You really stand out in that outfit."

"Yes, you do! And that's why we have an extra special

favor to ask of you," Gibraltar added.

"We're part of the show tonight, the opening act, in fact, and we lost one of our performers. We were wondering if you'd help us out," Alcatraz asked.

"What kind of show is it?" Big Daddy interrupted.

Before Alcatraz could answer, Bobby jumped in, "I used to be in shows!"

"Perfect! All you have to do is stand there and show off your body. We'll do the rest," Gibraltar replied.

Bobby looked at Big Daddy with eager eyes.

"Sure, baby, you can be in the show. I think you look beautiful tonight and should show everybody. Here, don't forget your pill." The Beverly Hillbillies slugged back their Ecstasy.

"OK, you need to come backstage with us so we can get you ready. The show starts in less than half an hour," Alcatraz said.

***

"You're not going to believe this," Big Daddy shouted over the music to the boys as he passed out the waters. "The Rocks just invited Bobby to be in the show."

"What does he have to do?" Rob asked cautiously, knowing what the Rocks had been rehearsing all week.

"They said he just has to stand there and look fantastic," Big Daddy said, barely audible above the pounding rhythm.

The boys were feeling the first wave of their Ecstasy when the lighting changed and the sounds of Carl Orff's "Carmina Burana" began. Flickering orange flames projected onto the curtains. Two bodybuilders appeared at opposite sides of the stage. Big Daddy and his group applauded wildly when they recognize it was the Rocks. Wearing nothing but black leather jock straps and black gladiator sandals tied up to their knees, they met center stage, grabbed the curtains, and pulled them back to reveal the set - ancient Rome burning in ruins. The flames were painted scarves that naked dancers were fluttering to the music, producing the overall effect of an inferno. Tied to a central column was Bobby. His hands were bound overhead by a gigantic knot of rope that secured him to the stone pier.

Big Daddy leaned over to Tomàs and pointed up to the stage. He shouted over the music into his ear, "My boy looks like saint what's-his-name. I want you to paint a portrait of him, like that."

214

Tomàs nodded in agreement. "Sure, why not?" His Ecstasy made him agreeable to anything.

The Rocks fell to their knees in front of the bound boy. They licked and kissed their way up his legs as he writhed in ecstasy. Obviously, Bobby's E was kicking in. His cock pushed his leather pouch out and away from his body. The Rocks worked their mouths up to his balls and start licking the leather pouch. Then they reached up and pulled down the pouch. Out sprung Bobby's raging hard-on. The crowd went wild. Bobby, who was blindfolded, started writhing in pleasure as his long cock dripped precum. It glistened as it caught the spotlight. Gibraltar rolled a black condom down the length of Bobby's cock while Alcatraz continued to lap at his balls. They started spitting on Bobby's shiny black cock. It throbbed to the beat of the music. Gibraltar bent over in front of Bobby, giving the audience a view of his ass. He then pivoted and impaled himself on Bobby's hard dick. The audience cheered.

"I love watching my baby have a good time. He's so hot, isn't he?" Big Daddy raved.

"Oh, yeah. He certainly looks like he's having a great time," Tomàs responded, but Big Daddy was lost in the onstage spectacle.

The Rocks were taking turns bouncing on Bobby's dangerous-looking cock. It looked massive sticking out from such a short muscle boy. First, Alcatraz shot his load into the air while riding Bobby, showering the audience. Then it was Gibraltar's turn. His load shot even further. The crowd didn't seem to mind being hosed down with the performers' DNA. Then the Rocks removed Bobby's condom and started using their mouths in unison to bring him to orgasm.

Meanwhile, Big Daddy had slowly moved toward the stage, unconsciously making his way through the crowd. He was almost at the edge of the stage when Bobby erupted and managed to splatter Big Daddy's black cowboy hat and shirt with thick white jizz. "Now that's my boy!" he yelled. Rubbing the white cum into his black shirt Big Daddy hollered to no one in particular, "It's raining men, hallelujah!"

Jake & Luca

They arrived at the Black Party at least an hour later than they'd promised Karl. When they approached the entrance, the beat of the music was so strong that they could feel it before they actually heard it. It pounded in their chests. Then the immense rusted door swung open, and they were overwhelmed by the sound. Pumping music pummeled their ears. It sounded like a factory full of wildly crashing machines, all with an underlying rhythm.

The air was warm and humid. It smelled like a men's locker room. The lighting was all red pinspots. Waiting for their eyes to adjust, they realized that they were being sized up. Men were everywhere, dangerous and exotic. Some were cloaked from stem to sternum in leather. Like others around them, Jake and Luca wore nothing but black jockstraps and black combat boots. Luca looked on in amazement at the tattoos and body piercings that surrounded them. Entire backs were inked with angel's wings. Others had intertwined bodies of snakes or dragons. One man had a steel bar that passed through one prominent nipple across his chest to the other. Some men had rings hanging from their noses.

Jake and Luca moved through the industrial space, eating up the attention. Returning some of the glances thrown their way, they locked eyes with men of every color and physique. There were huge white men who looked like they lived life in underground gyms, their pale skin glowing in the dimness, and black men whose ripped muscles were oiled to ebony perfection. Hungry eyes were everywhere.

The crowd got thicker enroute to the bar. Jake and Luca were shoulder to shoulder, balls to ass. When Luca's chest brushed against the bare back of the man in front of him, the stranger reached around and squeezed Luca's crotch. Finally, Jake made eye contact with the bartender and ordered two Coronas. Then he and Luca merged back into the throng.

At last, they emerged into a three-story space. The heat and humidity increased as they moved toward the heart of the dance floor in search of their buddies. There was a lighting grid up in the rafters. The flashing, spinning lights and the size of the crowd made it impossible to find their friends. Jake and Luca gave up the hunt and gave in to the unstoppable force around them. Everyone was moving to the beat in a way that went beyond dancing. The musky smell of sweat and sex was overwhelming. It was the primal scent of males. The animal connection was tangible. They danced for what seemed like hours.

Jake and Luca swam through the sea of men to grab an ice

216

cold beer. Suddenly, they heard the sound of naked flesh being slapped. A man with black rubber boots up to his thighs was suspended in a leather sling. His booted feet were spread apart in stirrups. He was covered in tribal tattoos. One butt cheek was flaming red from the big hands of his Master who was slapping his ass. The rough hands of his Master were forcing Crisco straight from the can into his sling pig's hole. The Master started greasing his own hand with it, continuing up his hairy forearm.

Luca noticed something odd about the Master's earlobes – they were stretched with silver dollar-sized black rubber plugs. *He looks like the Wild Man of Borneo*, Luca thought. His face had several piercings, too. His big hairy cock had been pierced along its entire length with a series of bars. A heavy Prince Albert hung from his piss slit. He started to swirl his greasy fingers around the sling pig's hole, teasing him. He opened him up with four fingers, and the rapt audience grunted in approval. Then his thumb slid in as well and he started twisting his hand. The pig in the sling loved it and pushed down. *Whomp!* In went the entire hand. The crowd cheered. The Master started pumping and twisting his arm. It slowly sank in.

The Master removed his arm and greased up a bright orange traffic cone. The sling pig's hungry dilated hole pulsated in anticipation. Jake and Luca were so engrossed by the main attraction that they'd barely noticed the side show. A man with an enormous hard-on and balls like a bull was being shaved from head to toe while restrained on a slanted table. As shaving cream was wiped off the guy's crotch, several men advanced with thick white candles and began dripping hot wax over his just-shaved genitals. The restrained guy's huge hard cock started bouncing up and down. He howled and shot his load all the way up to his chin.

Their thirst still unquenched, Jake maneuvered his way through the crowd with Luca holding his hand. Seductive smiles and lingering pats on their asses accompanied their progress toward the bar. These bartenders were all wearing black rubber aprons and boots. Long rubber gloves protected them as they searched the barrels of icy water for bottles of beer. Every time one of them turned around and bent over, there was the shock of seeing a naked body against black rubber. These men must have been chosen for their spectacular asses. Each one was a prize winner. These boys could put themselves through college with the tips they were raking in tonight.

When one of the boys turned around, he and Luca instantly locked eyes. It was New Face, his co-star from the Priapus shoot. Despite the unpleasant incident with Southern Discomfort, they'd connected with one another on the set and enjoyed each other's company. "Luca! What a great surprise. I should have known you'd be here," cried out New Face. With that he jumped over the bar to offer up a hug. Looking over Luca's shoulder, he saw Jake. "You must be the boyfriend. I'm pleased to meet you."

Jake knew exactly who New Face was. He'd seen him in action in Luca's video.

"So, what are you guys up to? 'Cuz I'm done my shift," he said with a mischievous grin. New Face reached across the bar and one of the other bartenders handed him his bag of clothes. He dropped his rubber apron and got dressed, holding onto Jake for balance.

Luca couldn't help but notice the smile on Jake's face. "I have an idea," he suggested to New Face. "I think we've had enough public entertainment, now it's time for some private fun. Want to join us?" Luca checked his watch. He was amazed at how time had flown. *Is it really near dawn?*

"Count me in," New Face said with a smile. "Can we go back to your place?"

They headed toward the exit. Jake and Luca fished for their coat-check tickets down in their socks. They found the soggy remnants. Handing over the barely-readable stubs, they were amazed that they yielded anything. They quickly pulled on their track pants, t-shirts, and jackets. Making their way through a dark tunnel, the three of them eventually came to the enormous rusted door that opened to the outside. They stepped into the harsh light of day. All three squinted as they searched in their pockets for their sunglasses. Suddenly, they were surrounded by everyday people going about their everyday lives, oblivious to what was going on behind the nondescript rusted door.

Luca hailed a cab and the three of them piled into the back seat. "The Paramount Hotel, please," he told the driver.

New Face was beaming from ear to ear. "Have I got a surprise for you boys!" he exclaimed. "All night long guys would go to pay for their beers and when they rummaged around for bills, all sorts of things fell out of their pockets. I nearly twisted my ankle when I stepped on one of these." He reached into his sock and pulled out two bullets filled with white powder. "I'm not certain what's in them. Cocaine or

218

Special K? Wanna give them each a try and find out?"

Jake grimaced. "No thanks." He didn't care for either drug.

"Are you sure?" New Face asked. "It'll put us in the proper frame of mind for some serious playtime. I want you boys to do me every which way possible!"

Luca shook his head. "Shouldn't we wait?" he asked, dead set against the prospect of getting fucked up before they reached the safety of their hotel.

"A little bump won't hurt," responded New Face. "I think I'll start with the blue one. It's my favorite color." He tapped the bullet and snorted some of the powder. "I'm pretty certain this is Special K. Here," he said as he reloaded the bullet and handed it to Luca, "do a bump and tell me if this is coke or K."

"Sorry, I'm not an expert at these things," Luca answered. He handed the bullet back to New Face.

"Well, no sense in having it go to waste," he responded. New Face raised the bullet to his nose and took another snort. "Definitely Special K," he stated with no uncertainty. He placed the blue bullet in his jacket pocket. "Now let's see what the pink one has in it." New Face began to load the second bullet.

"How about if we assume they're both filled with Special K?" Luca suggested.

New Face was undeterred. "Don't worry it's just a little bump." he responded. He raised the pink bullet to his nostril and snorted. "You sure you don't want to try some?"

"No thanks, one of us has to stay sober to pay the cab driver," Luca laughed, trying to make light of what was becoming an uncomfortable situation.

"Wow . . . ," slurred New Face as the drug began to take effect. "The pink stuff is a lot stronger than the blue. I can barely see straight." At that moment the cab hit a pothole. The three of them slid across the seat and slammed into each other. "Oh fuck," burbled New Face as he hit Luca's shoulder and slumped forward.

"Come on, puppy. Get your act together," Luca said. He tried to maneuver New Face back into an upright position only to have him slump against Jake. His eyes had a glassy faraway look.

"What the fuck . . . ?" Jake said. He grabbed New Face and shook him. He got no reaction.

Luca noticed the cab driver glancing into the rear view mirror to see what was going on. "Roll down the window and get some cold air in here," Luca barked.

"But he's in a K-hole," Jake answered, the panic in his

voice rising.

"I know that," answered Luca. "The cold might help bring him around."

"We can't drag him into the hotel like this. What the fuck do we do?"

"Calm down," Luca insisted through gritted teeth. He quickly assessed their options. They were several blocks from the Paramount. If he didn't act fast, the cabbie would order them out of the car. "Driver," Luca commanded, "take us to the nearest emergency room."

"What are you doing?" Jake asked.

"I'm taking control of this mess," Luca responded.

New Face began to come around just before they pulled into the emergency entrance. "Unnnhha," he mumbled, and drool spilled from his mouth.

"Wake up," Jake demanded. He raised his hand and slapped New Face with enough force to leave an imprint on his cheek.

New Face popped open his eyes and took in the unfolding scene. "Wow, where are we?" he asked.

"We had to take a little detour. Are you OK?" Luca calmly asked.

"Yeah, sure. What a cool out-of-body experience that was!" he proclaimed. "Can't wait to get to your hotel. You boys ready to play?"

"Not today, big boy. You need to rethink what you just put us through," answered Luca. He eased New Face out of the cab and closed the door.

April 1995 - *One Month Later*
Beverly Hills

Ira & Beau

"Beau tells me that you have a proposal for us," Ira said in his business voice. He was eager to hear what the Party Promoter was offering in exchange for Fuji's images of Beau.

"I think Beau represents the epitome of the kind of guy that every one of my attendees aspires to meet," replied the Party Promoter. "I'd like to make him the face of all of my parties, starting with the upcoming one in Palm Springs."

Beau could become the face of his generation, thought Ira. *Stranger paths have led to stardom.* "OK, I can understand why you'd want to use those images. But initially, Beau signed a release for use by Fuji solely for his

220

calendar, not advertisements. What's in it for Beau?"

"I have an idea that we talked about," Beau jumped in. "I'd like to get involved with the promotion of the parties. I want to add my name as co-host. That way everyone will know I'm involved. The possibility of meeting me in person at one of the parties could be a big draw," Beau said without embarrassment.

"As you can imagine, I have to invest quite a bit of capital to get these parties off the ground," the Party Promoter stated. "There's the rental of the space, the equipment, the set up. There's advertising. And that's an area where I think Beau could be advantageous. He could do interviews with the gay press. Who wouldn't want to print those photos along with comments by the model?"

"I can also imagine that you make a nice profit, otherwise you wouldn't be in the party business," stated Ira.

"Yes I do, and I make a point of donating a portion of the net proceeds to local AIDS charities," the Party Promoter explained.

"How much do you want Beau to contribute to have his name alongside yours as party host?" Ira asked point blank.

"The initial outlay would be minimal compared to the possible profits we'd be sharing. I'm sure we can arrive at a figure that both of you will be comfortable with."

"Before I commit to a number, I'd like to see figures from previous parties. You know, how much outlay versus the cash coming in from ticket sales and your percentage of the bar," Ira answered.

"No problem. I can get you the info by the end of the week." The Party Promoter knew full well that his profits were never shown on paper. The cash collected from tickets sold at the door was stashed in a safe deposit box, away from the prying eyes of the IRS. For a nominal investment, he could guarantee a nice return on Ira's money, while still keeping the lion's share of the profits for himself.

The Party Promoter thanked Beau for selling the deal to Ira by giving him a small bag of white powder. "Remember, just do one small bump," the Party Promoter said, "it's potent stuff."

May 1995 - *Six Weeks Later / Memorial Day Weekend*
Fort Lauderdale
Thursday

Big Daddy & Bobby

"We're really looking forward to it," exclaimed Big Daddy. He lay naked on Jake's massage table. The Beverly Hillbillies were already packed for the big party weekend in Palm Springs. Bobby had placed their suitcases by the front door. Jake was horrified at the thought of Big Daddy dancing in public in nothing but his Calvin Klein's at the weekend's highlight, the Underwear Party.

When asked if he and Luca would be attending, Jake simply said, "No, Luca has to work." He thought it best not to mention that Luca had already left for Palm Springs to shoot a video with David Fujimoto. With any luck, their schedules would be at such odds that they'd never cross paths.

"Bobby and I have a surprise for you and Luca!" Big Daddy announced while the three of them relaxed in the hot tub looking out over the Intercoastal. Jake got goose bumps in spite of the hot water swirling around him. *With these two, almost anything is possible,* he thought.

"Go ahead, Bobby, tell Jake," Big Daddy said with a big grin.

"We're going to Ibiza! Big Daddy's rented a villa on the side of a mountain for the first two weeks of August. We'd like you and Luca to come along!" Bobby squealed, bubbling over with excitement.

"Everything is our treat! Even the airline tickets!" Big Daddy seemed as excited as Bobby.

"Wow! I don't know what to say." *Honestly,* Jake thought, *this was the last thing I expected.* "I'll check and see if it works with Luca's schedule."

"Well, let us know as soon as you can so we can book the flights," Big Daddy said, sounding a little miffed that he hadn't gotten an instant, enthusiastic yes.

"I just want to run it by Luca. You know, the exciting life of a porn star, and all," Jake said, thinking, *Oh, God! What if Luca says absolutely not?*

"It's going to be so much fun!," Bobby exclaimed. "We can't wait. The Brazilians have already confirmed. You don't know the other guys yet, but you'll like them. They're so much fun. It's my workout partner, Bluto, and his boyfriend."

Are we all expected to have sex with you? Jake wondered. The prospect of the trip delighted and horrified him at the same time.

222

South Beach
Friday

Jake

He was getting into his car when a young lady walked up the driveway behind him.

"Excuse me, are you Jake Smyth?" she asked.

What's this about? Jake wondered briefly before answering, "Yes, I am. Can I help you?"

"I have a registered letter for you," she said. She gave Jake a clipboard and a pen. He signed his name and she handed him the envelope.

It was from a law firm in downtown Miami. *Maybe it's about Sean's will. It's about time I heard something final.* Jake wanted the security of knowing that everything Sean had wanted was settled. Since he was already running late for his massage appointment with Hunt, and knew he was going to hit traffic, he'd open it when he got to Hunt's.

***

Jake drove up to the gate of Hunt's estate and pushed the button on the intercom.

"Hello!" Hunt said in a cheerful voice. The heavy gate rolled back on its tracks. Jake parked in front of the garage door behind which the Rolls Royce was kept. Hunt only used the Rolls to drive to the ballet. The BMW sedan, the Mercedes coupe, and the Jaguar convertible were behind the other garage doors.

"I got some kind of registered letter from a law firm and haven't opened it yet. I'm hoping it's about Sean's will."

"Well, come on in and we'll read it together," Hunt said.

Jake followed Hunt down the entry hall and into the master bedroom, where he set down his massage table. They both sat on the edge of the king-size bed. Hunt put on his reading glasses while Jake opened the envelope.

He read it through quickly and handed it to Hunt. "I don't understand," was all Jake could manage.

Hunt read the letter carefully. "Well, honey, it looks like the executors of Sean's will are suing you to recover your house as part of the estate."

"But they were his best friends - how can they do that? They knew that Sean wanted me to have the house. He had it all planned out. I don't understand this." It felt like the house was all that Jake had left of Sean. There was no way that he'd let them take it from him.

"Don't you worry. I'll get my lawyer to take a look and see what we need to do. If worse comes to worse, you can always live here with me," Hunt said, unaware of the fact that Jake and Luca were now living together. Hunt's solution was no solution at all. Jake was not about to leave Luca.

Palm Springs
Friday

Ira & Beau
Who would have guessed when local boy turned Party Promoter started his Underwear Party in Palm Springs that it would grow to thousands of attendees, bringing in over a million dollars in revenue? Beau intended to increase those numbers and truly put Palm Springs on the international party circuit. He'd blanketed all the gay venues in LA with flyers and posters. He gave interviews to all the gay rags. The press ate it up. After all, he was David Fujimoto's star model and his photo was on every piece of promotional material. He was making a huge splash as Fuji's poster boy.

Ira watched as Beau intently reviewed his notes. He was pleased to see him applying himself to something. Maybe this would turn into an income for Beau. It didn't matter to Ira. He was just happy to see him focused. What Ira didn't know was that instead of a morning cup of coffee, Beau started most days with a bump of Tina. It kept him going all day. He believed it made his thinking clearer. He scribbled endless lists of ways to help promote the parties and improve them. Beau was an unstoppable ball of energy.

Ira had rented a spectacular home built in the '50s for a prominent member of the Rat Pack. He and Beau would be staying there for a week before and a week after Memorial Day. The sprawling ranch was in remarkable shape, considering it hadn't been renovated in several years. All the rooms had sliding glass walls that retracted and opened to the pool.

After unpacking, Beau dressed and borrowed the car. He wanted to hit the gym and start spreading the news that he, the poster boy and co-promoter of the Underwear Party, was in town. First, he'd stop by the host hotel and see how things were coming along, then he'd hit all the bars to make sure they had their posters and flyers. Maybe he'd get lucky along

224

the way.

Big Daddy & Bobby

They felt like they were returning home when the taxi dropped them off in front of Inn Exile. They both loved nude gay resorts like the one where they'd originally met in Key West and this one where they'd first met the Brazilians. The Beverly Hillbillies enjoyed the Brazilians' company and the guaranteed sex that came with their acceptance of invitations to join them on trips and vacations. Little did they know that the Brazilians would rather be checking in with the Fashionistas at the ever-so-chic health spa across town, but artists didn't have that type of money. Sweat equity was another matter. If a little sex got them to Palm Springs on Big Daddy's dime, then so be it.

The Beverly Hillbillies had booked poolside rooms, affording them beautiful views of the Inn's infamous waterfall as well as the best vista for scoping out the poolside action. Big Daddy would send Bobby out as bait to lure the hot boys back to their suite. He expected the Brazilians to be quite a draw as well. If all went according to plan, there would be hot and cold running boys throughout their stay.

While the Beverly Hillbillies were getting settled in their room, Fuji was checking in at Inn Exile's front desk. The following day he was set to shoot a video of his models splashing in and around the resort's waterfall and pool. He'd come up with the idea after talking to Ira.

He'd told Fuji that he was missing the boat by just shooting still photos. "Film a video of one of your photo shoots. Who wouldn't want to see beautiful young men in action as they pose and play in front of your camera?"

The Fashionistas

They generously tipped the bellman, who swept away their Louis Vuitton luggage, and scurried out of the desert heat and into the lobby of the Twin Palms Spa. The smell of eucalyptus mixed with the heady perfume of rich women. When the Brazilians suggested that they stay with them and the Beverly Hillbillies at Inn Exile, the Fashionistas knew exactly where they *didn't* want to be. They were not about to stay at some nudist resort. Twin Palms was the new hot spa for all of their clients, the women who had made an art of spending their successful husband's money. Karl and Curt had to check it out.

Both boys eyed the roly-poly grand dame checking in ahead of
them at the front desk. They both recognized her from the
columns of *Women's Wear Daily*. She was one of the ladies
who lunch. Karl's first thought was, *She's got one of those
cutesy names that only WASPs can get away with.*

   "Welcome back to Twin Palms, Mrs. Conrad-Wright.
This young lady will escort you to your bungalow. If there's
anything I can do for you, please feel free to call on me."
Barely acknowledging the man behind the desk, the human
beach ball waddled after her tall blond escort. The
Fashionistas marveled that Chanel suits came in such large
sizes.

Saturday Morning

Luca arrived at Inn Exile at 6:00 am, an hour before the shoot
with Fuji was to begin. Luca loved being photographed. He
intuitively understood how to look into the camera and seduce
the photographer. Due to his burgeoning career in porn, he
knew how to work in front of video cameras as well. He was
told he was to be re-teamed with Beau. Luca was looking
forward to perhaps getting some private performance time
with Beau, whom he hadn't seen him since his abrupt
departure from Miami's White Party.

Beau had been up all night, first hitting all the hot spots to
make sure they had plenty of promotional material for his
party, then spending the rest of the night fucking a guy who
had shared some Tina with him. He was still flying when he
arrived at Inn Exile.

All of the models were gathered poolside, knoshing on bagels
and drinking coffee, when Beau arrived at 7:00 am. He wasn't
hungry in the least.
   Then Fuji arrived carrying several cases of video and
photographic equipment. He looked around, greeting all the
models with a big hug. When Fuji saw Beau, he froze. "Are
you OK?" he asked.
   "Sure. Never been better. Why?" Beau replied.
   "Your whole body is shaking. I know you can't be
shivering in this heat," Fuji said. He then turned to the other
models, "Speaking of heat, let's get things rolling before it gets
too hot. I want to get a few hours in before we all take our

226

midday siesta. We'll resume shooting as the sun sets," he said to the assembled boys. "OK, enough eating. I want flat tummies."

Several naked guests were taking in the sights of the models stripping down. The Beverly Hillbillies were among them. The Brazilians were still sound asleep. This was a detail that Big Daddy would have to take up with them. As long as he was footing the bill, they could damn well get their asses out of bed at an appropriate hour so they could all eat breakfast together.

Fuji watched Beau fold and refold his shorts and tank top in a pile with his sneakers. Something wasn't right, but he couldn't quite figure out what it was. When Beau stood up straight, Fuji was concerned. Beau was more ripped than ever, but gone were the voluptuous muscles that had made him a cover boy. Now Beau's body was all sharp angles.

Is he sick? was the first thought that ran through Fuji's mind. Pulling Beau aside, he asked, "What's wrong, Beau? Talk to me."

"I told you, nothing's wrong. Why do you ask?"

"You've lost weight. I can see it in your face. And you've lost some muscle mass, too. Is your health alright?" Fuji asked, concerned.

Something inside Beau snapped. "What exactly are you accusing me of?" he snarled.

"Nothing. It's just that you won't photograph as well as before. You're a little too lean."

"Are you talking about not shooting me? I'm your star, your poster boy. Remember? It's my face and body that got you where you are. How dare you think of not using me!" Beau screamed.

Luca couldn't believe the hissy fit Beau was throwing. *Is he crazy?* Luca thought. *You never bitch at the man who's pointing the camera at you.*

Beau was fuming. He stormed off stark naked carrying his clothing. *Wait until I tell Ira that Fuji doesn't want to use me. I look better than ever!* He got several odd stares as he dressed in the lobby.

***

"Well, look who decided to wake up," Big Daddy growled at the Brazilians when they joined him and Bobby poolside with their morning coffee at 8:00 am.

"Good morning," Paolo mumbled, not quite awake yet.

"The early birds sure caught the worm today," Bobby chirped.

"Huh?" Tomàs asked as he slugged down his java

"One of the models over there just had a shouting match with the director. He grabbed his clothes and left in a huff, without a stitch on!" Bobby exclaimed, thrilled to have witnessed the whole scene.

Tomàs and Paulo turned to look. "Sounds like we did miss out. How long has this been going on?" Paolo asked.

"Oh, for at least half an hour. That's why it pays to get up nice and early. You missed all the drama, but you're just in time for the action by the looks of things.'

"The guy sitting with his back to us looks familiar. Isn't he Jake's boyfriend, Luca?" Bobby inquired, straining to see if it was who he thought it was.

"Bobby honey, swim over and find out if that's him? Wouldn't it be fun to watch Luca shoot a video?" Big Daddy asked with a leer.

Without a moment's hesitation, Bobby dove into the pool and swam over to the model. When he came sprinting back he said, "It is Luca! He didn't say much but said he'd stop by when he got a break. I think we've met the guy who stomped off. We saw him with Luca in the pool at the LA fundraiser and again at the Barbra Streisand concert with the guy in the Panama hat. He looked terrible. That's why I'm afraid to miss even one day at the gym. I'm scared I'll fall apart and Big Daddy won't love me any more," Bobby confessed a bit too honestly.

"Don't be silly, baby. I'd love you no matter what. But you look so pretty, it would be a shame to let it all go downhill, now wouldn't it." Big Daddy stated. "You wouldn't want to end up looking like me, now would you?"

The Fashionistas

Karl and Curt let the heat sink in as they settled into their outdoor mud baths. They sipped ice cold mineral water garnished with thick slices of cucumber and wondered what the Brazilians were up to across town. Just then, an enormous woman in a pink sweatsuit went trudging by. The poor thing's face was as fuchsia as her ensemble.

Jogging in this desert heat? Is she crazy? Well, it's one way to lose fifty pounds of baby fat, Karl thought.

Ira & Beau

"What are you doing home so soon?" Ira asked

innocently.

Then the bomb exploded, "That asshole so-called friend of yours said I wasn't good enough for his video shoot!" Beau screamed, the veins standing out on his neck.

Ira had never seen Beau in a state like this. "There must be some misunderstanding."

"Oh, no. I understood him perfectly. It was my photos that made him famous, and this is how he repays me? My photos are all over town. HOW DARE HE!" Beau screamed, spittle flying from his mouth.

"Calm down. I'll straighten it all out with Fuji. You go take a shower and a nap. I'll wake you up when lunch is ready," Ira said.

Beau stormed off down the hall. Although he wanted neither a nap nor lunch, he decided to take a sleeping pill and a hot shower to relax. Maybe he'd been working too hard. He needed some rest.

Ira convinced the desk clerk at Inn Exile to carry a message out to Fuji.

In less than five minutes, Fuji returned the call. "Ira, I'm so sorry," Fuji began.

"What happened?" he asked. "Beau was so angry he could hardly speak. I want to hear your side of the story."

"Well, when I hugged Beau, I thought something was odd. He was shaking. Then he stripped down, and I was shocked."

"What do you mean?" Ira asked.

"He's lost a lot of weight. So I asked him is he was alright. I mean, right away I thought of his health."

"His health?" Ira's face turned ashen.

"Yes, even his face looked thin. Maybe it's none of my business, but he created quite a scene. I'm worried about him, Ira."

"I know he's been working hard on this Underwear Party, but I haven't noticed any weight loss."

"Maybe it's because you see him every day. For me, it's been a while. If it's not his health, could it be drugs? You know, a lot of these boys party too hard."

"Well, I know he's in perfect health. He hasn't even had a cold since I've known him. He goes out at night a lot, but he's working the bars to promote this party. I think I'd know if he was using drugs. Maybe I haven't been paying close enough attention. If it's drugs, I'll send him straight to Betty Ford. I have plenty of friends there," Ira answered with a hollow laugh.

"Ira, I didn't mean to upset him, but honestly, I was

shocked. I just blurted things out. I'm so sorry. Please, let me know if there's any way I can make it up to Beau. Maybe I can use him tomorrow. You know, the camera does add ten pounds or so," Fuji said, trying to sound optimistic.

"I'll get back to you after he settles down. He's taking a nap right now," Ira replied, trembling when he hung up.

Beau didn't have any sleeping pills, and he wanted to take one before his shower. No problem, he'd get some from Ira's stash. Naked, he padded down the hall. He opened the medicine cabinet and found it empty. *Where would Ira put his travel kit?* he wondered. *Under the sink? Bingo!* There it was right next to a stack of fresh towels. He pulled out a bag of pills. *Damn, Ira came prepared.* Beau read the labels, looking for a familiar name. What he read took his breath away. One large container had Retrovir printed on it. *Why would Ira be taking Retrovir? That's an AIDS drug.*

Shaking with anger, he clutched the bottle and went to confront Ira. "What are these?" Beau asked, shaking the bottle of pills.

Ira broke out into a cold sweat. "How dare you snoop around in my bathroom!"

"I wasn't snooping. I was looking for a sleeping pill. Why are you taking Retrovir?" Beau demanded, on the verge of hysteria.

Ira fell silent. What could he say? All thoughts of Beau's possible drug problem evaporated in the face of his own guilt.

"You have AIDS and you haven't told me?" Beau screamed.

"I'm HIV-positive. I've never had any symptoms. My t-cells are high. I don't have AIDS," Ira insisted, his eyes filling with tears. His worst fears had come to pass. His dirty little secret had been exposed.

"You liar! You could have given me AIDS!" Beau threw the bottle at Ira. It hit the wall and shattered, pills flying everywhere.

"That's not possible. I've never fucked you," Ira sobbed, trying to defend himself. "I'll take you to my doctor and have you tested. You can't be positive. I know it."

"How do you know? What else have you lied to me about?"

"Nothing, I swear. I'll do anything to make it up to you," Ira pleaded. Tears rolled down his face. He couldn't remember the last time he'd cried. No, that wasn't true. He'd cried ten years ago when his doctor had told him that he was

230

positive.

"You bet you'll make it up to me, or I'll tell every one of your big shot Hollywood friends that you gave me AIDS!" Beau turned and practically ran back to his bedroom and slammed the door.

My life is over, Ira thought. *I might as well be a murderer.*

Saturday Night

Big Daddy & Bobby
At 10:00 pm sharp the Brazilians headed out to join the Beverly Hillbillies in the limo that Big Daddy had hired to take them to the Underwear Party. While they thought it ridiculous to arrive at any party before midnight, their hosts thought it was imperative to be there before the crowds arrived. As expected, the Beverly Hillbillies were impatiently awaiting them. Big Daddy was wearing a matching white Polo shirt and shorts.

Tomàs's first thought was, *How many "X's" are there before the "L" on that label?*

The Brazilians tried not to cringe when they checked out Bobby's ensemble. He was wearing a white headband. They hadn't seen one of those since *Flashdance*. His barely-there tank top looked more like two shoelaces. He was wearing Daisy Duke shorts over his white g-string. The icing on the cake? A pair of white cowboy boots.

What, Paolo thought, *no leg warmers?*

Apropos of nothing, Bobby sang out, "These boots are made for dancin'," as he rolled back on the seat, kicking his heels in the air.

"They sure are," Paolo said, unable to think of any other response.

Fuji
He had taken his Ecstasy with a vodka gimlet before he left the resort. As he walked across the parking lot to the host hotel, he could feel the day's heat rising in waves from the asphalt. The sun had set several hours earlier and he could feel the cool, dry desert air against his skin. Suddenly, an electric spark ran down his spine. His E was kicking in.

Earlier that day, Fuji had asked what his models were wearing to the party. He wanted to fit in and decided that he

231

too would wear nothing but white Calvin Klein boxer briefs, combat boots, and a tank top. At first, Fuji had felt foolish going out wearing nothing but underwear, but compared to some of the outfits he was seeing, he was appropriately attired. Fuji was proud of his body. He worked hard to stay trim and fit. He had a body that most men half his age would kill for. Like most of tonight's guests, Fuji had chosen to wear a cock ring to make sure he showed a nice basket. Now he was glad he had. His considerable package was attracting some hot and heavy stares from the cute young boys who were walking toward the party with him.

He handed his ticket to the massive bodybuilder at the door. A special band was attached to his wrist and he was pointed in the direction of the VIP area. Handsome young muscle studs, lost in their own worlds, were flagging to the music alongside the main entrance to the dance floor. Fuji looked around and saw his image of Beau riding the shoulders of Luca on every wall. The photo had been made into huge posters. He felt excited to be a part of something so big, something that drew thousands of young gay men together to celebrate life. Chills ran up and down his entire body as he felt the heat emanating from the crowd. He slowly circled the dance floor, watching the tribal ritual that was taking place before him.

God, this is amazing! Fuji could feel an extraordinary energy connecting him to all these beautiful young men. He felt himself being pulled toward the mass of bodies but wanted a friendly face to smile and invite him in. He studied the dancers - many of them looked as if they were being transported to another place. He wanted to go there with them.

Luca

I see your picture everywhere, sang RuPaul.

Luca was dancing with the Brazilians and some of the models from the photo shoot when, out of nowhere, Beau appeared. "Hey everybody!" he said enthusiastically. "Having a good time?"

They all nodded in affirmation.

Then, like a magnet, Beau zeroed in on Luca. He started grinding his pelvis against Luca's leg as RuPaul sang about *a million dollar derriere.*

"Are you alright?" Luca asked apprehensively, flashing back to the poolside drama that morning and wishing Beau would disappear.

232

"Yeah, I'm doing great. Just taking a break from my duties and checking out the dance floor," Beau explained, speaking a mile a minute. He scanned the crowd, all the while bumping Luca's hip with his dick and balls.

RuPaul continued singing about *making love to the camera*.

Luca took a hard look at Beau. He could no longer see the resemblance between the two of them. Then Luca saw Fuji. He was standing at the edge of the dance floor staring intently into the crowd. Their eyes connected. *Oh, shit!* Luca said to himself as he saw Fuji smile in recognition and start making his way toward their group. "Heads up," he said to Beau. "Fuji is coming our way. Please be nice to him."

"Hi guys! Mind if I join you?" Fuji asked innocently, hoping Beau had cooled off since that morning's blowup.

Luca felt Beau's body go rigid and thought, *Uh-oh! Here we go again.* Beau spun on his heels and confronted Fuji. "What the fuck do you think you're doing here?" he shouted. Everyone around them turned to see what was going on.

"I want to apologize for today," Fuji said, swallowing his pride. "I feel terrible. I never meant to hurt you. I was just concerned. I did it out of love," he said, expressing the emotion in his heart. Or was it the Ecstasy speaking?

"LOVE?" Beau hollered over the music. "What do you know about love? All you know about is using people. You've used all of us. We're nothing but bodies to you, bodies to photograph and throw away. Isn't that what you did with me? You used me to make yourself famous, and now you've decided I'm not good enough anymore." Beau's anger was ferocious.

"That's not true," Fuji protested. "You're all so beautiful. I want to share that beauty with the world. I'm not using anybody." No matter what he said, Fuji felt as if it was all coming out wrong.

"I've got news for you. The only reason us pretty boys have anything to do with you is to use *you* on our climb to the top. We have something that you can never have. Youth! Look at you. Boots and underwear? You look like a fool. And there's nothing more pathetic than an old fool!"

With that last remark, Beau pushed his way past Fuji and stormed off the dance floor. Fuji looked around at all the boys dancing, boys he'd squired to many a famous *fete*, boys whose bodies he'd photographed in intimate detail. All around him, he saw blank stares from eyes fogged over by drugs. He felt

233

stupid and naked. Beau was right. There's no fool like an old fool. The only friendly face in the crowd was Luca's. He reached out in an attempt to comfort Fuji, but the crowd pushed him away from the photographer. Fuji pulled out the tank top that was tucked into the rear of his waistband and slipped it on. He walked off the dance floor with his head hung low. He wasn't part of this tribe. No matter how he tried, he would never belong. It had all been an illusion.

Fuji

After Beau's scathing attack, Fuji could only assume that Ira's talk with him hadn't gone well. Now Fuji realized that the problem was bigger than just Beau. He'd seen the truth tonight, and it wasn't pretty. Now that his eyes had been opened there was no closing them. He dialed his friend, the editor of a national gay magazine. "Hello?" Fuji said.

"Who's this?" the magazine editor asked.

"It's Fuji. David Fujimoto."

"Are you alright, Fuji? What time is it, 1:00 am?" he asked trying to wake up.

"I'm fine. It's just that I've had an epiphany and need to talk to you. I have an idea for an article," Fuji said.

"An epiphany? At this hour? Are you sure you're fine? Because I have to tell you, on this end you're not sounding fine," the editor replied.

"Really, I'm fine. I'm in Palm Springs. I just left the Underwear Party. And I'm shocked by what I've seen," explained Fuji.

"What are you talking about?" asked the editor.

"I'm talking about the truth. There's nothing glamorous about these circuit parties. They're simply an excuse for all these muscle boys to get fucked up on drugs and then have sex with as many guys as possible, and the sorry joke is that these parties are raising money for AIDS. Well, as far as I can see, more guys are getting infected at these debaucheries than can possibly be helped by any charity. It's all blood money," Fuji insisted.

"Why are you so worked up, Fuji?" asked the editor, now wide awake and listening intently.

"I've helped promote this cult of muscle fascists with my photography. I've glorified these boys. And now I've come to realize that they want nothing to do with you . . . unless you can make them famous. I'm through with it all."

"Are you sure about this?"

"I have no doubts," Fuji insisted. "I'm leaving Palm Springs tonight. Can we have lunch tomorrow?"

234

"Sure, I'll meet you at The Abbey at 12:30. How's that?"

"That's great. I'll see you then," Fuji answered.

"And Fuji, please drive safely. You're scaring me," the editor said to a dial tone.

Big Daddy & Bobby

Big Daddy was sitting in the VIP lounge of the Underwear Party attempting to be polite to the Fashionistas as they chattered on about their day at the spa. It all sounded unbearably boring to Big Daddy. *Why would anyone sit buried up to their neck in mud?* Big Daddy looked around to see if Bobby was anywhere in sight. He was out on the hunt, having been given specific instructions to find a hot muscle boy for Big Daddy to play with. Someone in the VIP lounge did catch his eye. "Oh, my God isn't that Armando over there, the old COLT model?" he asked the Fashionistas. Armando had always been one of Big Daddy's favorite porn stars.

"You mean the one with the salt-and-pepper hair and furry chest?" Karl replied.

"He's friends with Jake and Luca," Curt remarked. "We met him on the dance floor at White Party in Miami. When is he going to shave off that tragic '70s mustache?"

The Fashionistas were quickly bored with Big Daddy and left the VIP lounge to see if they could find the Brazilians. Just after they left, Big Daddy saw Bobby approaching with a handsome muscle boy in tow, but the security guard wouldn't let him bring his guest into the VIP area. The boy didn't have the required blue wristband.

Big Daddy knew how to solve the problem. He got his massive bulk out of the seat and walked over to the guard. "This guy's a guest of ours. We'll just have a drink and then we're out of here. Do you think you can help us out?" Big Daddy asked. He slipped the security guy a $50 bill.

"Sure, chief, no problem. Come on in," the guard replied.

"Thanks, Big Daddy. This is Mr. B. He's a porn star, and he wants to come home with us," Bobby said, thrilled that he had found exactly what Big Daddy was looking for.

Well this changes the equation, Mr. B thought. *I would've fucked this hot boy for free, but it looks like the meter is running from this point on.*

"Have you boys had enough of this loud music? How about we take our limo back to the resort and get the real party started?" Big Daddy announced. *The Brazilians can fend for themselves,* he thought.

"Sounds like the perfect plan, Big Daddy," Mr. B said picking up on Bobby's nickname for this whale.

Enroute to the resort, Big Daddy asked Mr. B, "So, what videos have you been in?"

"All of them," he laughed. "I've worked with all the studios. But I came out here this weekend to film with David Fujimoto," Mr. B said proudly, as if he'd worked all day with Ingmar Bergman.

"What a small world. I thought you looked familiar, but I didn't recognize you with your underwear on," Big Daddy quipped.

Bobby laughed a little too loudly at Big Daddy's joke.

"We were at the pool today while you guys were filming. I want all the porn gossip," Big Daddy said

After a ride through the dark empty streets, the limo delivered its passengers to the front door of Inn Exile. Big Daddy took care of the driver's tip and followed the boys through the lobby to their poolside suite.

Damn, how much does this place cost? Mr. B wondered. *I might make enough money tonight to cover my whole trip.* He felt like he'd hit the jackpot

"Bobby, fix us something to drink while I shower," Big Daddy instructed once inside. "You boys can shower in the other bathroom, but don't get started without me."

Mr. B got the gist: *Big Daddy is paying the bill, so Junior isn't allowed to sample the goods without him being there.*

"What would you like to drink?" Bobby asked Mr. B. "We have champagne, beer, soda, and water." The Diet Coke and bourbon was reserved for Big Daddy.

"Water, please," Mr. B responded. "I don't want anything to ruin the roll I'm on. This E is still hitting me pretty hard.

"Why don't you jump in the shower first," Bobby suggested as he turned the water on.

"Cool. Are you sure you don't want to join me?" Mr. B asked as he slipped out of his white Calvins. His dick was slightly fluffed. He pulled on it suggestively, trying to entice Bobby.

"No, that's OK. I'll go bring Big Daddy his cocktail. I'll jump in when you're done."

Mr. B stepped into the stream of hot water and felt his E kick in even more strongly. He lathered up and gave himself a raging hard-on. *Perfect, just what the customers*

236

want. He rinsed and toweled off. The air conditioning was making his nipples hard. Then he heard a knock on the door.

"Are you done in the shower?" Bobby asked.

"Sure, come on in," Mr. B said. His cock throbbed as he watched Bobby undress. *Damn, this boy could do porn. He's got a killer bod and a huge cock.* Mr. B's butt quivered at the thought of riding Bobby's monster. He was glad he'd douched before heading out to tonight's party. He knew he wanted to be ready to go with whatever came his way. *Let's hope Big Daddy's a bottom and muscle boy's a top. That's a combo I can handle,* he thought.

"Why don't you go into the bedroom?" Bobby suggested. "Big Daddy's waiting. I won't be long."

Mr. B swaggered into the darkened room. Big Daddy was already naked on the bed stroking his beer-can dick. Mr. B approached the side of the bed and stood with his cock jutting out toward the beached whale. "I need to let you know upfront that I charge $200 an hour," he said. Mr. B liked to get the business part of his job out of the way as soon as possible. He was not about to harpoon this one for free.

"That's not a problem. How many hours can you stay?" Big Daddy asked without missing a stroke on his hardening member.

"Hey, I'm yours all night if you want me."

"Perfect, now come over here and let me suck on that famous dick of yours."

Mr. B kneeled down on the bed with his dick in Big Daddy's face. He closed his eyes as the hot wetness engulfed him.

South Beach
Monday

Jake & Luca

"Honey, I'm home!" Luca called out. He set his luggage down just inside the front door.

Jake practically ran to give Luca a big kiss and hug. He realized at that moment exactly how much he depended upon Luca for a sense of security. He hadn't told him about the letter, afraid it would ruin his time in Palm Springs.
"Well, I have both good and bad news, and a surprise for you. But first, tell me how your weekend went? I can't wait to hear about it."

"Palm Springs is beautiful. But it's so damn dry in the desert. I think I used an entire tube of Chapstick every day,"

Luca said.

"Maybe one day we'll do the party together," Jake replied, feeling as if he'd missed out on something big.

"Honestly, I wouldn't waste the money. It was fun, but compared to parties in Miami and New York, it was disappointing. Holding it in a hotel ballroom, with low ceilings and chandeliers, made it feel like a big bar mitzvah. And then you have to deal with all the bitter LA queens. Those boys are beautiful in a scary artificial way but fucked in the head," Luca said. He flopped down on the bed and looked out at their gorgeous pool.

"How so?" Jake asked.

"You know the guy I posed with on my shoulders? LA has gone to his head. He thinks he's famous now that he's got his name up in lights as oo promoter of the Underwear Party. So we all show up in the morning for the video shoot, and he's a mess. When it comes time for us to all get naked, he strips and looks like he hasn't eaten in days. One of the models suggested that we throw him in the pool to rehydrate him. When Fuji asked him if he was alright and made reference to the fact that he'd lost some muscle, he snapped."

"Snapped?" Jake asked, sitting down on the bed. This was getting juicier.

"As in, lost it."

"Sounds like he's fitting into LA perfectly."

"Fame and drugs. He had to be on something."

"No wonder he looked so bad. That must have made for a little tension on the set," Jake noted.

"Wait, that's only half of it. He had another melt down on the dance floor when Fuji showed up. Read him mercilessly. And after the dust settled, you'll never believe who appeared out of the blue. Turns out Raul is an old 'business associate' of the Party Promoter, if you get my drift. He flies Raul out every year to appear as "Armando" at the official party, then keeps him around for his own private after-party."

"Sweet deal for him," Jake laughed.

"When I filled Raul in on what he'd only seen from the DJ booth, he couldn't wait to talk to the Party Promoter. You know how much he loves gossip."

"So what's your news?" Luca asked. "First, the good news."

"OK, hold onto yourself. Just after you left, I went up to work on the Beverly Hillbillies," Jake began. "They want to take us on vacation, all expenses paid, to Ibiza in August!" Jake said, trying to make it sound enticing.

238

"Are you serious?"

"Before you say no, the Brazilians will be staying with us. And Raul will in Ibiza, too. The Beverly Hillbillies have rented a villa on a mountain with a cook and servants and everything. Please, say yes. It'll probably be the only way we'll ever get to go."

"OK, if you want to go, fine. But they had better not expect me to have sex with them," Luca insisted.

"Don't worry. I'll take one for the team. You won't have to play with them. I'll call Big Daddy and let him know we're a go."

"And the bad news?" Luca asked, looking concerned.

Jake felt a catch in his throat. "I got a registered letter on Friday." He went over to the dresser and picked up the envelope and handed it to Luca. "It's from Sean's executors in London. They want to take the house away from me," Jake couldn't help but get emotional saying those words aloud.

"They can't do that."

"Hunt's lawyer is looking into it," Jake continued. "I'm scared."

Luca put his arm around him and started reading the letter. When he was finished, he held Jake close and tight. "Don't worry," Luca whispered into his ear. "We'll get through this together, no matter what.

"I guess now would be a good time for the surprise," Jake said.

"I don't know how much more my heart can take, but go ahead," Luca smiled.

"Don't worry. I think you'll like this surprise." Jake pulled a small box from the dresser. "Open it."

Luca's face brightened when he saw what the tiny box held - a ring identical to the one Jake had worn since Sean's death. "Oh, honey! It's beautiful."

"I had my buddy, Kenny, the jeweler make it. He copied the Cartier ring that Sean gave me," Jake said happily, knowing that Luca was pleased.

"I'll never take it off." He knew how much that ring meant to Jake.

Beverly Hills
Tuesday

Ira & Beau
Beau hung up the phone after talking to his supposed

business partner, the Party Promoter. "Hung up" was putting it nicely. So was "talking." It was more like screaming and slamming down the receiver. Someone had poisoned the Party Promoter's mind with questions about Beau's drug use. The Party Promoter had had the gall to ask Beau if perhaps he was doing a little too much partying. *Partying? Wasn't that their business? Wasn't it the Party Promoter who'd introduced him to Tina?* Now Beau, whose image had made them the talk of the gay party circuit, was being told his services were no longer needed. *Fuck him. I'll outdo him.*

Since Miami's White Party, all he'd been hearing was how all the rich and famous gays spent the month of August in Ibiza. Beau decided that he would throw his own fabulous parties for the gay jet set on that little island. He knew he could do a much better job on his own. He'd have men like the Movie Mogul begging to come to his parties. He was startled from his reverie by a knock on his door.

Ira was standing there. He was crying.

Beau was in no mood for this drama. "What is it?" he snapped.

"My doctor called. He said he has the results of your blood test," Ira said in a near whisper.

"Well, what is it? Did you give me AIDS?" Beau spat out.

Looking as if he'd been slapped in the face, Ira sobbed, "He wouldn't tell me. He said he had to see you in person to speak to you. You can go to his office this afternoon."

"Oh, look who's worried about my health," Beau said, the vitriol in his voice rising. "It's a little late for that, isn't it? Please! We both know what you did to me, and you're going to pay for it. Starting with my trip to Ibiza. And you're not going to stop me. I have important business there," Beau said, his mind swirling with lists of details that had to be attended to.

"Please, please," Ira begged. "Before you do anything or go anywhere, see the doctor. Then you can go on vacation. I'll pay for everything."

"You're damned right you will!" Beau shouted. He stormed into his bathroom and slammed the door behind him. He turned on the shower and stripped. In the slowly fogging mirror, he studied his naked body. *I don't know what they're talking about. I look better than ever. I'm shredded, not an ounce of fat. A few solid nights' sleep will get rid of these circles under my eyes. A vacation is exactly what I need.* The shower's steam continued to cloud the mirror, obscuring the sight of his body completely.

240

New York
Wednesday

Rob

The phone rang. Rob picked it up and at first heard nothing. "Hello? Is anyone there?" he asked. There was the sound of a deep breath being drawn.

"Rob?" a weak voice asked.

"Yes, who is this?" He couldn't identify the caller. It was as if they were struggling to speak.

"Rob, it's Ellis. I need your help."

"What's wrong? You sound terrible." Rob's heart began to pound in his chest. A wave of guilt flooded him. It had been way too long. He'd let the bar and his life with Erik make Ellis a stranger.

"It's Baby," Ellis managed to get out before breaking down into sobs.

Oh, God, Rob thought. *She's finally thrown him out for being gay.*

"She's dead."

"What? How did it happen?"

"I got a call from the hospital in Palm Springs. She was out there at a spa. She collapsed while jogging, had a massive coronary. God, what am I going to do?" Ellis sobbed into the phone.

Rob was stunned. "You know I'll do anything for you, Ellis. You're family. How can I help?" He could hear Ellis crying on the other end of the line.

Haltingly, Ellis continued, "I was supposed to go into the hospital this week."

"Why, what's wrong?" Rob asked, his guilt deepening.

"Well, I wanted to keep this to myself, but you're all I have now." Ellis started sobbing again.

"Anything, Ellis. Tell me."

"I have CMV."

"What's that?" Rob had heard the condition mentioned in passing as it related to HIV.

"Cytomegalovirus. I'm going blind. My doctor wants to implant the medication. It's supposed to be the best treatment available. But now with Baby gone, I don't know."

"Ellis, listen to me. You are going ahead with the procedure. I'll go with you to the hospital. Erik and I will do anything we have to. I'll grab him and we'll be right over."

"Thank you Rob. I feel so alone right now," Ellis said through sobs.

Rob's heart was breaking, but he would be strong, maybe stronger than he'd ever been. He owed so much to this man who had asked for so little in return. "I love you, Ellis. I always have, and I always will."

***

"I can barely see through these dark glasses," lamented Ellis. "I feel like I'm living in a cave." According to the doctor, there was little chance that Ellis's diminished eyesight would ever improve. The dark glasses were certain to become a permanent fixture to protect his sensitive eyes from the harsh glare of sunlight.

"How am I going to live like this? I don't know what to do without Baby to help me."

Rob wiped a tear away from Ellis's eye. He hated to see him in this state. Rob knew there was little that he could do to improve matters. "Well . . . ," Rob began, trying his best to sound upbeat, "to begin with, you've got live-in help. They're here 24/7 to assist you with anything you might need. Plus you've got me and Erik. Whatever needs to be done, we'll be more than happy to take care of. You know you can count on me, don't you?" Rob asked.

Ellis nodded his head, but Rob could tell that his thoughts were elsewhere. "I can't ever go back to the firm again, can I Rob?" Ellis asked, the sorrow in his voice echoing in the large townhouse's living room. "I can barely read *The New York Times*, let alone architectural drawings. Everything's changed forever."

There were no words that Rob could summon up to comfort Ellis. Everything had indeed changed forever. He leaned in toward Ellis and wrapped his arms around him. "We'll get through this."

Fort Lauderdale
Thursday

Big Daddy & Bobby
It had to be some mistake. Big Daddy couldn't believe the charges he saw on his American Express bill. It infuriated him even further that he didn't recognize the name of the company that was billing him thousands of dollars. American Express was less than helpful. They told him they'd look into it, but they couldn't yet give him much information other than that the company did business on the Internet. Big Daddy could feel his anger rising. No one pulled the wool over his eyes when it came to money.

"Bobby, did you buy anything on the Internet?" he

242

asked, fuming.

"No, only that porn site, the one where we watched Mr. B having sex in different rooms of that beach house in Laguna. Remember?" Bobby answered, not understanding why Big Daddy was so angry.

Big Daddy called his lawyer in Atlanta. "Put me through to the boss," he told the secretary, not bothering with any pleasantries. Although he'd spoken to the woman for years, he wasn't about to waste time.

"Right away, Mr. Mercer," she answered without having to ask his name. She knew him quite well from his rudeness over the phone. She'd bet money that after twenty-some years, he didn't even know her name, which was fine by her. She'd read enough in his legal files to curl her hair.

Big Daddy got right down to business. "I need you to look into something for me. Judging by my AmEx bill, somebody's trying to rip me off - an Internet company. A few months back we signed up for some porno site. Anyway, it was a waste of money. I canceled our membership after the first month. Is there any way these people are running up a huge bill on my credit card?"

"Give me all the details, including the name of the website, so I can contact these people," the lawyer said, wondering what kind of perversion lay ahead for his viewing pleasure.

Summer 1995

August 1995 - *Two Months Later*
Ibiza
Saturday

Jake & Luca
They were exhausted by the time they reached the tiny airport, which more closely resembled a bus station. It had been a long uncomfortable flight from Miami to Madrid on Iberia Airlines. The plane was dirty and the flight attendants were like surly waiters. At one point, Jake came out of the restroom to find one of the attendants clipping his fingernails onto the floor of the galley.

Luggage in hand, they made it through customs. Bobby was waiting outside to greet them wearing a sarong and sandals. He looked like he was ready for a luau. The boys looked around. They realized Bobby wasn't the only one dressed that way. It seemed that everyone who wasn't a new arrival was pretty much wearing as little clothing as possible.

"Hey y'all!" he shouted. "Big Daddy and the gang are waiting for us by the pool. We're not very far away." He grabbed one of their bags. It was amazing how easily he slipped back into his role of houseboy. Bobby packed the tiny rental car's trunk with their luggage and the overflow onto the back seat practically on top of Luca. Because of Jake's long legs, he got to sit up front with Bobby. The Peugeot had no air conditioning. None of the rental cars on the island did. So down came the windows in the blazing heat.

Jake looked on in horror as Bobby abused the manual transmission, grinding from one gear to another.

"I haven't driven a stick shift in years," he said with a grimace. He tried to put the car into reverse.

Lucky us! Jake thought. *Let's hope we make it to the house in one piece.* Finally in gear, they were off through the barren countryside, passing one giant billboard after another advertising nightclubs. Jake's favorite was for Space. Its slogan was "Happy People in the Morning". He wasn't sure what that meant, but it definitely sounded like fun.

***

The house was situated on the side of a steep hill. Jake and Luca could see the ocean from the open front door. They followed Bobby through the living room and out onto the deck that overlooked the pool.

"Hello, strangers!" Big Daddy shouted. "Welcome to Ibiza!"

Everyone by the pool waved at the new arrivals. The Brazilians had arrived the day before. Bobby pointed out the other couple, whom Jake and Luca had not yet met – Bluto and his boyfriend Bill. Bobby told Jake and Luca that they owned an insurance company in Fort Lauderdale. Bluto was Bobby's workout partner. He was as hairy as a beast, had a black beard, and was one of the most massive bodybuilders they'd ever seen. Bill was about Jake's height and build, all-American looking. Everyone was nude.

"Take off your clothes and join us," Big Daddy shouted up to them.

"We'll be right out after we put our bags away," Jake replied. They ducked inside with Bobby who led them to their room. It was furnished with a queen-size bed surrounded by mosquito netting. A simple wooden dresser with an oscillating fan on top of it stood alone on the terra cotta tile floor.

"At night, there's a great breeze. You won't even miss air conditioning," Bobby said with a smile. "See you down at the pool. Don't dawdle, Big Daddy's waiting."

Jake and Luca looked at each other in amazement. After Bobby was gone, Jake exclaimed, "No air conditioning in this heat? And let me guess, the mosquito netting isn't just decorative."

"It's stifling," Luca complained. "This feels like Palm Springs. The air is so hot and dry. I feel like I'm standing too close to an open flame."

"Well, we're here. We need to make the best of it," Jake said. In defiance of Big Daddy's edict, they put on bathing suits. Luca wasn't about to walk around naked just because an overweight water buffalo commanded it.

***

"I hate you already!" laughed Bill, one half of the Insurance Guys. "Aren't those Gaultier bathing suits? They must have cost a fortune. I love them!"

"Oh, come on, boys. Get comfortable. This is no place for designer bathing suits. Get naked like everyone else," Big Daddy insisted with more than a little bit of irritation.

Jake and Luca reluctantly removed their trunks and settled down onto chaise lounges.

Big Daddy came over and plopped down on the foot of Jake's lounge, threatening to tip it over. "You're the last in our group to arrive, so let me bring you up to speed. If you want to hit the gym, you'll need to go with Bobby at 7:00. Breakfast is at 9:00 sharp. Then you can relax around the

248

pool while we go shopping with the chef. We were told he was a gourmet chef who had cooked for Paul and Linda McCartney, but we were very disappointed in our first dinner. It was something foreign with rice and chicken and clams. Can you believe that?" Big Daddy exclaimed.

"I think it's called *paella*. It's kind of the national dish of Spain," Jake said, incredulously.

"Well, whatever it was, we're not eating it again. So every day I go to the market and pick out something that's not so foreign. You know, like steak and potatoes," Big Daddy smiled.

Jake and Luca were appalled that they would hire a world-class chef and then force him to cook the most mundane of meals.

"We hit the beach around 1:00. We like to stop at Pizza Hut on the way for lunch," Big Daddy continued. "You guys can drive over with us."

Jake and Luca's hopes of an exotic Spanish vacation began to fade. "There's a little restaurant out at the gay beach, but you have to wear clothes to be served," he said.

Jake thought, *Gee, you have to wear clothing to be served in a restaurant? How novel!*

"We head home around 6:00 so we can relax with a cocktail before dinner at 7:00. Then after dinner we play hearts for a few hours before getting a good night's sleep."

Hearts? I've never played cards in my life. And how good a night's sleep are any of us going to get without air conditioning? Jake thought, his frustration mounting.

Luca spoke up, "Do you guys plan on going out and enjoying any of the nightlife that Ibiza is famous for? We must have passed a dozen billboards for clubs. Our friend Raul has raved about how amazing the gay bars are here."

"Oh, we're not much for nightlife, but maybe one night we'll get crazy and go out on the town."

Jake and Luca were speechless. They had come halfway around the world to an island that existed as an excuse to party all night long, only to be trapped with people who were happy doing exactly what they did at home in Fort Lauderdale.

***

>CREAK<

"Move over," complained Jake. "You're hogging the bed."
>CREAK<

"I wish I could move over, but there's no more bed on

this side," muttered Luca. "This isn't a king-size like at home," he complained. "And I'm sweating bullets."

"So am I," answered Jake, "but what're we going to do about it? The tiny fan on the dresser is set on 'high' and I've got the sliding glass door open as wide as it'll go."
>CREAK<

"Who builds a million-dollar vacation home on a sweltering island without air conditioning? Or ceiling fans?" snarled Luca. "It's nearly midnight and it's got to be over 80 degrees."
>CREAK<

"I don't know what to tell you," answered Jake. "All I know is that this bed is too small for the two of us. And the mosquito netting is doing nothing more than trapping the mosquitoes inside with us. I'm being eaten alive."
>CREAK<

"Enough of this!" Luca growled. He kicked the netting aside and got out of bed. "Do you think we can cool off in the pool without waking up half the house?"
>CREAK<

"It'd be hard to be noisier than this pathetic excuse for a bed," said Jake. He tried to untangle his long legs from the swirl of sheets and netting gathered at the end of the mattress. It was futile trying to keep the bed quiet. No matter which way he moved, the metal frame creaked like the Tin Man in Oz.

Luca went to the bathroom and grabbed two towels. In order to reach the outside staircase that led down to the pool, they'd have to walk along the terrace past their hosts' bedroom with its open sliding glass door. Their only other choice would be to climb down the steep hill. Jake fumbled in the dark looking for their flip-flops. One false step on a sharp pine cone would foil their plans for a midnight swim.

With towels slung around their necks, Jake and Luca helped each other half-walk, half-slide down the slope to the dark unlit pool. Fortunately, the moon was nearly full in the star-filled sky and illuminated the nightscape. Better yet, there was a slight breeze. It felt glorious against their sweat-soaked bodies.

"Don't make a sound," whispered Jake when they reached the end of the pool where steps led into the water.

Luca nodded his head. The last thing either of them wanted was to have their hosts wake up and join them. Like two Navy SEALS trying to elude detection, they slowly immersed themselves in the cool water. "This is wonderful,"

250

Luca whispered. "I could spend the rest of the night in here."

Jake could feel the stress of 12 hours of travel begin to lift off his shoulders. His entire body began to relax in the dark water. He swam up behind Luca and gently grabbed his torso.

Luca turned and their lips met. It was a slow luxurious kiss.

"No matter how awful this trip may seem right now, we'll find a way to make the most of it," offered Jake. He reached out and stroked Luca's hair with his wet hand.

Luca wrapped his legs around Jake and the two of them floated in the pool, oblivious to everything around them.

***

They began to climb the steep slope back to their bedroom, "I can't get any traction in these flip-flops. How are we going to make it back up this hill?" asked Luca.

"We have to take them off or we'll never get back up," Jake answered.

"Shit! That's gonna hurt."

"It's either that or walk up the stairs and past their open door."

"Then that's what we have to do," Luca responded. Like two cat-burglars, they stealthily made their way back down to the pool, over to the stairs, and tip-toed their way up. Big Daddy was snoring like a tuba in a marching band. They silently slid past his open door.

"I think we're home free," Luca whispered when they reached the open door into their bedroom.

"I want to pick up where we left off in the pool," Jake said. "I have some impure thoughts I want to share with you."

"That creaking bed will wake up the whole house."

"How about we put the mattress on the floor?"

"I like the way you think, big boy."

Sunday

"We were about to begin without you," Big Daddy announced. "I told you, breakfast is at 9:00, not 9:01."

Luca looked at his watch. It read 9:05 am. He and Jake took their seats. Everyone else was already assembled

Then Bobby piped up, "Can you believe I had to stand there and wait for the guy to open the gym this morning? The owner didn't get there until a quarter after 7:00. Doesn't he know that some people need to get an early start?"

"I've heard that everything runs late here. People go to dinner around 10:00," Jake commented.

"What kind of weirdos eat dinner at that hour? That's ridiculous," Big Daddy said with contempt.

"I think it's the custom here," Luca responded. Everyone stared at him for challenging Big Daddy.

"Well, we're Americans and it's not our custom. And as long as we're paying with our American dollars, they can play by our rules."

The table went silent.

After breakfast, Big Daddy and Bobby left to go grocery shopping. The boys headed out to the pool for some morning sun. The pool was tiled in deep turquoise and had an infinity edge that created the illusion of the water spilling over into the horizon. Looking out over the island from their perch, they could see blue sky meet blue ocean. The Brazilians and the Insurance Guys were already swimming. Jake and Luca tested the water.

"Come on in, it's really warm," Paolo said.

"Do we have the cement pond to ourselves now that Jed and Jethro have gone shopping for vittles?" Jake laughed.

"Yes. I wonder what part of the cow we'll be eating tonight?" asked Bill. "Isn't this an island? Don't they have great seafood here?"

"Of course, but Big Daddy doesn't like anything that's fishy. You heard him about the *paella*," Bluto said. "I thought it was good. We ate it up. I wish they were a bit more adventurous."

"Yeah, I mean, I like pizza, but every day?" Paolo complained. "That little restaurant on the beach looks like fun. All the boys are eating there except us."

"How do we get our hosts to enjoy some of the local nightlife?" Jake asked.

"I think it's up to us to talk about how all the gorgeous guys go out to the bars and the clubs," answered Tomàs.

"A good friend from South Beach who's been coming here for years will point us in the right direction," Luca added. "Raul's here for the next two weeks. I'm sure we'll bump into him at the beach. He's got the whole island schedule down."

"Great!" Tomàs exclaimed. "You pump him for info and all of us will talk it up. Big Daddy can't resist going for the eye candy and Bobby loves to show off his perfect little body. Getting them to go out on the town should be a breeze."

"I don't know. Big Daddy seems a bit fixed with his schedule," Jake replied.

252

***

Bobby pulled off to the side of the road behind a long line of parked cars. The Insurance Guys, with the Brazilians in tow, parked behind them. A sign up ahead read, *Playa des Cavallet*, with an arrow pointing to a distant stand of pines trees.

"This is it! Everybody out!" Bobby announced.

Big Daddy slowly worked his enormous bulk out of the front seat, freeing Jake and Luca, who were crushed together in the back. It was a sweltering 90-something degrees.

"OK, everybody ready for a walk through the woods to the beach?" Big Daddy asked. The smell of the scrub pine forest was refreshing and at least provided some shade from the broiling sun. Along the way, they caught glimpses of guys disappearing down narrow paths into the woods. Raul had said that the woods were active all day with guys cruising for sex *al fresco*.

A cool ocean breeze met them when they climbed up and over the dunes. As they made their way onto the beach itself, it became apparent that clothing was just an option and was worn mainly in the restaurant. No one seemed to have any visible tan lines. Jake liked the sexy relaxed atmosphere.

"We're finally here," Big Daddy announced to his group, out of breath from the trek.

Jake looked at his watch. It had been at least 45 minutes since they'd left the car. He couldn't believe that guys made this journey every day. If he'd known, he would have voted to stay back at the house.

Big Daddy started talking to the young man who ran the concession for lounge chairs. Jake saw some cash trade hands. The young man started dragging white plastic lounges down to the water's edge for them. Big Daddy led the way, dictating to his group, "OK, everybody strip!"

Jake and Luca glanced around, hoping that none of the naked guys around them had heard the "ugly American." They looked at each other, then at the Brazilians and the Insurance Guys.

There was a group shrug. *Oh, well. Everyone else is naked. Why not go with the flow?*

Later when everyone was asleep in the sun, Jake and Luca slipped on their trunks in order to treat themselves to a little snack at the café. It gave them a chance to strut their stuff in their Gaultier bathing suits. They walked along the makeshift boardwalk that led up to the café. An adorable young maitre d', all smooth tan skin and giant sunglasses, led them to an empty table and dropped two menus. Jake couldn't help but notice the double "G" logo on the boy's sunglasses and tiny bikini. Gucci Boy was the epitome of style.

The menu was in Spanish, with some rather odd English translations. The *emparedado de jambon y queso* (ham and cheese sandwich) had been translated into English as "pig and Switzerland." They perused the crowd, which looked and felt different from anything gay in the States. There seemed to be a vibe of unspoken wealth and understated chic.

Even though he was accustomed to South Beach prices, Jake thought the numbers on the menu were staggering. *How do these guys afford this day after day?* he wondered.

Luca asked their server-of-indeterminate-gender what the frosty mugs of cloudy looking beer were.

"A Shandy," he/she said with a strong Spanish accent.

"What's in it?" Luca asked.

"It's half beer and half Fanta Limon," he/she answered. "It's very refreshing. You should both try one."

"Great! We'll take two."

"Beer and lemon soda?" Jake asked. "Are you sure?"

"When in Ibiza, do as the Ibizans . . . ," Luca laughed.

Jake and Luca finished the first round of their new favorite beverage. Indeed it was quite refreshing. It would be pretty easy to get crocked on these in the overwhelming heat.

Looking around to see what had happened to their food, Luca spotted the last person he expected to see on Ibiza. "Oh, no!" he whispered to Jake. "Don't look now but you'll never believe who's headed straight for us. Pray that he didn't see us."

"Who?" Jake barely had time to say before a buzzing ball of energy swept down on them and pulled up a chair.

"It's great to see you guys!" Beau said a bit too loudly. Jake looked around to see if anyone was staring at them. "So nice to see some familiar faces," Beau added, drumming his fingers on the tabletop. Gucci Boy dropped a menu in front of Beau and vanished. "I'm starving. Have you guys ordered yet?"

"Yes, about a half an hour ago," Jake said, staring at the white crust caked around Beau's nostrils. It looked like he was breathing through two powdered donuts. The server-of-indeterminate-gender took his order.

Beau never stopped talking about the parties he was

throwing at every nightclub the boys had seen billboards for. Space. Amnesia. Privilege. He seemed to be a busy boy. Both Jake and Luca felt uneasy sitting next to him. Amazingly, all three orders arrived together.

The minute Beau had finished eating, he jumped up. "Well, thanks for lunch," he said. "I'll take you guys out to dinner one night this week." And he was gone.

"What the hell was that?" Jake asked.

"Like I know?"

"Did you see his nose?"

"Are you kidding? I couldn't stop staring. I thought sooner or later he'd realize and wipe it."

"At least it explains his behavior."

"And he stuck us with his lunch. Lord only knows how much that'll cost. And why? His Sugar Daddy has more money than God," Luca grumbled, remembering the houses in Laguna and Beverly Hills.

"Do you really think he's doing all those parties?"

"Maybe all that's left for him is Ibiza since he burnt his bridges in Palm Springs," Luca answered, thinking back to the scene with Fuji.

"He's burning something. He never stopped moving or talking," Jake said with distain.

"I kept thinking he was going to have a heart attack."

"Speaking of heart attacks, let's pay up. Luckily they take American Express here," Jake laughed. He retrieved his card from the tiny pocket in his bathing suit.

"Let's be big sports and bring a Shandy back for everyone," Luca suggested. "Ask the server-of-indeterminate-gender to add them to our bill."

"Great idea. Maybe it'll soothe Big Daddy's ruffled feathers. I don't think he'll like our going off to have a bite to eat without his approval."

"I know. It's beginning to feel like we're on a school trip and he's our chaperone."

As they were leaving the restaurant, someone called to them. They turned back and couldn't believe their eyes. It was Mr. B. Was there anywhere on God's green earth where this second-rate porn star didn't show up?

"Hey guys! How are you?" he asked, kissing them both on each cheek like a real European.

"What are you doing here?" Luca asked, dumbfounded.

"Oh, you know me. I work the circuit. If it's August, then I'm in Ibiza. I run my ads in the international gay rags saying I'll be here and then get a handful of bookings to cover my costs. Hey, speaking of cost, I rented a minivan so I can shuttle people back and forth from town to the beach. I only charge $5 for a one-way trip. It's a real bargain!" Mr. B said, sounding like a used-car salesman. Luca took the lead, "Well, thanks. We'll keep it in mind, but right now our hands are kind of full. We need to get these Shandies back to our hosts."

"Oh, sure, I understand. I'll see you guys around. I'm here for the next two weeks," he said with a smile and headed back into the shade of the restaurant.

They gingerly made their way back across the scorching sand.

"That guy turns up everywhere," Jake said.

"He's always working it," remarked Luca. "Never stops. Can you imagine, the poor boy is so into being a porn star that he legally changed his real name to his porn name."

"Talk about believing your own hype."

"And what do we have here?" Big Daddy asked.

"They're called Shandies. It's half beer and half lemon soda," Luca explained as he handed them out.

"They're perfect for the beach!" Jake added.

"That sounds disgusting," Big Daddy sneered.

Ibiza
Monday

The Velvet Mafia
A warm sea breeze made the crisp white linen table cloth flutter. The polished silver ice bucket shimmered with water droplets. The Cristal chilled. They were all reclining on chaise lounges covered with enormous towels of thick white Turkish cotton, protected from the blazing midday sun under an elegant white canvas tent, its side panels carefully rolled up to provide a spectacular 180 degree view of the white sands of *Playa Salinas*, the most exclusive beach on the island.

The maitre d' handed each of his pampered guests a menu and went over the day's specials. "May I suggest the Andalusian gazpacho? It's one of our chef's specialties, served in the traditional style with chopped cucumber, tomato, and peppers on the side. Also today, I would highly recommend the lobster salad. They were caught this morning and are very sweet. Perfect with ice cold champagne," he added.

"Thank you," responded the Movie Mogul. "Give us a

256

few moments to decide."

The maitre d' disappeared with a nod of the head. He would have clicked his heels together in another place and time. Here on the beach, wearing espadrilles, he couldn't have made it work.

"I wonder how the ceviche is prepared," pondered the Lesbian Designer. "It's must be exquisite, don't you think?"

"I understand the chef trained with Joël Robuchon in Paris, so I'm certain everything is done to perfection," answered the Media Mogul, a man proud of his knowledge of French wines and restaurants.

"Well, here's to perfection," the Movie Mogul offered up. He raised his champagne flute and the assembled guests followed suit.

A young waiter moved among them with a sliver tray of chilled oysters spiked with a hint of lime.

"Speaking of perfection, who's this bronze angel heading straight toward us?" asked the Media Mogul. "Is one of your models joining us for lunch?" he inquired of Mr. Underwear.

All eyes were on the angel who was wearing nothing but a Versace bathing suit and a smile.

"That's Ira Gould's current boy," realized the Movie Mogul, before Mr. Underwear could answer, and nodded to his security person to allow the young man to enter.

"Hello everyone!" Beau greeted them. "It's so nice to see you all again. It's been, let's see, since the White Party in Miami. I guess we're all on the same circuit," he said, talking a mile a minute. While Beau may have appeared to be a bronze angel from fifty feet away, up close it was clear that this angel's wings had been clipped. Beau hadn't shaved in days. It was doubtful he'd even taken a shower.

"Why yes, I remember. We were all together on Ira's boat, right?" the Movie Mogul noted.

"Yes, we were. Ira's consumed with business in LA so I'm here throwing fabulous parties. In fact, I'm hosting one tonight at Amnesia. I'd be happy to put your names on the guest list," Beau said without taking a breath.

"Thank you," answered the Movie Mogul in as noncommittal a voice as he could muster. "Will you and Ira be out on the Island for the Morning Party later this month?" he asked, trying his best to make conversation.

"I'll be there staying with friends. You must know them. They own Jocks in Manhattan," Beau replied while fidgeting with the flyers in his hand.

"Yes, I've heard of that bar. Well then, I'll look for you

out on the Island." Beau put several of the flyers down on the clean white linen table. "Perfect. I look forward to getting together then. Oh well, I'm off. No rest for the wicked!" he said in farewell.

No sooner was Beau out of range, when the gossip began. "He's delusional," the Lesbian Designer declared. "My friend, Jade Jagger, is hosting tonight's party at Amnesia. Look, he's written his name on these flyers in magic marker. See how it reflects purple in the sunlight?"

"He wasn't lying when he said no rest for the wicked. He looks like he hasn't slept a wink in days," the Media Mogul commented.

"Still, I wouldn't kick him out of my bed," laughed the Movie Mogul. "That Ira has a real eye for trophy-boys with trophy-cocks. And that bathing suit was well packed!"

"Cheers!" sang out Mr. Underwear, raising his champagne flute. "Here's to trophy-cocks!"

The Lesbian Designer shot him a bemused look.

"And trophy-twats!" he laughed, clinking his glass with hers.

Thursday

Jake & Luca

"Not again," whispered Luca to Jake.

"Oh, yeah. Here we go," he replied under his breath. "It's show time."

Each night during cocktail hour Big Daddy would make an announcement, "Ladies and gentlemen, it gives me great pleasure to introduce the worldwide singing sensation, Cherry Delite!"

Bobby would then lip-synch to "Somewhere Over the Rainbow." Every evening he'd add a new piece of drag, purchased that morning while out shopping for dinner. Stiletto heels one night. A feather boa the next. Each night it was the same performance. Afterwards, Big Daddy would lead the applause for his little superstar. Jake and Luca were ready to stick pins in their eyes.

Saturday

Raul had arrived a few days after Jake and Luca and was livid that they were missing out on all the nightlife. The three of them passed the time chatting out in the ocean away from Big

258

Daddy's ears hatching a mutiny. The boys suspected the Brazilians would have no part of their scheme, but maybe the Insurance Guys would join in.

***

Raul stopped by the Beverly Hillbillies' villa shortly after breakfast. The hosts were away shopping for dinner and drag. Raul told the Brazilians and the Insurance Guys to explain to their hosts that he'd kidnapped Jake and Luca, but would bring them to the beach later that afternoon. He got Jake and Luca to pack their beach bags and throw some shorts on over their bathing suits.

Before they started Raul's car, he opened a Tic Tac container and gave them each an Ecstasy. He claimed the E on the island was fantastic because it came straight from Amsterdam. "I bought it last night from my favorite drug dealer." They swigged theirs down with the bottles of water they carried with them everywhere. "I'm taking you to meet happy people in the morning!" Raul exclaimed, his excitement overflowing.

"You mean Space? The place out by the airport?" Jake asked.

"The one and only! You guys are gonna love it. You'll kick yourselves for not going there every day this week.

***

"OK, take a deep breath and pray that we find a parking space," Raul said. "This place is bound to be packed with all the people who went out last night and then came here."

"My heart's pounding with anticipation," Jake laughed.

"No, that's your E kicking in. You boys should be rolling by the time we hit the front door."

They left their t-shirts in the car and floated their way across the enormous parking lot. Before they reached the entrance, a jumbo jet took off from the nearby runway and zoomed over their heads.

After the roar passed, Raul hollered out, "Did you feel that vibration? Wasn't that amazing? If that doesn't get your E rolling, nothing will!"

"Oh, it got my E rolling alright. I feel like the top of my head's about to lift off," Jake said.

"Me, too," was all that Luca could manage to say.

"OK, my buddy should be at the entrance gate," Raul said. "Follow me."

Raul led the boys past a long waiting line and went straight to the front.

"Raul, my friend!" called out a short man with a shaved head wearing a Space t-shirt.

"These are my friends from South Beach, Jake and Luca. I've told them all about how fabulous this place is. They can't wait to see it."

"I'm honored to have such handsome Americans come to my humble little club. Please, be my guests. Come in and have a wonderful time. And remember to tell all of your friends in South Beach about Space!" he said.

The three of them were swept past security and onto a large open terrace. Raul went up to the nearest bar, and ordered three bottles of water. "I saved us each $40 US at the door," he said proudly. "Can you believe the prices here?"

Luca took that as a hint and stepped up to pay for the waters. They were $8 each.

"You guys shouldn't drink any alcohol this afternoon. It's too easy to get dehydrated in this heat. It's deceiving out here because of the cloth overhead."

The boys looked up, and indeed the entire terrace was shaded with camouflage netting.

"Those fans produce a great breeze, but still, keep drinking water. You're sweating and the fans are making it evaporate. If you don't drink up, you'll fall down and go boom. Got it?"

"Got it," answered Jake.

They made their way through the crowd of beautiful boys and girls to an area that was mostly guys. Most were muscular, all were handsome, and all seemed quite happy to welcome them into their midst. Raul introduced Jake and Luca to a dozen guys he seemed to know. It was impossible to hear names over the loud music.

At one point, a guy shouted into Jake's ear, "The DJ is Danny Tenaglia. He's an American from Miami, like you."

At one point, Jake turned his back to the group and began dancing with a boy and girl he assumed were Brazilian. Both had smooth caramel skin and short curly hair. The girl's ample breasts were held aloft by a crocheted gold bikini top. The boy was wearing long surfer shorts and flip-flops. They were very smiley and started grinding their bodies against

Jake's.

The boy shouted over the music, "I love you, big American muscle boy. You look like the Billy Doll. You know this Billy Doll?"

Jake nodded yes as the apparently straight boy leaned forward to kiss him full on the mouth. When the boy finished, his girlfriend kissed Jake just as fully. Then they danced their way off into the crowd. Jake turned back to Luca and Raul.

"What was that about?" Luca asked.

"That straight boy said I looked like a Billy Doll and kissed me," Jake said with a huge grin.

***

Finally, their last night in Ibiza arrived. After the Beverly Hillbillies and the Brazilians finished their game of hearts, Big Daddy surprised everyone when he suggested they all have some strong coffee and head out for a night on the town to see the hot boys. Jake and Luca put their mutiny plan into action. While the rest of the house was getting ready for their big night out, they packed their bags. They placed their traveling clothes on top so that they could make a quick change of attire at the airport in the morning. Under cover of darkness, they snuck their luggage out of the house and into the trunk of the Insurance Guys' car. Bluto and Bill had agreed to join the mutiny.

***

Big Daddy insisted on leaving the house at midnight.

"We're here," Bobby said. He parked the car outside the city walls.

Jake and Luca, having already gotten the lay of the land from Raul, knew exactly where to go. Jake proposed that they walk up into Old Town. "There are supposed to be a few small gay bars along the *La Avenida de la Virgen*," he informed them. They trudged up the steep cobblestone ramp and through the enormous wooden gates that historically guarded Old Town. It felt like they were entering a time warp. Had they been wearing togas, they'd have fit right in. They wobbled their way up the cobblestone street.

At one drag bar, queens tried to pull the muscle boys in. Only Bobby was interested in these kindred spirits. He made sure to tell them all how beautiful they looked.

Jake and Luca gave each other the eye. *Beautiful? How about frightening?* They were not-so-pretty men made up

261

to look like not-so-pretty women. Each tiny bar was a disappointment since they were all empty. The restaurant tables lining the tiny old street were jam-packed. "Can you believe how late these people eat?" Big Daddy asked.

The answer being, *Yes, we told you so.*

After their tour of Old Town, they made their way to Dome Bar just outside the city walls. It was the most popular of the "early" gay bars on Ibiza. Jake asked if the owner was around. He was setting up the bar. Jake introduced himself and asked if by any chance he'd seen Raul.

"Your friend Raul won't be here for another hour or two. Didn't he tell you how late the scene gets started here?"

"Yes, he did. Unfortunately our hosts wouldn't take my advice. They wanted to come out early," Jake said, feeling stupid and American.

"Well, let me start your evening off on the right shoe!" he said, mangling the colloquialism. "I'll bring out a tray of shots for all of you. How many are in your group?" he asked.

"Thank you very much, but there are eight of us," Jake said, not wanting to overextend their welcome.

"Then nine shots it is! I'll join you. If you are all friends of Raul then I must show you this courtesy."

Around 2:00 am, when the bar was just starting to get crowded, Big Daddy announced that it was time to depart for Privilege, the island's big disco. It was somewhere on the outskirts of town. They'd seen signs pointing to it on their daily pilgrimage to Pizza Hut. After what seemed an eternity of twisting, pothole-ridden, dark roads, they came upon a massive billboard pointing the way to "The World's Biggest Nightclub." Both cars pulled off the road and drove down a narrow dirt path, steep hills on either side of them. Arriving at the parking lot, they looked over acres of empty asphalt to what appeared to be a sports stadium.

"We'll get a great parking space right up front," bubbled Bobby.

Jake and Luca just looked at each other.

There were fewer than thirty cars parked in the lot. When everyone's shirts were tucked in and pants smoothed, they walked up to the entrance. A few people were milling around under a canopy that led to a long flight of steps down into the club.

"Hello, my friends!" said the doorman. Jake and Luca recognized him as Gucci Boy from the beach café. Even at night the pretty boy was wearing his designer sunglasses.

For what he paid, he probably sleeps in them, thought

Jake.

"You look fabulous in those tattoo shirts," Gucci Boy exclaimed to Jake and Luca. The boys beamed. They had bought them in South Beach specifically for Ibiza. "Aren't they Jean Paul Gaultier? I am so envious!" He ushered in Jake, Luca, and the Insurance Guys. The four of them took a few steps down the staircase. When Big Daddy stepped up to the entrance, Gucci Boy held out his hand. "You need to see my friend over there for tickets," he said unabashedly.

"What do you mean?" a surprised Big Daddy asked.

"Tonight there is a cover charge of 60 US dollars. You can pay in pesos if you have them," he said, his eyes masked behind his sunglasses.

"60 bucks? You have to be kidding! How many drinks does that include?" Big Daddy demanded in an embarrassingly loud voice.

"No drinks are included in the cover price," Gucci Boy said matter-of-factly.

"No drinks? What exactly do we get for our money then?"

"You get entrance to the world's biggest nightclub. That's why we call it Privilege."

"Well, I'm not paying 60 bucks just to walk in the door!" Big Daddy announced. "That's highway robbery. And why do we have to pay when you let those guys walk right in?"

"They are my friends. I see them everyday at the beach café. You, I've never seen," Gucci Boy said with no small touch of distain.

"Well, I refuse to be ripped off like this," Big Daddy fumed. "We're going home. Are you coming with us?" he asked, looking first at the Brazilians, then at the Insurance Guys, and finally at Jake and Luca.

Tomàs stepped in, "Listen, we'll ride home with you guys, and they can go in and see what all the hoopla's about."

Big Daddy just glowered.

"We'll take a look around and maybe have a drink," Bill said. "We shouldn't be out too late. Anyway, it looks like it'll be just us and the bartenders. We'll see you guys back at the house."

Jake was glad that one of the Insurance Guys had taken the reins on that one. He didn't think he or Luca had any more rope to hang themselves with Big Daddy. The four of them turned and started down the steps. They could hear Big Daddy complaining all the way back to the car.

"Thank God!" laughed Gucci Boy. "I should have told them it was 120 US dollars. We don't want anyone like *that* in here. Big American muscle boys are always welcomed with open arms."

Jake, Luca, and the Insurance Guys made their way down the stairs into the bowels of a building that was indeed the size of a small sports stadium. They stopped at the first bar they came to and ordered four Coronas with lime. The bartender seemed surprised to see any patrons at this early hour.

Jake checked his watch. It was 3:00 am.

"I'll be right back," Luca said. "I have to piss. I've been holding it in the entire way, and those bumpy roads didn't make it any easier."

Between the men's and women's bathrooms he saw a little old lady sitting at a small table. She was methodically folding small portions of toilet paper. She also had a small stack of paper towels for drying hands. On the wall above her was a hand-made sign that listed prices.

Is this possible? In a nightclub that charges a $60 cover, they actually sell you toilet paper and paper towels?

While using the long communal trough that served as a urinal, Luca became aware of someone mopping the floor behind him. He shook off his dick and zipped up his fly. He turned and was startled to realize the mopper was an old woman. *In the men's room?* It was kind of like having your grandmother in there with you. Luca passed the sinks without washing his hands. If he understood the signs above the sinks correctly, they said that the water was not drinkable. *Well, that's one way to keep guys from refilling their water bottles from the tap.*

Luca passed the old lady and her table of toilet paper on his way to the stairs. He climbed to the top and was met by Jake and the Insurance Guys.

"The bartender told us we're at least an hour early. The crowd doesn't start to arrive until 4:00," Jake said, disappointed by their big night out. "Shall we go for a look around?"

"Sure, we might as well kill some time until Raul shows. I hope we're still awake by the time he gets here," Luca laughed. They toured the club, which had several levels, and wound up in the very heart of it on a totally empty dance floor. Although the DJ was playing kickass music, there was no way they were going to dance all alone. From the dance floor they had an amazing view of a gigantic stage big enough for a theatrical production. Behind the stage were three-story tall floor-to-ceiling windows. Raul had told Jake you could

264

dance and watch the sun rise. In front of the stage was the club's most unusual feature – an Olympic-size swimming pool bisected by a catwalk. On the left end of the catwalk was a stand with a lifeguard in a bathing suit sitting watch.

"I wonder how many people fall in during the night?" Bill asked.

"Or get pushed in?" Bluto added.

"Drunk people and swimming pools aren't a good mix," Luca stated.

Jake went to the nearest bar to grab them each another beer. He returned with Raul!

They all jumped up as if he was their lord and savior.

"Ugh! I can't believe you guys had to go out so early with those hicks. I stopped at Dome and the owner told me you had been there and left. Anyway, I have some good news! There's an amazing party happening tonight. Now chug those beers and let's get going," he said impatiently.

They followed Raul out of the club.

"Where are you going, my friends?" Gucci Boy asked.

"The beach party," Raul answered.

"Lucky you! I wish I could go, too. It's the best thing going on tonight. I'm jealous."

When Jake and Luca got to Raul's car they stopped in their tracks.

"Look who I picked up at Dome," Raul said. "He was wondering where the action was tonight so I thought I'd bring him along for the ride." Beau was sitting in the passenger seat.

What the fuck is this mess doing in Raul's car? Please let him be wearing pants instead of that goddamn Versace bathing suit, thought Luca.

"What took you so long? I've been sweating my balls off out here." Beau complained. He was shirtless. "Let's get this party rolling. I've got a busy night of promoting ahead of me," he said with barely concealed irritation.

"Follow me or you'll get lost," interrupted Raul. "The party is on the other side of the island at a beach club that's usually straight. But tonight anything goes."

Jake and Luca squeezed into the back seat of the Insurance Guys' car while Raul climbed behind the wheel of his car.

At times it seemed like Raul was intentionally trying to lose them. They went uphill, downhill, through valleys, and at times they swore they were driving through farmers' plowed fields before reaching a spot on the edge of a steep slope.

Raul pulled over and parked. "Well, boys, this is it. Every August on the full moon, they take over this daytime beach club and turn it into Shangri-La," he said as he swept his hands through the air. Down below they could see a rocky cove. A full moon in the clear sky reflected off the water that calmly lapped at the beach. "Can you hear the drumming circle?" Raul asked. "It's over there around that campfire," he said, pointing to a flickering light on the beach. "I'm telling you, this is the one party of the season that everyone talks about. You guys lucked out on your last night. Did you bring along your bags?"

"Yes, Raul, they're in the trunk of their," Jake answered, pointing to the Insurance Guys.

The scene before them was surreal in its beauty. The entire landscape was dotted with flickering golden lights. Brown paper bags filled with sand and votive candles illuminated their walk. There was a kind of excitement in the air that was hard to explain. As the boys walked down the candle-lit path, the drumming grew stronger and blended with the dance music that was being played in a large pavilion that looked out over the beach.

"You guys are in for a treat," Raul gleamed. "Boy George flew in from London to be the DJ tonight. This party will last until the sun comes up. I'm so glad I could bring you guys to see this. It's something you have to experience to understand." Raul was beaming.

The boys were not the only ones traveling down this magically lit path to the beach. They were surrounded by boys and girls all drawn to the beat of the drums, all eager to dance under the full moon. Their tanned skin glowed from days spent baking in the sunshine and splashing in the surf. They arrived at a pair of gates at the base of the path and entered a romantic heaven. Thatch-roofed huts were sprinkled across the sand. Their hanging candle-lit lanterns cast a warm glow. The main pavilion held a thundering sound system and a dance floor big enough for hundreds. Above it all, Boy George was wearing a gigantic rhinestone-covered black top hat that glittered in the darkness.

"Now take your vitamins," Raul said. He handed each of them an Ecstasy from his Tic Tac container. "I want you to remember this night forever. This is one of the reasons I keep returning to this island. It's like no other place on earth. You'll see." Raul and Beau headed for the beach. "If you think this is wild, you should check out the action in the dunes down at the far end of the beach, past the drumming circle. Boys, girls, it's a fucking orgy where anything goes," Raul said with a big grin that was a little scary. The two of them disappeared into the darkness. The Insurance Guys headed for the dance floor.

Jake and Luca walked toward a rock jetty that pushed its way into the shimmering ocean. They sat on a large boulder that radiated warmth from a day in the sun. Water lapped around the rocks at their feet. Madonna was singing about *how someone had come into her life and touched her soul, changing everything.*

"Do you have any idea how much I love you?" Jake asked.

"I think so," Luca replied. "The same way I love you. I feel like I've found my soul mate."

"Losing Sean taught me what I was capable of. Of how much I could love and care for someone."

"With you I feel safe and grounded." Luca answered. "I feel like you'll always be there for me."

Jake wrapped his arms around Luca's shoulders.

Luca sat peacefully, letting himself be loved.

Sunday Morning

The sun was high in the sky when the Insurance Guys pulled up to the drop-off lane at the airport. All four boys climbed out of the tiny car to exchange sweaty bare-chested hugs. They were still in a state of nirvana from the night's party.

"Thanks for last night, guys," Bill said.

"And make sure to thank your friend Raul if he ever surfaces," Bluto added.

"You're very welcome. I'm sure you'll see him at the beach if Big Daddy allows you two to go," Jake laughed.

"Fuck him and Miss Goody Two Shoes! They tried to ruin this vacation. You saved it for us."

"Well, give our best farewells to the Beverly Hillbillies!" Jake and Luca shouted over a loud plane taking off. They grabbed their bags out the trunk and headed into the terminal. Inside the men's room, they shed their nightclub clothes and changed into jeans and t-shirts for flying home.

Beverly Hills – *One Week Later*

Ira & Beau
When Beau returned from Ibiza, he was more tan than ever, but he looked thinner and older to Ira. Beau had lost that youthful glow that Ira had found so irresistible. Blind to Beau's growing drug habit, Ira pinned it all on his health. He couldn't look at Beau without feeling guilty.

Although Beau looked tired, he was a bundle of energy. He regaled Ira with tales of the extraordinary parties he'd thrown on Ibiza. According to Beau, he was now an international celebrity on the gay party circuit. Everyone was begging him to produce parties for them. He let it casually slip that he'd had lunch on the beach in Ibiza with the Velvet Mafia and that the Movie Mogul had invited him to his Fire Island home for cocktails at the end of the month when everyone would be there for the Morning Party.

While Beau had been in Ibiza, Ira had been occupied with some unpleasant business. His lawyer had called to tell him that his involvement in an Internet company had gotten inquiries from the Federal Trade Commission. It seemed that someone was accusing him of fraudulent billing practices. An Atlanta lawyer had come up with a breakdown of how fees for viewing the site were handled.

Ira was mulling over what to do. He should have known it was too good to be true. While he'd been assured that no one ever questioned a discreet porn billing charge on their monthly credit card statement, this lawyer had a client who had the balls and the bucks to pursue the matter. Now Ira's attorney wanted to know how he wished to proceed. For the first time in his life, Ira was uncertain of what to do next.

Fort Lauderdale

Big Daddy & Bobby
I hope he says yes, thought Bobby. He had an idea he wanted to share.

"Big Daddy?" he asked tentatively.

"Yes, sweetie?"

"I've been thinking."

"Does your head hurt?" Big Daddy asked, jokingly.

Bobby looked at him quizzically then continued. "I saw a poster at the gym about a gay church here in Fort

Lauderdale. Do you think that maybe we could go sometime?" he asked. "I really miss going to church. Growing up, I never missed a Sunday."

"Well sure, honey," Big Daddy responded, figuring this little idea of Bobby's would pass before Sunday rolled around.

"Great! Tomorrow night they're having a service. I'd love to go and hear what the preacher has to say," Bobby said excitedly.

"Shit," Big Daddy muttered to himself. "Sure, honey, we can go," he reluctantly agreed.

***

Bobby was looking around the parking lot to see if he recognized anyone from the gym while Big Daddy looked for the ideal space to park his new BMW 740iL. Big Daddy parked as far away from the other cars as possible, for fear of someone putting a scratch on his dream-mobile.

So this is where the movers and shakers hang out, Big Daddy noted when he noticed how many other BMWs and top-of-the-line cars filled the lot.

***

The congregation rose to its feet and applauded wildly when the pastor took the pulpit. Big Daddy, unaccustomed to such displays in church, took a while to stand. He applauded politely while scanning the crowd. They reeked of money. Big Daddy's gears began to turn. This could be the ticket to meet people who actually mattered.

The pastor, a tall elegant man, cleared his throat. "I stand before you this evening to speak the truth. I am gay. I am proud. And God loves me without reservation," he said.

For Bobby, those words rang true. He'd always known that sweet baby Jesus loved him exactly as he was, but from where he came from, there was no way he could be gay and Christian. This was a whole new world for Bobby, a world in which he could fit in.

The pastor continued with his sermon. He spoke about how God had chosen to create all those assembled as gay. And to deny one's sexual orientation was to deny a gift from God. Once again, the congregation rose to its feet. He finished by stating, "We must stand united to reclaim our rightful place at our Father's table. We are all created in his image. And that image is perfect. We can be Christian and

269

gay because we are all loved equally by God." His concluding remarks brought thunderous applause.

After the service ended, Big Daddy pushed his way through the crowd toward the exit where the pastor stood. This was his opportunity to make an impression.

"Your sermon was very eloquent. Allow me to introduce myself. I'm Otis Mercer, but everyone calls me Big Daddy," he said, offering his hand.

"A pleasure to meet you," said the pastor, shaking Big Daddy's huge paw.

"I was successful at fundraising for my old church in Atlanta. Perhaps I could be of some use here," Big Daddy said as humbly as he could.

"Well, we're always in need of volunteers," the pastor politely replied.

"I'm not talking about volunteering. I'm talking about spearheading a campaign to expand this church."

"How so?" the pastor asked, taking a bit more interest in the giant Southern gentlemen.

"Well, perhaps if I made a generous donation, we might be able to get like-minded church members to follow suit in matching my gift," Big Daddy suggested.

"I am intrigued. Perhaps we should arrange lunch later this week."

"Lunch at my home would be perfect. It's not far from here. Are you familiar with the islands off of Las Olas?"

The pastor's eyes lit up in recognition of the pricey waterfront neighborhood.

"Here's my card. Give me a call to set it up." Big Daddy shook the pastor's hand and motioned to Bobby that it was time to leave. Bobby fell in behind as Big Daddy strode triumphantly out of the church. If the preacher was any indication, Big Daddy could win over the entire congregation if he played his cards right. Now, he had to find a way to make a big splash.

***

For months Tomàs had been working on a portrait of Bobby. Big Daddy's drug-induced request at the Black Party had indeed been serious and a sizeable check had exchanged hands. Tomàs had agreed to deliver the painting by the end of October. A grand housewarming party would be perfect for the unveiling of the portrait.

"Bobby, get in here!" Big Daddy shouted.

270

Bobby arrived, dripping with sweat. "Did you call me? I was out working on the pool. Can I get you a something to drink?" he asked.

"Sure, I'll take a Diet Coke, no bourbon. I have to watch my weight with the big Fire Island weekend coming up," Big Daddy replied. "I want you to go to the printers. They called and said the invitations are ready. I figured you'd hand them out this weekend since everyone will be there."

"That's a great idea! I can't wait to see them. Who all are we inviting?"

"We're sure as hell not inviting Jake and Luca. They turned out to be the worst kind of houseguests in Ibiza. Couldn't even be bothered to say a proper thank you and good bye, let alone put out," Big Daddy fumed. "We'll invite every one of their friends and see how they like being left out in the cold!"

"Won't the Brazilians say something to them?" Bobby innocently asked.

"I'm sure they will. Now don't forget my Diet Coke."

South Beach

Jake

He caught the phone on its last ring before the answering machine picked up. Jake recognized the voice of Hunt's lawyer. "I'm sorry," he said. "I have some bad news."

Oh God, please don't say Hunt is dead, flooded Jake's head. "Is Hunt alright?"

"Yes, of course. I haven't spoken to him. I wanted to call you first. It's about the house." *Not "your" house but "the" house,* Jake would always remember. He felt numb as Hunt's lawyer relayed the judge's decision. He could hear him speaking, but after the initial impact, the words had no meaning. Jake had never felt more alone. Now, the last part of Sean that Jake had, their house, was going to be taken from him. He felt lost, like his world was crumbling.

With Luca away shooting another video, Jake had to talk to someone. He dialed Hunt.

"Hello?" said Hunt. He sounded like he'd just awoken from his afternoon nap.

"Hi, it's me . . . ," Jake said.

"You sound so sad. What's wrong, honey?" Hunt asked, his voice rising in concern.

"I lost my house," was all that Jake could manage.

"What? You lost what?"

"I got a call from your lawyer. He told me the judge ruled against me. They're going to take my house away." He lost the ability to speak. He could only sob.

"Stay right there. First I'm going to call him and find out what went wrong. He assured me that you had a strong case. Then, I'm coming over."

Hunt arrived within the hour. Jake was sitting in the same spot where he'd taken the lawyer's call. Hunt confirmed everything that the lawyer had told Jake. Even though Jake and Sean had formed a company that owned the house, and Sean had signed over all the shares in the company to Jake, Sean's will hadn't been updated to show any of this. The judge ruled in favor of Sean's executors.

Hunt told Jake that he could move in with him.

"That's a very generous offer, but I can't, Hunt," Jake explained. "I need to have my own home."

***

After Hunt had left, Jake realized that he had to call Karl and cancel his and Luca's plans to go to Fire Island for the Morning Party.

"No fucking way!" Karl nearly screamed into the receiver when Jake told him the bad news. "Oh, honey. I am so sorry. This is so unfair. Sean must be furious looking down on this and seeing what his 'best' friends have done to you. He trusted those assholes to protect you from his family. Instead they turned on you. Oh, God! I can't believe this."

"I know. It all seems like a bad dream. And Luca's not here. He's working," Jake sighed.

"Do you want me to fly down there?"

"No, no. I'll be alright. It's just such a shock. I don't know what to do."

"You sit tight until Luca comes home. And we'll see you in a few days for the weekend," Karl said, trying to be upbeat.

"Oh, no. I couldn't after this. There's no way we'll be able to make it."

"Of course you're going to make it. You have to. All of your friends are here. You're coming up, and that's that. Besides, everyone's talking about the HardBodies party that you're throwing at Rob and Erik's. You can't cancel that and disappoint the entire gay community, including those of us who don't make the cut," Karl chuckled.

"OK. I'll talk to Luca when he gets home. I'll call you

to let you know what we decide," Jake said feeling overwhelmed. Maybe Karl was right. Jake didn't know what to think. He just knew he missed, loved, and needed Luca right now.

Beverly Hills

Ira

He sat there at his big desk in utter silence. Ira had just hung up the phone. He'd gotten a surprise call from an old friend from his Naval Academy days. These days, his friend was working for the California State Attorney's office. While thrilled at first to hear his old pal's voice, Ira was blindsided by the information he was given. By the end of the conversation, he felt like he was suffocating. He could barely thank his friend for the warning.

Ira felt like all his options had run out. *How could I have been so stupid? Get in on the ground floor of the Internet porn business. Charge the website customers at every turn. They'd be too embarrassed to complain.* All that he had worked for was in jeopardy.

South Beach - *One Week Later*

Jake & Luca

Luca hung up the phone and turned to Jake, "We're all set, with one little hitch. Erik won't be joining us. He's got a buddy visiting from out of town and is going to stay in the City on Saturday night. He'll meet us at the Morning Party on Sunday afternoon. Anyway, Rob said the Rocks would be there to help out with the HardBodies party as would - are you ready for this - Beau."

"Not again! Crazy crack-head Beau from LA?" Jake exclaimed.

"Well, I'm afraid we have to take the good with the bad. Rob has agreed to invite the hottest muscle boys in the City."

"I know you're right," Jake said, "but that Beau works my last nerve."

"We should be able to pretty much neutralize him," Luca replied. "I mean, this is our party. He can't make any claims on it. It's not like we need him for anything. We've got the Rocks to man the door. And, by the way, I volunteered us to bartend at the Morning Party with Rob."

"Are you serious? What a buzz kill!"

"No, Rob promised it will be fun. We get into the party for free, work the first shift before the party really gets going, flirt with every cute boy who wants our attention, then enjoy the afternoon with our friends," Luca assured Jake.

"Now that you put it that way, it does sound like the perfect plan."

Luca nodded his head then lowered his voice. "Just so you know, I didn't say anything to Rob about losing the house."

"Good. I only told Karl, who I'm sure told Curt, who probably told the Brazilians, who I'm certain told the Beverly Hillbillies."

August 1995 – *Two Weeks Later / Morning Party Weekend*
Fire Island
Friday

Jake & Luca

After landing in Islip, Jake and Luca took a van to the ferry. At the dock they met up with a large group from the City that included Rob and the Rocks. "Has Rob done something else to his face?" Jake asked in a whisper.

"I'm not sure, but it doesn't hold up well in daylight," Luca responded.

The ferry whistle blew and the boys picked up their luggage. Jake and Luca's entourage stepped aboard the ferry and made their way to the upper deck where they could ride in the open air and enjoy the view as the ferry crossed the bay from Sayville to the thin barrier island. Just as the boat pulled away from the dock, the Beverly Hillbillies climbed out of a white stretch limo with piles of luggage, enough for an African safari.

The summer sun felt strong. Most of the guys on the upper deck took off their shirts. Conversation dwindled. The passengers relaxed, closed their eyes, and leaned back against the hard benches. The boat moved away from the harbor and out into the open water. The frantic pace of the City fell away. They knew they were going someplace special, a place like no other. A lot of Fire Island regulars often joked about talking to guys for the first time out on the Island, guys they'd seen for years in Chelsea without ever approaching. Somehow being in this unique place allowed these jaded, insulated New Yorkers to drop their guard. The twenty-minute ferry ride made all the difference in the world.

274

Disembarking on a big holiday weekend was always an event. Full-time residents and already-arrived-housemates flocked to greet the new arrivals. When Jake and Luca stepped onto the wooden dock, they heard a familiar accent. "Jake!" Tomàs shouted, waving frantically. Both looked around to locate him. It wasn't easy. He was a pocket gay, hidden by taller muscle boys. Finally he broke through the crowd, pulling a little red wagon behind him. He dropped the handle with a clank and threw his arms around Jake. "Oh, it's so good to see you," he said, hugging him hard. "I'm so sorry to hear about your house." If Tomàs knew the news, then everyone knew.

Jake chose to change the subject. "You look great! You've really been hitting the gym," he observed.

"I've been training so I can get into the HardBodies party everyone's been talking about," he said with a sly grin. Jake and Luca piled their bags into his red wagon and made their way to the house. Creeping along the wide wooden walkway, they followed the parade of new arrivals down Pines Boulevard to houses buried in the pine forest. "You guys are the first here. Why don't we get you settled in before we have lunch. Paolo and the Fashionistas will straggle in later, after they've put in a day of work. Can you imagine that scene, coming out to the Island at rush hour?" he asked. Tomàs spent the entire summer on the Island painting and doing his illustration work.

After a short walk, they turned off the Boulevard and headed uphill toward the beach. They stopped before they got to Shore Walk, where the expensive beachfront houses were located. Their more humble house was on the corner of Neptune and Shore. How appropriate. Their outfits for the Morning Party were "Buck-Rogers-meets-Tom-of-Finland." They'd be the star troopers from Neptune tomorrow.

Jake thought back to his first summer on the Island. Someone in their house had pulled out a white tutu and worn it with a thick black leather belt and combat boots to go to a party. It was cute and kind of sexy. An idea was born. What if every guy in the house wore the same outfit for the upcoming Morning Party? All they would have to buy was a tutu. Each guy already had his own boots and a black belt. The rest of the day became legend. Everyone practically bowed down to the House of Tutus. A house outfit became tradition.

Tomàs slid aside the wooden front gate to the deck surrounding the pool and led the boys into the house. "You guys have the big room with the view," he said with a laugh as he helped the boys with their bags. "Curt has declared that you get to sleep on the living room floor."

Luca looked around at the all-white living room with its pale wooden floors. As if reading his mind, Tomàs continued, "the cushions from this sectional sofa make up into a nice bed. Trust me, it's probably the most comfortable bed in the house. Not to mention you get to sleep under the stars." He pointed up to the twin skylights in the peaked ceiling. "It'll be beautiful."

Big Daddy & Bobby

After Bobby had cleared the dinner dishes from the dining room table, the doorbell rang. Their porn star guest had arrived.

"It's nice to see you again," the infamous Mr. B said when Big Daddy greeted him at the door.

"Bobby, get in here and greet our guest," Big Daddy bellowed.

Bobby came at a clip, still drying his hands on a dish towel. "Hi! I think we've rented all your videos since we met you in Palm Springs. It's a real thrill to have you staying with us for the entire weekend," Bobby said, trying his best to sound enthusiastic.

"Well, thanks! I've been out here before but never on Morning Party weekend," Mr. B replied. "I couldn't believe how crowded the ferry was. I was afraid I wouldn't get on."

"Well, we're sure glad you did. Bobby, I'll show our guest to his room."

"Okie dokie!" Bobby said with a smile that seemed a bit forced as he headed back to the kitchen.

Big Daddy walked Mr. B to his room. Once in the room with the door closed he laid down the rules. "OK, here's the deal. Since I'm paying for your time this weekend, I expect your full attention. That means you go where we go. If we invite some boys by to play, you join in. Understand?" he said in a business-like manner.

"Yes, sir, Big Daddy. I understand completely. You can count on me," the porn star said as he took in his plush surroundings. *I could get used to this lifestyle,* he thought.

"Good, now let's get you settled in and out of those clothes," Big Daddy said with a hungry look.

276

The Beverly Hillbillies showered together while Mr. B prepared himself in the guest bath. As per usual, Big Daddy started hosing out his ass just as Bobby was stepping out of the shower to dry off. Bobby would never say a word, but he'd hurry his way out of the bathroom before he had to bear witness to the sights and sounds of Big Daddy's ass gushing filthy water. He could remember the first time Big Daddy started douching in front of him. He hadn't said a word, but the look of horror on his face clued Big Daddy in to his disgust. "Well, I gotta clean it out it you're gonna stick your big dick up there, don't I?" Big Daddy had barked.

At a loss for words, Bobby had simply nodded. Tonight he had a sick feeling in his stomach. Usually he was as excited as Big Daddy to play with a porn star, but this was different. None of the others had been invited to stay overnight. And this was a repeat performance. *What if Big Daddy likes him better than me?* Bobby worried. *His dick is thicker than mine.*

Big Daddy shouted through the steamed-up shower door, "Sweetie, fix me a Diet Coke and bourbon. Ask Mr. B what he'd like."

"OK, Big Daddy," Bobby said, wondering what the porn star might request. *I hope he doesn't ask for anything fancy that we don't have.* He hung up his towel and walked buck naked down the hallway to the guest bedroom.

Bobby's knock on the door caught Mr. B as the last big gush of Fleets shot out of him. He looked down between his legs. It was clear. His cleanup job was complete. He was glad he'd closed the bathroom door before he started. No one wanted to see their porn fantasy sitting on the can.

"Big Daddy asked me to find out what you want to drink."

"Oh, I'm drinking water," Mr. B responded.

"OK, water it is," Bobby said, relieved. "Meet us in the master bedroom when you're ready."

Mr. B hopped out of the shower and went searching through his shaving kit. He located several tiny bottles of Liquid Ecstasy that he'd brought with him. He unscrewed one and slugged it back. The bitter salty taste lingered in his mouth. He took a swig of mouthwash, swished it around, and spit it out into the sink. With no reason to get dressed, he headed down the hall toward the master bedroom.

When Mr. B stepped through the bedroom door, the Liquid Ecstasy hit him with a warm rush that quickly spread throughout his body. The drug made the scene before him wildly erotic. Instead of viewing the beached whale on the bed with disgust, he focused on Big Daddy's dick and headed straight for it. He practically impaled his mouth on it, stretching his jaw to its full capacity as he tried to stuff its girth into his mouth.

"Damn, you're a hungry boy," Big Daddy declared as the ravenous porn star devoured him.

"Unnnhha," Mr. B mumbled.

Bobby entered and was unpleasantly surprised that they had gotten a jump start without him. He put the small plastic tray bearing their drinks down on the night table and climbed onto the bed. He laid a hand on Mr. B's ass and stroked the tight round muscle.

Mr. B groaned when Bobby's fingers grazed his hole.

Bobby took it as a sign to go further.

Big Daddy nodded approval.

Bobby moved behind Mr. B and buried his face between the smooth twin globes. When Bobby's tongue made contact, Mr. B instinctively spread his legs further apart. Without moving his mouth away from its target, Bobby groped around on the bed for a condom. He felt Big Daddy place one in his hand, followed by a bottle of lube. Bobby kept munching away at Mr. B's butt. It opened willingly for his tongue. With his free hand, Bobby rolled a condom down the length of his now hard-as-a-rock member. He poured some lube into his hand and coated his sheathed dick. He removed his mouth from Mr. B's ass and lined up the head of his dick with the pink pucker in front of him. Before he could push forward, Mr. B pushed back onto the entire length of Bobby's dick and started bucking on it in rhythm to his sucking of Big Daddy.

After all three of them had shot their loads, they lay back on the king-size bed. "That was incredible," Mr. B said. He grabbed a hand towel to wipe the cum off of his chin.

"You're telling me!" Big Daddy exclaimed between giant huffs and puffs. He was still red in the face from blowing his load down the porn star's throat.

Bobby was silent. Finally he spoke up. "You're a wild man," he quietly said.

"Thanks!" Mr. B said, slightly out of breath. "Wow, I've only just started using this stuff. It turns you into a sex maniac.

"What stuff?" Big Daddy asked.

"Liquid Ecstasy," Mr. B replied. He rolled over onto his back. "It's new on the West Coast. I'm not sure you guys have it here, yet. It's got some long complicated name, so

278

they call it G for short."

"G?" Bobby asked, embarrassed that he wasn't in the know.

"I'd offer you some, but I've heard you're not supposed to mix it with alcohol," Mr. B said. *Actually I didn't bring enough to share with you guys,* he thought. *And I'm gonna need it to get through this weekend with Orca and Rebecca of Sunnybrook Farm.*

"We've done Ecstasy before," Bobby said proudly.

"But we've never heard about this stuff," Big Daddy interrupted. "It sure turned you on. We'll have to look into it. Why don't we cool off and take a swim?"

"Sounds good to me," Mr. B answered. He felt the glow of his G fading.

"Me, too," Bobby said. As he climbed out of bed, he carefully removed the cum-filled rubber from his still-throbbing cock.

With the last glimmer of G pushing him onward, Mr. B asked, "Oh, is that for me?" He grabbed the cum-filled rubber from Bobby's hands. He and Big Daddy watched with amazement as Mr. B emptied the contents into his mouth.

I like this one. He's a real pig, Big Daddy smiled to himself. With a grunt, he got off the bed and waddled off to the shower.

Horrified, Bobby's mind reeled, *How do I top that?*

Mr. B looked around the bedroom, "This is some setup you've got here," he said.

Bobby's face went red. This was the last straw. "Huh? What do you mean by 'setup'?"

Mr. B tried to cover his gaffe. "I meant this house must cost a bundle to rent out here this week. What did you think I was saying?" he asked Bobby. "I'd never be so rude to talk about your Sugar Daddy."

Bobby felt like he'd been slapped in the face. "For your information, he's not my 'Sugar' Daddy," he practically shouted. "He's my Big Daddy. And it's not a 'setup.' We're in love," Bobby concluded and stormed out of the room.

New York
Saturday Night

Erik & Tzoni
The way Erik's heart was pounding, you'd think it was his first date. In a sense, it was. Tzoni was the man who had first awakened Erik's long-suppressed desires. He'd come

into Jocks for a beer, saw Erik behind the bar, and sparks flew. In the years since they'd met, Tzoni had grown even more handsome. He was the epitome of what Erik considered masculine - muscular and hairy. This was to be a reunion, an affirmation that Erik's life had taken the right turn after he'd met Tzoni.

The doorbell rang. Erik stubbed out what was left of the joint he was smoking and slugged back a shot of tequila. He opened the door and without a word, they embraced and began to kiss. Erik's nose picked up that dark musky smell that had triggered so many fantasies, a smell that he remembered from his college wrestling days. He had long ago stopped using deodorant in hopes of achieving the same ripeness that he found such a turn-on. Alas, his blond all-American armpits never seemed to measure up to those of darker, more ethnic guys. He pulled Tzoni inside the apartment and kissed him again, pushing him against the wall. Their bodies ground against each other, hardening cock against hardening cock.

"Damn! You're a great kisser. I bet you've learned a few other tricks as well," Tzoni said.
"And I intend to show you each and every one of them," Erik promised. "Can I get you something to drink?"
"Sure, how about a beer?" Tzoni replied as he took in the spectacular view through the wrap-around windows.
"I have a better idea. Let's kick things off with a tequila shot and then a beer. It's an old bartender's trick. For some reason, tequila acts differently than regular booze. It really loosens you up."
"I'm all for loosening things up."
"Good, because I have a few surprises," Erik smiled.
"I'm up for anything. I'm yours all night if you'll have me."
"Great! That's what I intended. Rob doesn't expect me out on the Island 'til tomorrow afternoon. Let me go get our drinks. Why don't you get undressed? You're wearing way too much."
"How about I strip down to my boots?"
"Perfect!"

Erik entered the living room to find Tzoni out on the terrace, enjoying Manhattan by moonlight. He handed him a shot glass and a pill. "Tequila and Ecstasy!" Erik toasted. He washed down the little pill with his shot.
Tzoni followed suit.

280

"I'll be right back with our beers."

"You're a very lucky guy," Tzoni said when Erik returned.

"I know. Sometime I can't believe how lucky I am. I've got a wonderful life. I have the perfect partner, a great job, and I live in the sort of place that I used to only dream about. And I've found myself. I'm a pig bottom and proud of it!" Erik clinked his beer bottle against Tzoni's.

"Here's to proud pig bottoms!" Tzoni clinked back.

Erik led Tzoni along the balcony to the guest bedroom. He slid open the glass doors and they stepped inside.

"Damn! This is some playroom!" Tzoni laughed as he finished his beer.

"Another round?" Erik asked. Tzoni nodded and Erik slipped out the door for refills.

While Erik was gone, Tzoni inspected the playroom. There were condoms and latex gloves, butt plugs and dildoes of varying sizes, and a few bottles of poppers next to spray cans of ethyl chloride. Tzoni loved using both poppers and ethyl. A variety of containers holding pills, liquids, and powders sat on a tray with a pile of joints. About a dozen cum towels were stacked neatly in a pile.

Erik nudged open the door with a chilled six pack in one hand and a bottle of Patrón Gold in the other.

"You're quite the host," Tzoni said.

"It comes from being in the bar business. We always have free booze around, and you'd be surprised at the drugs the cleaning crew finds after closing," Erik smiled. He picked up two tiny bottles of clear liquid. "This was a gift from a porn star who was traveling through town this week on his way out to the Morning Party. It's Liquid Ecstasy. It's all the rage out in LA, or so I'm told. We never got around to trying it. We'll save that for later." Erik lit a joint and passed it to Tzoni as he poured shots of tequila and opened two new Coronas.

After sharing most of the joint out on the balcony, Erik took Tzoni's hand, brought him back into the playroom, and laid him down on the bed. He climbed on top of Tzoni and kissed his way down to his fat uncut cock. He swallowed it in one gulp, down to Tzoni's enormous balls. Erik inhaled the deep musk of Tzoni's crotch. Instantly, he was transported back to that time they'd wrestled. His cock was instantly hard.

Tzoni allowed himself to enjoy Erik's blow job while he slugged down his beer. Then, putting the bottle on the side table, Tzoni pulled an old wrestling move that brought him face to face with Erik's crotch. Not to be outdone, he went to work on Erik's dick. The two of them were sucking and licking as if it were their last meal. Eventually they worked their way down to each other's balls. They tongued away until both of them were dripping precum. They lapped it up like bears to honey. Finally they came up for air.

"OK, it's time for you to give up that ass to me. How about you show me what you've learned? Then I'll show you what an accomplished fisting bottom, I've become," Tzoni said. Erik got off the bed and into the leather sling, He adjusted himself so that his butt was hanging over the bottom edge. Tzoni made sure Erik's feet were up and out of the way in the leather stirrups. He reached over to the dresser and held up the poppers and ethyl chloride for Erik to choose.

"I'll alternate."

Tzoni handed him both. Finishing off his Corona, Tzoni lubed up both of his hands.

Erik took a hit of poppers. "It's all yours, buddy."

Tzoni took in the sight of this big handsome brute lying back exposing his ass. "Damn, what a pretty hole you've got."

Erik smiled. His thick hairy legs gave way to a white butt that looked like it had never seen the sun. The perfect muscle butt split to reveal a perfectly shaped, pink rosebud.

Tzoni could no longer keep his hands off of it. At first he started massaging it with his fingers one at a time, taking turns dipping in and out. Gradually he worked several fingers into him.

Erik sprayed some ethyl onto a cum towel and held it over his mouth, inhaling deeply.

Tzoni waited for Erik's body to relax before sliding most of his hand into him.

"More," Erik insisted.

Tzoni smeared grease up both of his forearms and proceeded. He could feel Erik bearing down on his hand, pushing his ass down around him. Wet heat enveloped him. He felt Erik's sphincter close around his wrist. His entire hand was up inside him. Tzoni knew from experience to allow Erik's body to relax and get used to the girth of his considerable fist.

Erik reached down to spread his ass cheeks as wide apart as possible. Tzoni started to move his fist deeper into

282

Erik's guts. He slowly slid his other hand into Erik's ass alongside the first. "Damn, boy. You're one talented pig. Fuck! That is amazing." Tzoni was sliding one hand is as he slid the other hand out, never quite leaving Erik's hole.

"I told you I was proud to be a pig bottom!" slurred Erik.

Tzoni was impressed. He pulled out and admired Erik's dilated hole. Then Erik snapped it shut using his well-trained muscles.

The combo of drugs and booze had Tzoni half cross-eyed. He reached over, grabbed a condom, and rolled it down his throbbing hard-on.

Erik took another hit of poppers and Tzoni slid his thick cock in alongside his hand. Erik could feel Tzoni's fist close around his cock and start jacking himself off inside his ass. It drove Erik wild. One more whiff of ethyl and he was in outer space. The sounds around him seemed to warp. His body went limp. All he could feel was the rhythmic pumping of Tzoni's cock-wrapped fist. His mind reeled from the pleasure.

Erik grunted when he felt Tzoni pop out of him. "Fuck! What happened?" he asked.

"I came jacking off inside you is what happened, you hot pig!" Tzoni explained as he pulled the condom off his bright red cock. "And when I popped, so did you. Look at the load you shot!"

Erik looked down. His furry abs were covered with cum.

"Here let me add to that," Tzoni said. He dumped the thick white contents of his condom, adding to Erik's own puddle.

"Damn, look at all that!" Erik said.

"Yeah, can't waste it." Tzoni bent down and lapped it all up like a hungry animal.

"Woof!" Erik growled. "Round one!

"Yep, let's take a little break and refuel. Next, it's your turn to work my ass. And damn, I've got a long way to go to top that one." Tzoni gave Erik a hand up out of the sling. They both grabbed cum towels to mop up their sweat and wipe the lube from their hands.

"Let's wash down another hit of E with a shot of tequila. Then we can sit out on the terrace and smoke another joint," Erik suggested.

After Erik fucked and fisted Tzoni in the sling, they toweled off before yet another round of drinks and another joint under the gorgeous full moon. They were both exhausted when they returned to the bed.

"Oh, I almost forgot," Erik said through a haze of tequila and beer.

"What? I think we may have invented a few things tonight," Tzoni said groggily.

"How about the Liquid Ecstasy?" Erik asked.

"You still want to do more?" Tzoni marveled at Erik's energy.

"Why not? It'll be the perfect way to finish off the night." Erik grabbed two tiny bottles from the bedside table. He handed one to Tzoni who took a tiny sip and grimaced.

"Fuck, that's so salty," he complained. He reached for a beer to wash the awful taste from his mouth. "That stuff is foul. I can't drink it."

"Oh, don't be a pussy," Erik said as he slugged back his vial.

They both lay back in each other's arms as they felt the wave of heat flood their bodies.

"See?" Erik said. "I told you it would be amazing!"

They kissed and their bodies fused into one.

Fire Island
Saturday Night

Jake & Luca
The muscle boys started to arrive at Rob and Erik's house at 10:00 pm. Word had spread quickly in the tiny community. If you wanted to attend the hottest sex party of the season, you had to show up at the right time and the right place to be considered for admission. Jake and the Rocks were at the door. Most of the "applicants" wore tank tops or no shirts at all.

Thank God our phone message is tough, Jake thought. *I hate turning guys away.* He let in small groups of three to five guys at a time who then proceeded to the dining room table where Luca sat. He gave them the waiver to read and sign: no unsafe sex and no drugs. After they had processed over a hundred guys - all extraordinary examples of hours spent pumping iron - it was time to close up shop. The doors locked at 10:30 pm. No exceptions.

"You guys have quite the system," Alcatraz said.

"We're fast learners," Luca replied. "There should be 112 by my count."

"It's time to start this party," Jake announced. "Let's get naked."

Jake, Luca, and the Rocks entered the foyer and started to strip. They looked around them and were amazed at the mountain of white trash bags with names written on them. They stashed their clothing into bags and hid them under the steps. The Rocks handed Jake and Luca towels and the four of them headed to the pool to get a drink.

For a brief moment they saw Rob followed by a guy who was so handsome, even in the flickering candlelight, that it looked like he was wearing a Clark Kent mask. They watched Rob lead his prize into the house and caught a glimpse of the enormous piece of meat swinging nearly down to Clark's knees.

He's got himself a winner, thought Luca.

Rob
He led the tall dark stranger upstairs to the second-floor master bedroom and locked the door behind him. He didn't want to risk having anyone follow them and think that the party was in the private part of the house.

Leather-scented candles filled the room with a musky aroma. Tribal music played in the background. Rob turned toward Clark and took in his beauty. Clark's body was naturally smooth and chiseled into defined mounds of muscle. Rob envied his abs. While he had a six-pack, this guy had a rippling eight-pack. Rob was stunned when Clark stepped closer into the relative brightness of the candlelight.

His first thought was, *I want that face.* No matter how many little "tweaks" he did, Rob knew in a flash that he could never top Clark's natural beauty. His square jaw met in a perfect cleft chin and his strong angular nose was a masterpiece that no surgeon could ever create. Long, thick, dark lashes surrounded huge black eyes that sparkled. Rob stood there as the naked beauty moved closer to join him by the side of the bed.

Jake & Luca
Jake was sitting in a wicker chair while a short Latin, with a Mohawk dyed fire-engine red, kneeled before him and sucked

happily on his cock. While he enjoyed this oral expert, Jake watched Luca pound a muscle muffin's bubble butt. Without a drop of jealousy, he found watching his boyfriend fucking another man very arousing.

Jake's ego was strong enough to deal with the attention that Luca got from being a porn star. It was odd and sometimes uncomfortable when strangers approached Luca as if they already knew him. Some fans would politely acknowledge Jake's existence while recounting their tales of jacking off to Luca's videos. Others acted as if Jake were invisible. Luca was always polite to his fans, thanking them for their support while excusing himself from the conversation because his boyfriend was with him. These encounters drove home the difference between Jake's job and Luca's. While Jake had sex with one, sometimes two massage clients in the privacy of their home, Luca was viewed having sex by thousands of men who watched his videos repeatedly, memorizing every detail of his body. Jake understood that Luca was his in a way that none of those viewers would ever know.

***

The parties that Jake and Luca had created with South Beach HardBodies were the fulfillment of what most men's fantasies of making porn were like, but Luca knew the difference, and it was a big difference. All he had to say was, "Imagine having someone tell you how to have sex, with someone you don't like, for hours on end in front of a camera crew." That pretty much summed it up and most guys got the point. A career in porn was good for one reason and one reason only: the money to be made from escorting. Luca wanted to make as much money as possible while he was still highly sought after.

He was lucky to be in his 30s with a bit of life experience under his belt when he began his porn career. Younger guys often began to believe their own hype. Luca had seen one such character getting off the ferry the day before - the infamous Mr. B.

When Luca invited him to the HardBodies party, Mr. B brushed it off with, "I'm working. If I'm getting laid, I'm getting paid."

Mr. B had pinned all his hopes on his fame, fleeting though it might be. After the adoring crowds had had enough of his face, body, and dick, they'd move on to the next face, body, and dick. As with any porn magazine or video, the viewer eventually loses interest. The poor boy failed to see that he was a commodity with an expiration date. Where would he be when those fans stopped adoring him?

Mr. B bragged to Luca about how he'd lucked out with his living arrangements. He'd rented out his LA condo because he was spending so much time living at Jabba the Hut's online Laguna beach house. Mr. B was living there for free and fucking all the hot porn boys he wanted, but he had bigger plans. According to him, the owner of the Laguna house would stop by regularly to check out the boys. The way Mr. B figured, it wouldn't be long before the guy with the Panama hat was his new Sugar Daddy. Luca never let on that he knew the man in the Panama hat.

Beau

He put on his lucky cock ring, a faded pair of jeans, flip-flops, and a brand new Versace shirt that he'd bought in Ibiza. He thought his outfit struck the right note of casual elegance. He figured it was the way the members of the Velvet Mafia dressed, or at least the way their trophy-boys did. If all went according to plan, he'd be sleeping in a new bed on Pratesi sheets tonight.

It was easy to find the Movie Mogul's newly purchased beach house. Everyone on the Island knew it. A landmark ever since Mr. Underwear had bought it and remodeled it, the place was the Buckingham Palace of Fire Island. All Beau had to do was make a few turns and then walk toward the ocean. There it stood, a clean cedar-clad box perched high on the dunes overlooking the Atlantic. Beau felt his heart pounding as he walked toward the big hulk guarding the gate.

"May I help you?" asked the Hulk.

"Yes, I'm here for the party," Beau said proudly. He took a step toward the gate.

The Hulk stood rock solid, blocking Beau's access. "Your name please?" the Hulk asked as he raised a clipboard and flashlight.

"First name, Beau. Last name spelled F-O-U-R-N-I-E-R," he replied patiently.

After a quick flash of light, the Hulk said, "Sorry. You're not on the list."

"Could you please check again? I saw him earlier this month in Ibiza, and he personally invited me," Beau said confidently.

287

The Hulk flashed his light on the list again, taking his time to prove to Beau that he was indeed checking it. "Sorry, nothing under Fournier or Beau," the Hulk said, extinguishing his light.

"He will not be happy if I don't attend his party tonight. He was very specific in his invitation."

"I'm sorry." The Hulk remained motionless.

Beau felt the heat rise in his face, and he was glad for the cover of darkness. "I came all the way from LA to attend tonight's party. You have to let me in. Perhaps you could get someone who could verify my identity?"

"Please sir, I'm just doing my job. I can't leave my post. Perhaps if you went back to your home and called him, he could send someone out to add your name to the list."

"Well, I guess I'll have to do that. I don't think he'll be happy with the way you're treating his friends," Beau added, trying to control his anger.

"Once again, sir, my apologies. I'm just doing my job."

I'll call Ira and get the Movie Mogul's number. This is ridiculous! Beau muttered to himself all the way back to Rob and Erik's with nothing but the sound of his footsteps drowning out the curses and threats he would direct at the Hulk upon his triumphant return to the party. Once engulfed by the darkness of the pine forest, Beau took out his bumper and did a quick snort. The smell of pine mixed with the antiseptic sting of the Tina.

The dark woods became a surreal jungle as Beau made his way back to his hosts' home. Moonlit shadows played tricks on his eyes. He thought he saw people, or maybe animals, moving just beyond his vision. Every snap of a twig or rustle of the wind through pine branches made him jump. At last he rounded the corner to Rob and Erik's.

He turned the knob of the wooden gate that guarded the front walk to the house. It wouldn't budge. *That's odd,* he thought. *They're having that HardBodies party tonight.* Beau could hear the thump-thump-thump of the music that was playing over the poolside speakers. *They have to be home.* Beau rang the doorbell. He waited for what seemed an eternity. *This is fucking insane! If I have to climb the goddamn fence, than that's what I'll do.* Beau held onto the gate and slowly stepped off the landing into the wooded darkness. He gasped as cold wet mud swallowed his foot. Abruptly he hauled himself out of the stinking muck. "Shit!" he hollered into the deserted forest. Beau shook as much of the slime off of his foot as possible, losing his flip-flop in the darkness.

"How dare they lock me out of the house, out of their fucking party!" he caught himself shouting. Realizing there was no way to get into the house without sinking into the marsh that most of the Island's houses were built above, he kicked off his remaining flip-flop and left it by the front gate. *Now what?* He reached into the front pocket of his jeans and did another bump. *OK, can't get into the Movie Mogul's party and can't get into the HardBodies party. I'll have to make the best of it and have my own party.*

By the time Beau had reached the end of Pines Boulevard, his bare feet were numb to splinters and the odd popped-up nail head. There was something driving him. He needed to lose himself in the anonymity of the Meat Rack. This wooded tract that separates the Pines from Cherry Grove was known by several names, among them Judy Garland Memorial Park and the Enchanted Forest. Crisscrossed by paths and ramshackle bridges, these wooded acres had been a sexual playground for gay men for decades.

He stayed on the cool white sand path that seemed to glow in the moonlight and made his way deeper into the woods. Everywhere he looked he saw figures. Some were solitary, lit only by the flare of a lighter or the glowing tip of a cigarette. Others were huddled in groups. No one spoke, but the sound of sex filled the summer night. Beau came to a small opening where several paths converged. He knew the men standing in the shadows were waiting for him to signal that he was available, so he stood under a thick tree branch and took off his shirt. He unbuttoned his 501 jeans and slid them down to his knees.

Men slowly approached him. Hands, too many to count, caressed his pecs, twisted his nipples, glided down his abs, swirled around his ass, cupped his balls, and encircled his rock hard dick. Beau's moans of pleasure mixed with sounds of approval from the shadowed men. Hands were replaced by mouths. He felt warm lips start to suck on his nipples. Someone was licking his sweaty armpit. A talented throat swallowed his hard cock down to his balls.

He arched his back when he felt someone lick the crack of his ass seeking his sweaty pucker. "Ahhh!" he moaned when the hot, wet, tongue found its target. Consumed by pleasure and pushed on by the Tina, Beau lost himself to the strangers in the dark woods. He felt hot cum shoot onto him. It splashed on his chest, followed by a tongue lapping it up. He felt hot cum splash on his ass, on his legs. He felt it run and drip, mixing with his sweat. He felt the pressure of a fat cock head against his spit-washed hole. After a moment, it popped its way inside him. He pushed back and fucked himself on the mystery dick. Beau then reached up and hung onto the large limb over his head while the crowd feasted on him.

Sunday

Beau looked around in a daze as dawn began to break. *How long have I been here? Where are my clothes?* In the early morning light, Beau spotted his jeans and shirt in a pile by a tree. He walked over to the heap. His dick slapped against his leg. *Damn, that hurts!* He looked down to see his dick bright red and bloated. Beau had no idea how many times he'd been sucked off, fucked, or shot his load. The entire evening's adventure was a dark blur. He bent over to pick up his clothes and the dried cum that covered his body pulled at his skin. He felt all "crispy." He tried to shake the dirt off of his jeans before he put them on, but too many combat boots had ground the swampy marsh-muck into them. He was repelled by the smell and feel of the caked-on filth. Then he picked up his $1,400 Versace shirt. *Ruined!* He decided not to even attempt to wear it on the "walk of shame" back to Rob and Erik's. He simply tied it around his waist. *No great loss. The Movie Mogul will buy me all the Versace shirts I want,* Beau thought confidently. Now, if only he could find his flip-flops. Then it hit him. He had lost one in the muck and had left the other at the locked front gate. His anger flared as he got his bearings and headed out of the woods back to his host's home. He was ready to strangle whoever answered the door.

The walk back to the house was long and painful. Beau's feet were a mess. He stopped a dozen times to pull splinters out of his shredded soles. *What was I thinking last night walking barefoot?* His rage was subsiding. All he wanted was to take a hot shower and lie down in a clean cool bed.

He arrived at the house to be greeted by his lone flip-flop. He turned the knob and the wooden front gate swung inward. *At least they unlocked it for me.* Beau was relieved. Then he looked down the walk and saw his duffel bag by the front door. When he approached, he saw no note, no nothing.

Beau tried the door and found it locked. He pounded on it with his fist, his anger rising. No one answered. Beau stood dumbfounded. Nothing was making sense. *This is all some sort of joke to get back at me.* He looked around. *First things first. I need to shower and change. I can do that at the gym.* Beau picked up his bag and tried to calm down. His heart was pounding like it was about to burst.

***

The lone soul at the outdoor gym's front desk stared at Beau but didn't say a word as he stripped off his mud-soaked jeans and scrubbed himself clean of last night's debauchery. There was no hot water in the poolside shower, but the cold water was bringing Beau's thoughts into focus. When he was sure that he was evidence-free, he dried himself with one of the t-shirts from his bag. He pulled on his Versace bathing suit and gingerly tucked in his raw dick. He tossed his cock ring into his bag. It felt like it had worn a permanent groove around the base of his cock and balls. He put on clean white socks and laced up his combat boots. He pushed his filthy clothes into his bag. Then he reached back for his jeans and found his bumper of Tina. *Gonna need that to get through the party.*

The guy behind the desk took it all in, watching Beau pick up his bag and head out. *Just another crazy motherfucker,* he thought.

When Beau got to the party he exchanged his ticket for a wristband and headed to the first bar he could find. "I need a bottle of water," he demanded and pushed his way to the front of the line.

"Sure, be right with you."

Beau recognized the bartender. It was Luca. He'd know what was going on. "Hey. Where's Rob? I need to talk to him," Beau insisted.

"I don't know," Luca answered, his hands digging down into the ice-filled barrel of bottled waters.

"He's supposed to be bartending with us," Jake said. "Where were you last night? You missed our party."

"I had other more important plans," Beau stated. "You know the Movie Mogul was throwing a party that I was invited to. Meanwhile, I have to find Rob. He must be pissed at me for skipping your party last night. Can you believe he locked me out of the house?" he said, his voice dripping with disdain. Beau asked Luca if he'd hold his bag under the bar for him. He handed it over without waiting for an answer. Beau then snatched the bottle of water from Luca's hand and without paying walked away from the bar. He disappeared into the crowd, uncapped the bottle, and poured some directly up his nose. It burned like a son-of-a-bitch. He'd done another bump of Tina on his way to the party. The water flushed the caked powder down Beau's throat. It tasted like poison. His stomach heaved. When had he last eaten? Beau pushed his way through the crowd, determined to get some answers.

Jake & Luca

They finished bartending the early shift at 1:00 pm and rushed back to the house.

"Thank God! We're all ready to go. Grab a Caipirinha and take it with you into the shower. You have to catch up with the rest of us," Curt ordered. He was done up in full drag as the Queen of Outer Space. His full-body, iridescent silver lamé cat suit was topped off with a giant Plexiglas helmet. The heavy false eyelashes he was wearing were tipped with sparkling rhinestones.

Jake stifled a laugh.

Curt always did drag, no matter what the event. And no matter who he was supposed to be, he always wound up looking like Liza.

Jake and Luca stripped, showered, and joined their housemates to don their spaceman apparel. They were in such a rush that they began to sweat as they pulled up their iridescent silver tights. They crouched down to lace up their silver spray-painted combat boots. Karl was standing by with their obscenely padded codpieces. Cock rings snapped on, they stuffed their dicks and balls into their space jocks. Thickly padded cuffs and collars finished off their uniforms.

"Here, rub this all over your chests," Karl instructed. He shook a bottle of baby oil mixed with iridescent body glitter and gave it to Jake.

"Karl, don't forget their ray guns!" Curt hollered. Karl fetched two silver water pistols and snapped them into place on Jake and Luca's hips. "OK, are we ready to rock and roll?" Curt asked, surveying his starship troopers. "Everyone take their E and let's go to the party!"

Jake, Luca, and Karl - the three strongest guys – each held up a corner of her majesty's litter. Tomàs and Paolo, the pocket gays of the house, struggled to keep the fourth corner aloft. Several weekends had been spent assembling this mini parade float. Two-by-fours supported a plywood base that held a throne. It weighed a ton. Everything was spray-painted silver and finished with tons of glitter. Surrounding Her Majesty's seat were Styrofoam balls all painted and glittered to resemble the planets of the solar system. The Queen of Outer Space climbed aboard and adjusted the Plexiglas bubble on her head.

After trudging through the sand, the entourage arrived at the entrance to the party. The cheer that went up from the crowd was deafening and drowned out the thumping dance music. The adrenaline rush that they all felt was incredible. Or was it the Ecstasy and Brazilian booze kicking in on their empty stomachs? Either way, the crowd parted like the Red Sea. The Queen of Outer Space and her hunky spacemen cut a wide swath across the center of the dance floor.

***

After hours of dancing in the sun, the boys of Neptune were beat. They'd had their fill of adulation and flirting. Besides, their synthetic tights were soaked to the skin. It was time for a change of outfit and scenery. The Queen's entourage marched back down the beach toward their house.

They'd stripped and jumped into the pool.

Then Karl pulled Jake aside. "We've all been invited to an after-party at the Beverly Hillbillies' place," Karl said rather uncomfortably.

"Oh, that's cool," Jake replied, anticipating what was coming next.

"But . . . ," Karl hesitated.

"We're not invited. I know we're *personae non gratae.* That's OK. Luca and I want to go back and enjoy the party by ourselves anyway. Don't worry about us," Jake told his relieved friend. After changing into cargo shorts and feet-cushioning sneakers, Jake and Luca split an Ecstasy and headed back down the beach.

They showed their wristbands and were readmitted to the party, which if anything had kicked into an even higher gear. With bottles of water in their back pockets, the boys hit the dance floor.

"Follow me to the center," Jake said. They made their way through the sweat-soaked crowd, rubbing sunburned shoulders with thousands of guys. They kissed old friends and greeted half-remembered acquaintances.

"Happy Morning Party," was the refrain.

Jake and Luca finally made it to their destination just as the DJ started playing one of their favorite songs. They had danced to it on the deck of the *Intrepid* when they fell in love. The lyrics were about *helping each other through bad times, knowing that things can only get better.*

Their bliss was interrupted when a short muscle guy worked his way in between them. Jake and Luca quickly realized it was Mr. B. He was in rare form. His hands were working their way down the front of Jake's shorts.

Jake gave Luca a surprised look as if to say, *What the fuck is going on?*

Mr. B was a mess. "I want you both to fuck me at the same time," he slurred.

"Let's not go too far here," Luca cautioned. He pulled Mr. B's hand out of Jake's shorts.

The porn star nearly toppled over his own feet when he stood up straight. "Come on, let's go back to your place," he insisted. Mr. B tried to take a step toward Luca but stumbled. Jake caught him before he hit the ground.

What the hell is he on? thought Luca.

"Let's get you some fresh air," Jake suggested. He began to guide Mr. B to the edge of the dance floor.

"We can't go back to my place," he shouted out like a drunken sailor. "My clients wouldn't be too happy with the three of us showing up to fuck." The porn star's eyelids fluttered as if fighting off sleep. "But fuck them! I'm here for the party on their dime. Sweet, huh? Besides, they already paid me." Mr. B tried to say something else, but his eyes fluttered again and he crashed headfirst into Jake. He was dead weight and slid out of Jake's arms onto the sand.

Luca, always good in a crisis, looked at Jake. "Help me get him to the medical tent," he ordered. Jake grabbed Mr. B's right arm while Luca grabbed his left arm and they half-carried, half-dragged him.

In the tent, someone shouted, "Bring him over here." They laid Mr. B down on a cot. "What happened?" asked a familiar face. It was Jake's buddy, the volunteer EMT.

"We were leaving the dance floor and he passed out," Luca said. The EMT took Mr. B's vitals.

"His eyes kept fluttering like that," Jake said, pointing to Mr. B's face. His eyes continued to flutter as if he was trying to wake up.

The EMT heard a gurgling sound and rolled Mr. B onto his side just in time for the contents of his stomach to be expelled into the sand.

Jake jumped back to avoid being covered with puke.

"Yep, another G overdose. We've been seeing it all day." The EMT yelled for a bag of ice. "Help me pull down his shorts," he said to Jake. After fully exposing his crotch, the EMT emptied half a bag of ice onto Mr. B's dick and balls.

He woke up with a start. "What the fuck?" he mumbled. "What happened?"

"You passed out," Luca said.

"You took G, didn't you?" the EMT demanded, his voice nearly cracking.

"Yeah, Liquid Ecstasy," Mr. B slurred.

"That's bullshit! G is an industrial solvent, and it can KILL YOU!" he barked. "You guys know Rob and Erik, right? Well, guess how I had to start my day at 6:00 this morning? I had to wake Rob up to tell him that Erik was dead! He died in the City from an overdose of this shit," the EMT said on the verge of tears.

Jake and Luca stood in shocked silence. They couldn't process what the EMT had just said.

"Can I leave?" Mr. B asked, breaking the silence.

"Yeah, get out of here," the EMT said without any attempt to hide his disgust.

Once outside in the harsh sunlight, Jake bent over and heaved. Then he broke down. "No, this can't be happening," he sobbed unaware of the looks he was getting from the partiers who were passing by.

Luca comforted him. "We have to tell the others," he said. They stumbled along the sand until they reached the stairs back up the dunes to the Boulevard. It felt like they were climbing Mount Everest.

Mr. B trailed behind them. "Where are we going?" he asked.

"Back to your place," they answered in unison.

They walked in silence to the Beverly Hillbillies' beach house.

When they opened the front wooden gate, Big Daddy immediately jumped up from his chaise. "What the hell do you think you're doing here?" he hollered like a madman.

Luca could see all of their housemates and friends lounging around the pool naked. "We have terrible news," he said in a low voice.

"You're not welcome in my house," Big Daddy shouted. "And as for you!" he yelled at Mr. B, "Bobby packed your bags after we discovered that you'd gone AWOL. You can leave on the next ferry."

Mr. B slunk away to retrieve his belongings from the

guest room.

"We're not here to crash your party. We're here because . . . ," Jake burst into tears.

The Fashionistas got up and came over to him.

"Erik's dead," Luca said, loud enough for all of them to hear. "He overdosed last night."

"Oh my God," Karl gasped.

"We should go back to the house," Curt said.

The Brazilians started putting on their bathing suits.

"Wait, don't leave. The party's just getting started," Big Daddy said, trying to sound jovial but hitting all the wrong notes.

"The party's over," Curt declared as he swung open the gate.

Monday

The ferry was unusually quiet. Everyone on the Island knew Rob and Erik, if not directly then by reputation. As the crowd piled onboard, heading for destinations around the globe, for many, it felt like the end of something. Jake and Luca climbed the steps to the upper deck to join the Fashionistas and the Brazilians. They all sat in silence. Like Jake and Luca, the other couples had their arms around each other. Today the sunshine and warm sea breeze offered no comfort. The ferry's horn signaled that it was pushing away from the dock.

Luca was startled when someone plopped down next to him on the hard fiberglass bench. It was Beau. Dark circles ringed his eyes. His lips were cracked and peeling. His hair was dirty. If he hadn't known better, Luca would have thought him a homeless derelict. In front of everyone, Beau took out a bullet and snorted a bump of Tina, and with that something inside Luca snapped. He smacked the bullet out of Beau's hand. It skittered across the deck.

At the top of his lungs, Luca yelled at Beau, "Look at yourself!"

Beau stared at Luca with pupils the size of dinner plates.

"Does anyone exist in your demented universe besides you?" Luca was livid, his face was red. "One of your friends is dead. Does that even register with you?" The entire boatload of people was riveted.

Beau tried to say something.

"I don't want to hear it," Luca roared before Beau

could get a word out. "You're nothing but a drugged-out mess!" Luca took a breath and roared on, "You need to take your sorry self back to LA and stay there! I don't wanna be around when *you* overdose!"

Beau sat with his mouth open, not quite understanding what had just happened.

"I can't even stand looking at you!" shouted Luca.

With that, Beau stood up and stumbled to the back of the boat. His legs were trembling as he struggled to walk a steady line.

Islip

Beau

He arrived at Islip Airport and headed to the snack shop for something to eat. He was starving. After grabbing as much junk food as they had to offer, Beau slid the cashier his platinum American Express card.

"I'm sorry, sir, but your card has been declined," the sunburned teenager told him.

"What? There must be a mistake." Fishing around inside his wallet, he pulled out a Visa card. "Here, try this one."

The cashier ran it through and made a funny face. She tried it again. "Nope, sorry, sir, but that one is being declined, too."

"This is crazy! Here," Beau said. He put down a handful of crumpled-up bills. The teenager hunted through the wad for enough cash to cover his tab and pushed the remainder back to Beau. There would be hell to pay when he got his hands on Ira. *How dare he put me through this embarrassment?*

Los Angeles

Beau slept all the way to LA, not even waking for the in-flight meal. Groggy from his five-hour hibernation, he was one of the last people to deplane. He made his way down to baggage claim to look for Ira's houseman. After a twenty minute wait, he called the house.

The houseman answered the phone, "Gould residence."

"Where are you?" Beau demanded, trying to keep his anger in check. "I've been waiting for you to pick me up at the airport. Did you forget I was coming home today?"

"Oh my," the houseman muttered under his breath.

"Let me speak to Mr. Ira," Beau insisted.

"He's not here. He's gone," the houseman said in a voice barely loud enough for Beau to hear.

"Fine. How soon can you pick me up?"

"I don't know where Mr. Ira is. All of his things are gone. I came in this morning to an empty house. And then the police arrived. They won't let me take the car to pick you up."

"What? What are you talking about?" Beau shouted into the phone.

"They said they wanted to talk to Mr. Ira, but he wasn't here. They asked if I knew where he was, and I told them I didn't."

"This makes no sense whatsoever! What am I supposed to do? I have no cash for a taxi and neither of my credit cards are working." A feeling of dread washed over him.

"I'm sorry, but there's nothing I can do. Maybe you should call Mr. Ira's friend, the photographer."

***

"Hello, Fuji?"

"Speaking. Who's this?"

"It's Beau. I'm stuck at the airport."

"I'm sorry . . . , Beau?"

"Beau Fournier. You know, Ira's Beau."

"Oh. It's been a while. Are you OK?"

"I'm fucking stranded at LAX with no money and credit cards that are worthless."

"Have you called Ira?"

"Of course. I called him first. But the houseman said he's gone missing and the police want to talk to him."

"What? Is he alright? What's going on?"

"I don't know anything. I just flew back from Fire Island."

"Another party?"

"Yes, another party."

"The last time I saw you . . . ."

"Yes, I know. We didn't exactly part as friends, but I have no one else to turn to, Fuji." Beau broke down. "Will you help me?" he sobbed.

South Beach

Jake & Luca

They flew back to Miami together, but returned home separately. Hunt had insisted on picking up Jake. He was waiting curbside for him. Luca took a taxi home. After only the vaguest of questions about his weekend on Fire Island, Hunt said, "I've got something I want to show you." They made their way to Jake's South Beach neighborhood and parked in front of a white, nondescript house. "I want you to take a look at this place," Hunt said. Jake had driven by the house innumerable times. A large front lawn led up to a ranch home built in the '50s. The closer they got, the more rundown it looked. The foliage that crowded around the house's foundation hadn't been trimmed in years. They climbed white terrazzo steps and looked through a black iron gate into a courtyard. "Do you like it?" Hunt asked.

"Yeah, it reminds me of my house. It looks like it might have a similar layout," Jake answered tentatively, unsure of what Hunt was up to.

"Good. I thought you'd like it," Hunt replied. He handed Jake a set of keys.

"How did you get the keys?" Jake asked.

"From an old friend, a real estate agent who I've used in the past." Hunt had bought and sold so many houses in Miami, each time trading up, that he'd lost count. Jake unlocked the front door and they stepped inside. The painted walls were scuffed and peeling in spots. It was a plain house but had good bones. "It's not in very good shape. It's been a rental for many years," Hunt said. "Let's take a look at the backyard." They walked through a rickety blue wooden door. There was no pool, just a mowed lawn surrounded by a hedge badly in need of clipping. Like the inside of the house, it was a blank slate. "Well, do you think we could do something with this place?" Hunt asked Jake.

Jake hesitated. "What do you mean?" He saw a look on Hunt's face of complete joy.

"It's yours," Hunt announced.

"Mine?" Jake was confused.

"As soon as I saw it, I knew it was perfect. It's actually bigger than your current house. It's just waiting to be turned into something special. We can put in a pool with a lanai and landscape the place to make it every bit as beautiful as your house is now."

Jake was overwhelmed. "I don't know what to say. I can't believe you've done this for me!" But his mind immediately went to Luca, *How will he fit into all of this?* He'd have to remain a "roommate" as far as Hunt was concerned. Jake didn't welcome the deception but Hunt had painted him into a corner.

"I know how much your house meant to you. And I know how terrible it's been to lose it. I also realize that you couldn't afford to stay in my house after I'm gone. You're right, you need your own place. Here, you can start your life again. I want you to be happy," Hunt beamed. "So, did I do the right thing?"

AUTUMN 1995

October 1995 - *Two Months Later*
Fort Lauderdale

The Insurance Guys
White silk flower petals tumbled out when Bluto opened the envelope. The room was immediately engulfed by the cloyingly sweet scent of magnolia blossoms in full bloom.

"What's that smell?" called out Bill from the kitchen.

"I just opened an invitation to a Halloween party from the Beverly Hillbillies," answered Bluto. "And . . . are you ready for this . . . it's a *Gone with the Wind* theme. Wanna go as Mammy?"

"Let me see that," demanded Bill. The front of the engraved invitation was the original movie poster, with Bobby's face superimposed over Vivien Lee's. *Margaret Mitchell must be twirling in her grave,* he thought. The reply card featured what appeared to be a picture of Little Black Sambo in the upper right corner. *Well, if you're going to be tasteless, you might as well go all the way.*

Bill was shocked that they'd even received an invitation. He was certain that he and Bluto were on the never-to-be-included list. After all, he'd seen Big Daddy erupt like a volcano in Ibiza when he realized that Jake and Luca hadn't provided a proper good bye and thank you. It wasn't pretty. But Bill and Bluto knew they'd done the right thing. They felt like they'd helped two innocent men escape from prison that night.

Bluto continued to be Bobby's workout partner after Ibiza, so he wasn't at all surprised. "Do we send our regrets or do we go to this thing?" he asked.

"How can you ask such a question?" replied Bill. "This is going to be the South rising up again. I'm not gonna miss this one."

***

"How much money do they have?" asked Bill when they drove up to the guardhouse of the island that Big Daddy and Bobby lived on. In front of them was a waterfront palace with a huge yacht moored beside it.

"Bobby drives to the gym in a Jaguar," offered up Bluto. "I think Big Daddy is the paper king of Atlanta or something like that." They drove into the community.

On their left was a faux Mediterranean monster of a home, garish in every respect. It looked like some Colombian drug dealer's idea of Barbie's dream castle. "I swear I see gun turrets on the roof," said Bill. "I had no idea there was so much money in this town."

"It's all about the water," answered Bluto. "You can get to the Intercoastal and ocean from here."

"None of these houses have numbers, only names," noted Bill. "Do you have any idea where . . . ," and with that, he stopped talking.

Bluto slowed the car. There were movie-premiere search lights in front of the house at the end of the street.

A handsome young black man dressed in a valet uniform opened the door to their car. The Insurance Guys, dressed in their opposing Union and Confederate uniforms, immediately recognized the sweeping orchestral theme music from *Gone with the Wind*. It was being pumped through loud speakers. Then they stopped in their tracks. The front of the house had been made to resemble an antebellum plantation. It was a remarkable illusion. It had to have taken carpenters and painters days to complete the facade. They passed between tall Corinthian columns.

A black uniformed butler with silver hair opened the front door with his white-gloved hand. "Welcome to Tara," he said.

Uniformed maids greeted the Insurance Guys with trays of champagne and hors d'oeuvres. An unusual selection of Southern food was presented - hush puppies, fried catfish, fried chicken fingers.

"So where's the watermelon?" asked Bill under his breath.

"You're evil!" answered Bluto.

"They must be saving it for dessert."

The Insurance Guys explored the main part of the house and were astounded by the décor. It was as if there'd been an explosion in an Easter egg factory. Everything was a hideous mix of pastels. Over in the corner of the massive living room was a grand piano that had been painted an oh-so-lovely shade of violet. The custom carpeting – baby blue with swirls of lavender and pink - complemented the inlaid springtime flowers on the pale yellow dining room table. "Who was their decorator?" asked Bill.

"Apparently, My Pretty Pony," Bluto replied.

"I need a drink," said Bill. They headed outdoors to the pool and patio area. In contrast to the film score that had greeted them upon their arrival, the sounds of disco past

304

pumped out of stadium-size speakers at the rear of the property. The thump-thump-thump beat of the Weather Girl's "It's Raining Men" pounded out around them. *The police are going to shut this party down if the neighbors complain,* thought Bill. Little did he know that Big Daddy had put his neighbors up in suites at the Diplomat Hotel for the night. They zeroed in on the nearest bar, where there was nothing but top shelf liquor in the biggest bottles available. If their hosts meant to impress, they were certainly achieving their goal. "I'll have an Absolut and cranberry," Bill asked one of the bare-chested black muscle boys who was serving cocktails as fast as the crowd could suck them down. "Look at the size of those bottles!"

"Fuck the bottles, look at the size of his biceps," Bluto remarked.

"I wonder if . . . ,"

"Stop!" Bluto laughed.

"What vault did they dig this music out of? Are these 8-tracks?"

"Please," Bluto answered. "Take a good look around you. This music is from the glory days of most of these old queens. Don't you recognize some of them? Like what's-his-name, the gay mayor, over there, and the pastor from the gay church."

"Something tells me that Big Daddy's invited every gay mover and shaker in Fort Lauderdale," Bill responded.

"Bobby told me that Big Daddy got onto the fundraising committee at the gay church by promising the first $100,000 to build a new chapel. To be named after him, of course."

"Oh, no he didn't!" Bill exclaimed.

"Oh, yes he did! Then, according to Bobby, he offered to match any other funds committed to the chapel. How do you like them apples?"

"So let me guess," Bill asked, "in return he got to use the church's mailing list for this party? Brilliant!"

"Yeah, this is his and Bobby's official introduction to Fort Lauderdale gay society," Bluto answered.

"This is some fuckin' introduction. Damn!" Bill laughed, almost spilling his cocktail.

"Oh, my God!"

"What?"

"I didn't realize until just now," Bluto observed, "the only black people here are the help."

Scanning the crowd, Bill realized the truth in this. "Are they supposed to be slaves?" he whispered.

"Oh, that's so wrong!" Bluto said, loud enough to attract a few inquisitive stares.

***

"Welcome, welcome! I'd like to thank you for all coming to what we hope is the first of many fantastic celebrations!" Big Daddy announced in his Southern drawl. He was positioned on a stage that had been built atop the raised hot tub. The Insurance Guys' jaws dropped when they caught sight of him. They weren't the only ones staring in shocked amazement. There Big Daddy stood, dressed as Mammy, his caramel-colored skin covered with black-face makeup. "If everyone would gather in the living room, we have a *big* surprise for y'all. Now I know what you're all thinking, and the answer is no. We won't be birthin' no babies!" Big Daddy laughed. He dismounted the stage and headed inside.

At first the crowd was silent. Then the buzz started.

"What was he thinking?" Bill asked Bluto under his breath. He strained to hear what everyone else was whispering about. "A black man doing black-face?"

"It's social suicide. Even with this group of old white queens," Bluto whispered. He dared not meet the eye of any of the staff.

He and Bill pushed their way into the house through one of the many open sliding-glass doors. Big Daddy was standing by the fireplace. Swathed in red and white gingham, he looked ready to start flipping flapjacks. It was hard to take your eyes off of him. Everyone was straining to catch a glimpse of the unfolding horror.

"And now ladies, gentlemen, I'd like to present the world-renowned artist, Tomàs Carvalho," announced Big "Mammy." The entire room politely applauded. No one had ever heard of him. "When Tomàs first met Bobby, he was taken by his beauty," stated Big Mammy. "It was then and there that Tomàs insisted on painting Bobby's portrait. Tonight, he's here to unveil his masterpiece. Tomàs, I'll let you do the honors."

Tomàs stepped forward with a perplexed look on his face. He had no idea where Big Daddy had come up with all that crap, but he really didn't care. He had the five-figure check in hand. With a tug on a long tasseled cord, the drapery covering the six-foot tall portrait fell away. There was an audible gasp from the assembled crowd.

The full-length portrait was an amazing creation, photo-realistic to a fault. Tomàs had taken countless photos of Bobby to get all the details of his body just right, but then he hit a wall. Big Daddy didn't find a single pose that he liked among the photos. Tomàs was stymied.

"You need to make Bobby look his best," insisted Big Daddy, "like those guys on the book covers that you do."

So that was the game, realized Tomàs. Big Daddy wanted Bobby to look like Fabio. Back in his studio, Tomàs had a moment of inspiration. He sketched out a drawing to show Big Daddy. Using Botticelli's painting of Venus rising out of the ocean on a half-shell as a starting point, Tomàs pulled out all the stops.

There above the fireplace, in near-naked glory, was a larger-than-life Bobby standing on a beach. Like Venus, his flawless body was barely concealed by a floating drape of sheer golden chiffon, but it was a bit too see-through. Bobby's pendulous cock and low-hanging balls were clearly visible. It was as if someone had pulled aside the shower curtain to expose the host in all his nakedness. It was so wrong on so many levels. There were several seconds of dead silence.

Then Big Daddy started the applause.

The entire room joined in uncomfortably. What other options were there? In its own way, the painting was indeed beautiful. Tomàs's skills were supremely evident. Bobby looked like a god. Bathed in early morning sunlight, Bobby's body glistened. The wind ruffled his red curls so that a perfect lock fell across his forehead. His eyes were as aquamarine as the sea behind him. The painting was luminous, but like a traffic accident, no one could take their eyes off of the dead-center, in-your-face cock and balls.

Before the applause died down, Big Mammy announced, "And now it's show time! Everyone head out back!" The crowd obediently filed out toward the pool.

"There's more?" Bill asked.

While they'd all been inside, mesmerized by the unveiling, a barge had been towed into place behind the house. On the deck stood Gloria Gaynor, the original disco diva. Her black skin stood out in contrast to her billowing white caftan. "Is everybody having *fun*?" she shouted over the PA system. The crowd stood there transfixed by the tableau. Surrounding Gloria were her backup dancers, a dozen black bodybuilder go-go boys, dressed in white g-strings. "Good, 'cause it's time to get this party started! Mr. DJ if you please!" Gloria commanded. With that, the music kicked in with a bass beat that nearly knocked down the less stable and slightly snockered older men in the audience. The young boys started bouncing to the beat and the go-go boys shook their moneymakers. Gloria started singing the disco version of "Summertime" from *Porgy and Bess*.

Bill could hear Gershwin cursing from his grave.

Gloria sang *about the livin' bein' easy and Daddy bein' rich* to a pounding dance beat.

The half-drunk crowd went wild.

The Insurance Guys thought it was brilliant high camp. They were wrong on that score. They had no idea how dead serious Big Daddy and Bobby were about tonight's entertainment, but they were about to find out.

After finishing to thunderous applause, Gloria said, "Thank you, thank you, ladies and gentlemen! And now it's my honor to present the star of the show." She took a dramatic pause then announced, "I give you Scarlet O'Hara!"

"Oh, no! That's Bobby," Bluto blurted out, not even bothering to lower his voice. "He said he was going to be the belle of the ball and he wasn't kidding."

Resplendent in a replica of Scarlet's infamous drapery dress, a fabulous brunette wig balanced on his head, a beautiful figure stepped into the spotlight. When the first strains of the all-too-familiar tune began, Scarlet looked over at Big Mammy with blue eyes filled with tears of joy. This was Bobby's big moment, the chance he'd been waiting for since he'd started his journey from Pensacola. Scarlet looked out at her adoring audience and began to lip-synch to Judy Garland's trademark song.

Bill's jaw dropped in horror as Bobby opened his mouth and a little girl's voice emerged, singing about a fantasy land located *over the rainbow*.

Bobby's painted lips sang about *dreams coming true*. Rainbow-colored fireworks lit the night sky over Fort Lauderdale's Intercoastal Waterway when he mouthed those last few plaintive lines. Bobby knew in his heart that he'd finally arrived at his destination. It might not be Oz, but it was the closest to it that he'd ever get.

SUMMER 1996

1 June 1996 - *Eight Months Later*
South Beach

Jake & Karl

Jake opened what he thought was a wedding invitation. The thick white envelope held an engraved card with a poem on its face. It spoke of the importance, not of one's date of birth or date of passing, but of the dash in between that represents one's life.

> *Please join us for a celebration of Erik Christiansen's life. White attire requested.*

Jake called Karl that evening. "I got an invitation to Erik's memorial service in the mail today."

"Yeah. I think it's nice that they're holding it on his birthday," Karl said. "Are you guys are planning to make it?" he asked.

"We'll definitely be there," Jake replied. "I've spoken with Rob a few times since Erik's death. I understand what he's going through."

"Wow. I didn't think you'd want to drag all that up again."

"He was a friend in need and I had to help. You'd be surprised at what you're capable of doing when the situation calls for it," Jake answered.

"I don't know how anyone can get through it. I don't know what I'd do if anything ever happened to Curt."

"You'd do what I did, turn to your best friends for support and somehow move forward."

Hearing the sadness in his best friend's voice, Karl changed topics. "Did you notice the address?" he asked. "It's on the Upper East Side. Curt and I walked by the other day to check it out. Oh my God! It's a double-wide, five story townhouse, around the corner from the Met. Who does it belong to?"

"All I know is that a friend of Rob's owns it."

"I can't wait to see the interior! I bet it's *FABULOUS!*"

"Only you!" Jake brightened. "You'd sleep with Yoko Ono!"

"Of course! Just to see the apartment," Karl completed the tired joke.

"It'll be nice to spend some time together. I've miss you," Jake confessed.

"I've miss you, too," Karl admitted. "Give Luca a big kiss for me."

"And hugs to Curt. I love you."

"I love you, too."

29 June 1996 - *Four Weeks Later / Gay Pride Weekend*
New York
Saturday

Jake & Luca

Jake turned to Luca as the cab they were in sped up Fifth Avenue toward the Metropolitan Museum of Art. "I'm not certain I'm ready for this," he said in a low voice.

"What's wrong?" asked Luca.

"I thought all my conversations with Rob would make this easier, but it hasn't," Jake replied.

The cabbie turned at the corner of 76th Street and pulled up to the address that Luca had given him. It was Ellis's townhouse.

"We need to do this for Rob. Trust me, you're stronger than you think."

"I don't know," replied Jake. "What if I lose it when I walk in the door?"

"And if you do," Luca responded, "that's alright."

Jake closed his eyes and took a deep breath.

"We're here," Luca said.

Jake leaned over and kissed Luca. Then he opened the door and got out of the cab. He stood still for a moment to collect his thoughts while Luca paid the driver.

"Jake!" yelled out Karl. He was waiting with Curt and the Brazilians by the stairs leading up to the grand entrance of the Belle Époque residence. "It's so good to see you boys." He rushed up to Jake and Luca and gave them both a long hard hug. "Come join us," he said.

"Can we wait a moment before going in?" asked Jake.

"Of course we can," answered Karl. "Are you alright?"

"Just a little overwhelmed. I really thought death was behind us," Jake sighed. "What with all the new meds that are out there . . . and then this. What a needless tragedy. I feel so sorry for Rob."

"We all do," replied Curt. "Just when you thought we'd turned a corner, just when you thought we had something to celebrate, it all falls apart. I mean, wasn't Stonewall 25 supposed to be a new beginning?"

"It's pitiful that we're uptown going to a memorial service instead of downtown at the Gay Pride parade," said Paolo. "I have friends . . . we all have friends who've struggled

312

to stay alive and Erik does himself in with a stupid drug overdose. I'm not sad, I'm angry. Look at what all the partying led to."

"Careful where you go with that," answered Tomàs. "We all indulged in plenty of drugs along the way. Erik just didn't know that what he was taking could kill him."

"Gentlemen," interjected Luca, "we can debate all of this at another time. Our job right now is to go inside and be supportive of Rob."

Karl turned to Jake. "Are you ready?" he asked.

"Yeah, I am," Jake answered. "Life staggers forward."

"And people still fall in love," said Luca as he grabbed hold of Jake's hand.

Many familiar figures were milling about in the enormous foyer. "I see a lot of old faces," Karl said.

"And a few new faces on old faces," Curt shot back. The friends tried not to laugh. Conversation ended when they stepped out of the foyer and into the main part of the house, taking in the impressive surroundings. It had been a showcase for the French and Belgian antiques that Baby had collected over the years. Ellis had sold them all at auction. His friends thought it was his way of moving forward and somehow reconciling with the loss, but other reasons had motivated his decision to renovate the townhouse. CMV had robbed him of much of his sight. So the interior, from top to bottom, had been painted bright white. In place of the dark furnishings that had previously filled the townhouse were modern sofas and chairs, all upholstered in brightly colored silk fabrics. Hot pink. Brilliant turquoise. Lime green. Everything popped against the white walls and white floors. Ellis was able to maneuver easily about the place despite his diminished vision.

Sunlight flooded the living room through a bank of French doors that led out to a courtyard. There were white flowers everywhere. The fragrance of Casablanca lilies, tuberose, lily of the valley, and hyacinths was intoxicating. On a modern steel table covered with blossoms were small white note cards. A faceted crystal cup held silver Cross pens. A small sign read:

> *Please write down your favorite memory of Erik
> and place it in the bowl.*

A large glass bowl, surround by votive candles, was already filled with note cards. Jake wrote of meeting Erik at

Jocks and how genuine his smile was. *"Erik radiated positive energy,"* wrote Jake.

What most guests didn't know was that the cards would be burned and their ashes mixed with Erik's. Half of Erik's ashes were to be given to his family, who wanted to scatter them in the lake of the summer wrestling camp that Erik's grandfather had built. The rest of Erik's remains Rob would take to Fire Island and scatter into the bay. It was the most peaceful place that Rob could think of. He liked the idea of always being reminded of Erik when he made his favorite voyage.

A small television monitor sat next to the glass bowl. The monitor showed a continuous loop of Erik. You could hear Rob's deep voice off-camera saying, "Let's see how this new video camera works. Tell me something I don't know about you."

Erik, deeply tanned from a summer out on the Island, broke into a smile from ear to ear. "When I was a kid, I spent summers at my grandfather's wrestling camp. He named it after his favorite Olympian, Johnny Weissmuller. It was called Tarzana." Everyone who watched the loop smiled along with Erik. Over and over the image of a smiling Erik filled the hearts of those gathered to remember him.

"If you would all take a seat, we would like to start the service," began Rob's best friend Charles. "We are here to celebrate life. That is why we chose Erik Christiansen's birthday for this gathering of his family and friends. Today is not about loss but about the gift that Erik shared with us. Each of us will carry that gift with us forever in our hearts."

The room quieted. Everyone took their seat. To Rob's right was a smaller man in dark sunglasses. They spoke softly to each other. He was pointed out as Ellis, the owner of the townhouse. Next to him sat a distinguished older gentleman with a white crew cut. He was introduced as the General. The Rocks were seated next to him. Clark Kent sat behind Rob and put a comforting hand on his shoulder. An older woman and two Nordic-looking young men - Erik's mother and his twin brothers - sat to Rob's left. The rest of the seats were taken by friends from the City and the Island, along with every employee of Jocks. There were well over one hundred people in attendance.

Rob, elegant in white, stood up to speak. He was visibly shaking. When he stopped to pull himself together, Erik's mother rose and hugged him tightly. At last Rob

314

turned to address the gathering. "Often we react to a personal loss with anger. When we love, we want more," he said. Tears rolled down his cheeks. "It's not always easy," he continued in a quavering voice, "but we must learn to turn that anger around and thank Erik for having been a part of our lives, no matter how brief. His is a light that will shine on inside each of us."

The guests choked back tears as Rob returned to his seat.

Charles rose again and began to speak. "Let our love for Erik help us to see how important it is to move forward, to live life, to carry on. And now, if you would be so kind as to follow Rob and Erik's family out into the courtyard."

The open space was filled with white linen-covered tables overflowing with even more fragrant white flowers. As if on cue, birds chirped in the blossoming trees. On the tables were crystal flutes filled with bubbling champagne. The central table was covered with elegantly folded, small, white paper boxes. Each box was hand-inscribed with Erik's name.

Charles spoke loudly so that everyone could hear. "If you would each take an origami box and hold it gently in your hands." Everyone helped pass the delicate boxes around. "Now, in your mind, visualize Erik. Remember a particularly happy moment that you shared with him. And thank him." After a moment of silence Charles spoke again. "You may each open your box now."

Each simple box opened to reveal a beautiful white butterfly. A warm summer breeze blew through the trees and the butterflies took flight. As they fluttered upward, the guests gazed up and saw several young men wielding enormous white fans, flagging from the balconies that looked out over the courtyard. The young men, all dressed in white, looked like angels ascending. Gracefully they beckoned the spirit upward to the heavens, into the sunlit blue sky of summer.

EPILOGUE

29 June 1996
Grand Cayman
Saturday

Ira

He'd never seen anything like it. Dozens of hummingbirds were flitting about him as he made his way, from the dinghy that had brought him ashore, along the garden path that led to his cabana. He was astonished at how much noise their almost-invisible wings made. Their iridescent bodies, pink, turquoise, and lime, hung in the air, then darted off in a blink. They shimmered like jewels against the blue sky of the island's eternal summer. Ira's yacht bobbed offshore in the crystalline water.

At first he was hesitant to move, afraid he'd collide with one of the delicate creatures, but when he slowly reached out to touch one hovering before him, he realized that the tiny birds could maneuver around him effortlessly. He was mesmerized. The sound of their buzzing wings became a drone in the background and Ira's focus, if only for a few seconds, was on something other than all that he had lost.

***

An ocean breeze ruffled the cabana's white canvas roof, and a sliver of bright sunlight fell upon Ira's white chaise. He adjusted his Panama hat and took in the view. Sensuously curved palm trees cast dappled shade on the powdery white sand, just like in a postcard. The canvas roof of the cabana fluttered again as the ocean breeze picked up and cooled the beach. Ira closed his eyes. He could picture a Manhattan penthouse with a view of Central Park, smell the dark blue ocean of the Laguna coast, feel the cool morning air of LA.

"Sir?"

"Yes," Ira said as he awoke with a start.

The young waiter was standing in front of him holding his Caesar salad with grilled chicken. "Your chilled bottle of Dom Perignon will be here momentarily."

Ira gave a wan smile. No matter how hard he tried to recreate his glamorous life of privilege, no one would be joining him for lunch. There was no one worth knowing on this island of thieves. Surrendering to reality, Ira had torn up his return ticket. He was under no illusion that he would ever leave.

"Will there be anything else, sir?"

Ira was barely listening. He couldn't take his eyes off the boy. Dressed in nothing more than a swimsuit and flip-flops, he looked like a bronze statue with his glowing tan. "What's your name, young man?" Ira inquired.

"Amante," answered the waiter. "It means . . . ," he began.

"I know what it means." Ira smiled to himself. Here he was with the perfect boy, with the perfect name, on a perfect afternoon. "Have you ever been a model?" asked Ira.

29 June 1996 - *Gay Pride Weekend*
Toronto
Saturday

Beau

Tibia? Fibula? Which one is it? thought Beau as he tackled the next question on the exam. He'd been under the impression that his anatomy class would be a breeze. The leg bone is connected to the hip bone, the hip bone is connected to the back bone. But it had proven otherwise. Beau struggled. It seemed to him that everyone else in the class had covered the subject before and he was playing catch-up. He left the exam room uncertain if he would pass the course.

Don't worry about it. It'll be what it'll be. If he had to repeat the class then that's what he'd do. He'd resolved that failure was not an option. It was a mantra that had been driven into him by his support group. When he felt overwhelmed he turned to them to keep focus. It would be too easy to fall back into old habits without them. He'd failed too many times already. Rehab followed by relapse followed by rehab.

He stepped outside and his spirits lifted. It was a stunning day, too perfect to take the subway. *It's not a long walk to Yonge Street.* If he picked up his pace he could be there in 15 minutes with plenty of time left to find his friends among the throngs of men and women gathered for today's parade. A light breeze rustled the leaves in the trees and made the rainbow flags on every lamp post flutter like brightly colored birds. Toronto's all-to-brief blue summer sky was ablaze with rainbows as the city celebrated.

When he rounded the corner he saw a massive banner on the side of the Art Gallery of Ontario. The sheer size of the banner stopped him dead in his tracks. He let out a gasp. It was as if he'd been sucker-punched and had all the wind knocked out of him. *Let's Get Physical* read the top line of the banner. *Male Photography: 1975 – 1995* was printed along the bottom. Beau read the words but they barely registered. It was the image that riveted him. There, looming over him, was Fuji's iconic photo of Beau sitting atop Luca's shoulders.

A dam of memories and emotions burst and flooded his senses. His dream had come true. His larger-than-life image dominated the street. But somehow it felt all wrong. Someone brushed by him on the sidewalk. "That's me up there!" he wanted to shout out to them, but his voice caught in his throat. New York, LA, South Beach, Ibiza. It all came rushing back – the good, the bad, and the ugly. Hadn't he left that life behind? Hadn't he stumbled his way out of that abyss? Beau took a deep breath. *The past is always with you,* whispered a voice in his head. *The best you can do is to make peace with it.* In that fleeting moment of clarity Beau saw a way forward. He continued his walk and the banner receded into the distance.

CPSIA information can be obtained at www.ICGtesting.com
Printed in the USA
LVOW041928021111

253232LV00001B/115/P